I0749315

THE OCTAVIAN LATTICEWORK

THE OCTAVIAN LATTICEWORK

JACK BELMONTE

Voltaire Publishing

The Octavian Latticework

Published in the United States of America by Voltaire Publishing.

ISBN: 978-0-9891775-1-1

Library of Congress Control Number: 2013946835

For my grandfather

Chapter 1

The gunshot exploded within the subject home and ripped through Johnny Luca's ears at 1:00 A.M. the morning of November 18, 2022.

The twenty-four-year-old surveillance technician for the U.S. Anti-Subversion Authority clutched his headset and lurched forward in the driver's seat of the armored SUV, knocking over a cup of coffee. "Goddamn it," he said, coffee pooling around him on the seat.

Why hadn't he heard any approach? Footsteps, bedroom door opening, a struggle? They'd set up microphones all over the subject's house. Yet Johnny had only heard the shot—nothing before, nothing after.

He reached for the handheld radio wired to the truck and clicked it. "Fullerton," he said. "Come in."

"What's up, Luca?" replied Julius Fullerton, a twenty-seven-year-old Authority agent supervising the operation from the duty desk at the Newark field office.

"I just heard a gun go off," Johnny said. *What do you even do when you hear a gunshot from inside somebody's house?* he thought. *What if the dude's bleeding to death up there?*

"You heard *what*?"

"A gunshot, man. I think—" Johnny stopped himself and donned a professional law enforcement tone. "Suspected point of origin, the master bedroom."

"Come correct with it, Luca, none of that robo-cop bullshit. You heard a shot? Did you hear anything before that? What's going on now?"

"I didn't hear anything before. And now…" Johnny strained to listen—nothing. He punched a button and switched to the microphone in the hallway outside the bedroom, and now there were footsteps, creaking along the corridor.

"Footsteps," Johnny said. "Out in the hallway, real slow."

"Leaving the scene. Or maybe… Maybe the subject's shooting up the place?"

"Shooting up his own place? I don't think so. I think… someone just broke into the house and shot him. Shot him right in his sleep."

"Either way… you need to get out of there. Right now."

He's right, Johnny thought. He shifted in the seat and felt the coffee soaking the backside of his pants. He studied the subject's house, a center-hall colonial, a flight of semicircular brick stairs bowing out from the long front porch.

Johnny was parked in a tony New Jersey suburb, snooping on a professor with terrorist ties from an armored truck parked across the street. Earlier in the day, Authority agents had planted surveillance all over the house, and tonight Johnny had been manning the listening post and making sure that the recording equipment was working. The professor had put his young children to bed early in the evening, and had retired himself about an hour before. And now a gunshot had gone off, and…

The kids. They're in there with whoever fired that shot.

"I can't leave," he said. "What about the kids?"

Fullerton groaned. "I'm not trying to leave them there," he said. "I'm just... You need to get out of there. The op's going to get fucked up if you stay parked in front of that house. And if you go inside, Peterson will fire both our asses tomorrow morning, if he doesn't do it in his sleep tonight. Get on back here."

Johnny looked around, his face flush now. He couldn't hear anything. He punched buttons, cycling through the other microphones, through the kids' bedrooms, the other rooms—nothing.

What's going on up there?

"You there, man?" Fullerton said.

"I need to go in and help those kids, I—"

"Are you armed? Answer me. Are you? No, you're not armed, and you're not trained. You can't do a damn thing to help those kids. I don't know what in the hell just happened in that house, and you don't either. Maybe the subject is high and shooting the goddamn place up. Or... maybe he *is* dead and you're going to bust in there and make those little kids think you're the dude who just popped their daddy. Get out, man. Someone's going to call the five-o, and we can't get involved in that shit. Peterson's orders. *No compromising the operation.*"

Johnny punched the steering wheel. How could he leave?

But this investigation, unlike the other graveyard shift surveillance ops they'd tossed him out on, seemed serious. The professor was suspected of belonging to a terrorist group. Johnny wanted to be an agent someday, and this was what guys like Fullerton had to do every day. He had to stand down.

"I'm coming back to the field office," Johnny said.

"Come on back safe," Fullerton said. "Turn on the ignition, turn on the lights, and pull away real natural." He paused. "Stay calm, and come on back safe."

Johnny bit his lip one more time, then clicked the radio. "Copy."

He turned the key in the ignition, felt the engine roar to life, and flicked on the lights. Just then, he saw a light flash on in an upstairs window in the house next door. He had to get the hell out of here.

Johnny pulled off the curb and started back, drifting up the block, still cycling through the microphones and straining to listen—nothing. As soon as he was a bit more up the block, he'd be out of range, and he'd be leaving those little kids alone to face the night.

This isn't right. This just isn't right.

He shook his head, then throttled up the pace as he escaped from suburbia. He passed driveways jutting up hills, manicured shrubs and bay windows, bird feeders and stone fountains.

Suddenly an SUV shot out in front of him, zooming through a stop sign on a side street. The dark blue truck righted itself, slowing down to about Johnny's speed.

Johnny squeezed the steering wheel and narrowed his eyes. The driver was trying a little too hard to look normal after whipping out into the street like that. And something seemed... Johnny studied the truck, with its tinted windows. Something seemed government-issue about it.

He reached for the radio receiver, then dropped it. *Fuck Fullerton. He'll just say something like, "It's not safe, man, come back to the office so I can make you cookies and milk." No way. I'll handle this myself.*

Johnny was a surveillance bitch, and his job was to... What was the word? *Surveil.* So he would surveil the shit out of this truck before he went back to the office tonight—see where it was headed, get the plate.

The truck in front turned right at a stop sign, in the direction of the highway. Johnny followed.

He wasn't trained for this, but instinct took over. Hang back, slip behind another car if he could. Signal turns before the other truck did, make it look like he just wanted them out of the way so he could get home. Mix in the occasional lane change.

Johnny and his new subject whirred out onto the main drag in town. Gas stations flashing blue, green, and gold, the Burger King marquee burning brown, the supermarket sign buzzing red, everything glittering. They were headed for the interstate.

Johnny edged up near the truck from the right as it approached a left turn. Then, just as it headed into the turn, he zoomed up straight and bent towards his driver's side mirror, staring in at the front of the truck he'd just passed. *Holy shit.* There were light bars behind the grill—definitely law enforcement.

What was another government vehicle doing around here tonight, peeling out like that? Nosing in on Johnny's case, maybe?

The Authority had this professor dude good. First they'd sent him an email advertising some political science symposium, but in fact exporting spyware which recorded every keystroke he made on his computer. Then case agents harvested all of his email passwords and began reading his incoming and outgoing mail, until their suspicions were confirmed: The professor was a member of the deadliest homegrown terrorist group in American history, Brigade 910—an anarchist group that had announced its arrival in 2018 by lacing an Iowa town's water supply with ricin, and had followed up with a wave of bombings in several cities.

And now, it turned out, maybe Johnny wasn't the only one snooping on the professor tonight.

Johnny drove on, no longer in front of the other SUV, having gone straight when it turned left. But he guessed it was headed east towards either Newark or New York. If he was wrong, he was wrong. But if he was right—he damn sure owed himself some frozen pizza before he went to bed for his fine investigative work. Maybe even a beer or three.

Johnny approached a sign for I-280. *This is it*, he thought, racing towards an alternate on-ramp for the interstate west. This was strictly movie-level now, and it was turning into the most exciting night of his life. Air bolted down his throat, cascaded through his chest, swirled in his stomach.

And in that instant that he reveled in his first non-mundane task on the job ever, he thought of those kids again, and of how he was getting deeper into an unauthorized reconnaissance mission even though he was just a twenty-four-year-old rookie hired to do surveillance work, not fight crime. He was not supposed to think for himself.

But Johnny couldn't help it. His dad had been a cop, and that blood pumped in his veins more than ever. Investigations opened up in front of him the way the field opened up for a quarterback right before he lasered a touchdown pass: he saw all the moving parts, had a feel for what would go where, when it was going to go, and when to go for broke.

Johnny flew onto the highway, westbound. He rocketed along the raceway, dropping into the left-most lane and then wrenching the truck left in a U-turn, bouncing across the shoulder and then through a cut-out in the divider. He surged into the left-most lane of the other side, now headed eastbound.

Not bad, Luca. Johnny slowed down and nosed into the middle lane. If he had guessed right about where that other truck was headed, it would be along shortly.

Johnny thought about the investigation of the professor. According to Hunter Peterson, the Special Agent in Charge of his office, the Authority had him nailed on material support, conspiracy, and a lot more. Johnny had even heard a little of his terrorist banter as he eavesdropped earlier tonight. *Would you die for this tonight?* the professor had said over the phone earlier. *If it came to it, would you give your life?* There was a pause. *I know about all their plans,* the professor had continued. *And believe me, if we don't stop them, it'll be the death of us all.* The words weighed on Johnny now as he drove: *The death of us all.*

Who was Brigade 910, anyway? The group probably numbered a couple of thousand at this point, and was mostly made up of nihilistic twenty- and thirty-somethings who'd warped into militancy in a country struggling with fifty percent youth unemployment. The group's credo was that the government must roll back its foreign policy and domestic security tactics to those of September 10, 2001—hence its name.

Johnny shook his head as he drove. He let a couple of trucks whip around him on the right, but that was it—his subject wasn't coming. He bit his lip. *Time to head back and apologize to Fullerton for being late. I can be a real dumbass sometimes.*

But then he saw a pair of wide headlights streaming up the left lane in his side mirror. Johnny tilted the wheel and faded into the right lane. *No way. No goddamn way.*

But there it was, the same truck that he was after, racing up the left lane and then passing him. Johnny squinted, made the license plate, and sounded the number to himself.

Now he'd hang back and let them get away—he didn't need this to turn into a game of who's-making-who. But who the hell were they?

Johnny clicked the radio. "Fullerton," he said. "I need you to run a plate."

"A plate? What for?"

"Don't worry about it. Just let me give you the numbers."

"I'm about to worry about it, Luca. Why in the hell am I running a plate?"

Johnny sighed. "Because I saw a suspicious vehicle back in the professor's neighborhood, and I tailed it awhile."

"You tailed it." Fullerton laughed, a this-shit-just-keeps-getting-worse laugh. "And what made you do that?"

Johnny feathered the steering wheel with one hand, coasting along the highway. "I think the vehicle was law enforcement, and it was leaving the scene the same time I did."

"It looked like an undercover vehicle? For real?"

"Check the plate. You'll see."

Fullerton groaned. "Give it up."

"J-K-G, 2-1-Y. Jersey."

There was a pause as Fullerton ran the license plate. Johnny was closing in on Newark now, just a few minutes out. He looked down at the row of switches, fastened to the dashboard above the console, for the different lights on the vehicle, the front strobes, the rear strobes, the red and blue flashers. He had driven this stretch of highway at this hour plenty of times over the years. But he never imagined he'd be driving it in an armored truck, doing surveillance for a top-secret government agency. Johnny fingered one of the switches as he drove. *What a trip.*

"I'll be damned," Fullerton said over the radio. "You little punk. You're right."

Johnny felt a rush in his stomach; blood flooded his face. "Who is it?"

"It's... us. It's the New York field office. One of their undercover g-rides. It's in our database."

"New York? You mean the Authority? Us?" What the hell did Johnny just break?

"That's right, the Authority. It's NYFO, man."

"Any idea what it was doing there?"

"I don't have a damn clue," Fullerton said. "Did you see it there while you were parked?"

Johnny was just thinking that himself. He *hadn't* seen the truck while he was working. If they were casing the house too, where were they? "I didn't see it at all. Maybe they were bugging the subversive down the street."

Fullerton didn't laugh. "Just get on back here. And if any aspect of your trip changes again, you make radio contact, you dig?"

Johnny squeezed the transmitter. "Dig."

He flew through downtown Newark, the sleeping office buildings snoring with loiterers and private security. He turned off the street, dipped into a parking garage, and at the gate swiped his index finger over a scanner. The barricade swung upwards to let him through, while an aluminum barrier to the right rolled upwards. He thumped over a speed bump into a fenced-in portion of the garage and backed into a spot. As the aluminum barrier started to roll back down, Johnny walked to the far corner of the pen, let himself out, and hopped in an elevator.

A few moments later, the elevator doors squeaked open, and Johnny stepped out. Dim light misted through the corridor, sprinkling off the gold-plated "United States Anti-Subversion Authority" sign inlaid into the wall. He swiped his finger over a sensor and yanked open a ballistic door.

Johnny stepped into the field office lobby. To the left was the receptionist's desk, encased in bulletproof glass. To the right were leather chairs arranged around a mahogany table. And on the right wall were pictures of the two most powerful men in the United States: President Reed Wilkins, his brown face glowing in a mustachioed smile, and Authority Director Alexander Bryson, stoic behind fair skin and ice-gray eyes.

Johnny opened another ballistic door. He walked straight ahead to the duty box, the partitioned-off surveillance organ of the office with a wall of monitors broadcasting video from all over the building. Fullerton was glancing up at a flat-screen monitor in which eight different sections of the office, each in their own box, were on camera. He spun around in his swivel-chair. "Welcome back, young buck," he said, smiling.

Fullerton was African-American. He stood six-one, a couple of inches taller than Johnny, and weighed about one hundred eighty-five pounds, a little thicker than him. His brown skin shined atop his closely-buzzed scalp.

"Yesterday in Cincinnati, police put down a college protest over the Total Information Awareness Act," a reporter said on the television that swallowed half the wall above, "using stun grenades and tear gas..."

Fullerton muted it and leaned closer. "Do either of us know what happened back there?" he asked.

Johnny dropped the SUV keys on the desk. "Not me," he said.

Fullerton nodded. "Me neither."

"Hear anything over the scanner?"

"Just the dispatcher, telling the local P.D. about a shot. Nothing since. But they've got to be there by now." He shook his head. "You just heard one shot?"

Johnny nodded. "Just one."

Fullerton leaned back. "Maybe he popped himself?"

Johnny shook his head. "Then what were those footsteps I heard? I think someone just… murdered our subject." He paused. "What are we going to do?"

"See what the locals come up with. We'll tell Peterson tomorrow morning and keep our ears open to find out what the P.D. found on the scene. We'll reach out to one of our boys in the department."

Johnny folded his arms. "What about that truck I saw?"

Fullerton furrowed his eyebrows. "We've got to tell Peterson about that, too. I mean... we've got to tell him everything. You shouldn't have tailed them, man." He shook his head again, but then he smiled. "But you damn sure picked up a pretty important piece of intel. Good looking out, kid."

"But what does it mean? What was a New York field office truck doing there?"

"I... I don't know, Luca. Maybe they were just trying to steal one of our cases. Wouldn't be the first time."

But something seemed off for Johnny. He had pulled away natural and slow. That other truck seemed kind of... rushed. "They shot out of there pretty quick," he said.

"They must've been shook up by the shot. Just like you."

But there was another thing which bothered Johnny. "They didn't come out the same way I did. They cut through the streets a different way. They were parked somewhere else." He bit his lip, then made a reach. "And I think they got a little bit later of a start then I did."

Fullerton looked into his eyes. "You think they know something about what happened tonight?"

Johnny had thought it, but... it was impossible. "There's no way they can," he said.

Fullerton stood up and clapped him on the shoulder. "Listen... You head on back to your place tonight. Come in tomorrow morning, and we'll fill out a report on all this and take it to Peterson. Get here early."

Johnny nodded. He was just now starting to feel tired. "All right. I will." The two slapped hands, and Johnny made his way towards the door. He took a step out of the duty box, then ducked his head back in. "Fullerton," he said.

"Yeah?"

"We need to tell Peterson they were driving fast."

Fullerton looked into his eyes again, and he understood. "We will, young buck."

Chapter 2

Johnny kicked a fragment of a broken bottle and walked over to his building, through the vestibule, past the sleeping elderly security guard inside. The elevator grinded and hissed the whole way up.

Finally home, he stood in the dark in his studio, his bed in the near left corner, his couch straight ahead, his kitchen to the right. He edged over to the far left corner, towards his desk, his hand groping the darkness so he didn't bang his leg on the coffee table. Johnny flicked on his desk lamp, and light streamed out to the edges of the room.

His bed wasn't made, and there was a mess of clean laundry on top of it that he didn't have time to put away. Yesterday's breakfast sat on the coffee table, an empty plate with a fork and some crumbs on it, an empty glass with milk caked around the rim beside it. A twenty-inch television sagged on a stand his mother had bought him last Christmas. A couple of stray socks lined the floor.

But up on the wall, everything sparkled: above his bed hung a plaque celebrating the 1998 Yankees, World Series winners the year Johnny was born, Mariano Rivera dropping to his knees on the pitcher's mound, the scores of every playoff and World Series game etched on the brass below. On the next wall hung one picture of Babe Ruth embracing Lou Gehrig and another of Yankee Stadium on Opening Day 1923, sandwiched around a dartboard bearing the Red Sox logo. Above Johnny's desk was a framed picture his brother gave him, a volcano erupting into a blackened sky, lava searing down the sides of the mountain.

Johnny powered up his laptop and headed to the bathroom. He peeled off his sweater and looked in the mirror.

He stood five-foot-ten, one hundred seventy pounds filling out his frame. Lack of sleep bled around his brown eyes. Beard stubble spotted his face– he hadn't shaved in three days—and his short brown hair clung to his scalp.

Returning to his desk, he plopped in the chair. He stared at a picture of him and his father in a digital photo frame, his dad holding him up on his shoulders under the bat at Yankee stadium. The digital clock burned in front of him: 11/18/22, 2:33 A.M. Johnny took the frame in his hands and paused the shuffle. So today was the day, after all.

One year ago tonight, Johnny's father had said goodnight to the guys around the stationhouse, then headed out for the night. Giovanni Luca, Sr. then parked in an abandoned lot, stuck a revolver in his mouth, and pulled the trigger.

Johnny stroked the LCD screen. In the picture, he was eleven. His father was big—an inch taller than Johnny was now, about 40 pounds heavier, broad-shouldered, thick brown hair tinged with silver—and Johnny was so little, swinging on his shoulders.

Johnny and his father weren't talking much at the time the old man ended his life a year ago, not since Johnny had told him he wanted to join the Authority. He was supposed to go to law school. "Don't join up with that damn nonsense," his father had said. "Do you have any idea what you're getting yourself into?"

They argued for a couple of months, and then Giovanni Sr. resigned himself to it. He told his son he was making a terrible mistake, that he was giving up his entire life to "be a cop." Funny, he was a cop himself. *But I raised you to be better*, he told Johnny. *So you don't have to chase around... what I chase around.*

Johnny put the frame back on the desk. *I just wish I knew why you did it*, he thought.

Even though it was two-thirty in the morning, Johnny still had work to do. He swiped his finger across a biometric sensor on his laptop, then fired up a secret program embedded in the computer. He snapped on a pair of headphones. *Another late night at the office*, he thought.

Johnny sat back and listened. *Let's see what you're up to, douchebag.* But only snoring crackled over the headphones.

The program that Johnny was running could remotely access the microphone on a subject's computer and then transmit audio back to a surveillance technician like Johnny. All the Authority needed was an IP address.

Johnny clicked a button, and a window reading "Live streaming" popped up. The Authority could also access a video feed from a subject's webcam, which Johnny was doing now. A sea of black rolled in the window. *Lights must be out.*

"We are approaching the dream of total information awareness," Director Bryson had said in a video address to Authority personnel last week. "We need only Congress and the President to take the necessary steps to allow us that power."

This might be a little less than total information awareness, Johnny thought as he stared at the black video stream, snoring cascading in his ear. He double-clicked on the name of another subject; late-night television mumbled in the background, but nothing else. There was no webcam.

It was Johnny's job to double-click down the list of subjects and monitor them for five minutes each, allowing the program to capture a "fingerprint" of the audio and video. He then had to upload the "fingerprints" to an Authority database, at which point another program would assimilate the data into master profiles of each subject—common sights and sounds in the residence, such as television viewing habits, music tastes, telephone conversations.

Johnny collected the "fingerprints," then uploaded the data and closed the program. Next he visited a website he'd been assigned to monitor, some subversive hangout called "Clocks Striking Thirteen."

Johnny couldn't help but smirk at the content. "The time has finally come to rise up against the criminal regime occupying the seat of power in Washington," read the homepage. "And the modern-day Lexington and Concord must be a rebellion against the rule of the Anti-Subversion Authority."

Nutjob.

He then moved on to a newspaper columnist who was on the Authority's watchlist. "Midnight in the Valley of No Heroes," blared the headline at the top of the screen. "The hour grows darker, and America's slumber deepens," the column began. The writer was no ordinary columnist; it was Gordon Bragg, billionaire media mogul, and avowed enemy of the Authority and Director Bryson. "Yesterday, the Total Information Awareness Act made it out of an important House subcommittee. Passage of the most draconian bill ever seen this side of the Atlantic is inching closer to reality..." Johnny had to summarize the column and grade it on a scale for such categories as "Degree to which article undermines public confidence in the Authority" and "Capacity to embolden or encourage terrorist groups." *Someone's getting bad marks tonight.*

Then he pulled up a bookmark for the sports section of the *New Jersey Tribune*. *Hey, pretty lady*, he thought, poring over the headshot of a brunette female columnist with rectangular glasses. *I know you.*

But he didn't just know her. It was Elizabeth Heathrow—Lizbeth—his best friend from college, now the best damn sportswriter for the paper. "Darnell Williams doesn't care much for turkey this Thanksgiving," she wrote. "But the Linden High star quarterback cares about the fixings—fixing to lead his team to a championship, that is."

Johnny laughed. *Love those leads.*

He gazed at the headshot for another moment. *This is about as much as I see of you these days,* he thought as he closed the page.

He pulled up his email, and there was a message from Lizbeth in his inbox. Johnny smiled, then double-clicked on the message. *Hey Gio*, it began.

Lizbeth was the only person in the world who called Johnny "Gio." His real name was Giovanni, like his father, but everyone called him Johnny. Except Lizbeth.

Hey Gio, the email read. *I know today is going to be hard for you, with your dad and all. But I just wanted you to know I'm thinking of you. Actually, I wanted you to know I'm always thinking of you. I miss you like crazy, I haven't seen you in forever! Love, Lizbeth.*

Johnny looked to the bottom of the message: *P.S. Just remember that when you lay down to sleep tonight, I'm thinking of you. You can get through this, you always have.*

Johnny started to reply, but instead put two fingers to his lips, kissed them, and laid them on the message. "Good night, beautiful," he whispered.

He'd have to email her back another time—when he *had* time. *There's so much to tell*, he thought.

Johnny looked out his window. On a clear night like tonight, he could see all the way to New York. The Empire State Building, the Chrysler Building—and the most majestic of all, One World Trade Center, rebuilt in 2013, swirling 1,776 feet into the vault of the sky.

Perched on the top floors of that building, on the same site where terrorists had rained death on Manhattan twenty years earlier, was the Authority New York field office. The agents on those floors—maybe even right now, as Johnny yielded to sleep—tangled with the biggest anti-terror cases in the world. They were out on the 2022 battlefield, breaking down doors, raiding safehouses, taking down subversives.

Johnny stood up and gazed out at the skyline. That was where he belonged, across the Hudson, serving his country. *Someday*, he thought, drawing the shades and cutting off the desk lamp.

As he lay down to sleep that night, Lizbeth was almost the last thing he thought of. He tried really hard for her to be. But every night he ended up in the same place, more so tonight than all the others.

How come you never told me? Johnny bit his lip and heaved, then shook it off. *All you had to do was tell me, Dad, I would've straightened out, we could've made everything better…* Johnny turned over. *Why, Dad? Why did you do it?*

He floated to sleep, his question pouring out the window, out onto the street below, dying on the cracked pavement that offered no answer.

Chapter 3

"Damn, you could have at least worn a tie," Fullerton said as Johnny strolled up to the duty box the next morning. "We've got to sit down with the boss."

Johnny glanced down at his khakis and button-down shirt with an open collar. "You mean you don't dig my style?"

Fullerton looked him over again and groaned. "You need to buy an iron, kid, for real."

Authority agents buzzed in and out of the duty box, flashing .357's on their hips and barking requests for equipment and surveillance vehicles to a second duty agent. As they cycled through, Johnny fixed his eyes on their weapons. His own hip was bare—surveillance guys didn't carry.

"Find anything out about last night?" Johnny asked.

"I did," Fullerton said. Strain cut across his face. "The cops found the kids hiding under their beds, terrified. And the professor was DOA at the hospital."

Johnny felt his face kindle. He'd heard a shot... and he'd known he had to run inside and save those kids. But he left them in there with whatever monster killed their father. Thank God they were alive.

"How do you know?" Johnny asked.

Fullerton gestured to the television on the wall. "Local cable's all over it," he said. "It's a big deal around here. I mean, he was a professor." He slapped Johnny on the shoulder. "Look, Luca... We did the right thing last night. You've got to believe me." Just then, the phone rang. "Duty desk," Fullerton answered.

Johnny dropped his shoulders. *DOA at the hospital. Who the hell killed our subject?*

"Peterson wants to see us," Fullerton said. "Let's hustle up."

Johnny followed him into the hallway. The two walked along the carpeted corridor to a conference room and sat down in leather seats at a roundtable. Johnny ran his fingers over the finish. Everything in the room was so new.

Congress had created the Authority with the Anti-Subversion Act of 2018, while the nation writhed in the mania of the Iowa ricin attack. "An entire town... wiped off the face of the earth," one cable news reporter said at the scene.

But the identity of the culprits was what jolted the country. The federal agencies had stormed off in search of Arab terrorists, only to find that the killers had sat in the back of American classrooms, had loitered in front of American 7-11s, had butchered thousands of "people" in American video games since the time they were seven. Not only that, but they'd immersed themselves in a sea of polemical websites branding America as an imperialist dictatorship, controlled by a military-industrial complex bent on oppressing the developing world. With an ugly world of unemployment, poverty, and war above, this black sea was inviting and never-ending.

And when these college-aged youth came up for air, they found terror-cell leaders beckoning them ashore: the founding fathers of Brigade 910. These leaders were soon amazed at their recruitment success, at how easily they could set up an "antiwar" or "anti-imperialist" meeting at a college and then break off the one student in the room alienated and empty enough to embrace militancy. Alienation and emptiness, as it happened, were increasingly easy to come by in the America of 2016-17, with the nation still writhing in the wreckage of the depression that began in 2008, and once a member was recruited, mind control drugs did the rest. The drugs, mixed into drinks at meetings in trace amounts and then directly administered as recruits became compliant, whipped members into paranoia, sapped their short-term memory, and broke down their minds into mush that the leaders molded.

The group declared war on the federal government with the Iowa attack. Congress smashed back the volley by creating the Authority—an agency that would rip out subversion at the roots. "For too long, we've coddled anti-American venom as 'free speech,'" said the senator who'd drafted the Anti-Subversion Act. "This is our moment. Either we begin to destroy the subversive element now, or we'll bury our dead by the thousands."

That senator was Alexander Bryson, now Authority Director, the second most powerful official in the United States. Johnny looked up at the picture of the Director on the wall, his thin silver hair swept to the sides of his thick bald scalp, the wrinkles on his sixty-year-old face edging into a smile through pursed lips. He was 6'4", his broad frame bursting against his suit when he walked, his swagger betraying a military man who'd notched more than a few kills in his career. Bryson's gray eyes looked like ice shavings.

"I want him on the phone in twenty minutes," a voice said at the door of the conference room. "Look, I know he's a congressman, but I want you to tell it to him just like that. I'm not some local cop from his district. Tell him I'm Hunter Peterson, and I work for the President, not him."

Johnny and Fullerton looked up at the Special Agent in Charge of their office. The SAIC was forty-eight years old, six-foot-two, nearly two hundred pounds, cords of neck muscles stacked on wide shoulders beginning to soften with age. Silver shone across his light brown hair. Lines eased across his face, at the corners of his mouth. He was clean-shaven—always—and everything on him was right where it should be. Diagonal blue stripes on his tie embraced his white collar in a full Windsor, silver cufflinks clasping at his wrists, leaving just enough room to let slip a silver-faced watch.

Peterson closed the door, then turned to face the young agent and the young surveillance technician. "So can someone tell me exactly what the hell happened last night?"

Peterson had called Johnny into his office his first day, about eight months ago, and given him some talk about "the mission" and the importance of doing the job right. He had read his name off a piece of paper, and hadn't uttered it in any of their meetings in the elevator or the parking garage since.

"Fullerton here told me the whole story," Peterson said to Johnny. "But now I want you to tell the story yourself."

Johnny winced. He should've just filled out a report last night. *Goddamn it.* "Well, sir—"

"Before you entertain me, what's your name again?"

Johnny stopped himself and took a breath. "Johnny Luca, surveillance technician."

"All right, then." Peterson walked over to a window, looking out at the New York skyline. "Go on."

Johnny looked over at the boss. Everyone knew he was a hardass, but damn, he was worse than his father. "The subject was in his bedroom at one o'clock last night, and the kids were in their rooms.

Then–"

"Based on what intel?"

"The last activity that the mikes picked up was subject putting his kids to bed. I heard him read them a couple of stories. Then he went back to his room. Nothing after that."

Peterson nodded, still looking out at the skyline, his back to Johnny and Fullerton. "The girl on News 12 says that the neighbors called police about a gunshot sometime a little after one. I'm going to assume you heard the same gunshot they did." He turned around and looked right at Johnny. "And I'm going to assume you were not asleep."

Johnny stiffened, then returned the look. "You assume right."

"Fullerton, what time did Luca contact you?"

"Right around one o'clock, sir," Fullerton said. "He told me he heard a shot."

"And you told him to leave?"

"Affirmative. I didn't want local police up on him during an investigation."

Peterson turned back to the window. His shoulders heaved once. He stroked his chin, started to say something, then stopped. He turned back around. "I know who you tailed last night, Luca."

Johnny's eyebrows flared up. "You do?"

"You goddamn near destroyed the most important investigation we have going on inside this office, but you just handed me something on a silver platter." He laughed to himself. "You might've handed me everything."

"What do you mean, sir?"

"There are a lot of things going on that you don't understand," Peterson said. "Things you and Fullerton are too young to understand. Do you know the mission of this office?"

Johnny remembered the oath he'd sworn. "Defend the Constitution against all enemies, foreign and domestic, defend—"

"Right, right, all that. All enemies, foreign and domestic. Domestic, boys. Remember that." Peterson pointed out the window. "You caught a vehicle from the New York field office leaving the scene last night. But there weren't any Authority agents inside."

"There weren't?" Fullerton asked.

"No. They were Brigade 910 terrorists who stole the truck so they could use the anti-bugging equipment inside to get into the house without Luca detecting them. They killed Professor Jacobs."

The words struck Johnny like a live wire whipping into a puddle. "But—" He turned to Fullerton, but his face was sunk in puzzlement. He turned back to Peterson. "But I thought the professor was a terrorist himself?"

"He was. But he knew too much about a major attack they're planning, and they knew we were after him."

"But how?" Fullerton said.

"That's for me to know. But the trail's going to go cold for awhile. They struck us a big blow last night."

The three were silent for a moment, until Johnny spoke up:

"Then we should strike one back, sir."

Peterson smiled. "You hear that, Fullerton? The kid's looking for a little action." He looked Johnny in the eyes. "And you're going to get it. Because I'm putting you and Fullerton together on this one. You two are going to make the trail warm again." Peterson held the gaze. "You showed a lot of stupidity last night, Luca. But a lot of guts, too. Sometimes they're two of the same thing."

Johnny tried not to smile, but he couldn't help it. SAIC Peterson had just sent him to the stratosphere. "What do you want us to do?" he asked.

"You'll be getting surveillance assignments with high-level targets. And Fullerton will be out in the field with you. He'll be the only one armed, and he'll be in charge. You're there for surveillance only."

Johnny nodded. *Good enough for me*, he thought, a smile still burning off of him.

A pretty middle-aged woman, blonde and smiling, ducked her head into the conference room. "Mr. Peterson, Congressman Sanders is on the phone," she said.

"Tell our friend I'll be with him in a moment, Cynthia." Peterson walked to the door, then turned back to the two young men. "Remember your oath," he said. "I've taken you both into my confidence, and I expect you to understand what that means. No chirping to your buddies around here, to your girlfriends, your boyfriends, whatever. The two of you witnessed something last night no one was meant to see, and now I'm going to work with that. If either of you breach my confidence, you can consider your career over." Peterson smiled. "Oh, and Luca?"

"Yes, boss?" Johnny said.

"You're on car wash duty for a month for disobeying Fullerton's orders last night." With a nod, Peterson was gone.

"Sorry, dog!" Fullerton said, laughing.

Johnny shook his head, then grinned. "Did any of that shit just happen?" he said.

"Something's up," Fullerton said. "Something's so up we'll break our necks trying to look at it."

Johnny looked at him. *Then I guess we'll just have to find out what it is.*

Chapter 4

That night, Johnny went for a walk around his neighborhood. He stopped at a lamppost with an "Impeach Wilkins!" sticker slapped on it. Except it wasn't just a lamppost: there was a camera inside the bulb above. And there was one on the next block, and the block after that, and throughout most of the city—and throughout most other cities these days.

Johnny ducked into a corner store, which was freezing cold inside. "No heat on in here, buddy?" he said to the man behind the counter.

"No heat, no nothing," the man said. "You know how is the price."

"Yeah, I do. It's bad, everything's bad." Johnny plucked a coffee pot and poured himself a cup. "But what are you gonna do?"

"Not everything is bad," the man said as Johnny approached the counter. "If you have family, you have everything you need already. You have family?"

Johnny thought of his brother away at college, and his mother in her little garden apartment. "Yeah, I have a family," he said.

"Then you are lucky man. This no heat, this cold, it means nothing. It may seem very bad, but there is always a way to make the good."

Johnny smiled. "You're right. Goodnight, buddy." He walked away.

He headed back, thoughts of his father rushing in as he walked. Johnny sighed. Just a few more hours, and he could toss November eighteenth away and get on with the rest of his year.

He reached for his radio key fob at the entrance of his building. He could hear the security guard laughing inside. *The dude's actually awake for once.*

"You are one pretty girl," the guard said as Johnny shouldered open the door. "Your friend is going to be real happy to see you."

Johnny pivoted inside, his eyes scanning left to right, first across the elderly, bald, drooling security guard, then across the figure of Elizabeth Heathrow.

A chill bolted down his spine, surged through his stomach and then back up to his throat, sucking out all the air. His knees buckled;

a smile spread across his face.

"Surprised, Gio?" she said.

Lizbeth smiled, and the lobby shone. She stood five-foot five, her slim body nestled in a light purple wool coat and blue sweater, jeans clinging to her legs. Her light brown hair fell in ribbons around her shoulders. A painter had colored in her bright face, stroked her thin eyebrows, fanned out her eyelashes, crafted her lips. Her cheekbones edged up, setting her eyes back, casting her forehead so that her olive skin poured past her eyebrows, leaving as a droplet her nose and splashing across the rest of her face.

Johnny looked into her green eyes, sparkling behind rectangular glasses. He half-laughed. She'd hated herself in those glasses ever since her boyfriend told her she looked better without them. But Johnny loved them, and she was wearing them tonight.

"Just a little," Johnny said.

"Well I knew you'd never respond to my email, or text me, or call. So I thought I'd corner you in your own building and force you to hang out with me. Oh, the horror!" Lizbeth giggled. "I've finally got you!"

Johnny threw up his arms. "I surrender. You got me."

"Where have you *been*? It's been months, man. Totally unacceptable."

"Just... you know. Busy with work." Johnny winced. Authority policy dictated that he not reveal his employer. There was a two-step approach: first, tell an inquirer you worked for "federal law enforcement"; and then if pressed further, say you were an office support technician for the FBI. And that's what Lizbeth thought he did.

Lizbeth got up, crossed the lobby to him, and hugged him. "Well I'm not going to let my best friend bail on me. I could never let that happen."

It was Johnny's fault. He'd gotten so wrapped up in work, everyone was hunting him down all the time. But it was kind of hard to be around Lizbeth when she was with...

"So how's Dick?" Johnny asked.

Lizbeth narrowed her eyes. "*Richard*," she said, "is doing just fine."

She'd been dating the same Red Sox fan jerk-off for almost three years, since senior year. Johnny grinned. "Tell him it's too bad about the playoffs this year." The Red Sox had been swept in the first round.

Lizbeth rolled her eyes. "Are we going to Coogan's or what?"

Coogan's was the pub around the corner. Johnny smiled. "Let's go—I haven't had a beer in days!"

And he was out into the street again, this time with Lizbeth by his side.

They had met in the first week of their freshman year, Lizbeth whispering to her roommate about the cute guy down the hall and Johnny telling his roommate about the hot chick he'd just smiled at. They rocketed into friendship that fall, keg-standing together, sleeping in each other's rooms, marveling at their mutual love of pizza burgers and professional wrestling. It was Johnny who knocked on Lizbeth's door one afternoon that fall and found her crying, having just broken up with her high school boyfriend. He sat with her on the floor, rocking her in his arms, stroking her hair just once. *This is the kind of stuff that has to happen,* he'd told her. And then, reaching down for the only thing he could come up with next: *Wanna get some pizza?* Lizbeth smiled just then, sunshine through rain.

One night, just once, they'd nearly gotten together. Johnny and Lizbeth went to the winter ball together in senior year, pregaming with friends in Lizbeth's suite and then dancing themselves into a sweat at the ball. *You've been positively charming,* Lizbeth said as she threw her arms around his shoulders for the last dance that night. *For a lush.*

Darlin', I'm not drunk, Johnny said, easing in step with her. *I'm completely wasted.* Johnny swung her back out, still dancing in step, and smiled. *Follow me. I want to show you something.*

He led her out onto campus, her heels clicking on the pavement winding along the tree-lined path, ankle-height lamps pouring yellow vapor into the December night. *I noticed this on the way over to your place tonight,* Johnny said, gesturing to a branch tilting with snow.

Lizbeth bundled up in her coat. *You mean you noticed that it's twenty degrees?*

Johnny tapped her shoulder. *Man up, Heathrow. You see, just when the wind blows...* The air was still; anticipation hung on her face. He looked skyward. *A little help down here!* he said.

Just then, the wind blew, and snowflakes drizzled about them. Johnny grinned.

What are you up to? Lizbeth asked.

Johnny threw his arms around her and started slow-dancing again, the snow misting onto their hair, their faces. *I thought this would be better than that dance back there,* he said.

Lizbeth buried her head on his shoulder. *It's beautiful,* she said, dancing with him.

Johnny drew her close again. *You know, I picked up a few things in that French class I'm in.*

Lizbeth laughed. *The one you took to meet chicks?*

Johnny rolled his eyes. *I was going to say I took it to impress you, but then you'd know I was lying.* Then he feathered Lizbeth's chin upwards with his finger, his mouth drawing nearer to hers. "*Vous êtes jolie,*" he whispered. "*Tres jolie.*"

Lizbeth leaned in as another wind swept through, more snow flakes drifting around them. "*Merci,*" she whispered back.

Her lips edged towards his, closing the cold between them, sealing in her breath on his. Lizbeth turned her head, her lips now before Johnny's, her eyes gliding up and down his face one last time. She closed her eyes.

Hey Luca, you guinea bastard! a voice yelled from across the lawn. *Are you coming to the party, or what?*

It was Johnny's mad dog of a roommate, Billy. He and Lizbeth held their positions a moment longer, their lips almost touching. One of them laughed, then the other. They went to different parties that night.

The two chalked it up to drunken weirdness, and that was it. Not like Johnny didn't think about it in the days and weeks after—how she fit into his arms just right, how her lips were melting onto his when Billy yelled for him—but he'd catch himself. Date Lizbeth? His beer pong teammate? And besides, Johnny was a little shy, shy over a girl for the first time in his chick-chasing career. Maybe she wasn't into him. So when she started dating Richard a couple of months later, Johnny swallowed it down and went back to hooking up with girls at parties.

Johnny looked at Lizbeth tonight as he held the door open for her at Coogan's. She looked the same as she did the night of the ball, even down to the glasses.

She almost skipped inside, hooking her arm in Johnny's. "You don't know how much I've needed this," she said.

Well, with Dick for a boyfriend, probably pretty badly. "Yeah, me too," Johnny said. Twenty-four hours ago he was parked in the truck in front of the professor's house.

He wondered if Lizbeth would eventually figure out the whole truth about what he did. She was pretty sharp as a journalist, and she knew her Gio Luca 101.

They glanced at the college kids jostling around the bar to the right, then sat down at a table to the left. A mural of a map of Ireland was plastered on one wall, and shamrocks and photographs of 1890s men with handlebar mustaches were everywhere. A rock song overlaid the hum of the crowd.

A waitress in a green apron walked over. *Two Newcastles*, Johnny thought.

"Two Newcastles, please," Lizbeth said.

Johnny smiled. "You can mix it up sometimes, you know? Maybe a Yuengling or a glass of milk or something."

"But Newcastle's the best!" Lizbeth fell silent for a moment, plaintiveness starting to streak across her face. "You know why I came to see you today, Gio."

Johnny nodded. "I know." *Because it's a year ago tonight. A year since Dad… did what he did.*

She brushed his hand. "How's it going?" she asked.

"Oh, you know. I'm too busy to even think about it."

Lizbeth looked into his eyes. "Are you going to tell me the truth?"

Johnny sighed. "It's the same as it always was. Just another day, nothing really new about it. What can I do?"

"You can talk about it, if you need to. You can always talk about it with me."

"I don't know if there's anything to tell." Johnny forced a smile. "So how's your column coming? I caught it yesterday. Darnell

Williams cares about the fixings—that's gold!"

Lizbeth groaned. "I knew you'd change the subject. You're such a mystery, you know that?"

"What do you mean?"

"I don't know. It's… it's so hard to track you down, I guess. I can't get you on the phone, or even get a text or an email back. Where do you go all the time?"

"I just have a lot of work." Johnny thought back to the night before, and Peterson's assignment that morning. "A lot. Long hours."

The waitress plopped the beers on the table. "Maybe you have a lot of work, or maybe you're avoiding me," Lizbeth said. "I hope it's not because of Richard."

Johnny threw back some Newcastle. "Dizzle has nothing to do with it. Don't worry." *'Dizzle" is definitely my favorite nickname for Dick.*

"'Dizzle.' Cute." Lizbeth pursed her lips. "I think he's going to propose soon."

Johnny took a swig to keep from gulping. *How about that.* "Are you excited?"

She looked down, then back at him. "Yeah, I am."

You don't look it. "Then I'm happy for you, dude." Johnny smiled. "Everything's coming together. The big-time lawyer and the Pulitzer-winning journalist, getting married."

"Yeah, with Darnell Williams and his fixings," Lizbeth said, laughing.

"And getting married… You're down with that?"

Lizbeth took another gulp of her beer. "I think so."

Johnny narrowed his eyes. "You *think* so."

Lizbeth sighed. "I don't know, Gio. Sometimes… sometimes I dream, you know?"

"Dream of what?"

"Of another life, dude. Writing about more serious stuff… traveling the world… catching the Roman sunset as it glints off the Coliseum. Stuff like that." Lizbeth slapped Johnny's arm. "And what about you? You don't dream of adventure out in the stars?"

"I think I'm happy with adventure here on earth."

A shroud of seriousness fell across Lizbeth's face. "But you can do more than that, Gio."

Johnny swigged his beer and sighed. "Maybe someday."

Lizbeth shook her head. "You're living in this 'someday' cloud. You don't have to wait. You can just… reach out and grab whatever you want." Her hand brushed Johnny's. "We both can."

The hairs on Johnny's hand tingled to life. "And you're thinking… you might do that?"

Lizbeth paused, and in that moment her eyes betrayed her. But her words didn't: "No," she finally said. "I just lose my head sometimes. I've got a good thing going, you know?"

Don't we all. "Yeah, I know."

The first round gave way to four more, but the conversation only got lighter as the beers got heavier: the Yankees and the Mets and Thanksgiving plans.

When they were finished, Johnny led Lizbeth back to his place. "I'd better get going," she said when they arrived. She stumbled, then fumbled for her car keys.

"I don't think so," Johnny said, catching her. "Maybe you should come up and get some coffee before you try to drive."

Lizbeth laughed. "God, when are we ever going to grow up?"

Johnny opened the door. "Hopefully never," he said.

They went upstairs, and he started making coffee. She leaned back on the couch, picked up her phone to call Dick, then tossed it aside. Her eyes fluttered. "Gio?" she said, half-asleep.

"Yeah?"

"The reason... why I came... to see you was to make sure you're doing okay because of your dad. Are you really doing okay? Are you hurting?"

Johnny looked away. "I'm all right." *That's true, isn't it?* he thought.

"Because you know you mean everything to me, right? If you were ever sad or upset, I would drop everything just... just to make you smile..." Lizbeth sank into the couch and yawned. "You don't fool me," she said, the armrest muffling her voice. "You're the sweetest guy in the world. Or maybe... just for me... you are..." She snuggled up on the couch.

Johnny looked down on her as she slept. *Is it lame to feel really lucky that I get to watch her sleep?* Her arms clutched the arm rest, her legs draped in, a little smile resting on her face, tangled in her dreams.

He gathered her in his arms, laid her in his bed, and draped a blanket over her. "Goodnight, dork," he whispered, taking off her glasses. He sighed. Maybe this week would get normal at some point?

Johnny lay down on the couch. It was way past midnight now—a year without his father had passed.

When Giovanni Sr. left him, Lizbeth was there more than anyone, every day, every hour. *We don't have to say anything, she said to him one night*, laying his head in her lap and stroking his hair. *Just sit here, and everything will be okay.*

Johnny glanced at her one last time as she slept. It wasn't November eighteenth anymore, and Lizbeth was here. For now, everything was okay.

Chapter 5

Hunter Peterson, clutching a glass of scotch on the rocks, stalked around the study of his townhouse. Photos of presidents filled his walls, with Peterson men beside them—first his father, then himself, over sixty years of defending the Chief Executives of the free world and earning their confidence. He glanced at the picture of his father Hank with Eisenhower, the young Secret Service agent shoulder-to-shoulder with the President, Hank smiling straight ahead, Eisenhower keeping his chin tight. Peterson poured down some scotch, felt it dance in the back of his throat and steam its way down.

The next picture was of his father and Kennedy. Hank Peterson beamed, face-to-face with the President, who smiled in reply, his head thrown back a little, his hand tapping Hank's elbow. The Oval Office desk was behind them, but Peterson liked to think of his father and President Kennedy as buddies in polo shirts on a yacht at Hyannis, about to jump overboard for a swim.

On the intersecting wall were pictures of the younger Peterson with every President in the line from Clinton down to Wilkins. But he stopped in front of the Wilkins picture, only because that was the only one where he had a smile like his father's—returning a smile from a man who felt like his friend. When Peterson had arrived for the photo-op, Wilkins was poring over his papers, his forehead resting on two fingers of his right hand, his sleeves rolled up, his tie dropped below his open collar. The President rose to his feet and asked for a moment to button up and throw on his suit jacket, but Peterson said that if it were all right, he'd actually like to take a picture with a working President—all the others had seemed so... handled. Wilkins understood. *Reed Wilkins*, he said, extending his hand. *The working President.*

That was almost two years ago, just after Wilkins's inauguration. After serving on detail for candidate and President-elect Wilkins, Peterson would be leaving the Secret Service. He was headed to Newark to be Special Agent in Charge of the Newark field office of the Anti-Subversion Authority, now the most elite civilian agency in the government.

Peterson studied Wilkins. He was African American, tall and

broad, his graying brown hair hugging his brown scalp. They had told him to ditch the mustache, but he would hear none of it. *I've worn this mustache from Baghdad to Washington*, he told his advisors. *And I don't reckon the voters will hold it against me now.* He was right.

Back then it was all pomp, with cable news carpet-bombing viewers with the astounding tale of the kid from Ohio who had become the tough-on-terrorism President.

Now everyone was after him. The plotters were twisting the elements against Wilkins, stirring winds of public resentment and raining fire on his presidency. The unemployment was his fault, the surging oil prices, the terrorism, the rioting, the gradual breakdown everywhere of everything. One side blamed him for anti-terrorism laws which dammed back free speech and had chewed up thousands under tasers and tear gas canisters. The other side blamed him for not capturing or killing every member of Brigade 910 in the United States—and for his opposition to the Total Information Awareness Act.

Peterson gulped the rest of his drink and slammed the glass on his desk. The slamming wouldn't wake anyone up—Patricia had passed away five years ago, and he had no children. He headed to the basement.

The plotters had done this to President Wilkins, like they had done everything to him from the beginning, first because they thought he'd be their boy in the White House and then because they knew he wouldn't. They couldn't derail him in the 2020 election, but they weren't going to wait for 2024.

As Peterson yanked on the pull-chain light in the basement, he realized that this was the two-plus-two that both he and Professor Anton Jacobs knew equaled four. What separated them now was that the professor had been killed.

He thought of turning the fans on, that maybe the basement was bugged and he needed to mask the sounds of his movement, but fans in November would be too suspicious. He had thought of using anti-bugging equipment to jam any motion detectors and listening devices, but the possession of such implements was criminal. Peterson couldn't take the equipment from his office, because the surveillance cameras were always on and the thugs manning them were bound to report any breach, even by a SAIC; he couldn't buy materials to design his own such equipment, because a purchase by credit card would throw him on a secret Authority grid tracking Americans' credit-card transactions; and any merchant nowadays was sure to report a purchase in hundreds of dollars of cash as suspicious.

So Peterson slid aside a weight tree in the gym he had furnished in the basement. He peeled back a section of rubberized track, then pulled out a section of linoleum which was underneath. Below was a two-by-two concrete shaft, and a safe. He took a deep breath, then pulled out the safe. Its contents could kill him.

He stuck his thumb over a reader, and the safe beeped and clicked from within. Peterson pulled it open.

He reached inside and removed a poster, rolled and jammed in there. He unrolled it, setting a weight at each corner to keep them from rolling back, and clicked on a flashlight.

Below him was an investigation flow-chart, like they used to make in the old days, and on the chart were arrayed headshots of administration officials, military men, senators, corporate executives, and journalists—the plotters.

Peterson reached into the safe and pulled out another poster, which he unfurled and weighed down with more iron plates. This was not a flow chart, but rather an appendix. It was arranged into columns: federal agents, police officers, politicians, executive branch functionaries, journalists, academics—obstacles to the plot who were dwindling by the month.

The ones who had died, whether by suicide, or robbery, or car accident, or allergic reaction, or food poisoning, or drowning, or otherwise, had a red "X" slashed through their faces. Peterson pulled a red marker out of his pocket and found Professor Jacobs's picture on the poster. *I was so close*, he thought. *So close... to finding out what you knew.* Peterson stroked one line across Jacobs's face, then another diagonal to it. A red "X."

Really, there were two plots, not one—two tumors metastasizing side-by-side that would soon pump toxins into the republic. The first, however gruesome, at least made sense: Brigade 910, according to intelligence reports, was preparing for a massive spring offensive which could slaughter tens of thousands in simultaneous attacks, an offensive which they called "Project Orion."

But to Peterson, the second plot was the more treasonous. It had revealed itself to him pixel-by-pixel since he'd joined the Authority, like a picture crawling down the screen over an old dial-up connection, the last sliver flashing before him with Luca's revelation about the Authority truck fleeing the scene last night.

If his intelligence was sound—if his informants, some of whom now had red X's across their faces in his appendix, were credible—and if he hadn't gone crazy—Peterson could now conclude that a band of ultra-nationalists within the government was planning to assassinate President Wilkins for being too soft on the terror war.

Peterson stared at his flow-chart. *Maybe I am crazy*, he thought. *But if Luca really saw what he says he did…*

Professor Jacobs was no terrorist; Peterson had fed that line to Luca and Fullerton to co-opt them into the surveillance op. But the professor knew something about the Authority plot to kill President Wilkins, and last night he ate a bullet for it.

It was Authority agents from the New York field office—not Brigade 910 terrorists, as Peterson had told Fullerton and Luca—who had broken into the professor's house and murdered him in his sleep. *They're executing dissidents now. This is way beyond drone strikes in Pakistan.*

And with Jacobs gone, now Peterson was back to scooping sand in his hands to pick out the one grain that held the truth.

He pulled a manila envelope out of the safe, fished out a headshot, and pinned it to the top of the chart. It was Shepherd Moloch, the SAIC of the New York field office, who Peterson now knew had dispatched the assassins across the river last night to Jacobs's home. In the order to come, he was to be entrusted with enforcement of the Total Information Awareness Act.

Peterson fished out another headshot and then pinned it above Moloch's. It was Alexander Bryson, Authority Director, former senator and army officer bent on the brutalization of subversives—Alexander Bryson, leader of a cabal of hyper-jingoists who'd decided to murder their President for his weakness in the face of the new homegrown terror threat. It was to be a very public execution, not just of Wilkins, but of democracy—and blamed on Brigade 910, of course.

This was zero hour for America, here in 2022— two plots mushrooming into reality independently of each other, one engineered by the terrorists, the other by those sworn to defend America from them. And Peterson had to stop them both.

He thought of his father, who resigned after Kennedy was shot and never told stories about his Secret Service days. Years later, when he was dying of cancer, he brought up Kennedy to Hunter. *That was the most false-flag bullshit that ever was*, the old man said, using the intelligence term for an attack staged by one party and then blamed on another. *The whole thing was a goddamn frame-up, ordered by all those bastards on the inside.*

Peterson had thought his father's mind was in its last jumbled throes, and he let it go. But tonight the words came back to him: *false-flag.*

It all went in a straight line: The assassination of President Wilkins; the passage of the Total Information Awareness; the construction of a surveillance state by the Anti-Subversion Authority.

Peterson knew it by what they called it: "Operation Reichstag."

Chapter 6

There was no radio in the truck, no lights or sirens, and Johnny and Fullerton carried no identification of any kind. This was a "black bag" operation.

"Black bag," as Peterson had explained it, meant this: take your black bag of equipment, do the job as ordered, and prepare to be completely on your own no matter the eventuality.

Johnny tensed in the passenger's seat of the black SUV, parked in the woods in upstate New York, awaiting the sight of a sedan pulling out of a gated driveway. He and Fullerton had rolled up about seven o'clock this mid-December morning, snaking around bends on the county highway and dipping down hills, gliding by woods, over brooks, and along farmland. Before them a long driveway wound up to a red house sitting on a lawn stiff with frost, a backyard of hills bridging their way to the horizon; no other houses were around. At the front of the driveway was a black wrought-iron gate with motion detectors on top, fanning out to enclose the property.

Peterson had told them to wait for the subject to pull out of the driveway in a blue pickup around eight-thirty that morning; sure enough, at eight-thirty-one, a blue pickup came tumbling out of the gate. Next up was his wife, due to leave the property in a red sedan around ten-thirty.

Johnny clutched his black bag. Peterson had dispatched him and Fullerton to this outpost, a farm owned by a terror suspect, and they were to string up the house with surveillance devices. They'd parked the car in the woods across from the front of the property, camouflaging it with brush.

Johnny checked his watch; ten-thirty-four. Fullerton was trained for this, and he was not. But Peterson had told him that he'd better start getting used to planting surveillance if he wanted in on this operation. *On-the-job training*, he'd said with a smile.

"Fullerton," Johnny asked, "what are we supposed to do if one of them comes home while we're inside?"

"It's a black bag, man," Fullerton replied. "We'll do what we have to do."

Just then, the gate swung open, and a red sedan slipped out, the gate closing behind. Fullerton turned to Johnny. "Let's do this," he said. Johnny grabbed his bag and poured out of the truck, running after him. He wondered if this was what his father felt like the first time he chased down a bad guy.

Black bags in hand, clad in camouflage gear, they bounded up to the gate. Fullerton unsheathed a slender radio transmitter and pushed a button, the gate's motion detectors blinking twice and then dying. Johnny hit the fence mid-jump and threw himself over the top, his partner landing a step behind. He charged up the driveway as Fullerton ran behind him, holding up his transmitter as if lighting torches, jamming all the residence's motion detectors.

Johnny pulled an infrared heat-sensor from his bag as he reached the door, swabbing it over the wooden structure with three panels of glass cut into it. He gave a thumbs-up, then raced around to the right as Fullerton dropped his bag on the front step. He waved the sensor over an outside wall—nothing. "All clear," he said into his headset. He scanned the exterior walls around the perimeter of the home, reporting into the headset that there was no one inside, and then rejoined Fullerton on the front step.

"Get your disabler out," Fullerton said as he jammed a tool into the doorknob. "Knock out the alarm."

Johnny removed a slender transmitter of his own from his bag, fumbling and then dropping it. Fullerton grabbed it and flipped it back to him in one motion, not saying a word. Johnny caught it and punched a button, a beep letting him know the alarm had been powered down. His partner held up his hand, wrenched his tool a few more times, and then pushed open the door.

"Now remember the most important part," Fullerton said. "You've got to leave everything the exact damn way you found it." He pulled off his shoes and threw them in his bag. "Do the same with yours," he said.

Pretty nice for an old farmhouse, thought Johnny as they ran across white tile at the landing out onto hardwood floors. To the right was the dining room, a green china closet towering above the rectangular wooden table gilded with two candlesticks and a bowl of gourds and squash, a window framing twisting leaves of yellow and orange outside. Fullerton grabbed a chair, set it under the china closet, and toed the upholstery. "The highest points are always the best," he said, pumping himself onto the chair and peering over the top of the closet. "Impossible for the subject to detect." He reached into his bag and pulled out a clear plastic bag without rummaging. "There's no door in this room, but we're going to need to set up a detector and code it so that it shows up as a different room on the grid. We need to establish different rooms so we can pinpoint location during the op, so the mikes can follow movement from room to room." He whistled as he embedded a piece of equipment, too small for Johnny to see, into the cabinet.

Damn, he's good at this. Fullerton had set up the surveillance for Professor Jacobs's house. Here he was now, standing in a room in a house he'd never been in, with the chance the owner could come back at any second, and the dude was whistling. This was the picture of the agent Johnny wanted to be.

"This is only a sliver, nothing but a little trifling piece," Fullerton said. "Smaller than your fingertip, kind of like a contact lens. It's lying flat on the surface of the wood up here, but it's going to shoot an infrared beam out to the entrance of the room once I code it. It's programmed to melt into the surface precisely at twenty-four hours, or longer, if I ask it to. It doesn't make that ticking noise when it's tripped and it doesn't smell or stain anything when it melts– just a little droplet. This is a fifty-thousand-dollar piece of equipment here, Luca."

Johnny nodded. *Some contact lens.*

"We're not going to be able to hook up any cameras," Fullerton said. "It takes too long. So we're going to have to rely on motion detectors and audio." He hopped down, set the chair back in place, and stood in the threshold of the room, holding up a device that flashed green or red in response to his movements. "I'm coding the detector. Watch me."

Johnny looked over Fullerton's shoulder as he lined up the transmitter with the motion detector on top of the china closet, punching buttons on a keypad first to tell it that the contact would be across the threshold of the room, then to tell it that this would be a room that was to be partitioned off as a separate room on the monitoring system out in the truck.

Next was the listening device. "Always put it inside something that won't be opened anytime in the near future," Fullerton said, waving Johnny over. He dropped to his knees at the dining room table, took apart one of its joints, slipped a microphone inside, and screwed the joint back up.

"You'll hear the sound of this dude's voice in your ear just like he was with us out in the truck. The wood of the table doesn't do a damn thing but conceal the mike. The mike costs more than the detector."

Fullerton then coded the microphone to transmit to the truck on a certain channel at all times, where every minute of dead and live air would be digitally recorded. He next coordinated the detector, the listening device, and the command center in the truck, setting it up so that whenever the room was breached, the channel would switch to the microphone in this room so that he and Johnny could listen in.

"Now we do this in every room," Fullerton said.

They padded through the house, sticking detectors and listening devices on top of the refrigerator, inside chairs, bed frames, and smoke detectors, in the fireplace. "The mike is fireproof," Fullerton said.

While they were working in the last room, the master bedroom, Johnny glanced at a picture frame on one of the night tables, a picture of a blonde in a graduation cap and gown.

He looked at the picture next to it. It was a little girl, a blonde—probably the same girl—in a ballerina costume, with pink angel wings. A man with light brown hair and glasses stood behind her with one hand on her shoulder and the other around a woman's waist, smiling. The woman, her curled blonde hair falling around her slight shoulders, looked down as she played with the girl's hair.

Johnny recalled the briefing for today's subject. The husband was a money launderer for terrorists, occasionally hosting Brigade 910 meetings in the house.

Johnny stared in at the man in the photo. He didn't look like a terrorist—he looked like the kind of guy who pushed his glasses up on his nose every two minutes as he read a history book in between sips of tea.

After Fullerton finished, they headed down to the front door.

"We're going to leave real natural, real smooth," he said. "I'm going to open the door, we're going to put our kicks back on, and we're going to do a nice brisk walk. I'm going to un-jam the motion detectors, turn the alarm back on, set everything back the way it was. You just keep walking."

Fullerton popped open the door, and they moved just as he'd said, down the driveway, across the narrow street, into the woods, and into the truck. He dropped into the driver's seat, pulled the door closed, and checked his watch. "Forty-two minutes," he said. "About what I expected." He laughed. "You try an exercise like that down at training, you're lucky if you do it in less than three hours." He laughed again. "Forty-two minutes. That's what I call total information awareness, bitches."

Everyone's favorite phrase.

What else could you call it, anyway? The only difference between the proposed law and what the Authority already did was that most of the stuff the Authority did was illegal. The new law would change that for good.

"You need to understand, something like that don't come off unless there's solid intelligence," Fullerton continued. "Peterson gave us perfect intel—how many rooms in the house, when they'd be leaving, and the most important thing—when they'd be back."

"Which is when?" Johnny said.

"Wifey'll probably be back in about ten minutes."

"*Ten* minutes?"

Fullerton chuckled. "That's right, young buck. Too close for you?" He didn't wait for Johnny to answer. "That's what our job is. You get these little windows. Little windows to investigate, little windows to plant your surveillance, little windows to make an arrest before an attack happens. We work right on the edge all the time. And damn, we violate some serious constitutional rights along the way."

"What do you mean?"

"Well take this place, for instance. Where's our warrant at? Did Peterson go to the magistrate and show him what probable cause we got?"

"I don't know, did he?"

"He damn sure did not. Way things are these days, if you want a warrant, it don't even matter a goddamn if you've got probable cause, if you can show your investigation is related to terrorism. But us? We didn't even bother. We just broke into a man's house and fucked with his papers and effects."

"We did? I thought we just bugged him."

Fullerton laughed and shook his head. "I was quoting the Fourth Amendment. They teach you anything at Ravioli U?"

Johnny rolled his eyes, then sharpened them. "Fuck that shit. He's a terrorist scumbag. We're out to catch him, not wait until people get killed."

Fullerton shook his head again. "That's right, Luca. Fuck all that shit like the Constitution. Maybe I'm the only one, but I thought that's the only reason why there's even such a thing as the Authority right now. To defend the Constitution, to stop those dudes who would take shit over and go breaking into people's pads in the middle of the night... or the morning."

"Then why are you an agent?"

"Honestly? Money, man. The economy's so fucked up now that I can make more in the government than for a company, if I could even find a job at all."

Bullshit. You're in it for a lot more than the money.

In fact, Fullerton sounded just like someone he knew very well.

Every night before you go to bed, thank God you're born in the land of the free, Johnny's father used to tell him all the time when he was a kid. *The greatest country in the world.*

Giovanni Sr. spent his spare time reading books about the Founding Fathers, watching specials on the History Channel about the Revolution and the War of 1812, studying biographies of every President, poring over tomes about constitutional crises, great compromises, and war.

It was a funny hobby for a guy who investigated drug dealers and racketeers during the day. Sometimes he took ugly things home from the job—things that wired his mouth shut during dinner, made him pound the table just a little harder when Johnny or his brother played with their food or cursed in front of their mother—but at night, he'd be on the couch watching more History Channel, or debating on the phone any of his friends who were feeling political that evening. It was the kind of thing that made Johnny feel secure in the world before he fell asleep at night, the way his father should be.

He only saw it abate after the Iowa attack. When the television pounded his father with images of protesters clashing in the streets, of mounted police restoring order with tasers and tear gas—when the cable news channel led with a graphic that asked, *Cracking republic?*—when then-Senator Bryson gave a speech declaring that now was the time to go about *re-calibrating our conception of our rights*, Johnny saw his shoulders sag. Just in that time.

Johnny leaned back in the passenger seat and glanced at Fullerton. *Just like Dad.*

Johnny was glad he thought differently. Twenty-one years ago, the World Trade Center collapsed onto the ideals Fullerton and his father clung to. And if anything remained, the Iowa attack pulverized it.

There was only terrorism and counter-terrorism. He didn't like thinking of the world that way, but that wasn't Johnny's choice—it was the terrorists'. He was only three years old when the towers collapsed, and his mind couldn't form a single pre-War on Terror memory—as far back as he could remember, there was Iraq and Afghanistan, suicide bombings and IEDs and drone strikes and televised beheadings… and then the Iowa attack, and the emergence of a homegrown enemy that could wreak far more havoc in America than al Qaeda.

Maybe it was time, after all, to recalibrate Americans' conception of their rights, like Bryson said.

Chapter 7

"You look more bored than a chick out with you on a date," Fullerton said to Johnny as the two sat in the truck out in the woods some seventeen hours later in the pre-dawn darkness. "What were you hoping for, a pornographic experience?"

Johnny grinned, then rolled his eyes. They'd sat in the woods since eleven-fifteen the morning before. After the wife came home, they picked up her movements through the house, room-to-room, the microphones transmitting the vacuum cleaner, the squeezing of the mop, and later, the clanking of pots and pans. At one point, there was a phone call: "Hey sweetheart... good luck on your last final. . . yeah, noon would be good... I'll see you then, Sarah. Be careful driving... I love you, too." Must have been the daughter. Other than that, it was daytime TV.

Around six o'clock, the blue pickup truck came rumbling back up the driveway. A portly man in a shirt and tie dropped out. "Hi Chub," the wife greeted him.

Chub. Pretty badass nickname for a terrorist.

After that, there was just shuffling in and out of the different rooms, clattering of silverware at dinner, and small talk that almost put Johnny to sleep. Work was fine, the general contractor was a real asshole, a snowstorm would be blowing in over the weekend, Sarah would be home for winter break tomorrow, and no, she wasn't bringing that emo freak she'd been dating, they broke up. And for Chub's information, the wife said, he wasn't an emo freak, he was a nice boy.

Johnny and Fullerton waited on into the night, past the made-for-TV movie about Brigade 910 operatives bombing soft targets, past bedtime for Cheryl and Chub. As the latter's snoring drifted through their headsets, Johnny leaned back and closed his eyes for a moment.

"You got big plans for Christmas?" he asked Fullerton.

"Just me, my brothers, and my mom. How about you? Big Italian thing going on?"

"No. Just me and my brother, and my mom."

"Where's your old man at?"

Johnny bit his lip. "Where's yours?" he asked.

"Not around, man. He was never around. You know the deal." Fullerton paused. "Same deal with you?"

"No. He passed away about a year ago."

Fullerton nodded in understanding. "Sorry, Luca."

Johnny and Fullerton agreed to take turns sleeping; Fullerton was to go first. "You make sure your ass stays awake," he said. "You fall asleep, and I swear, man, I'll take out my gun and shoot you. I will cap you."

Johnny leaned back. Staying awake wouldn't be a problem. He'd gone through nights like this, not allowed to listen to music or dedicate brain cells in any way other than to listen to that snoring on the headset. He was keeping America safe.

Johnny thought of the time he and Lizbeth read each other's palms one afternoon in her dorm freshman year. *I see big things for you*, she said, tracing a fingertip over a line in his hand. She paused, biting her lip. *Rodeo clown, I think.*

Johnny rolled his eyes, then grabbed her hand and traced a fingertip over her palm. *Hmm*, he said. *I see you becoming… someone who tells better jokes. In like fifty years, anyway.*

Lizbeth's green eyes met Johnny's. *I'll be an investigative journalist first*, she said. *And I'll travel to track down the truth, travel all over the world. And someday… I'll break a huge story, something that'll change everything.*

Johnny wondered what she was up to about now. She was probably sleeping at that ass-pirate Dick's apartment. Or maybe working late on a story. Or maybe—

A green light flashed on the panel.

Johnny bolted upright and stared in at the monitor. The back door, leading out from the kitchen, had been breached. There wasn't snoring on his headset anymore. Instead there was a padding of feet and a ruffling of clothing.

He pushed Fullerton, then shook him. No car had pulled up, it couldn't be the daughter or anything like that—

"What, man?" Fullerton said, thrashing awake.

Johnny pointed at the monitor. "The back door, the back door—"

"What?"

"Listen."

Footsteps sprinkled across the airwaves. It had to be more than one person—it sounded like a march. There was bustling in the kitchen.

A green light now flashed at the threshold of the living room.

There were still no words, only footsteps. "What do we do?" Johnny asked. "What now?"

Fullerton raised a finger. "Quiet," he said. "We just sit here and take our surveillance. Those are the orders."

There was creaking on the steps now. The microphone tracking the march was so sensitive, Johnny figured, that they probably heard that creaking better in the truck than anyone in the bedroom would. He strained his ears. First there was a chorus of footsteps; then a duel of taps on the stairs; then a single specter of footsteps mounting. *Four of them.*

"Switch your headset to the master bedroom," Fullerton said. "Tell me what you hear."

Johnny switched over. Chub's snoring cascaded into his ears, Cheryl's light breaths breezing between the eruptions. "The same," he said. He grabbed Fullerton's arm. "Look, man, no car pulled into that driveway, there's a bunch of intruders in the house—"

Fullerton ripped his arm away. "Are you going to bust in there? Or are you trained to sit your ass in that chair and record what's going on inside?" His eyes darted at the panel; Johnny's followed.

The bedroom door, flashing green.

The door creaking. Footsteps across the room. Then a thud.

"Cheryl... Cheryl, is that—what the—" A crack.

"Honey? Is everything all ri—" A woman's scream.

"Please, take anything you want..."

There was another crack, then a crash on the hardwood floor, then a scream rising over the other sounds like smoke over an explosion.

"Get out of my house!" Chub yelled. There was jockeying on the floor, footsteps crashing back and forth, objects shattering, falling—but no voices of the intruders. And then, a new voice:

"Now, do them!"

A shotgun exploded in Johnny's ears. Cheryl screamed. Then there was a cocking, and another explosion. No more screaming.

Johnny's insides collapsed; he felt himself turn red. *What the fuck is happening*, his mind mumbled to itself.

"Check them," said the voice that had given the order to kill.

More footsteps. "He's done," another voice said.

"So's she," said a third.

"Are we ready?" asked a fourth voice.

"Affirmative," said the voice who had given the order. "You two go downstairs and start taking what you need. Remember—take everything of value. This is a robbery." A pause. "We'll stay up here and take care of our end."

Johnny punched the dashboard. "I'm going to take care of *you*, motherfucker," he said, grabbing the door handle.

"No, you're not," Fullerton said, yanking him back.

Johnny tore loose. "Get the fuck off of me!"

"They got shotguns, man. You wanna die?"

"Let them fucking kill me! We can't let them get out of here!"

"We don't have a goddamn choice!"

Johnny glared at Fullerton. For the first time, he saw fear dripping off his face.

"All right, give me the vial," the ringleader said over the headset.

"Listen," Fullerton said. Johnny sat up.

"Blood from an inmate at Riker's Island who got released last month—we've got a guard working for us on the inside. Poor guy just got cut while he was trying to rob these two, and now he went and shot them."

It was a set-up—a robbery by an ex-convict on the outside, and an assassination on the inside.

"They're professionals in there, whoever they are," Fullerton said. He groaned and lowered his head. "But who the fuck would do something like this?"

"The same people who did the professor," Johnny said. "Fullerton, if you have any balls, you'll come with me and stop them before they get away."

"If you try to go... I'll take you down. Don't try it."

Johnny grinned. "Why? Are you with them? Should I turn around so you can give it to me in the back of my head?"

"They've got an army in that house. They could have automatic weapons, body armor, who knows what the fuck they're carrying. We take our recording to Peterson as soon as we get out of here. That's our move."

Johnny sank in his seat. He had to fight whatever was inside. But it was like throwing himself in front of a tank; he couldn't win that way. And now he knew he had to win.

"Who are these people, anyway?" a voice said over the headset.

"I don't know," was the reply. "Octavian never tells us. It's not our job to know."

Fullerton snapped his fingers. "Nine-Ten," he said. "Right under our goddamn noses."

"How do you know?" Johnny said.

"'Octavian.' That's what the Nine-Ten guys call their leader."

"Who is he?" Johnny said.

Fullerton shook his head. "It isn't just one guy. Every commander in the chain is 'Octavian' to his subordinates." He grasped at air, trying to explain. "It's like, I'm 'Octavian' to you, but I'm just plain 'Fullerton' to Peterson. And I have to call Peterson 'Octavian.'"

Johnny nodded. "And do we know who this crew's Octavian is?"

"No clue."

Fantastic.

Fullerton clasped Johnny's shoulder and lasered a look into his eyes. "I swear to Christ, Luca—on my mother's life—on my own soul—that I didn't know this was going to happen. I don't know what the hell is happening, but I'm on your side. I will kill to save your life tonight."

Johnny nodded back.

Just then, he thought of Chub and Cheryl's daughter—of Sarah. "What if the daughter comes home?" he said. "What are we supposed to do? Let her die?"

Fullerton looked at him a moment, then bit his lip. "We'll leave when they leave. If the daughter comes home while we're still here, then… we'll protect her. She won't die."

Johnny looked into Fullerton's eyes. He knew that move alone would be risking both their careers.

"She's supposed to come home around lunchtime," he said.

"She's going to find them like this. Shotgun blasts, man. Their faces are blown off—maybe their heads. She's going to see her parents like that. Whoever the fuck did this—catching them isn't enough. We have to kill them."

Fullerton rubbed his head. "Killing ain't the only way, Luca. We do justice, not revenge."

"Two of the same thing. And you know it."

The two fell silent, helpless. They continued to listen to the twosome downstairs ransacking the house while the leader and his apprentice planted evidence above. "Let's go," the boss finally said. "We're done here."

The next sounds to whisper through the headsets were the same march of footsteps as before, followed by the door clicking shut. A few moments later, off in the hills, Johnny heard an engine roar to life, then trail off until it was gone, the last wisp of smoke drifting away from the wreckage that he and Fullerton now lay in.

Chapter 8

A few hours later, Fullerton was sitting on a leather chair in Peterson's office as the sun climbed above Newark, gold bouncing off the buildings. He'd sent Johnny home on their return to the office, telling him that he'd take care of everything.

"This is the audio," he said to Peterson, handing him the digital recorder.

Peterson nodded. It was a long office, with his desk at one end and a small conference table at the other, gray carpeting bridging the space between the mahogany. Pictures dangled on the wall, showing him aboard Air Force One, at White House press conferences, escorting the Pope.

"How'd the kid handle it?" Peterson asked.

"He lost his cool when we heard that shot. But besides that, he did all right."

"Fullerton, we're up against something more twisted than whatever you trained for."

"What is it, boss?"

"This Project Orion… It's more than a terror attack. They're calling it 'Nine-eleven squared.' It's their endgame."

"And tonight was part of that?"

Peterson nodded. "Had to be. Killing someone who knew too much."

Fullerton looked into Peterson's eyes. "It's gonna get rough, isn't it?"

"Very." Peterson paused. "This is your chance to walk out. You don't have to go any further than this."

Fullerton lowered his head.

"But you deserve to know," Peterson continued, "that I handpicked you for this. You're a damn good investigator." Peterson squared his jaw. He couldn't say the same about the kid, Luca. All he had to recommend himself was loyalty, and the spunk he showed the night Jacobs was killed. But in an office full of thugs loyal to Bryson, that was the best Peterson could hope for.

"What did you handpick me for?"

"Our own endgame. The answer to theirs." Peterson set his jaw.

"I'll tell you now, it'll involve more nights like last night. A lot more... ugly things."

Fullerton bit his lip, then looked up. "I took an oath," he said. "I stand by it."

Thank God for that. Peterson smiled. "Go on home," he said. "I'm going to take care of that surveillance."

Fullerton nodded. "Yes, sir."

Peterson leaned back as Fullerton strode to the door and walked out. The kid had been up for more than twenty-four hours, and he still had a little strut. *We're going to need that kind of energy.*

Peterson let his head drop for a moment. As if he didn't have his hands full with Operation Reichstag—now this. Every time his mind tried to buy him a drink and assure him Project Orion couldn't be real, the terrorists blasted their way back in with a shotgun.

Chapter 9

He slapped her face, threw her on the bed, and pressed down on her stomach, kneeling on the sheets, his arms pinning hers against the pillow. He felt his right fist clenching; it was trembling; he had to stop it. Not here, not tonight, no blood.

Shepherd Moloch surveyed his conquest, this twenty-year-old blonde from Ukraine, the girl who had spoken to him of the majesty of America after he had pumped her full of champagne the first night he paid for her. This whore, lured across the Atlantic by mafioso human traffickers promising her riches, lecturing him on the country which he had served for two decades. He'd almost laughed that night.

Tonight, in the moment he looked down at her, he saw the stillness that rippled through her blue eyes as she looked up at the ceiling and not at him. Back home she'd been a top student, at the top of her class in political studies; here she was property, sending money overseas to her orphaned brother and sister.

Moloch buried his lips in her neck, breathing heavy as he pawed her body. He was unstoppable. No one in New York, or in the whole country, he thought as his pawing became thrashing, could stop him...

There was a pounding at the door. Moloch clasped the girl's neck in his hand and looked around the hotel room. A single lamp was on, illuminating a queen bed turned down in sheets of blue, the lights of the city beyond bouncing through the sliver of window left exposed.

"What is it?" he called.

"Bryson, sir," came the reply.

The Director. Moloch rose, his hand still on the girl's throat. "I'll be right there," he said.

He looked down at her for another moment, then loosened his grip. He hoped to see a flash of defiance, a spurt of contempt, something to show she was worth conquering again. But she just stared ahead. Moloch plucked her from the bed and punched her in the stomach. "Call your pimp," he said, throwing her to the floor.

He gathered his overcoat and opened the door, leaving the girl a gasping heap. A tall young man with thick shoulders took the coat and wrapped him in it as another handed Moloch a leather attache.

"The Director called for you, sir," the first agent said. "He wants you to meet him at the Plaza."

"Then let's go," Moloch said.

Six agents flanked him as he walked through the corridor of the hotel, into the elevator, and out into the lobby. "Tell the bellman to clean up the mess in my room and throw it out in the alley," he said. "Give him a hundred bucks."

Moloch and his detail walked out into the December cold, snowflakes drifting about them and dying on the street. The Special Agent in Charge of the New York field office of the United States Anti-Subversion Authority straightened the collar on his white button-down shirt and threw back his shoulders. He stood six feet tall, imperially slim, tips of silver sprinkled through his jet-black hair. Sinews held his arms and legs together, ready to lash out in a fit of the combat training he'd received at the Secret Service academy all those years ago. The night hid his dark brown eyes.

Moloch stood for a moment on the sidewalk, the snow a pad beneath his feet. He fingered his cream-colored scarf, one half thrown around his neck, the other hanging by his waist. Steam rose from a girder next to him, up into the canyon of skyscrapers, as the honking of a taxicab's horn banged against the buildings down in the valley. Moloch owned this city, every pair of swinging hips in blue jeans, every bit of glass ground into the street.

He turned around and glanced at the window of a clothing boutique; a tarp covering the frame flapped in the wind as an armed guard stood post outside. Yesterday a band of subversives, screaming about the "corporatocracy," had smashed the windows. The police called in the Authority, which rounded up the offenders and spirited them to a temporary detention center that had been set up downtown. Moloch himself had asked Director Bryson to get the facility up and running; such incidents in the city were on the rise.

A black SUV came tearing up the street and then pulled over. One of Moloch's entourage slid open the door while another pulled up the middle row of seats. Moloch nodded and sat down alone in the back row.

As the truck wound through the city, he glanced at the mounted officers they passed every few blocks, maintaining order, moving people along. *I did this*, he thought—*I brought New York City under control.* Moloch had chaired a think tank called the Project for the Stabilization of New York, and Director Bryson had adopted his recommendations in full. Riot police now patrolled Manhattan daily, armed officers stood post on buses and subways, and uniformed personnel cradling submachine guns hulked in front of the most sensitive targets. A pedestrian could expect a stop-and-frisk or baggage search at any time.

The truck whirred through Times Square. The square dripped with red and blue splashed across video screens, a sea of pedestrians lapping against the buildings and ebbing.

After all the attacks and the riots, New York was still standing. As Moloch glanced out the tinted windows on the truck, he saw an old couple laughing and pointing, children on fathers' shoulders, carolers entertaining the crowds with their singing.

Moloch didn't like it. It made people restive when the authorities searched them, patrolled their buses, guarded the buildings. They loved their freedom and they hated order. Order had to prevail.

That's why Authority officers had been spilling into the city. The agency had spun off a Uniformed Division comprised mostly of mercenaries from private security firms, and with the largest federal appropriation ever for a law enforcement organization, it had pumped manpower into Manhattan. More and more, NYPD officers had been reluctant to get rough when... things got rough. The Authority in New York, under Moloch's supervision, did not hesitate.

"New York is under occupation," Gordon Bragg had wailed in a column only a few months before. "We must free ourselves of the unconstitutional menace among us."

You're the menace, Moloch had concluded when he read the article, you and everyone else who resists. In the order to come, the only constitution that would be left intact was that enshrining stability over chaos. Soon enough, they wouldn't be crying about constitutions. When the shock waves hit, the Gordon Braggs of the world would be the first ones ducking for cover. Moloch and Bryson and the others were going to wire the middle with explosives, stand back, and obliterate it. There would be no middle anymore—only subversives and those who obeyed.

The truck pulled up to the Plaza. Moloch stepped out under the green awning, strung with Christmas holly and white lights, and marched inside.

Moloch walked through the lobby flanked again by his detail. They marched in formation along the marble floors, past bellmen draped in red and partygoers in suits and evening gowns, up to another group of hulking figures at the elevator landing. There was a moment's pause, then mutual nodding, and then a parting giving Moloch and his men passage.

The elevator hopped as it hit the eighteenth floor. *A midnight summoning*, Moloch thought as he padded across the carpet. *There'll be a time when I do the summoning.*

He nodded at one of his agents, and the young man knocked on the door at the end of the hallway. A moment later, an agent within pulled the door open, and Moloch crossed the threshold.

Chapter 10

Director Bryson sat on a red velvet couch, watching a flat-screen television hanging on the wall. He wore a starched white button-down shirt, open at the collar, and a gray sports jacket. He turned and directed his gray eyes at Moloch. "Sit down," he said.

Bryson scanned the room as Moloch sat. When he started as a soldier in the field all those years ago, he never thought defending the country would take him to a room like this: Immaculate white carpets meeting a white fireplace jutting out from the wall, two pillars supporting a stone mantle, flames licking out from behind a screen, green curtains inlaid with gold resting against the azure walls.

Bryson waved at the armed guards in the room, including Moloch's, and they all filed out. "Look at this," he said after the last had left and closed the door behind him. He gestured at the television on the wall.

Moloch sat. The cable news channel was airing a clip of President Wilkins addressing the press earlier in the day.

"I've made my position clear," Wilkins said. "I want to capture or kill every terrorist on earth who has taken up arms against the United States. I think that's a view we all share. But I won't sacrifice the Constitution to do it. Our way of life is non-negotiable. And as far as I'm concerned, our freedoms are our way of life. As long as I have the veto pen, those freedoms are non-negotiable."

Bryson punched the power button on the remote. "He means it," he said.

Moloch nodded. "I know, sir."

"Then you know what has to be done."

"I do."

Bryson narrowed his eyes. "Do you know why Operation Reichstag has to happen, Moloch?"

"Because Wilkins is too weak to stay in office."

That's all Moloch understands, Bryson thought. *Weakness and strength.* He paused. "Do you know why Kennedy was killed?"

"The Bay of Pigs."

"Right. The Bay of Pigs. The Pentagon and the CIA trusted him to take out Castro, and at the last second he lost his nerve. A lot of people died—and a lot of people were embarrassed. All while the Soviets strengthened their hand. They killed him for that, gunned him down in the middle of the street like a dog."

But it wasn't because he was weak. It was because he was obstinate. Just like Wilkins isn't weak—he's headstrong.

"Do you know how they did it?" Bryson asked.

"A second shooter on the grassy knoll."

"Probably a second and a third shooter, actually. A triangulation. They stalked Kennedy for weeks with triangulation teams. Almost got him in Miami—but the Secret Service ring around him was too tight."

Moloch's eyes brightened. "Well, we won't have to worry about that anymore."

That was true. In recent years, the Authority had gradually usurped the Secret Service's role in protecting the President, to the point that the Service was little more than a figurehead.

Bryson nodded. "But that's not what I meant. The lesson of JFK isn't how they physically killed Kennedy—it's how they drew up the plans."

"Which was how?"

"Ultra-nationalists," Bryson said. "They recruited ultra-nationalists who shared their beliefs that Kennedy was a threat to national security. A lot of right-wing Cubans, for example, who escaped Castro, landed in Miami, and swore they'd follow the CIA into hell out of loyalty. And a lot of hardcore types in the CIA, the Pentagon, the State Department, who had training staging coups in other countries."

"And then they staged one here," Moloch said.

"Right. They assassinated the President and launched a coup. But do you know why the history books don't say that?"

Moloch shook his head.

"The patsy shooter—Oswald. Because there aren't really coups in the U.S., are there? No. To pull it off here, they needed to recruit a psycho Communist ex-marine boogeyman who'd be easy to sell to the public."

Moloch nodded. "And when he went on TV and started whining about being a patsy, they shot him."

Probably the most important moment in American history in the last sixty years.

Not Nine-Eleven, or Iowa, or the Kennedy assassination itself. But the moment that a mobbed-up nightclub owner plugged Lee Harvey Oswald on live television the day after Oswald threatened to start talking—that was the moment when they showed they were truly capable of anything, and that no one would ever be brave enough to stand up and stop them.

"We need a patsy, Moloch," Bryson said. "And it's up to you to find him. The President's allowing subversives to destroy this country, piece by piece."

"I'll find the shooter," Moloch said. "You know I will."

Bryson nodded. "These are tough decisions. But think of all the greatness we won through blood and treasure—the world wars, Korea, Vietnam, both Iraq wars. I'm a soldier, Moloch. And I love this country. And to think we're going to lose everything because the Commander-in-Chief himself doesn't have the guts to take charge and do what needs to be done—I can't accept that. We can't give up our place in the world—not now, not ever. And a lot of important people inside the government feel the same way." *And outside of it.*

Bryson studied his subordinate for a moment. Moloch would never acquire the skill of subtlety to go along with his serpentine cleverness—he was a killer, a sadist. He'd be the perfect man to enforce the Total Information Awareness Act, once it was enacted–but no more. In the future Bryson Administration, which would become reality after the 2024 presidential election, Shepherd Moloch would be pushed to the background, and if he made too much noise, eliminated.

"So what's our latest intelligence on Brigade 910?" Bryson asked.

"They're planning something," Moloch said. "Midtown. Probably a car bomb, going after Christmas shoppers."

"When?"

"Soon. It could be any day now."

Bryson nodded. "Then I should let you get back to that investigation." He stood up and shook Moloch's hand. "We'll be in touch," he said. "Tell the detail men to stay outside for a few minutes."

With a nod, Moloch turned and left.

Bryson dropped back onto the couch. *Moloch worships one god*, he thought, pouring himself some scotch. *Power.*

A man like Moloch didn't understand the modern world—he only saw an opportunity to wield more power, arrest more dissidents, open more detention centers in New York.

He didn't understand why Operation Reichstag *really* had to happen. America was a global empire, and the entire territorial U.S.—the homeland—was the capital city of that empire. And it was time to get control of the capital city.

For too long, America had coddled its citizens with more freedoms than it allowed the rest of the world, with more money and more luxury, financed by cheap credit—its way of keeping Americans distracted while exacting tribute from every other nation on earth. Except now the money was gone, the luxury was fading away, and the other nations were turning on America, trying to kick its military bases out of their territories, standing up to it in every corner of the world. And here in the capital city, people didn't have the will to play rough with the upstarts, to keep the empire strong.

Bryson would give them the will—by shoving it into them, like a steel skeleton replacing bone. The time for coddling was over. After he liquidated Wilkins, there would be two kinds of citizens in the country—the law-abiding, who support the empire, and subversives. The Authority would deal with subversives however it had to—by blacklisting them so they couldn't work, by disabling their bank cards so they couldn't eat, by executing them so they couldn't live.

Bryson sighed. He didn't always see the world this way; he didn't always know the truth. Even he was naïve once. Then his wife and daughter were killed in 2001… but that wasn't something he allowed himself to think about these days.

Bryson powered up the television again, and there again was the footage of Wilkins. Bryson stared in at the broadcast, stared so hard he could pick out the pixels. Preservation of the most glorious empire in history was worth blood, even that of the President of the United States.

Bryson glared at Wilkins on the screen. *Especially that of the President of the United States.*

Chapter 11

Johnny walked in the shadow of the Empire State Building, its spire glowing holiday red and green tonight. At the end of the block, there was a girl manning a stand signed "Freedom Now!" in block letters at the top. *Here we go.*

"Excuse me," said the girl, about eighteen or nineteen with reddish streaks in her blonde hair. "Would you like to sign our petition protesting the Total Information Awareness Act and demanding that Congress dismantle the Anti-Subversion Authority?"

But then I'd be unemployed. "No thank you," he said.

"But the Authority is arresting people on mere suspicion and holding them without charge," the girl continued. "Don't you want to strike a blow against the empire?"

What I want to do is get to the bar and get crunked already. Johnny narrowed his eyes. "Don't you need a permit to set this up over here?"

The girl threw up her arms. "Do I need a permit to exercise my freedom of speech in America?" She stepped closer. "Think about what you just said. That's why you should sign our petition. They've brainwashed you into believing you need a permit to think, to breathe."

Johnny's gaze softened, and he let slip a smile. *I miss college.*

"I don't want to sound lame about the permit thing," he said to the girl. "I'm just saying, the Authority is going to kick you out of here eventually."

The girl started to fire back, then lowered her head. "I know. But until they do, I'm going to stand out here and try. Even if I freeze my ass off."

"Well, I'll tell you what. If you're still standing out here when I come back, I'll get you a hot chocolate." Johnny smiled. "And another thing. I've got a brother. He's your age, and he's got all the same views as you, and he could really use a date—"

"Get lost," the girl said. "And you can keep the hot chocolate, too. I don't accept hot chocolate or hookups from proto-fascist sympathizers."

That's definitely the first time I've heard that sentence in my entire life.

Johnny smiled. "Good, you shouldn't. I was just testing you. I'm an Authority spy, you know."

Johnny smiled again and walked away. After a few blocks, he stopped in front of a pub and yanked open the door.

"There's the princess!" a fat guy yelled as soon as Johnny walked in. He turned to the bartender. "He'll have a shot of Jameson and a Guinness, like a real man."

Johnny smiled at Billy Hawkins, his college roommate, and joined him at the bar. He was Johnny's height, corpulent with blond hair, a red beard tracking down the sides of his face. He clutched a beer mug with a thick hand and heaved down a gulp.

"A real man, eh?" Johnny said. "Only a real man could drive the ladies crazy like you do."

"Fo shizzle!" Billy gulped again.

Johnny rolled his eyes as the bartender arrived with the shot and the beer. The tavern was dark, with Irish and English soccer on the televisions, and "Danny Boy" wafting through the speakers.

"So what's up, man-love?" Billy asked. "How's the job going?"

"It's cool," Johnny said. He plucked the shot glass, eyed the whiskey, and then hurled it at the back of his throat. *Maybe not so much.* Every night since the shootings at the farm, he'd lain awake in bed, obsessing over scenarios in which he could have disobeyed Fullerton and barged in, gun drawn. Then maybe that girl Sarah wouldn't have come home and seen… whatever she ended up seeing.

Johnny looked up at Billy, the shot burning in his chest. *I've known this guy for six years. And I can't tell him about any of this.*

"How are the ladies?" Billy asked.

"You mean besides your mother?" Johnny said. "There are none. Not these days."

"What? Why?"

Billy knew Johnny in college, when Johnny could toss a ball at a ceiling and have a new girlfriend by the time it fell back down. But thing had been different lately.

"Too busy." Johnny downed some beer.

Billy grabbed his shoulder and slumped down to look him in the eye. "You're still alive, right? No top-secret government experiments done on you?"

Johnny shook his head, laughing. "So how's work?" he said.

"That's actually what I wanted to talk to you about. I'm peacing out soon."

"You're quitting? Why?"

Billy put down his beer and shook his head. "Not quitting. I'm peacing out from *here*, I mean."

Johnny narrowed his eyes. "For where?"

"Party in the city where the heat is on, bro!"

Where Billy had wanted to go all along… "Miami?"

"Ye-ah!"

Johnny paused, then slapped Billy on his thick shoulder. "Holy shit, man. Finally."

"Yeah. The boss wants to set up a new Miami office, and he wants me to run it."

"Running the office—damn!" Billy did IT stuff for some firm. Whatever it was, he made damn good money.

"That's right. I'll be out of this hellhole in a couple of months."

"Hellhole! This is NYC!"

Billy rolled up his sleeve and made a pudgy muscle. "But there's no beach here!"

Johnny slapped the bar. "Can I get another shot?" he yelled to the bartender. "My buddy here is too sexy for me."

"So you've got to tell me one thing," Billy said. He pinched Johnny's cheek. "How's Lizbeth?"

Johnny shook him off. "She's fine, asshole. Why?"

"You hardly see her, for a girl who's your soulmate."

"Yeah, she's my soulmate. She's been going out with Dizzle for three years."

Billy grinned. "And like I said, she's your soulmate."

Johnny shook his head. "And how would *you* know when I see her?"

"Because unlike you, I actually talk to her."

"Well, I've been busy."

"No hetero man is ever too busy for a hot chick, even one as questionably hetero as you." Billy narrowed his eyes. "Listen, man. There's one thing I want to see before I move my game down to Miami, and that's you and her getting together."

"You know it's not going to happen."

"Well, I had one wish come true, maybe I'll get another. You two belong together."

Johnny couldn't help but ask: "Why do you say that?"

Billy leaned back and smiled. "One, because she's hot. Two, because I see how happy she always makes you. Even when we're talking about her now you've got a little smile on your face."

Johnny covered his mouth. "No I don't," he said.

Billy laughed. "Back in the day, you two were always so close. I know how close you came to hooking up that night and how I fucked it up. And she was there the whole time with your dad… the way she used to talk to me back then... It was all you. We'd be watching a movie, and 'Oh, I hope Gio's okay, I wonder how Gio's doing.' And now, dude, she's always asking about you when I see her. And you know something else?"

Johnny felt the wave picking him up. "What?"

"I saw her about a month ago, and she had the same stupid smile on her face when I talked about you."

"Really?"

Billy looked into Johnny's eyes and nodded. "She just digs you, man. All the way down to her soul."

Johnny paused. He wondered if Billy knew she'd be getting engaged soon. He gulped his beer and shook his head. "It was a long time ago."

"Oh yeah? Then prove it."

"Prove it? How?"

Billy gestured to two young women at the end of the bar. "Those chicks over there. I'm going to make your move, and then you're going to follow through."

Johnny glanced at the girls, a blonde and brunette, as Billy conferred with the bartender. *What's he up to?*

Billy returned. "You're going to have to make your move on the blonde," he said. "'Cause I'm going to tell the other one all about Miami."

"What did you do?"

"I told the bartender to have them buy us our next round."

Johnny furrowed his eyebrows. First a laugh came steaming from the corners of his mouth, and then it exploded into a bellow. *This fat fuck is nuts.* Johnny's eyes shot up to the bartender; he had to watch. "New York is going to miss your fat ass," he said to Billy.

He watched the bartender shuffle to the other end of the bar, make eye contact with the girls, and then lean close to them, gesturing back at Johnny and Billy. The brunette made a face; the blonde laughed, swabbing her eyes over Johnny.

"It's not looking too good for you," Johnny said.

"Bullshit," Billy said. "I'm invincible, man. I cannot be vinced."

The bartender walked back over. He was a college kid, in jeans and a long-sleeve polo, a wool cap plopped on his head. "The one on the left said you can go fuck yourself," he said to Billy. "The one on the right wants to know what your buddy here is drinking."

"Guinness," Johnny said, grinning as the bartender nodded and strolled to the tap. He winked at Billy. "Never doubt the skills."

"That's skills with an 's,' right? Because I spell it with a 'z.'" Billy smiled. "Get your ass over there."

"Why would I do that? She'll be here in two minutes."

Sure enough, just as the drink was getting to Johnny, the blonde started tugging on her friend's arm. He watched as she dragged her the length of the bar, giggling the whole way.

"There's no way you sent that bartender over," she said to Johnny, gliding her umbrella drink onto the bar and smiling at him.

"Why not?"

"Because you're the gentleman of this duo. I can tell."

Johnny grinned. "You know, I was about to get up to give you my stool, but I just changed my mind."

She folded her arms and smiled in a "You've almost impressed me" kind of way. He looked her over. She was tall and slender, with blonde hair that fell straight back past her shoulders.

"Don't let him fool you," Billy said. "He'll be pulling out chairs and holding doors the rest of the night. Perfect kind of guy to wrap around your finger."

Please shut up.

"My friend here needs to do some wrapping," the girl said. "I just want to buy a guy a drink. First time for everything, you know." She looked Johnny over again. "And since you'll be buying me the next round, call me Justine."

"I'll think about it," Johnny said, grinning. "I'm Johnny. This is Billy."

"His name's really Giovanni," Billy said. "He's *that* kind of Italian."

I really need him to talk less right about now.

"I'll bet you know your way around a can of tomato sauce!" Justine said.

Okay, she's either really drunk or digging me. "Yeah, and I can tell you some things about vodka sauce and puttanesca, too," he said. *Well, that sounded pretty stupid.*

Justine turned to her friend and then turned back. "This is Alissa. She's a little shy. Plus I've been pumping liquor into her all night."

The light bulb exploded above Billy's head. "Well, in that case!" he yelled. He flagged down the bartender, then turned back around. "So Alissa, have you ever been to Miami?" he asked.

Johnny popped off the stool and gestured for Justine to follow him a few steps away. "He's going to tell her all about his new job in Miami," he said. "It'll definitely be the most interesting conversation of her life."

Justine smiled. "I'll bet," she said. "You guys are close?"

"Roommates all four years of college."

"And now he's headed down to Miami?"

"He just told me tonight. He's going to be running an office for some IT firm. He'll be a millionaire in a few years."

"But you're going to miss him."

Johnny pulled out a stool for Justine, and she sat down. "I try not to miss anybody."

Justine bundled her legs in the crossbeams of the stool. "Ahh, the tough guy. You try not to miss anybody, but you can't help it. Because you're human and all."

Johnny sipped his beer. "What makes you think I'm human?"

Justine laughed. "Maybe you aren't. But you're definitely a smartass."

You know it. "Of course I'll miss him," he said. "But I can't say it."

"God, *men.* Why not?"

"Because... he knows. That's enough. He knows."

"I don't know. I'm a little more demanding than that." Justine sipped her umbrella drink. "I think I'd have to hear it."

Johnny smiled. "Then I'll remember to say it to you as I'm walking you out tonight." *Nice one, Luca.*

Justine arched her eyebrows, a "we'll see about that" look melting into another smile. "So what do you do, Giovanni?"

"Contract killer," Johnny said. *I really don't feel like feeding her the company line.*

"Maybe you are," Justine said. "You've got your leather jacket going on, you're in shape. You're some kind of man of action."

Johnny shrugged. "Actually, I'm a support technician for the FBI."

"Really? So what kind of stuff do you work on? Top-secret? Can't tell me?"

"You know, just work on stuff around the office. Fix this cable, clean this gun. Nothing fancy."

Johnny watched as the "man of action" image faded from Justine's eyes. *James Bond never told a hot chick he was an office support technician.*

"So what about you?" he asked.

"I'm in law school. Third year."

"Oh yeah? Going to be a millionaire like my friend?"

Justine laughed. "Not quite. I'd like to be a prosecutor."

Johnny nodded and swigged some beer. "So you can kick some terrorist ass?"

"Justice Department, Anti-Corruption Division, if I'm lucky." Justine shook her head. "I won't be kicking any terrorist ass. The Total Information Awareness stuff makes me feel uncomfortable. A little too much power, you know?" Justine paused. "Are you sure you're just an office support guy?"

No, Johnny thought. "Yeah, why?"

"Because you look like more. You just don't seem like the other guys here." Justine laughed at herself. "God, that sounds so lame. But I don't know how else to say it." She looked into Johnny's eyes. "I just noticed you when you walked in, that's all."

Johnny felt the smile flood off his face. But then he looked down for a moment. *She can never know me*, he thought. *Not after what happened on that farm. This girl can't ever know what I do.* He looked back up. "I'm not like most guys," he said.

Justine's blue eyes widened and then settled back on his. "Tell me how."

Johnny looked back into her eyes. He could forget it all for just tonight, just be a normal twenty-four-year-old at a bar... "Well, for one thing, I don't hate lawyers." He smiled; Justine giggled. *That's gold.* "And for another thing—"

A blast.

A boom ripped through the air, flung Justine off her stool, and threw Johnny to the ground. The floor shook as the lights flickered; the windows rattled and cracked; the stemware above the bar shattered in a row like a glass flare. Everyone screamed, thrashed about, bolted for the exit.

The lights settled back on. The explosion was outside, blocks away. Car alarms pulverized the air, laced with emergency sirens.

On the floor Johnny reached for Justine's hand. The crowd was still rushing the door; bodies fell, catching heels to the hand, boots to the face. Johnny's hand closed around Justine's. First he pulled her closer to him, then he pulled her up.

"Are you okay?" he asked.

"What's... what's happening?" she asked, tears in her eyes.

Johnny turned to Billy, who had fallen to the floor with Alissa and had helped her up. Then he turned back to Justine. "It was a car bomb. A couple of blocks away."

He glanced at the scene at the door. Women were crying, men were hustling their way through, New York-style "What the fuck"s were flying. He saw a musclehead-type throw a pencilneck out of his way as he grabbed at the door.

Then it hit Johnny. He had to run to the scene. He wasn't even sure why; he just belonged there. New York City had just been struck by a terrorist bomb, and he was only blocks away. He had to help.

"I've got to go," he said. He nodded at Justine. "Please, get home safe." Before Justine could answer, Johnny turned and grabbed Billy. "Ger her number," he said in his ear.

He rushed to the door as Billy, Justine, and Alissa looked on in silence. The musclehead was still grabbing at the door, jostling. Johnny grabbed him from behind and threw him to the floor. "Get the fuck out of my way," he said.

Johnny edged his way through the crowd and bolted out, looking back over his shoulder for a second. As a piece of New York burned up the street, he noticed Justine gazing from within the bar at the figure running to the scene.

Chapter 12

Johnny sprinted about a block and a half, weaving in and out of people darting in every direction, before crashing into the fortress that the Anti-Subversion Authority had ringed around the scene. Before him were riot officers on horseback, pounding back the panicked crowds. "What's happening?" people yelled. "What's happening?" Sirens tore through the air; four fire engines had already barreled through, police cars blazing the way for them. For a moment Johnny froze where he stood.

In the distance was tonight's terrorist attack on New York City. A wall of fire consumed a section of the street a couple of blocks ahead, pouring out of storefronts and reducing parked cars to shells. The rescue vehicles bathed the night in blue and red. A troop of officers dragged barricades around the perimeter.

It stank of gunpowder, like an entire army had spent its ammunition at close range under Johnny's nostrils. Car alarms banged against each other in dissonance.

And then there was another explosion.

Johnny crouched and turned his head, shielding his face. The street filled with screams. "Get *back*!" an Authority officer screamed.

Johnny glanced back, and there was another blast. He shriveled for a second, then looked up again; nothing. Just secondary explosions.

He stood back up. *Bastards, they must have cut down little kids in the middle of the goddamn street...*

The riot officers were prodding the crowds. The officer who had screamed beat one recalcitrant in the back of the leg with his baton and sprayed another in the face. "Get *back*! This isn't a fucking show!"

Christ, these people might know someone who just got blown up. They're not the terrorists.

The "Freedom Now!" stand was a wall of fire, and EMTs were wheeling a covered stretcher away from it. *My God.* Johnny remembered the girl circulating the petition. He crouched again, his legs weak. *Please, please tell me it wasn't her.* Johnny shook so hard he almost vomited.

Just then, a wave of legs knocked him over. A girl fell down next to him, no more than ten years old, blonde and pale. "Oh, my God... Oh, my God..." she said. "Oh... oh..." She started shaking. He scooped her up. "Come on, you've got to keep moving," he said. "You'll get hurt out here, sweetheart. Where's your mom?" The girl started convulsing; she must have been petrified.

Johnny sat up, cradling her as he caught glancing knees to the back of his head. *This girl's having a panic attack*, he thought. Then he looked up at a riot officer engaging a man trying to run through the perimeter. He hit him once, then unsheathed a taser and jammed it into his shoulder. The man wailed, then dropped to the pavement, thrashing.

Johnny clutched the girl. *They fucking tased her.*

"Caitlin!" a woman yelled, running up to him. "What did you do to my baby!" She pushed Johnny aside and swept the girl in her arms, picking her up and running off.

Johnny stood up. He lasered his eyes, past the madman on the horse and through the barricades, to the scene of the crime. He was in this business to fight terrorists, not stand on the sidewalk and watch. Some animal had bombed this street tonight, and he was going in to find out who.

He plunged his hand into his pocket and fished out his wallet. He flipped it open and pulled out his Anti-Subversion Authority identification. He had screwed up his face when posing for the picture, a tough guy look, just like the agents did. "This certifies," the card read, "that Giovanni Luca has been deemed worthy of trust and confidence by the United States Anti-Subversion Authority."

Johnny slid his "creds" behind a transparent sheet in his wallet and ran straight ahead, flashing his identification as he yelled, "Anti-Subversion Authority!" Johnny wove in and out as he surged ahead, sidestepping, whirling, ducking. He ran around the officer on horseback and headed for the barricade, stilling holding up his ID. "Authority!" he yelled. "Anti-Subversion Authority!"

He jumped over the barricade, pivoting over the block of wood painted blue. Johnny continued towards the scene, the smell of gunpowder burning his nostrils with each step.

"Hey!" he heard someone yell behind him. "Get back here!" And then: "Someone jumped the barricade, he's headed your way!"

Johnny flagged down two officers he saw ahead, waving his ID. They ran towards him; he held his wallet in front of him. "Hey, I'm–"

A baton bashed him in the back. He dropped to his knees and struggled before he was hit again in the skull. One of the officers in front snapped a handgun to his forehead as his assailant dug his knees into his back and wrenched back his wrists.

"What the hell do you think you're doing?" the officer with the gun asked.

"I'm... one of you..." Johnny said.

"You're under arrest," the man behind him said.

"My creds... Look in my right hand."

The officer with the gun pressed the barrel against his head as a third officer grabbed Johnny's wallet.

Johnny's back throbbed. *Well, this isn't how I expected the fucking night to go.*

"He's telling the truth," the third officer said. "He's with us."

"What the hell were you doing jumping over the barricade like that?" the man behind him said. He loosened his grip on his wrists and pulled Johnny up.

He stood straight up and then doubled over, his back wrenching. "Goddamn it," he said. "I... was just coming..." Johnny forced himself straight up and bit his lip. "I was just coming to support."

"There's smarter ways to do it," said the third officer, the one who had checked his wallet. "Riley, get him a bandage for his head." The one who had drawn the gun stalked off.

Johnny drew his fingers across his head and then looked. Blood.

"What the hell happened out here?" he said.

"Car bomb. About the strongest fucking one you can imagine."

"But who?"

"Some subversive shit who has to die," the one who had struck Johnny said. He walked away.

Johnny turned back to the third officer. "But any idea who?"

"I'm just a uniform guy," he said. "Let Moloch and his agents do the math. But we know who did it."

Johnny massaged his temples. "Brigade 910," he said.

That was what changed everything in America. When it wasn't

outsiders anymore—when it Americans themselves launching the terrorist attacks—nobody was safe anywhere, at any time. Everyone was a subversive. Tonight those fucking terrorists had taken it a step further, and tomorrow there would be more goddamn riots and blood.

"Goddamn Wilkins can't do shit," Johnny said as Riley returned with a bandage. Johnny took it and wrapped it himself. "The President just sits on his ass."

The officer who had checked the wallet smiled for a second. He was in his early forties, wrinkles cracking across his forehead, his blond hair thinning in the front. "I don't know the first thing about it, kid," he said. "I don't know about the President or shit else." He threw up his arms and shook his head. "I'm just a cop. They shrunk the NYPD down, and the Authority were the only ones hiring." He gazed at the fire, then turned back to Johnny. "Wake up," he said. "The President doesn't have anything to do with this. He's just... stuck. Everything is all fucked up."

Johnny stared out as the sign atop a bodega cracked off and crashed to the street as firefighters poured water into the flames. "I know," he said.

"And tonight Moloch and his boys will look at the scene, and they'll start looking for their suspects. And we know which way it's gonna come out, and who it's gonna be. No surprises."

Johnny nodded. "I guess not."

The officer studied him. "You're not an agent, are you?"

"Come on, I'm—" Johnny stopped. There was no fooling him. "I'm just a surveillance guy."

"Then you can forget about taking another step. They're not going to let you near there. They're not going to let *me* near there. They wouldn't let an FBI agent near there, for Christ's sake. Moloch's in charge." The officer grabbed Johnny's shoulder. "Let me tell you something," he said. "Between you and me, I think they're all animals."

"Who?"

"Half of the guys I'm working with tonight. Uniform guys, agents, whatever. The guys coming out of that academy aren't like any cops I ever worked with. Animals." The officer shook his head.

"Welcome to the new world order."

Johnny thought of the girl convulsing in the street. He couldn't argue. "But you're working for the Authority."

"I've got to feed my kids. What's your excuse?"

"I just want to..." There was another secondary explosion. Johnny rubbed his head again. "I just want to fight terrorism. That's all."

The man looked into his eyes, then nodded. "I know, kid. I know." He scratched the back of his head and wiped his brow. "But it's not going to be tonight. You may as well go home. All you got for your trouble was a nice bump on your head."

Johnny wanted to argue, but there was no point. The officer had a gun, and the ones ahead probably had machine guns. He smiled. "And a bump on my back," he said.

The man laughed. "Yeah, that too. Get out of here, kid. Go home and hold your little girlfriend a little tighter tonight. We're all lucky to be alive."

"Yeah, maybe I'll do that." Johnny wished he hadn't thought of Lizbeth just then, but he did. He started walking away.

Then he turned back. "Hey," Johnny called. "What's your name?"

"Duffy," he said. "And I hope I never see you again."

Johnny paused, then smiled as he rubbed his head one last time. "Same here."

He shuffled back towards the barricade, holding up his wallet like before. This time no one harassed him.

The frenzy had died down. The onlookers had become rubber-neckers at a car crash, silent and stationary. When he had flown over the barricade earlier, there was chaos behind him; now he melted into a sea of horror.

Johnny slipped his finger under his bandage and then drew it back out—still bleeding. New York City was burning, and he was bleeding. Could he die for this city if he had to? What if he cornered some Brigade 910 punk with a bomb strapped to his backpack? Could he take him down and give up his life?

He looked out at more bodies being hauled into ambulances and shook his head. He still didn't know.

Chapter 13

Johnny spent Christmas day at his mother's apartment. As he crossed into her building and ascended the wooden stairs to her door, creaking betrayed him; the door at the top of the steps flew open. "There he is!" yelled Marissa Luca. "There's my Christmas boy!"

Paul grinned behind her. "Wow, you're a big loser," he said.

"No, *you're* a big loser," Johnny said.

"That's enough of that," Marissa said, donning her teacher's voice. "For God's sake, why don't the two of you just sit down and eat something?"

Johnny stepped inside and hugged his mother. She was five-four, and two months into her experiment in cropping her hair that saw her looking like a flapper. Her blue eyes sparkled. When she smiled, she looked younger than Johnny.

Johnny looked at Paul, or Paolo, or the "Paulinator," whatever he was calling himself now. He was tall with blue eyes, skinny, his light brown hair jutting up in spikes. Sideburns edging past his earlobes framed his face, light and rosy and hairless. He was dressed in baggy jeans and a long-sleeved polo shirt, collar up.

The kid was a genius, especially at math and science—the top of his class in high school. He had appalled the graduation crowd by calling President Wilkins an "ass jockey" during his valedictorian speech.

Johnny sat at the table and chomped on a piece of bread. Marissa hustled off to the kitchen behind him, and Paul sat down across from him. "What's that cut on your head, dude?" he asked.

Johnny touched his hand to the wound the Authority officers had administered him. "I was moving some stuff in my apartment," he said. "A box fell out of the closet and hit me."

Paul narrowed his eyes. "Yeah, that's my excuse of choice when I hit my head passing out somewhere."

Johnny grinned. *If only*. "And when's the last time you passed out?"

"Right before the semester ended. It was insane."

"Oh yeah?"

Paul smiled. "Yeah, bro. You've got to come party next semester.

No excuses about work."

"You going to show me how much of a baller you are?"

Paul shrugged. "There might be some Paulinating going on."

Please don't ever say that again.

"I don't think I just heard references to prostitution and alcohol consumption," Marissa said from the kitchen.

"So who do you have your eye on?" Johnny asked.

"Don't worry about it," Paul said. "How's it going with Lizbeth?"

"Who said I wanted to hook up with Lizbeth?"

"She's such a nice girl," Marissa said from the kitchen as she slammed the oven door shut. "I really like her."

"Come on, dude," Paul said. "You've wanted that chick forever. Don't you think I know?"

"You don't know anything," Johnny said.

"The macaroni's ready!" Marissa said.

That was their signal to march to the kitchen, stand at attention, and load their plates. As the three settled into dinner, Johnny felt he could forget the world for just these few hours, block out of his mind the double-homicide, the bombing, the beating the Authority had dealt him. In Paul's sanitized version of things, school was good, his grades were all right, he was getting along just fine. Everything was okay for Marissa, work was the same, the parents at her school seemed to get nastier every year, her utility bills kept going up and up. Just like everyone else, she said. She wished she could see more of Johnny, but she supposed a lot of people were saying that about him these days.

Later, Johnny leaned back and sighed as Christmas dinner sat in his stomach, his mother back in the kitchen, Paul playing video games in one of the back bedrooms. Vanilla candles mingled with smells of coffee and freshly baked cakes. *Noel, Noel,* a choir cascaded through the stereo. *The first Noel... Born is the king of Israel...* His mother made Christmas so nice, especially in the last few years.

Marissa set a cup of coffee in front of Johnny and laid her hand on his. "You look so tired," she said.

"Mom, I'm fine—"

"I just wish I knew that you relaxed sometimes, you know? All this running around you do can't be good for you."

"I can handle it. And I relax sometimes." Johnny paused. "So you're really doing all right around here?"

"Yeah, I'm okay. Times are tough. But they've been tough before." Marissa traced her finger over Johnny's head. "I'd still like to know how you got that cut on your head."

"I told you." *I knew she wouldn't buy it.*

"Okay, then I'd like you to tell *the truth* about how you bumped your head. But that's okay." Marissa sighed. "My son, the superhero."

"What do you mean?"

"You're always running this way and that way. No one ever really knows where you are."

"You guys know where my place is."

"You're never home! And you never answer your phone."

"I'm just really busy, that's all. I'll try to slow down a little."

"If you slowed down, you wouldn't be Johnny." Marissa smiled.

Johnny smiled back. "I should get going. Busy day tomorrow." He paused. "Thank you, Mom."

"For what?"

"For… for today. Best gravy ever. But one of these years I'm going to convince you to make turducken."

Marissa kissed him. "And one of these years I'm going convince *you* to put in nine hours in the kitchen," she said. She smiled. "Merry Christmas, sweet pea."

"Merry Christmas, Mom. I love you."

Johnny swept out into the night and strode towards his car. Then he stopped. Everything was so quiet. No one was outside, and only an odd car or two whirred by on the road. This was the Christmas night still, and he loved it as much as he did when he was ten years old. All the world was asleep, everyone wrapped in contentment for one night.

Johnny walked on as the second Christmas without his father yielded to night.

Chapter 14

President Reed Wilkins glared across the long table at Director Alexander Bryson.

"What can you tell me about these riots in Los Angeles?" he asked.

The President sat in the taller chair at the center of the east side of the oval mahogany table in the Cabinet Room. On his right was the Secretary of State, a brown-haired, tight-chinned man, and to his left was the Secretary of Defense, a broad-shouldered, bald man whose eyebrows sharpened into sabers at the mention of the riots.

"More opposition to the Total Information Awareness Act, Mr. President," Director Bryson said.

President Wilkins glanced around the room. He didn't know any of the men and women here; they'd all been foisted upon him. The party had assured him it knew what was best. And now—a Secretary of Education who tied schools' federal funding to states' incorporation of anti-subversion lessons into their grade school curricula; a Secretary of Labor who boasted week after week of job growth and bursting prosperity, even as the average American household collapsed under $60,000 of debt; a Secretary of Defense who was privately lobbying members of Congress to repeal the Posse Comitatus Act of 1878 so that troops could patrol the streets.

I could gut this room, President Wilkins thought. *Clean out this den of lackeys, get some real people in here who are qualified and ready. This is my Executive branch.*

He stared at Bryson. The thick scalp; the frozen gray eyes; the set jaw. "And who mostly comprises these crowds?" Wilkins asked. "Criminal elements? Dissidents?" He paused. "Patriots?"

This debate had jolted the Cabinet for months now. As the riots radiated across the country from urban centers, the media had been quick to tag the rioters as "subversives." Wilkins, on the other hand, had rankled the men and women in this room, time after time, by wondering if any of them could be considered patriots.

"They can only be criminal elements, sir," Bryson said. "Subversives."

That's funny. I always thought that people who faced armed thugs in the street to defend freedom were called patriots.

He turned away from Bryson and looked across the table at Vice President Greenaway, another silver-haired white man, another brain-dead lackey. The party had forced Wilkins to name him as his running mate. For unity, the leaders had said.

Now it seemed the only people with whom the Vice President shared unity were those who wanted to crown Bryson as America's first emperor.

To the Vice President's left was the only one in the room whom Wilkins trusted, Attorney General Wilson Sharpe. They'd been best friends in law school, best men at each other's weddings, godfathers to each other's children.

Wilkins looked at Sharpe. "What do you think, Will?"

"The FBI has been saying it for months, and maybe even years now," Sharpe said. "Most of the people at these rallies are protesting what they see as the destruction of the Fourth Amendment."

"In case you've forgotten," Bryson said, "the FBI hasn't had jurisdiction in this area since the Authority was created. And I take offense that you would call these riots *rallies.* It's exactly because of those attitudes that the Justice Department doesn't matter anymore."

Wilkins' throat clenched to intervene, but he choked it back. *Wait for it*, he thought. *Wait for it...*

"It's exactly because of these attitudes that a majority of the American people see your agency as an army of thugs and want a return to the way things used to be," Sharpe said.

That's my Will. Give him hell, man.

"I'd like to know what polls you're reading," Bryson said. "Because the ones that come across my desk say that anywhere from two-thirds to three-fourths of the people are with us, and want us to go further in stamping out the subversive activity."

"I refuse to recognize the validity of polls that your agency sponsors. And frankly, I think we've reached a sad day in the history of democracy when we make policy based on polls that are as legitimate as the ones that used to elect Saddam Hussein president with ninety-nine percent of the vote."

"And I think it's a sad day in democracy," Bryson said, "when we let criminals smash store windows, pelt government buildings and elected officials with vegetables, and advocate armed uprising against the United States government, and *especially* when we let them detonate massive car bombs in midtown Manhattan."

"Gentlemen, please, enough," Wilkins said. He scanned around the room with the look of a disappointed father. "We're not delivering on the promises I made in my campaign to get everyone's lives back to normal. We've failed on every front. Inflation and unemployment are out of control. Infrastructure is crumbling. States can't deliver basic services, because they're broke. And Brigade 910 just pulled off its most brazen attack since I've been in office."

Brigade 910. The great specter of my presidency. I've got some group roving the country killing women and children, and to this day, I still don't know who the hell they are.

"Sign the Act, Mr. President," Bryson said.

Wilkins stared across the table. "I won't," he said.

Bryson's office had drafted the Total Information Awareness Act. He was the most powerful law enforcement official in America, and everyone in this room, and the country, was supposed to prostrate themselves and entrust him with the care of their precious flesh. Whoever refused was a subversive who should be thrown in prison... or assassinated.

Because that's what this dance was really about. The Authority now had the duty, by law, to "support" the Secret Service in its efforts to protect the President. But as with everything else the Authority did, "support" meant "control." Now Authority snipers patrolled rooftops along Wilkins' motorcades, brandishing long-range rifles as he passed. An Authority agent was beside him everywhere he went.

And they were all the same: all young, unwilling and unable to socialize, awkward without a gun in their hands. Wilkins had served in the military, and had never met anyone as cyborg-like as an Authority agent. Now he was trusting them with his life, and what was more, they had fanned out across the nation in waves of untold thousands, patrolling the republic's streets. Just how many were there? How the hell could it be that he was President, and he couldn't get a straight answer on how many were on the street? How many in the academy? Ten thousand? A hundred thousand? Or, as some blogs had rumored, half a million to be deployed after passage of the

Total Information Awareness Act?

Wilkins caught the grin which gleamed in Bryson's eye. That was the game—Wilkins' life in the balance. They both knew it, and there was no mistaking it. Bryson could have him killed at the snap of his fingers. *This interloper whom we let slip through the gates. And now he rules us all...*

"Tell me again what you consider the benefits of this law to be," Wilkins said.

Bryson squared his jaw. "Simple. Something better than the hydrogen bomb. *Information.*"

"I'll tell you what I see. I see the creation of a monolithic grid in the United States. And on that grid is every sort of communication and every sort of transaction which occurs in the country—many trillions of pieces information which we now have the technology to process instantaneously. Really the most enormous undertaking in the history of civilization. Am I right so far?"

Bryson gritted his teeth. "So far."

"And all of the information which travels along that grid will go through a government filter, and if it is not perfectly sanitized according to our standards, the grid will flash. Every text message, every email, every entry into a search engine will be monitored, and certain key words will alert local police of a potential subversive, with a record created in a central Anti-Subversion Authority database. Everyone who visits every website will be recorded, and a file of their internet traffic will be maintained by the most powerful computer ever designed. Please, stop me if I'm wrong."

"You're correct, Mr. President."

"But it goes even beyond that. We'll monitor every phone call, but we'll do more than just keep a database of every number dialed—we'll eavesdrop on every call, and our digital filters will intercept and report certain key words and phrases that'll alert us to potential terrorists in our midst. Every time an American swipes a credit card, a record of what he purchases will be beamed to the government. But it goes even farther than *that.* The real innovations of the Act are the location-based provisions."

Bryson nodded. "You're right, Mr. President."

"Right. And with the benefit of these provisions, and the satellite technology supporting them, we'll compel states to include a radio frequency identification chip in every driver's license, along with a DNA sample. This chip will feature a GPS tracking option that the citizen can't turn off. And everywhere he takes that license—out on the road for a Sunday drive with the family, to work in the morning, to the bar on a Saturday night—we'll be able to follow him. And if he doesn't carry it, we'll throw him in prison. But that's not all." Wilkins looked into Bryson's eyes. "Everywhere an American uses a radio tag to pass through an electronic toll– everywhere he uses a mobile phone—everywhere he drives, walks, breathes, and sleeps, we'll know exactly where he is and almost what he's doing. All of this information, the bill tells us, will be used to compile master terrorist profiles of only those Americans who are threats to freedom—all other personal information will be discarded after a few years. All without a warrant, and all with every single citizen knowing full well that we're watching and listening."

Bryson nodded again. "That's right."

"And after all that, if there's anyone left in the country who even dares to have an independent thought, well, we can fix him good without arresting him. We can scramble his debit cards so he can't buy food. We can mess with his credit rating so he can't get a mortgage. We can even crash the internal computer on his car so he can't drive anywhere."

Bryson stared back at Wilkins. "If it comes to that, Mr. President."

Wilkins returned the volley with his eyes. "I'll never sign that bill, Director Bryson."

Bryson paused, then curled his lips into a mold of enmity. "This is insanity. This would be like President Bush vetoing the Patriot Act after September eleventh."

"The Patriot Act didn't stop a handful of college kids from putting ricin in the water in Iowa," Wilkins said.

"And you think you can stop them from putting it in the water in New York? In Los Angeles?"

"I believe I can. And I believe I owe it to three hundred fifty million people to do it within the rights given to them by God." Wilkins paused. "I'll tell you what," he said. "I understand the act also elevates the position of Authority Director to a Cabinet-level position. If the Congress can pass it over my veto, I'll be more than happy to nominate you for the position. No one deserves it more."

Bryson narrowed his eyes. "Thank you, Mr. President."

Just try and threaten me. But if you kill me, I'm taking you down with me.

But inside, Wilkins trembled. Where was an honest man like Hunter Peterson when he needed him?

Chapter 15

Two beeps from Johnny's Authority two-way ripped through the silence of the apartment. "Luca! You there, man?"

Johnny grabbed the two-way, surprised. It was Fullerton, and it was almost midnight on a Sunday night in late January. "I'm here," he said, beeping back. "What's up?"

"Get on down to the office," Fullerton said. "We got business tonight."

"What kind?"

Fullerton groaned. "Didn't they teach you not to talk about this shit over the open airwaves? Meet me at the office."

Johnny nodded. "Copy."

He bolted from the apartment and out to his truck.

Johnny jumped in his old Jeep, fired it up, and peeled out. The Newark streets were empty, except for the usual cast of late-night characters: the man in rags sleeping on a bench, the man with a garbage bag wrapped around his head scurrying up and down the street screaming, the two young guys hustling some business under a streetlight.

Early in the new year, Peterson had called Johnny to his office and explained that he was going to make him an agent—without him being an agent. He was to be trained as such, but no one could know of his new status. "It'll take months," Peterson had said. "Take it from an old Secret Service guy. This is the best training in the world."

Johnny dared not ask what the secrecy was all about. Peterson arranged for Fullerton, who was qualified as a combat and firearms instructor, to train him. Johnny needed work with the combat; he could handle the firearms. When Fullerton handed him a machine gun on the firing range, he raced back to the fifty-yard line, dropped onto his stomach, and blasted a three-round burst through the heart of the target. "My old man was a cop," he explained.

Fullerton worked with him at a run-down Newark gym on fighting techniques. They focused mainly on defense—throws, blocks, and disabling grips. It wasn't easy, even for an eager student like Johnny. He went home every night bruised and stiff with pain.

He'd even gone out with Justine a couple of times. Johnny spent

New Year's Eve with her and her friends and then took her out to dinner the next two weekends. When she asked him why he limped when he walked, he said he'd just had a rough workout. She smiled and hooked her arm in his. "Let's get out of here, you wimp," she said.

Johnny turned into the Authority building garage and slipped his truck in the pen. He took a few steps through the near-darkness. "Don't move," a voice called behind him.

It was Fullerton. "Hey, what's—"

"Shut *up*, man. Follow me."

He'd been crouched behind one of the SUVs. He edged over to the driver's side of a black minivan, popped open the door, and pivoted inside. Johnny followed around to the passenger side and did the same.

Fullerton twisted on the ignition. "We're going to have to include some style training with all that other high-tech shit we're giving you," he said. He pulled out of the cage and exited the garage, out into the Newark night.

Johnny laughed. "Style?"

"Yeah, man. Acting all giddy and shit. You've got to be a professional, like me."

"Yeah, you're pretty professional when you prank me on the two-way."

"That's just babysitting, my brother, making sure you ain't getting into trouble. Or getting laid... but then again, we know you don't do that."

Johnny laughed. "For your information, I'm not doing too bad in that department."

"Oh yeah? What's the lucky dude's name?"

"Justine," Johnny said. "I've been out with her a couple of times."

"A couple of times, he says. And where did you meet her?"

"At a bar in the city. The night of the bombing, actually."

"Well, let's hope it goes a little better than that from now on."

Johnny examined the rear of the truck as Fullerton drove, and his heart jumped. Two shotguns rested in front of the liftgate.

"Fullerton," he said. "What exactly are we doing tonight?"

Fullerton sighed. "It's serious."

Johnny nodded, his eyes fixed on the shotguns. "What is it?"

"We found the one of the guys who did that dude and his wife up at the farm."

Johnny whirled back around. "How... how do you know?"

"A credible tip. At least that's what the boss thinks. All I've got is an address, a physical description, and when we can expect his ass."

"And... we're gonna arrest him?"

"Not exactly. It's more like a detention. Extraordinary rendition-type shit."

"Black bag?"

"Strictly."

Johnny sank back in his seat, clenched his fists, studied them. This was it. Nothing had been normal since that night on the farm. He still dreamed about it sometimes.

"So, black bag again," he said. "I thought you were all about doing things straight."

"This is different," Fullerton said. "We're in a war. The fight of our lives."

Johnny tried to steady his hands. So he was scared, a little. He'd never done anything like this before. "What do you mean?"

"I can't tell you that. I'm not authorized. Peterson said he'd brief you. But it's serious shit, man. Every move we make now... a lot of lives are at stake."

"A terrorist attack?"

"I said I can't tell you." Fullerton paused. "Listen to me, Luca. There's some shit you're going to have to learn. When I say I can't tell you, I'm not fucking around. You don't know something until you need to know it. That's how we operate, and if you want to do this shit and live, you've got to roll with that."

And live, Johnny thought. Fullerton was right. To be a professional like him, you had to be ready for anything at any time and move without asking questions. That had been the difference between him and Johnny all along. Fullerton moved when he had to move, and he stayed cool.

"You're right," Johnny said.

"Say what?" Fullerton said. "I didn't know Italian dudes ever said those two words."

"Fuck you. Black dudes don't say it either, asshole. But... I'll move when you tell me to move."

"You trust me, right?"

"Do I have a choice?"

"Come correct with the answer, Luca. It's the most important question if we're going to have a chain of command. Do you trust me?"

Johnny thought back to the farm. *I will kill to save your life tonight*, Fullerton said.

"I trust you," Johnny said.

Fullerton nodded, leaning back, gripping the steering wheel with one hand. He sighed. "It's about a terrorist attack," he said. "Multiple terrorist attacks... simultaneous attacks. That's what we're up against." He paused. "That's all I can tell you."

Johnny nodded. That's as far as it could go. "Where are we going?"

"Jersey City."

They fell silent. Johnny gazed out the window as the Turnpike miles rolled behind them.

"Now listen to me," Fullerton said as they closed in on Jersey City. "The dude we're going to take down tonight... I know he messed you up inside. But you need to leave that behind. Don't beat on him, don't say shit to him. He shot those people up at the farm, but we need him."

"I'm cool," Johnny said.

What had Fullerton been through, Johnny wondered, to become a "professional?" How did he get to the point where he accepted that he needed a killer more than he wanted to kill him himself? How did become more human than human like that, and how could Johnny do the same?

Fullerton pulled off the Turnpike and wound through Jersey City, past luxury condos, the hospital, then through decrepit streets. He parked in front of a crumbling apartment complex.

"This is his place," he said. "We'll wait here. When the dude rolls up, you take the wheel. I'll do the rest." Fullerton paused. "Unless he's not alone."

Blood flushed Johnny's face at the thought.

They didn't have to wait long. After a few minutes, a young man in a puffy blue jacket came trudging up the street, a gray sweatshirt hood yanked over his head. Johnny made out a red bandanna across his forehead. He was about Johnny's height, maybe shorter, built a little slighter.

"That's him," Fullerton said. "And he's alone. Get behind the wheel when I get out."

Johnny watched the suspect amble along in the dark, breathing smoke on the way to the building. They waited, waited...

When he approached the rear of the truck, Fullerton reached for the door handle. "Now," he said. He cracked open the door, slid out, and crouched on the street. He gestured for Johnny to wiggle behind the wheel. Johnny climbed over.

Fullerton coiled in his crouch for another moment, then jumped across the hood and pounced on the subject as he walked past the rear passenger side. The hooded man reached for his waistband; Fullerton grabbed his wrist and elbowed him in the head. Then he reached into his pocket and jabbed a clenched fist into the man's shoulder. Fullerton dug his fist into the shoulder as the man thrashed, still gripping his wrist, until he collapsed. He ripped open the sliding door, lashed a nylon zip-tie around the subject's wrists, fished a handgun out of his waistband, and then threw him in the back seat. He slammed the door, jumped into the passenger seat, and dropped the magazine from the handgun. "Back to the Turnpike," Fullerton said.

Goddamn, Johnny thought, firing up the truck and speeding off. "Where are we going?"

"Not the office. Head towards Irvington. I'll give you directions when we get closer." Fullerton held up a needle. "A paralytic and a sedative," he said. "His ass'll come to just when we need to talk to him a little bit."

Amazing. He did it all in a matter of seconds.

"Flow of traffic, Luca," Fullerton said. "No one saw us. Trust me."

Johnny drove on towards Irvington, a flattened town outside of Newark. It was a war zone, armed gangs roaming through the streets in broad daylight, some of whom pulled kerchiefs around their faces. It was a subversive hotbed, with hooded teenagers and young men destroying Authority surveillance cameras nightly.

It wasn't long before Johnny and Fullerton pulled into the city. It was nighttime in the dead of winter, and vagrants shivered on corners, collapsed on benches. Young men in small groups under street lights turned and bore into the truck with hungry eyes as it turned corners and drove on. Johnny and Fullerton continued past rusty wrought-iron gates guarding apartment complexes with busted front doors and bars in the windows. They bumped over train tracks which hadn't conveyed a train in decades, swept through traffic signals which didn't signal, passed decades-old cars on cinder-blocks.

Fullerton directed Johnny to park in a driveway leading up to a garage with wooden doors, attached to a two-floor sweatbox with a screen door swinging in the door frame which rested on a porch of termite-eaten wood. Fullerton jumped out of the truck, undid the padlock on the doors with a key, pulled the doors open, and gestured for Johnny to pull inside.

Fullerton opened the door as Johnny cut the engine. "Don't worry, it's abandoned," he said. "Grab the shotguns and a pair of night-visions in the back and follow me."

Johnny did as told, gripping the shotguns on the outer loops of their triggers. Fullerton threw their prisoner over his shoulder, slid the door shut, and then opened the iron door leading from the garage to the house. Johnny followed, crossing the threshold into darkness, and then Fullerton flicked on the light.

The basement was furnished with two couches and scattered chairs on its bare concrete floor, outfitted with laptops, flat-screen televisions, stereos, and other electronics, firearms scattered everywhere.

A chemical odor singed the inside of Johnny's nostrils, as if someone had bent his head back and poured a household cleaner down his throat. He scanned the room, his eyes settling on a sink in the corner of the room, a plastic basin with vapors emanating over the edges.

Fullerton secured the prisoner, sitting him in a steel chair, fitting his arms around the back, and slapping on a pair of handcuffs to go with the zip-ties. He then drew an extra length of chain which ran from the handcuffs, a manacle, and snapped it around a pipe behind the chair.

Fullerton crossed to Johnny and pulled him aside. "This is a Brigade 910 safehouse," he whispered in his ear. "That smell is bombs and chemical weapons that they've been testing."

"But this looks like a gang hangout," Johnny whispered back. "Look at all the electronics. It's all got to be hot."

"Where do you think Brig 910 gets their funding? Church donations? You're going to learn a lot of shit about this group. And the first lesson is that they raise money just like regular criminals do." Fullerton glanced back at the prisoner, then back at Johnny. "Now listen," he said. "We've got intel that says Brigade 910 abandoned this place. If there's one thing they're sloppy at, it's leaving their chemical testing shit in the sink like that, 'cause they always figure their safehouses are in the middle of nowhere and no one would ever snitch on them—safer to leave it here than transport it out and get caught, they figure. Judging by the merchandise they left behind, they must've felt the heat on them real strong, seeing as how they ghosted and left thousands of dollars worth of shit like we see here." Fullerton examined the prisoner again, nodded, and looked back at Johnny, grabbing his shoulder. "Your job is to take that shotgun and go upstairs. At the top of the stairs you'll find a window, right next to the front door of this place. You stand guard, man. I'll be able to hear you if you want to shout out to me, and I'll have my shotgun, too. While you're up there, I'm going to interrogate his ass. You might hear me say some strange shit. You just stay up there with your weapon and don't say a damn thing. We'll talk about it when the op is over."

A couple of hours ago, I was sitting on my couch getting ready to call Justine. And now—Johnny had to bite back a smile, even though they were deep in enemy territory in the dead of night—*now I'm doing what I signed up for.*

He handed Fullerton one of the shotguns. "Copy," Johnny said. He marched up the stairs, pushed open the door, and just as Fullerton said, he found a window. He pulled on the night-vision goggles and gazed outside, the bare street bathed in green. He crouched at his post.

"Do you know where you're at?" he heard Fullerton say downstairs. "No? Take a look around, man. You know where you're at."

Why were they interrogating this guy here? Why didn't they arrest him and bring him to the office? Johnny fixed his eyes on the street again. He was at the bottom of the totem pole, but at least it was a new totem pole.

"Tell me your name," Fullerton said.

"Fuck you, *puta*," a voice replied in a Latino accent.

Johnny heard a thud which sounded like fist meeting face, and then the legs of the chair scraping the cement floor.

"You can't get up," Fullerton said. "You can't move. Talk."

"I don't know shit."

"Bullshit!" Fullerton yelled. "Do you know who I am? I'm a commander, man. And you conducted an operation without our permission. I should pull that bandana off and choke you with it."

"What? What are you talking about?"

"You did those two upstate. And I want to know who gave the order."

"Did who upstate?"

Another thud. "Look, you're on my last nerve. A few weeks ago, you went into some dude's house, and you capped him and his wife in their bedroom. Am I right?"

"But... but I thought that was cool. I thought that was cool with you."

Johnny clenched his shotgun. *When is that ever cool, motherfucker?*

"You did someone close to the revolution. I want to know who gave the order."

Close to the revolution? *Goddamn it,* Johnny thought, *he's posing as a Brigade 910 guy.*

"And how the fuck do I know who you are?" the prisoner said.

"Because I'm the one with the shotgun, motherfucker, and you don't need to have a face right about now," Fullerton said. "Look where you are. You know who I'm with. But I don't know who you're with, and your ass will meet with the reaper tonight if I don't find out the truth."

"Tyranny, like hell, is not easily conquered."

Johnny turned towards the basement. What?

"Yet we have this consolation with us," Fullerton said, "that the harder the conflict, the more glorious the triumph."

Speaking in code.

"Tell me your name," Fullerton said.

"Guevara."

"Good. A good name. You took it from Che." Fullerton paused. "Who gave the order?

"Octavian."

"And that's all you know him by."

"That's all I would know *you* by."

"What does he look like?"

"I... I don't know, man. He's a white boy, a little older. About six feet. Light hair."

"They call him Sigma?"

"Maybe. I don't know."

"I want to know how he approached you."

"The way it always goes down, man."

"So you went to a meeting, you got your orders, and you found half your money waiting for you when you got home, along with a weapon," Fullerton said. "And then the night of the job, they picked you up, drove upstate, and you all did the job. And when you got back to your place that night, the rest of the cash was there."

"That's right."

Fullerton knows every detail of the way Brigade 910 operates.

"Someone's playing you," Fullerton said. "And I damn sure hope it's not the feds. Because if it is, you will die tonight. I promise you."

"I didn't pull a job for no pigs!"

"How do you know?"

"Because they was *us*, man. I've been working at this shit for two years now, I know a pig when I see one."

Not this pig, Johnny thought, smiling in the dark.

"How much paper?" Fullerton asked.

"Ten G," the prisoner replied. "They made it extra 'cause the dude's brother was some prosecutor."

"A prosecutor? What kind of prosecutor?"

"I don't know. Some kind of federal prosecutor. He was getting up in the revolution's business."

"So someone sent you to teach a lesson by doing his brother."

"That's right."

There was a lull. Johnny looked outside; nothing. He glanced at his watch. It was past two a.m.

"What's this shit on your hands?" Fullerton said. "Your fingers are all burned up. You been out testing shit tonight. Mixing bombs?"

"I wasn't—"

"Don't bullshit me, I know chemical burns, you don't think I get them on my own hands? What the fuck do you think is that smell in the room right now? Don't bullshit me. Who were you with?"

"Just... just regular dudes, man, that's it!"

"Listen, I don't know who in the hell you're working with now, but it's not the revolution. You pulled an op without our approval. Either you're trying to fuck with us, or you're with the government. And I'm going to decide what to do with you right now."

"They're not pigs, man! They're with us!"

"I don't believe you. And even if they're not pigs, then some new posse is starting shit inside the resistance, trying to take shit over. We didn't authorize that hit that night. And now we're going to send a message to whoever in the hell you're working for."

"Man, I got a little daughter," the prisoner said. "Please..."

That's right. Beg.

"Tell me everything you know about the project."

"What project, man?"

Another thud, like before.

"I told you to stop fucking with me," Fullerton said. "How long do you think we put up with this shit in the revolution? You should've been dead five minutes ago. You're a ghost to me. I will blast your goddamn face off if you fuck with me one more time. I want to know what you know about Project Orion."

"I don't know nothing!"

"We're planning the biggest operation in the history of the revolution, and you're making bombs. You know what I'm talking about. Have they sent you to recon any targets?"

"Buses and trains." The prisoner sighed. "They got me taking practice runs so I can leave a bomb in a bag and set it off after I get away. But I never heard of no Orion."

"We never authorized a train hit," Fullerton said. "That's not part of the plan. I'm telling you, you're a pig, and you're going to pay."

"I'm not! I swear to God." The chair scraped the cement again. "Let me out of here!"

"Come on, you're real bad, you blasted that guy and his wife, and now you're about to blow up some buses and trains. What are you afraid of?"

"Because I didn't do nothing, man! I'm loyal!"

"You're loyal," Fullerton said. "You're loyal." He paused. "What made you join us?"

"Because, man. So I could fight the fascist government that's keeping us down."

"You see, you're bullshitting me. You joined up for the paper. You do some bitch work, and you pick up some cash. You get good at it and they ask you to do more high-risk shit. So you do it and you make your score, and now you're going to look for more scores by blowing shit up. I've been telling everyone you're the kind I don't want, and tonight I'm going to lead by example."

"Please, man! Please!" The prisoner screamed, and then he said, "It's going down this spring."

Johnny turned his head towards the basement. *Fullerton broke him.*

"What's going down?" Fullerton said.

"I'm supposed to do my thing this spring. They told me there's going to be a signal."

"What signal?"

"I don't know. I swear. But there's going to be a day where I'm supposed to ride around town, and then there's going to be a signal to do it. And then I'm going to do it, and a whole lot of other shit is supposed to be going down that day."

"What day?"

Just then, Johnny saw two figures outside.

Kerchiefs covered their faces, pulled up around their ears. Each wore a handgun in his waistband. One of them gestured towards the house. The other nodded and burned a look into the window, right where Johnny was standing in the dark. And now they were approaching.

"Goddamn it, I said what day!"

"I don't know!"

"What's the signal, man! What is the fucking signal?"

Johnny ducked into the basement. Fullerton had a belt in his hands, clenched at the knuckles, his hand drawn back.

"Two at the door," Johnny said. "Headed this way."

Fullerton nodded, then lashed the prisoner in the face with the belt. "You hear that, man? We got pigs running up in here, and I'm going to leave you!" He looked up at Johnny. "Hold the door."

Johnny nodded, and the blood rushed to his face. This was it. He'd been in fights before, and he'd had some wild nights as a surveillance technician, but he'd never pointed a gun at someone. His innards scraped against each other like tectonic plates. This was it. He had to hold the door.

Johnny's finger curled around the trigger, his left hand clutching the barrel. What were the rules of engagement? He'd tell them to freeze, and if they moved for their weapon, he'd... He'd blast them.

The two outside stopped in their approach, then retreated to a position in front of the garage. One pulled out a cell phone and swept his fingers over the screen, texting.

"They're in front of the garage," Johnny called out.

"I've had it with you, man," he heard Fullerton say.

"I don't know nothing about no signal!" the prisoner said. "I ain't lying!"

"Then you're useless to me. Either way, you're fucked."

"They said they won't tell me the signal until right before it happens. And I heard some talk that other shit is going to go down, here, and in other cities. But it's all rumors, man. That's all I know."

A van pulled up at the mouth of the driveway, and the two in front of the garage ran out to meet it. They slid open the door, disappeared into the van for a moment, and then reemerged, now three strong. And armed with machine guns.

They ran at the house.

"Automatic weapons," Johnny said. "Coming right at us."

"Shit, we've got to get the fuck out of here," Fullerton said. "I'm coming."

Johnny clutched the shotgun. He gulped, and his teeth began to chatter. This wasn't a schoolyard fight; this was his death in front of him. He couldn't hold the gun steady; he couldn't breathe; he couldn't—

One of the figures outside raised his weapon. Johnny pulled the trigger.

The discharge blasted out the window and exploded at the feet of the gunman, knocking him down in a cascade of dirt. The recoil hurled Johnny backwards, and he hit the floor as glass shards drizzled on him.

"Holy shit," Fullerton said, leaping through the door frame. He tackled Johnny as he tried to get back up. "Stay down!" he yelled.

Machine-gun fire crackled, pelting the window and spraying the wall. Drywall poured off in sheets of dust.

Fullerton crawled to the window, and Johnny followed him. "Shit," Fullerton said, peering outside. "Get downstairs now!"

They turned, and each raised into a crouch and ran towards the door as more fire sliced into the house. A metal object dinked onto the floor and then exploded in light and smoke as Fullerton threw Johnny down the steps.

Johnny rolled down and crashed to the cement floor on his head. He pawed the floor, reaching for his weapon. He glanced upstairs—it looked like the sun had crashed through roof of the house and landed on the first floor.

"Stun grenade!" Fullerton yelled. "I can't see!"

Johnny felt lumps rising on his cheek and the side of his head, and the room swam in front of him. Then he shook his head and it all came clear.

He knew they were coming through the front door, and Fullerton was down and blind.

Johnny ran upstairs. The light was burning away, and Fullerton was on all fours, reaching out. There was a pound on the door, and one side of the frame split. Johnny raised his weapon and fired again.

The shot blasted the center of the door to fragments. Someone screamed outside. "Stay down!" Johnny yelled at Fullerton.

Just then, a bullet buzzed by Johnny's head, the velocity of the near-miss pouring air in his ear. He dropped back down, just in time to spy a leg pivoting through the window off to his right. He fired again, the shotgun slamming into his shoulder, but the shot missed the leg and blew out a part of the wall. *Goddamn it.* Johnny raised the shotgun again.

"Downstairs!" Fullerton yelled, surging to his feet. "I've got a plan. Let's go!"

They ran back downstairs, Fullerton closing the door behind them. "What's the plan?" Johnny said.

"We're getting in the truck," Fullerton said. "You're going to drive straight through the door, and straight out the driveway. Be ready for anything."

"But they've got us blocked in."

"Trust me, goddamn it! Let's move!"

"What's going on, man?" the prisoner said. "What's happening up there?"

Fullerton shook his head. "He stays," he told Johnny. "Let's go."

The door breaking open upstairs. Footsteps running across the floor. Different voices yelling. The basement door opening.

Fullerton yanked open the iron door leading into the garage, and he and Johnny jumped in the truck. Johnny jammed the key into the ignition, his hand shaking, and jerked the ignition to life.

"You've got to have faith, Luca," Fullerton said. "Put it in reverse and slam on the fucking gas, straight out to the back of the driveway."

Johnny grabbed the gear shift on the steering column, pulled it into reverse, and looked at Fullerton one last time. Then he pounded the gas pedal.

The truck flew backwards, crashed through the wooden doors, and bounced down the driveway. It t-boned the van blocking the driveway, slamming Johnny and Fullerton's heads back. Fullerton jumped out, pulled a handgun from his waistband, and fired two rounds at the driver's side window of the van; crimson sprayed onto the glass on the inside. Then he whipped around and peeled off two more rounds at the driver's side window of a car which had pulled behind the van; more crimson spray.

Fullerton jumped in the back of the truck. "Should've gone with the MP-5," he muttered, grabbing a machine gun. "Open the roof."

Johnny hit the button to open the moon roof. Fullerton was

totally calm now, and Johnny was plugging into that.

Fullerton stood up through the aperture in the roof with the machine gun. "Pull away," he said.

Johnny slapped the gear into drive and put some ankle into it. The wheels spun, then caught on the driveway and yanked the truck from the van which it had hit. Johnny whipped the truck to the left, cut across the front lawn, and bounded out into the street.

Fullerton ripped off fully automatic rounds as they pulled away, firing at the house. Then he dropped back into the truck, pulled out a cell phone, and hit the send button.

The house, now a block away, exploded into the night.

Chapter 16

Johnny swerved, the blast jolting him, bursting loose even more adrenaline. "What the fuck!" he yelled, speeding away. He glanced at the rearview mirror, throbbing red.

"Flow of traffic," Fullerton said.

"It... it blew up!"

"I bombed it, Luca. Just like we planned."

"We?"

"Me and Peterson."

"What the hell... was that..." Johnny was out of his body, floating above this night, looking down on someone who was not himself.

"Someone tipped them off. That's why they came at us like that. They figured we had one of their own with us."

"You... you planned to blow that place up?"

"The whole time. Peterson told me to make the judgment call to see if our collar had any intel value for us, and if not, leave him in there. Tonight we sent a message to Brigade 910."

"What message?"

"That someone is fucking with them. Maybe the Authority, maybe another faction. We straight disrupted their operations. It's like throwing a rock at a beehive. They're going to fly out in every direction and buzz at one another. And when they do, we're going listen."

"Every cop in the county is going to be there... and people saw us..."

"Look at you, man! We just killed like six dudes and the only thing you care about is getting caught by the motherfucking law." Fullerton laughed. "You really are an Authority agent now!"

"But—"

"No one's gonna pull us over. All the cops know that when we're in the area, strange shit happens. I guarantee you that tomorrow morning, the media will call it there a bad drug deal. Or if those corporate prostitute bitches have permission to be adventurous, they might report that a Brigade 910 dude blew up the house testing out a bomb."

The adrenaline bubbled in Johnny's stomach. Did he shoot a man back there?

"You were posing as a Brigade 910 guy," Johnny said.

"You may as well know now," Fullerton said. "I've gone undercover in a Nine-Ten cell before. A couple of years ago."

Johnny nodded, heading back onto the highway. How could he absorb any of this?

"Who are they, Fullerton? Brigade 910. Who the fuck are they?"

"Well, first you've got the foot soldiers. Pissed-off broke dudes, gang bangers, loners, all that." Fullerton paused. "But the commanders are different. Smarter—stronger. All kinds of training—weapons training, how to organize, how to indoctrinate, use propaganda, the whole terrorist playbook. And then there's someone at the top, someone we need to decapitate."

"Who?"

"Octavian."

"Why do they use that name?"

"It's the name of the first Roman emperor after Caesar. He ended the republic and started the empire."

"And that's what they want?"

"Damned if I know," Fullerton said. "They're an anarchist group. I think that all they want is chaos—to see the world burn." He sighed, then smiled. "You saved my life."

And in the agony of tonight's mayhem, Johnny smiled. He had.

Just then, a flurry of police cruisers whipped past them, lights swirling. Fullerton beeped his two-way. "Boss," he said. "Mission accomplished. Returning to Newark."

Chapter 17

"I've missed you so, baby," Mama Wilkins said, rocking in a wooden chair on her front porch, the last sunbeams of the day falling across her wrinkled face, thick red-framed glasses, gray hair, and print housedress.

"I've missed you too, Mama," President Reed Wilkins said, taking his mother's hand in his, rubbing his fingertips over her fingers. He could remember when they were the hands that healed him when he cried, soothed him to sleep. Now they felt like paper...

"You see, I'm always here for you, honey. I ain't never gonna leave you."

The President smiled. "I know... I know." He clasped her hand and then kissed it. In the sunset, she wasn't old anymore; she was young and beautiful, the prettiest mother in his Ohio hometown. "I came so far to see you, Mama."

"I know you did. Sit beside me."

At that moment, the President knew he was dreaming; his mother had been dead for almost five years now. *This isn't real*, he whispered into his own mind as he sat beside her. *This isn't real, but I can't help it, I need her so much...*

"Night be falling soon," she said. "Sometimes I just wanna take the old sunset in my arms and hold it tight, just so there'd be no night. You know the good Lord don't promise us nothing but now, honey. There ain't no guarantee on tomorrow."

"I know, Mama." Wilkins looked out at the sun, edging into the horizon, splashing red across the sky...

"Don't let it fall, baby."

"What?"

"That sun is falling so hard now, I'm scared there's gonna be night forever. Don't let it fall."

"But Mama... I can't keep the sun from setting." *This isn't real.*

"You can do anything, honey. You're my boy. And I know if you're facing down the night, you can keep the sun in the sky. Do it for me, please, sugar."

"But–"

"Mr. President," a voice cut through the sky. "Sir–"

The chair beneath him dissolved; his mother evaporated.

"Mr. President," the voice said again.

President Wilkins awoke in his bed in the White House, an agent of the Anti-Subversion Authority standing above him. His muscles tensed.

"I need to brief you, sir."

It was Agent Mitchell, leader of the Authority presidential protective detail. In the dark, he looked like a storm trooper hovering over the bed.

"What is it?" Wilkins asked.

"Sir," Mitchell said, "if you'd like, we can go to another room so we don't wake the First—"

The President looked over at his wife, her face eased into the silk pillowcase, her form cuddled in the blankets. "Is it an emergency?" he asked.

"No, sir."

"Then brief me here, but whisper."

"Sir, the New York Field Office is reporting that a Brigade 910 safehouse was destroyed in New Jersey tonight."

"Destroyed? How?"

"They're not sure, sir."

"And why is the New York office reporting it, if it happened in New Jersey? New Jersey is Peterson's office, isn't it?"

"Yes, Mr. President. SAIC Moloch is concerned that Peterson is conducting covert operations without your approval."

This was a trend. For months now, Authority figures—from agents on his detail up to Director Bryson himself—had been questioning Peterson's competence. *The son-of-a-bitch must be doing something right.*

"Well, I'll have to talk to SAIC Moloch about this," he said. "Tell him we'll have to see how we can keep SAIC Peterson in line." *I can play this game, too.*

"Yes, sir."

"Is there anything else? Anything I should know?"

"No, sir. Rescue vehicles are putting out the fire. We believe some terrorists inside were killed, but no one else. There's nothing else to do about it tonight."

"Okay, then. Tell Moloch that I want him down here tomorrow for a meeting with Director Bryson and me." *If Moloch wants to wake me up in the middle of the night to play games against Peterson, now he can wake up at five a.m. tomorrow and get himself to Washington.*

"Yes, sir." Agent Mitchell started to walk away.

"One more thing, Mitchell."

"Sir?"

"Don't come back in here tonight unless it's an emergency. You've given me a lot to think about."

"Of course, Mr. President."

That last part was a decoy. He was going to do a lot of thinking, but it wouldn't be here. It was time for another of his late night trips.

The First Lady stirred. "Baby, is every—"

"It's nothing, Delilah," Wilkins said. "You can go back to sleep, beautiful."

"Okay. I love you."

"I love you too."

Wilkins settled back into bed; he had to wait until she fell asleep.

He loved her so much, her and the kids. With three hundred fifty million Americans to fight for, there were three—Delilah, Garrett, and Gabrielle—who kept him going. *God, Delilah,* he thought. She'd waited for him when he was off fighting the first Gulf War, and even stuck by him when he got the cockamamie idea to go to law school. The U.S. Attorney's office, the House of Representatives, the loss in the Senate race, the win in the governor's race... and then the Presidency. All with Delilah by his side.

Wilkins waited until he knew she was asleep, when she started to ease her breaths into the pillow, the notes of a dream neither of them would ever know. He slid out of bed, felt around in the dark... and his fingers caught in the edges of an unmarked closet door cut into the wall.

The closet was no secret; it was a nineteenth-century designing trick. The trap door in the back of the walk-in closet, on the other hand, was a secret he guarded with his life—a twenty-first-century Reed Wilkins designing trick.

Wilkins slipped into the closet, huddled in a back corner, and felt around in the dark some more. He slid his finger under a piece of carpet, traced it over a button, and pushed. He kept his finger on the button.

Good thing this won't be in the history books. The President of the United States sneaking around in the dark like a kid up past his bedtime.

The button he pushed was a signal to a detail of Secret Service agents waiting in a musty chamber in the bowels of the White House mansion. If the coast was clear, the button would radiate heat to his fingertip; if not, it would prick him with cold. It was amazing.

A moment later, he felt a pulse of heat on his fingertip. *Thank God.*

In the black of the closed closet, Wilkins flipped up the piece of carpet, then flipped up a piece of tile cut seamlessly into the floor. He lowered himself into the hole, first one leg resting on the rubberized platform below, then the other. He tugged on a pair of ropes, pulling the piece of carpet above back down, sealing him in. The President then slid the tile back in place. He flicked a light switch.

He was in a stairwell, with every inch—the stairs, the walls, the ceiling, the landing—coated in black soundproofing rubber. Wilkins walked down a couple of steps and then flicked another light switch. The air behind and above him hummed. The switch had released an electromagnetic soundproofing wave so powerful that he had to stand clear of the secret "entrance" above before he activated it.

Kevin Chan, the Secret Service Director, suggested the secret garage to Wilkins a few months ago, right after the Authority had been invested with the duty of guarding the President's room. First Chan and a few other agents had swept an anti-bugging device over the President and discovered a homing chip implanted in the back of his neck. *The Authority did this to you while you were asleep*, Chan explained. We knew they would. *They're not trying to protect you, they're trying to track your every move.*

Chan then showed Wilkins dozens of replicas of the chip and explained to him that Secret Service agents would implant them throughout his wardrobe, to keep up appearances, he said. He next showed the President how to remove them at will. Finally, Chan floated the idea of the Lincoln-era trap door in the President's closet which led to a secret garage that was not in the White House blueprints, that in turn led to a secret tunnel that ran under

Washington. *We could wire the trap door with a button*, Chan had said, *which could give you a heat signal if it's safe to come down. Just leaving that out there, Mr. President.*

The whole setup was not new, according to Chan. The trap door in the bedroom was a means of escape for President Lincoln, if necessary, during the Civil War—except then it was the living room. It led to a barracks where Union soldiers awaited the order to spirit the President and the First Lady away to Maryland in a coach through a tunnel under Washington.

After Pearl Harbor, military engineers extended the tunnel to Virginia, paved the tunnel in asphalt, and fitted it with electric lights. Finally, decades later, in 2022, the Secret Service soundproofed the entire escape route in response to what it believed to be treason against the President by the Anti-Subversion Authority.

The funniest thing, Wilkins thought as he crept down the stairs, *is that the hardest part of this whole escape is getting past Delilah.*

He opened a rubber door at the landing, then looped down another stairwell, then another. He opened a final soundproof door, but this time there would be human life on the other side.

"Same place, Mr. President?" asked Chan, an Asian man in his early forties with straight black hair parted to the side.

"Same place," Wilkins said.

They were standing in a garage—cold concrete, yellow lamps, oil slicks, a fleet of black SUVs. Ahead was a rolling aluminum gate which gave way to a secret tunnel which snaked under the capital city. The tunnel emptied into a common parking garage, really a Secret Service front, in another part of town.

An agent rushed to the President with shoes and an overcoat. His military aide joined him at his side, carrying a briefcase bearing the launch codes for the nation's nuclear weapons. One of the SUVs then pulled up. "Arlington, sir?" the driver said.

"Arlington," Wilkins said.

As his vehicle carried him through the night, Wilkins thought back to the day Chan showed him the homing chip. The message had been clear: the Authority intended to track his every move, and the Secret Service intended to do what it had been sworn to do since the Teddy Roosevelt administration—protect the President. There was a difference, a border into sinister that the Authority threatened to cross, but that the Secret Service would police.

The tunnel frightened Wilkins, no easy task considering he had ten thousand nuclear warheads at his disposal. Pairs of rectangular yellow lamps lit the way, their vapors glowing against stone slabs. There were no signs, no lane markings—this was a tunnel built for one man in the world, the President of the United States.

The vehicle drifted to a stop, a few feet in front of a wall blocking its path. The driver then hit a button. The wall rumbled and rose– another Roosevelt-era addition– and the vehicle continued on. Wilkins was as amazed tonight as he was the first time he saw it.

The two trucks drove through the opening, emerging in a fenced-off corner of a parking garage. The President's driver hit a button, and the wall behind them closed again. He then hit another, and a section of the fence in front of them slid up. The drivers continued, wound through the garage, nodded to an undercover Secret Service agent manning the gatehouse, and emptied into northwest Washington, headed for Arlington.

Wilkins now knew the extent of the planning that went into these trips. First he had to remove the minuscule bugging device from his clothes and leave it in his bed in order to dupe the Authority. Then he had check in with the agents in the secret garage below, who had to make sure that the coast was clear, order the agents manning the undercover parking garage to clear the facility and shut it down, and alert the military guard at the National Cemetery not to interfere with the convoy.

I don't know what it is about this place, the President thought as his truck pulled onto the cemetery grounds. *It's just so pure... so noble.*

"Tomb of the Unknowns, sir?" the driver asked.

The President nodded. "That's right."

The truck continued along narrow asphalt paths. In the moonlight, Wilkins could see row after row of simple crosses marking graves of not-so-simple men. They might have died alone in the Argonne Forest. Or Normandy... or Iwo Jima... Korea... Vietnam... Afghanistan... Iraq. A man lying under one of those crosses may have been a fifteen-dollar-a-month private whose last moment on earth may have been choking on German mustard gas—or maybe he was a twenty-first-century jarhead from Alabama who lay writhing from an IED as he stared up at the Fallujah sky.

The President bowed his head, and a chill ran up his spine and across his shoulders. *Just one of those men is worth a thousand of me.*

The driver stopped the truck. "We're here, Mr. President," he said.

Wilkins nodded and stepped outside, the winter wind biting into his face. Director Chan walked before him, and his military aide walked alongside him. Other Secret Service agents fanned out around him and trailed behind him as he walked towards the Tomb of the Unknowns.

Wilkins stopped at the Tomb. The Army sentinel patrolled back and forth. Wilkins could trust him not to look up—not to pry—not to implant a homing device into his body. This young man—as unknown to his President as the soldiers in that tomb—was guarding so much more than his fallen comrades as he marched back and forth, so much more.

The President looked at the marker. *The men in that tomb laid down their lives. The thousands on these grounds laid down their lives, so many of them dying far from home, sometimes alone under a foreign sky, for duty and for freedom.*

Wilkins watched the sentinel. He knew what the young man was doing: he was marching twenty-one steps across the tomb. On the twenty-first step he would turn and look at the tomb for twenty-one seconds. Then he would switch his weapon to his outside shoulder and march twenty-one steps the other way.

This is the soul of this nation, the keeping of its time.

Wilkins looked out at Washington, glistening on the horizon. *The shining city on the hill. If we all only knew the strength that lies in us, the strength of the men buried here, we could stop Bryson and the rest of them.*

Wilkins could give them what they wanted, he could sign the bill, he could imprison three hundred fifty million people in a police state. Hitler would do it; Stalin would do it. But Washington, Jefferson, and Madison never would.

Or, Wilkins thought, he could continue to refuse. Eventually he would be assassinated, and the conspirators—whoever they were—would rain down oppression on a population still restive for freedom.

But a third choice seduced him. He could fight them—and win. He could first fight them behind the scenes—stop their assassination attempt, or survive it. He could then fight them out in the open—by exposing them.

Who was he to have such pretensions? It was narcissistic, on the one hand, and suicidal on the other. *I should sign the bill and beg for mercy.*

He gazed again at Washington in the distance, and his lip quivered. *But I won't.*

Wilkins sighed. *I don't stand much of a chance. But if I can stand up to them—I can prove to Garrett and Gabrielle that this isn't an iron cage locking us in, but just an old, rotten latticework... and if we all grab a slat and pull, we can rip the whole thing down...*

The President turned to Director Chan. "Chan," he said. "Do you know a man named Hunter Peterson?"

Chan nodded. "He's a great agent. Used to be on your detail, right?"

Wilkins smiled. "That's right. And you're right, he's a great agent... one of the best." He paused. "Do you ever talk to him?"

"Not really, you know, I might run into him at some dinner every couple of years, stuff like that. But I know people who talk to him."

"I want you to set up a meeting."

"A meeting, sir?"

"Yes. I want you to set up a meeting between myself and SAIC Peterson... right here, on one of these trips."

"Right here... at the cemetery?"

"That's right."

"I'll get on it right away, Mr. President."

Wilkins turned back towards the capital on the horizon. *Time is running out.*

Chapter 18

"You're really something," Justine said, narrowing her eyes and smiling.

Johnny raised his eyebrows. "Oh, am I?"

"I'm starting to think you are. I mean, you made reservations at this gorgeous restaurant, you pulled out my chair... and having the host put out my favorite flowers at the table was a pretty nice touch. I think this is the nicest Valentine's Day I've ever had."

"Well, you're the nicest Valentine I've ever had."

Justine kicked Johnny under the table. Johnny had all the right moves tonight: an elegant Italian restaurant in Manhattan, white tulips at the table, and a card with a stanza of her favorite poem inside—some crap about valediction and the morning.

Johnny took in the sight of Justine, her blonde hair falling past her shoulders, her black dress resting on her skin, diamond stud earrings sparkling in her ears.

"Who are you, Johnny Luca?" Justine asked.

"What do you mean?"

"I didn't think you had a night like this in you." She kicked Johnny again and looked into his eyes. "You totally surprised me with all this."

Johnny looked down a moment at the white tablecloth, then out at the waiters in blazers milling about the full dining room, the crowd of New York lovers waiting at the mahogany bar for a table. He smiled. "I'm just a regular guy, trying to show a girl a good time," he said, trying to believe it.

Justine studied him for a moment. "You're a regular guy, most of the time." She shook her head and smiled. "You know what I'm thinking of right now?"

"What?"

"The night we met. Right after... you know. After the bomb went off. The way you ran out of the bar and ran towards it."

"Yeah, it was a crazy night." *Here it comes.*

"Why did you run out like that?"

And there it is. "Because I wanted to help."

"But how could you help? Being a civilian and all."

"I had to try. It was just an instinct."

"Not getting enough action fixing stuff for the FBI?"

"I'm not getting *any* action with the FBI," Johnny said. "You know what they say, geeks with guns."

"I guess," Justine said. "You never say anything about it. How was work today?"

Well, today I briefed my boss on these Brigade 910 scumbags we've been investigating as part of the largest counter-terrorism investigation in American history. "Pretty boring. I mean, supervise this installation here, inspect this new fingerprint machine there."

"They've got you working weird hours doing that stuff. And sometimes I even think they beat you up at work." Justine giggled.

"What do you mean?"

"Well, take that huge lump you had on your head a couple of weeks ago. And that weird cut on your ear."

Johnny thought back to Fullerton throwing him down the stairs when the bad guys shot the stun grenade into the house. That was the lump. And the cut... that was the bullet that grazed his ear, a shot that would have killed him if it were a millimeter to the right.

"I'm getting into martial arts," he said. "One of the agents trains me on the side." *At least that's a little true.*

Johnny looked over Justine again. He couldn't fight it; he liked this girl. But he couldn't tell her about any of this stuff, not now, not ever. It was a part of him she couldn't reach.

"I know there's a lot you're not telling me," Justine said. "You can't fool me. I'll have you know that I'll be graduating with a completely worthless law degree this spring. You have to get up *pret-ty* early in the morning to fool me."

Johnny laughed. "So what aren't I telling you?"

Justine sipped her wine. "Let's just say that I already know. And when you feel comfortable enough to tell me, I'll be ready."

Johnny sipped wine himself. "You know, huh?" He folded his arms. "I think there's a lot you don't know about me, counselor."

"Then why don't you tell me?" Justine smiled. "I might even let you kiss me again, if you do."

"I'll be kissing you again tonight, even if I say there's nothing to tell."

Justine sipped her wine again and laughed. "You're so sure. Maybe you will, maybe you won't. But I'm going to get to the bottom of you."

Johnny grinned. "I hope you do."

She slapped his hand. "You're the worst!" she said. "Ugh, I don't know why I keep seeing you."

"Because I'm Italian, probably." Johnny took a slice of the piece of cheesecake they were sharing for dessert. "What about you? What do you have to tell?"

"You already know the basics. My soulmate is constitutional law, I hate tyranny and injustice, and I love the Mets. Everything else is a secret."

Johnny grinned again. "You should've kept the Mets part a secret."

Justine looked into his eyes with a half-seductive, half-longing gaze. "Some people keep different kinds of secrets than others," she said. "But I'll figure you out, I swear."

Is she on to me? No, she couldn't be. This isn't the kind of thing someone catches on to. Even if I do show up to our dates looking like I just got my ass kicked.

"So let me ask you something," Justine said.

Johnny grinned. "No, you can't have my autograph."

Justine threw up her finger, a little tipsy. "Shut up. I was going to ask you what you think of the Total Information Awareness Act."

"What about it?"

"Well, I went to a panel discussion on it at school today, and it seems pretty messed up. And since you want to be out on the front lines or whatever, I wanted to know what you thought."

Johnny gripped the stem of his wineglass with two fingers. "We need it. We need every tool we can get." He sipped the wine.

"But aren't there enough tools? They were saying at the panel today that the Authority already listens in on people's cell phone calls and monitors their web traffic. One expert thought they even use your laptop as some kind of remote microphone or something."

No comment.

"And so what if they do?" Johnny said. "The only people who have something to worry about are the terrorists."

Justine shook her head. "I knew you'd say that. But you're wrong. A lot more people should worry. This is our freedom we're talking about. It's like the President keeps saying—some things are non-negotiable. Sometimes I don't think we're a democracy anymore." Justine leaned a little closer. "Sometimes I think we aren't much better than countries like Uzbekistan or Azerbaijan. Ruled by criminals, nothing more than a dictatorship, no matter what we say." Justine studied Johnny a moment. "I'll bet that deep down, you agree with me. That second Johnny that's hiding in there. Some distant part of you that's actually sensitive and compassionate."

Later, when they were strolling through the city after leaving the restaurant, Justine kissed him on the lips. "Thank you," she whispered, blowing the last syllable against his neck. *Yeah, I like this girl*, he thought as he slid his eyes from her blonde hair to her peep-toed shoes.

On nights like tonight, life was normal. Johnny was a twenty-four-year-old guy out with his girl on Valentine's Day, and there were no bombs exploding, no one trying to shoot him. *I can get used to this*, he thought as they walked through the city.

"And when he shall die, take him and cut him out in little stars, and he will make the face of heaven so fine," Justine said as they walked.

It's from Romeo and Juliet, silly, she explained when Johnny responded with puzzlement. *You look so good tonight, you'd make the face of heaven so fine.* And then she kissed him again.

I could get used to this, Johnny thought again later that night, as they fell together into her bed in the sliver of streetlight that slipped through her window.

Chapter 19

"Project Orion is in the operational stage," a voice crackled over the headphones on Johnny's ears.

Johnny, sitting at the desk in his apartment one night in early March, checked to make sure the digital recorder was running.

"New York, Washington, Chicago, Los Angeles, San Francisco, Detroit, and Miami are all ready. We've had some trouble in Boston, where I'm going to send a couple of you, and Denver."

Johnny was listening in as a high-level Brigade 910 commander briefed a group of deputies. Everyone in the room called him "Octavian," but his file said that his superiors called him "Sigma"—the same man who had led the attack at the farm. "He's former American intelligence," Peterson had said to Johnny when he handed him the assignment.

"I know what some of you are thinking," Sigma said. "That we're going too far, we're taking too much of a chance. But Octavian gave me the order himself. There's no chance that's too risky, nothing that we can do that's too far. We're so close now we can taste it—the decapitation of this criminal regime."

That's what you think, asshole.

Peterson had come up with a novel way of snooping this time. He hadn't been able to penetrate the safehouse and plant listening devices, so he issued a subpoena ordering Sigma's wireless provider to bounce a certain signal to his cell phone. The signal activated the phone's mouthpiece as a microphone that fed audio to an Authority transmitter.

"So are the plans final now?" a voice asked.

"Here's what I'm allowed to tell you about Orion," Sigma said. "We'll use every weapon in the arsenal. This means all our truck bombs, all our chemical, all our biological, the one dirty bomb we have. Shoulder-fired missiles shot at planes, rocket-propelled grenades shot into office buildings, random shootings of civilian crowds. All in one day, at the same time."

Holy shit, Johnny thought, blood rushing to his face.

"What's happening in each city?" another voice asked.

"Octavian won't say yet. We may not know until a week before, or less."

"When will it be?"

"Spring. Probably late May."

"What about the signal?" another voice asked.

Johnny bit his lip. Peterson had told him this was the "trillion-dollar question which we *must* find out."

"I can't say," Sigma said. "Octavian may not authorize me to tell you until days before, or maybe even the day of."

Johnny shoulders sank. *At least we're on this guy. Thank God we know who this dude is.*

"But I can tell you this about the signal," Sigma said. "It's designed to trigger the attack *instantly*. It'll be definite and it'll be clear. It's something that's going to happen—and when it happens, I'll send out a confirmation to each of you, in each of your cities. Then you strike."

Johnny's hands were trembling. Even though Peterson had told him about a "massive act of terrorism," and Fullerton had mentioned "multiple terrorist attacks," he had no idea. This was no terror attack. This was total fucking destruction.

"What happens after Project Orion?" a new voice asked.

"I'm glad you asked me that," Sigma said. "The government will collapse. Riots will break out in every city. Prices will rise hundreds of times over. No one will be able to escape by car, train, or the air. There'll be no food, and after news gets out about a couple of water supplies we've poisoned, no water for days. That's what we've wanted from the beginning: to wipe this filthy empire off the face of the earth."

Johnny cringed. Even a fraction of all of that would be devastating.

"But what then?" the questioner persisted.

"Once we level this place from the inside, we win," Sigma said. "We'll wipe this country clean. No more imperialistic, meta-corporate oppression, from sea to shining sea."

These people are fucking psychotic.

"There's just one more thing to take care of," Sigma said.

Just then, a loud *clack* ripped over the headphones, and a chorus of shouts rose up. Johnny recognized the *clack* immediately; it was a firearm muffled by a silencer.

"Shut up!" Sigma yelled. The shouts fell silent. "He was working for the empire. So I executed him. Do you understand? *He was working for them, and now he's dead.*"

Peterson had told Johnny they were working with one of the deputies, who'd gotten nervous and tipped them off about Sigma...

"We're too close now," Sigma said. "If anyone else here wants to betray the revolution we'll find you. I promise you."

Johnny couldn't breathe; he had to breathe. He forced out a breath. Air burst in and out, he couldn't control it, in and out—

"Too much is at stake," Sigma said. "It wouldn't even matter if the enemy were listening in on us right now."

Johnny froze.

"Do you hear me? If you're listening, I'll find you, and I'll kill you, too."

Chapter 20

Peterson's and Fullerton's eyes were drawn as they looked at the twenty-four-year-old agent. Fullerton furrowed his eyebrows, started to speak, then stopped. He breathed deeply. "Luca, man," he said, "we didn't think that was going to happen. The dude we had on the inside... He was our source. He was all we had."

"We knew about everything you heard today," Peterson said. "We've known about their plans for a huge attack this spring in multiple cities. We knew they were going to use truck bombs, chemical, biological, and that they have a dirty bomb. What we need to find out is what the signal is, and who Octavian is. Without that, we're all dead. It's over."

Johnny nodded. "Is anyone helping us?"

Peterson and Fullerton looked at each other. "I just explained this to Fullerton," Peterson said. "We might have to go it alone, until I find help. You see, I don't trust the agency to handle this case."

"What do you mean?"

"Because I'm starting to think that Authority policy is to kill subversives first and ask questions later. And if I turn this case over to headquarters, or the New York office, they might trivialize this and just start shooting. 'Liquidate,' they call it. If they liquidate Sigma, it's over. They'll think they did their job, and our only contact will be gone. The Authority is convinced that Brigade 910 is too small to ever pull off a large-scale attack, and that we can win by just liquidating everyone."

"But what kind of numbers does Brigade 910 have?" Johnny asked.

"A couple of thousand," Fullerton said.

"But how? Who? You mean they've got two thousand guys who are going to blow themselves up and shoot civilians?"

"Not exactly," Fullerton answered. "The hardcore dudes are at the top and at the bottom. The Brigade 910 leaders are intense—they really believe this anarchist shit. And the punks at the bottom—the ones who do the attacks—are just as sick. They've got nothing going on in their sorry-ass lives but taking out their goddamn frustrations at the world on everybody else—and the commanders use heavy mind control tactics on them, secretly drugging them until they snap, then telling them the government did it to them, shit like that. But sometimes it's not even like that. We think that when they bombed the city a couple of months ago, they used a new tactic—they kidnapped some undocumented worker's family and told him they'd kill them unless he planted the car bomb. And then they killed him *and* the family."

"Christ," Johnny said.

"It's true," Peterson said. "Those are the soldiers at the bottom—whether they're natural born killers, or political extremists, or some poor guy whose family got taken hostage. The middle is different. In the middle is the majority of Brigade 910, contracted out to do the legwork. They raise money for the group through drugs, bank robberies, identity theft, money laundering. They spy on the bottom-level guys, keep tabs on where they go, who they're with, plant surveillance in their apartments. They buy arms, and components for bombs. A lot of the members in this middle group don't even consider themselves to be Brigade 910—a lot of them are just gangs who think they're helping some crime boss."

"Gangs are the perfect network for Brigade 910," Fullerton said. "They're loyal, they don't snitch, and they know how to get the streets open. And most important, they don't ask questions and they don't give a damn how they make their money."

"Just keep something in mind," Peterson said. "After Nine-Eleven, the FBI estimated that about one hundred thousand fighters trained in al Qaeda camps over the years. And in the end, it only took nineteen fanatics to destroy the World Trade Center. That's what we're looking at here, Luca. I believe Brigade 910 has enough fanatics to pull off this attack."

Johnny furrowed his eyebrows. He felt the world falling away from him. Everything he knew outside of this room—dinner with Justine, Christmas with his mother, hanging out with Lizbeth—was some sugar-sweet fantasy world. This was the real world, and it was getting uglier by the second.

Chapter 21

A couple of weeks later, in Arlington, Hunter Peterson looked down at President Kennedy's grave marker, the eternal flame licking the cold air. *My father protected this man until the day they shot him.* Then he looked up at his President, Reed Wilkins, standing tall in the March night.

"I'm glad you came, Hunter," Wilkins said.

Peterson nodded. "I'm glad you called on me, Mr. President."

Wilkins smiled. "You're a rare type. Men like you and Chan here—" Wilkins gestured to Director Chan—"are the type I need at a time like this."

"Just what sort of time is it?"

Wilkins sighed. "We're in trouble, Hunter. Trouble of the worst kind."

Peterson laid a hand on Wilkins' shoulder. It wasn't how an agent was supposed to touch the President; but they were friends, and Wilkins looked like he was in agony. "What's wrong?"

Wilkins sighed again. "You're here because I trust you. You know that, right?"

Peterson nodded. The air around them crackled with electricity. First he'd been summoned to meet with the President in front of the Kennedy grave at Arlington National Cemetery. Now here they were at 2 A.M., and Wilkins—the President of the United States—was asking him if he knew he trusted him.

"I know you do," Peterson said.

Wilkins turned to Chan. "And you know I trust you, right?"

"I do," Chan said.

Wilkins nodded. "I feel the whole government slipping away from me."

"What do you mean?" Peterson asked.

Wilkins paused, folding his hands to frame his words. "Hunter, what if I told you that I have the strongest feeling your agency is going to make a move on me?"

Peterson closed his eyes; his whole career had been moving towards this moment. "I would say you're right."

Wilkins turned to Chan. "What if I told you the same thing?"

"You'd be right, sir," Chan said.

"The Authority is going to assassinate me. After I veto the Total Information Awareness Act."

"So you're going ahead with the veto?" Chan asked.

"There's no other way. We're living under a Constitution here. I swore to God to defend it." Wilkins shook his head. "I think their plan is operational now. And if I'm guessing right, Bryson has already convinced the other conspirators that they have to get rid of me because I'm too weak on the terrorists and pose too much of a threat." Wilkins turned towards the Kennedy grave. "But there's another reason. It's that—"

"Bryson wants to launch a coup and start a dictatorship," Peterson said.

"*Right.* There's going to be a coup." Wilkins paused. "It'll come in a Trojan horse. They'll kill me, and then they'll force through the Act. The Act will make the Director more powerful than the President himself. The same system on the surface—President, Congress, courts—but Bryson will control everything."

"Fascism in America," Peterson said.

Wilkins snapped his fingers. "Exactly. And the best kind of fascism, too—with elections and a judicial system and every sign that we're still free." The President turned to Chan and Peterson. "Follow me."

Peterson and Chan followed Wilkins along the cemetery path to the Tomb of the Unknowns. Peterson gazed out at Washington sleeping in the distance.

"I've decided to fight," Wilkins said. "I've decided to veto the Act and stop their plot. But I can't do it alone."

"I'm up for a fight, Mr. President," Chan said.

"And so am I," Peterson said.

"Now hold onto yourselves," Wilkins said. "There's more."

"What is it?"

"I'm asking you two to do whatever you have to do to find out the who, when, and how of this plan. Now that they've postponed the vote on the law until April, it won't be until then. Rather than kill me now and install a lackey who'd sign the bill, they'd rather convince me to take their side and avoid the chaos of assassinating the

President. When I veto the bill, they'll make their move."

"So we've got to stop them," Chan said. "We have to start now, *tonight*—"

"I want you to catch them in the act," Wilkins said.

That's suicide. "Mr. President," he said. "We can't do that."

"Hunter, I know I'm asking too much already." Wilkins turned away, towards the capital. "I'm probably already dead, and if you can't crack this plot, it won't be your fault. It's my fault for asking this of you. But keeping me alive isn't enough. This doesn't end with arresting a lone gunman wacko Oswald-type. This ends with Alexander Bryson on trial for high treason."

"But that's imposs—"

"It's *possible*, goddamn it!" Wilkins said. Anguish cut across his face. "I'm sorry," he said, tears welling in his eyes. "But we have to try. You see, I've decided my life as President, my life as an American, doesn't matter unless we arrest Bryson and put him on trial. Look at where we are tonight. Think about the men buried here. It doesn't matter if I live or die, as much as I want to live—" Wilkins wiped a tear from his cheek—"as much as I want to grow old with my wife and see my kids get married and give me grandbabies. What difference does it make, if my grandchildren are born under the boot of a monster? Look at us. We're talking up here in the middle of the night because *I* can't talk to you in broad daylight. Do you know how I even got here tonight? I snuck out through a trap door through the closet in my bedroom, down into a secret garage, and then through a secret tunnel under the city. You didn't know that existed? Well, it does. We're at the end. We're in the twilight of republics and the rights of man, and night is falling. We can't let it. We can stop the night. *We can stop the night.*"

"Then let's grab Bryson now!" Chan said. "Let's arrest Bryson now for conspiracy. You're the President, if you support it publicly, we can build a case—"

"We can't do it that way," Wilkins said. "The people are with *him*, not me. He'll kill any judge who gives us a warrant or any prosecutor who puts him on trial. He'll kill the two of you. If we fight this in the shadows, where he's the strongest, he'll win—and we'll all die."

"Mr. President, what you're asking—" Chan put his head in his hands, then looked back up. "You're asking a Secret Service agent to stand down and let an assassin take a shot at you. I can't do it."

"I'm not asking you to let him take a shot. I'm asking you to crack this case—and move when the assassin moves. Arrest him when he's onsite and about to make his move. And use our best Secret Service agents to hit all the conspirators at the same time—including Bryson." Wilkins paused. "I know this sounds crazy... but think about it. If we act earlier, we tip our hand, and that gives them a free pass to go back to the drawing board and come up with a plan we can't crack. But if we act later—with the American people in an uproar over an attempt to assassinate their President—I can move against Bryson. We can win."

"Who else knows about this?" Chan asked.

"No one. Only you two." Wilkins paused. "Will you fight? Fight my way?"

"Are you asking me as the President, or as a friend?" Chan said.

"As the President."

Chan looked down, then back up. "Then I'm in."

Wilkins turned to Peterson. *Let's do it.* "I'm in, sir," he said.

Peterson looked out at Washington again. *The whole city's asleep tonight*, he thought. *And tomorrow, it'll be full of Congressmen and staffers, judges and law clerks, lawyers and bureaucrats. And none of them will ever know what we decided tonight.*

Peterson turned to the President. "There's more, Mr. President," he said. "There's something I have to tell you."

"Go ahead," Wilkins said.

"It's about Brigade 910, sir."

"What is it?"

Peterson sighed. "Our best intelligence tells us they're planning a massive attack this May."

"Massive?"

"Multiple cities, truck bombs, chemical and biological weapons, a dirty bomb."

Wilkins rubbed his grayish brown hair. "Can they do it?"

"I believe they can, sir."

"Jesus Christ," Wilkins said. "This is the first I've heard of it."

"That's what I figured. I didn't think Moloch or Bryson would tell you about it."

"They haven't told me... because they're planning for life without me." Wilkins shook his head. "And they want me to stay 'weak' on terrorism. But Christ, Hunter... why didn't you tell me?"

Because the dictatorship is already here. Because I can't communicate with you unless it's at a remote location in the middle of the night.

"I tried," Peterson said. "But there's no way to do it without being intercepted."

"And what's the progress of this plan? What are our plans to stop it?"

"It's in the operational stage. We think Brigade 910 is scouting targets and going on dry runs. But—"

"Who's 'we'?"

"Myself and two young agents. Two kids I trust with my life. All the other agents I have are thugs—and I think they might be spies for Bryson and Moloch."

"Peterson, I'm the Commander-in-Chief, and for something of this magnitude, you will *find a way* to brief me. Is that clear?"

"It's clear, sir," Peterson said.

Wilkins sighed. "What else were you going to tell me?"

"Brigade 910 will only launch the attack—which they call Project Orion—after a certain signal. We don't know what the signal is or when it's coming. We're listening in on a high-level operative they call Sigma. But we haven't been able to identify his superior... his Octavian."

Wilkins took off his cap again. "Good Lord," he said. "Brigade 910 is going to slaughter thousands of innocent people—and the agency that we created to stop them is plotting to kill me. Jesus Christ. Jesus Christ." Wilkins folded his arms and furrowed his eyebrows. "I suppose this is just one of those moments, you understand, one of those moments where a country either stands up or lies down forever. This is 1776. This is 1860. This is 1941. Either we stand and fight—or slavery and fascism for all of time."

"Then we stand and fight," Chan said.

"Right," Peterson said. "We stand and fight."

Wilkins smiled and rubbed his eyes. "All right, then, we stand and fight. Chan, you're in charge of cracking the assassination plot. And

Hunter, you're in charge of stopping this Project Orion attack." The President studied Peterson for a moment. "How did you get mixed up with an outfit like the Authority, anyhow?"

I wish I knew. "I thought I was serving my country, after the Iowa attack," he said. "I'm sorry."

"Don't apologize now. It turned out to be the one thing that might save us all. This is your chance, Hunter."

"I won't let you down, Mr. President."

Chapter 22

"Twenty-five," Marissa said, taking a forkful of cake. "A quarter of a century old!"

Johnny smiled. It was April 4, his birthday. "I'm a big shot now, Mom," he said. "For real. I think I deserve to walk with a little strut now. Twenty-five is not to be messed with."

Marissa rolled her eyes. "You already walk with a strut. And let's not get ahead of ourselves with the 'big shot' talk. When's the last time you played a video game, Mr. Big Shot?"

Johnny looked down, feigning shame. "Last night."

Marissa laughed. "Can the presidency be far off?" She sipped her coffee. "So how are things with you and Justine?"

"They're okay."

"It's been three months! I hope it's more than okay. I've got the under in the 'When will Johnny get married?' over/under pool your aunts and I have."

Johnny smiled. "You might lose. I'm not in any rush on that front."

Marissa slapped his arm. "Well *I'm* in a rush," she said. "You know who I always thought you should have gotten together with."

Let me guess. "Who's that?'

"That Lizbeth girl that you were so close with in college. You two were perfect together."

"Well, she's getting engaged to some lawyer."

Marissa threw up her arms. "Well scratch her off the list, then!"

Johnny laughed. Good old Mom, she always knew how to make him feel better. "Twenty-five years old," he said. "How come I keep getting older and you keep getting younger?"

Marissa smiled. "With charm like that, how could you *not* be married by now?" She patted Johnny's hand. "So I've got another a little present for you before you go." She slid a purple rectangular box across the table.

Johnny took the present in his hands. It wasn't a box; it was much lighter. "What is it?"

"Open it."

Johnny tore open the paper. As it gave way, a blue notebook

emerged in his hands. *Oh-kay.* "What is this?"

"It's... something your father wanted you to have." Marissa looked into Johnny's eyes. "A diary he used to keep."

"A diary?" *What the hell?*

Marissa smiled. "Yeah, a diary. And this is an amazing thing here, Johnny. It's a chance to know your father in a way you never imagined."

Johnny caressed the notebook. "I... I don't know what to say." *What's she up to?* Johnny looked up at his mother. "Thanks, Mom."

"I want you to read it, Johnny. Because you're right about what you said, about being twenty-five. You should start thinking about what you want the rest of your life to be like. I see you getting deeper into that job you have." Marissa paused. "Maybe this old diary can help you figure things out."

Johnny narrowed his eyebrows. "What do you think I need to figure out?"

"Just read it, sweet pea."

Johnny looked down at the notebook, then up at his mother. "I will, Mom."

Chapter 23

"I think someone's trying to kill President Wilkins," read the first line in Giovanni Sr.'s diary.

Johnny cast the notebook down on his coffee table. *What?* He picked it back up and read the first line again:

"I think someone's trying to kill President Wilkins."

A chill fell down Johnny's spine and splashed at the base. *Why would he write that?*

The entry was dated June 9, 2021. Johnny stared in at the date. *About five months...* he thought. *About five months before he... passed.*

Johnny looked up and sighed, gazing at Paul's favorite print in the room, the exploding volcano. Lines of red lava throbbing down the mountain...

This could be the start of something I don't want to read. This could be... oh, damn it. This could be the start of my father losing his mind.

Already, Johnny could tell what was lying on the coffee table. It was his father's secret world, a part of his life he'd shut his sons out of, kind of like what Johnny did to his mother and Paul and Lizbeth with his job.

But this... this was already too heavy. His dad was a detective. What would *he* know about a threat to President Wilkins?

Johnny picked up the notebook again.

***

We arrested a kid awhile back, and after everything that's happened lately, I have the strongest feeling that the President's life is in danger. It's so much that I have to write it down.

We raided the apartment of a kid connected with that group which did the Iowa attack. We suspect he's part of a cell planning something big in New York. He's about twenty-one years old, around Johnny's age.

We've got this kid solid. Machine guns, pipe bombs, biological agents—this kid could've started World War III tomorrow if he wanted, and he's got a whole group with him, how many, we're not sure. But what's got me is why he hasn't done it so far, what he's been waiting for. It's why I'm writing this tonight.

So we executed the warrant, found his stash, took him in. Then we brought him back to interrogate. At this point I know we're supposed to hand him off to the Authority, but the hell with that, he's my collar and I'm going to find out about terrorist activity in my town before I hand it off to some federal pencil neck who'll just fumble around and fuck it up.

So we're working him over real good, and this isn't a typical terrorist like they show you in the movies. He's not swearing that he'll never talk. He's pretty scared and he wants to deal with us. And for some reason he's scared– terrified– that he'll be killed. So we're asking him about the group's plans, and he says, "It's all about the President. The whole plan is about the President."

So I ask him what he's talking about. He says, "Someone is supposed to kill the President. Then we're supposed to act."

"What do you mean, act?" I asked. But we arrested the kid with an arsenal, for Christ's sakes, I knew what he meant. I wanted to hear it.

"I mean, start planting bombs," the kid said.

"Where?" I said. "When?"

"All over the city. But I don't know when."

I looked at the kid for a second. He looked like a regular kid, except, I don't know, his eyes were messed up. He didn't look at you, he looked through you, kind of. And his eyes were all bloodshot, and he couldn't stop shaking.

"Are you on dope?" I asked him. "Are you high? Come on kid, tell me the truth here. You shoot up?"

***

Johnny couldn't help but smile. Giovanni Sr. didn't limit "Are you on dope?" to his arrests; it was something he said around the house whenever he or Paul screwed up.

He scanned up the page. Where was it... "*We raided the apartment of a kid connected with that group which did the Iowa attack.*"

***

"Come on kid, tell me the truth here. You shoot up?"

"I don't know," the kid says. "Maybe. I don't know what he did to me."

"Who?" I say.

"Octavian," he says.

What the hell is this kid talking about, I'm thinking. "Who's that?"

"He gives me the orders. He tells me what to do."

"Octavian, what kind of name is that?" I ask. "That's not his real name, is it?"

The kid starts shaking. "I don't know... I don't know," he says.

I pat him on the shoulder. Now, I don't give a shit about this kid. I've made grown men, who turned out to be innocent, cry in this interview room before. But this one's got something I want. I need to coddle him.

"It's all right," I said. "What do you know about this Octavian?"

"He leads the revolution."

"The revolution?"

"The revolution to destroy the captains of industry who enslave us all."

This is word-for-word, now. I can't get a handle on the kid at this point. He started with me in the interview room like he wanted to snitch, and now he's giving me the terrorist poetry. He's confused. It's like his brain won't let him free. And he's still shaking and a little spaced out. Then he hits me with this line I knew by heart:

"Tyranny, like hell, is not easily conquered. Yet we have this consolation with us, that the harder the conflict, the more glorious the triumph."

***

Johnny stopped for a moment. He'd heard that himself somewhere before; where was it? He was out one night... working... He snapped his fingers. *That's fucking it.*

Those were the words Fullerton used with their prisoner when he posed as a Brigade 910 commander last month. How did Dad know it by heart?

***

That's from Thomas Paine, The Crisis. *I know the beginning of it by heart. Unlucky for this terrorist punk, I'm one patriotic son-of-a-bitch, and now I'm pissed that this group of killers uses Paine's words as some kind of treehouse password.*

"So Octavian leads the revolution," I say. "The whole revolution?"

"I don't know," the kid says. "I don't think so. I've heard him call someone else Octavian before."

So it's a code name, I'm thinking. Christ, am I the first one to hear this?

"Who does he call Octavian?" I ask him. "Other people like you, who fight for the revolution?"

"No. There's someone he talks about, like his boss or something, that he calls Octavian. Like, 'Octavian would be proud of this,' or 'Octavian wants to see this happen.'"

"And the Octavian who gives you orders," I ask him, "is he foreign? American? Black, white?"

"He's a white guy... an American."

"And what else can you tell me about him?"

The kid shakes more, then he looks down and takes a deep breath. I can see he's starting to cry. "They'll kill me," he says.

"No one's going to touch you," I tell him. "You're in my custody now."

And even if he is a terrorist, I mean it. I'm not going to let these scumbags lay a finger on him. He's with us now.

"There's a name I heard somebody call him once," the kid says.

"What's the name?"

He shakes a little more.

"What's the name?" I ask him again.

"Sigma."

***

Johnny dropped the notebook. The blood surged to his face, the synapses fired to his nerve endings. *Sigma.* The name of the guy who led the attack at the farmhouse, the one who executed the informant. *Sigma.*

This must be some other Brigade 910 code name, Johnny rationalized. *It can't be the same guy—Dad was writing two years ago. It has to be a code name.*

Johnny continued reading.

***

"So Sigma, or Octavian, gives you orders," I said. "And one of you is supposed to kill the President?"

"I don't know who." The kid cried a little more. "I just know it's going to happen."

"And then you start killing people?"

"No... no..."

"Because if we didn't pick you up tonight, that's what you were going to do."

"I don't know... I don't know..."

"How do I know you're telling me the truth right now?"

And then the kid looks right at me, and his eyes aren't so messed up anymore. He bites his lip, tries to get a hold of himself. He looks me square in the eye and says, "Because if they knew what I told you so far, they'd kill me."

"Kid, if they could kill you like that"– I snapped my fingers– "then what are you doing running with a crew like this?"

"I don't know how it happened... I don't know anything anymore..."

"Do you know the charges you're facing? Conspiracy to commit murder, conspiracy to use a weapon of mass destruction, material support of a terrorist organization." That was part one of the textbook interrogator's trick. And then

part two: "But we can try and get you out of some of that. Talk to me."

The kid shook his head. "I'm dead anyway."

"You're not dead. I told you, you're in my custody now. You're on the right side of the law. Octavian can't get you here."

And just then, the kid laughed. "Octavian can get me anywhere," he said. "He can get you."

I shook my head. "He can't get me… believe me. Now come on, tell me, how did you get mixed up in this?"

Textbook interrogation, here. Make it seem like it's not his fault.

"They just... kind of found me," the kid says. "I went to a meeting once..."

"What kind of meeting?'

"A meeting on... on campus... some group. Anti-Fascist Resistance, or something like that."

"Campus? What school?"

"I... I don't remember."

I'm thinking, this kid has to be high. Has to be. "You don't remember where you go to school?"

"I don't know... I don't go anymore... I don't remember. I just remember the meeting."

Okay, we'll play along. "What was the meeting like?"

"I remember I spoke up about how my big brother died in Afghanistan... how angry I was. How much I hated the government for killing my brother. And the next thing I know, someone's coming up to me on campus and asking me if I really want to fight the power, avenge my brother's death."

"And you said yes."

"Yeah... I thought we'd be protesting or something."

"When was this?" I asked.

"A couple of years ago... I think."

"Before or after they poisoned the water in Iowa?"

"I don't remember. But we didn't do that. Iowa was an inside job."

I never met anybody who was brainwashed before. But this kid was one hundred percent gone, mentally. "You believe that?" I asked him.

"The government did it," he said. "That's what Octavian told me, when I met him. They did it to discredit the revolution and impose martial law. We don't do things like that."

"No, you're just going to plant bombs around the city," I said. I shouldn't have said it, I was reeling him in now. But I couldn't help it.

"It's a war now," the kid said. "We have to fight them before they make us all slaves."

"So what happened after they approached you?"

"I got involved... I went to meetings where they talked about striking back, keeping America free... and then I left school..."

"Why?"

"I don't know... I don't remember." The kid shook his head. "I don't remember." He shook his head again and then he looked at me with tears in his eyes. "I think they've been drugging me... I think they've been drugging me since the beginning. Oh God, what have I done, what have I done!" He started sobbing.

He probably was high. But at that second, I believed him. Maybe I'm a sucker, but I can smell the truth. This kid... I don't know how to say it... he was some kind of mind control victim. He was a real, live Manchurian candidate, sitting right in front of me.

"Whatever they have planned," I said, "we can stop them."

"Maybe you can," the kid said. "But I'm already dead."

I grabbed him around the shoulders. "Nothing's going to happen to you," I said. "You're safe."

He started shaking again. I kept on interrogating him.

That night he gave me code names, meeting places, safehouses. He couldn't give me a date or anything about Sigma. And he didn't know when this attack was supposed to take place.

One funny thing he told me was that he told all of this to one of his old professors. But he didn't remember the name of the professor or where he taught.

And then, finally, the kid just broke down. "Save the President," he said. "God, please, save the President." And then he stopped talking.

***

Johnny put the notebook down. *So Brigade 910 was into killing the President. And damn, Dad actually interrogated one of their guys.*

He thought back to when Fullerton had done the same. He'd been so nuanced, so flawless. And Giovanni Sr. had been just as good. *Dad could really bring it.*

He traced his finger over the diary. Across years, and across death, they were working the same case.

***

The next morning, I went to my office, and the first thing I thought of was to read the report from the night before, which I'd locked up in my file cabinet.

So I went to the cabinet, and I unlocked it, and I pulled it open. The report and the tape were in there. But something had happened to the cabinet drawer, and that something is what made me start writing this journal.

See, I stick a fresh piece of double-sided tape on the inside edge of my report drawer whenever I open it. It's not a superstition. It's because one time about ten years ago, somebody stole a report out of my drawer and destroyed it. It turns out some big drug dealer scumbag I was after had paid off some lowlife to destroy evidence. The prosecutor had been making a big deal about nailing this guy, and I almost lost my job when we lost the evidence.

So it's real simple—I open the drawer, peel off the tape I'd slapped on there the last time I closed it, and stick on a new piece. It's really small, just a little pinch. It's enough for me to tell if someone tampered with the drawer or not.

And in ten years' time, no ever did. Until this time.

The tape was stripped. I noticed it right off, because it's the first thing I check. I'll be damned, someone had been in my drawer. The report and the audio tape were still there, but my little seal was broken.

My first instinct was to run outside and ask who'd been messing with my stuff. I put my hand on the doorknob, but I didn't take the next step. Asking around didn't seem like such a bright idea.

Why not? Because the last time this happened, a pretty powerful druglord was behind it. I heard years later that he'd paid off a young cop to get into my office. So whoever had pulled this off was a little too powerful to mess with at the moment.

That's a rule all cops learn eventually. At some point you'll meet the line you can't cross. You'll brush up against some case you're not supposed to follow too hard, because dark forces are at play. Maybe some of the boys in your department are on the payroll, or some politician is pulling crooked land deals, or some mob family is bribing somebody on the docks to smuggle in sex slaves. You hate it, it's wrong, but you have to let it go. Or the wrong people start to ask the wrong questions.

I wasn't going to make noise—I have a family. Whoever wanted that report so bad, they could have it, and shove it up their ass, too.

I sat down and got to work for the day, but I felt a little pit in my stomach, and I was shaking a little. Even if you know where the line is, it scares the hell out of you to bump up against it, even by accident. I don't give a damn how tough you are.

That really should've been it. But that wasn't it. Because today somebody shot the kid in broad daylight as U.S. Marshals were transporting him to federal prison.

***

This is crazy, Johnny thought.

***

A turf war over the suspect broke out in the last couple of days between the FBI and the Authority. The press had sniffed out the arrest and made a big deal of it because of the arsenal the kid had on him, so the Bureau and the Authority were slugging it out over who had federal jurisdiction. Director Bryson said the Authority should take the kid and hold him at a secret facility so they could get information out of him; Attorney General Sharpe said the FBI should handle the case with the kid awaiting trial in a federal prison.

A judge held a hearing and ruled that the suspect should go to a federal prison. The Marshals promised the judge they'd isolate the kid and keep a twenty-four-hour suicide watch on him.

The press swarmed around the courthouse, stuck cameras at the Justice Department attorneys, the Homeland Security attorneys—and at the kid. And then somebody ran right up to the kid and plugged him in the stomach.

According to the news, the shooter fled on foot, and a uniformed Authority officer shot him in the back. He was DOA at the hospital.

It's about eleven o'clock at night right now, and CNN just said the kid died in surgery. And what's more, they're saying the guy who shot him was in that Brigade 910 group. So that's the end of that.

But it's not the end. Because I know what the kid told me, and I know that someone broke into my office the other night, and now I know he's dead. I'm scared as hell and I'm confused.

I don't know why. But I feel like if I don't write this stuff here, I'll be letting go of something I can't let go.

***

That was the end of that day's entry. The end of June 9, 2021.

These weren't the ramblings of a crazy guy, this was… evidence. Johnny vaguely remembered the story of the Brigade 910 suspect getting shot in broad daylight in front of a courthouse.

Johnny read on.

***

June 10, 2021

I'm fifty years old, and I'm going over the line.

That line. The one I'm not supposed to cross. The line where good cops see bad things and decide to turn their backs because it's better to retreat than to fight. Well, I've decided it's better to fight.

I believe that kid was telling the truth in the interrogation room. Brigade 910 is plotting to kill the President. And yesterday, another terrorist killed the kid. Fair enough.

But no one is talking about a plot against the President—not the media, the Authority, no one. Something's not right, and I have to find out what.

The whole thing was too quick, too seamless. Suspect walks out of the courthouse with half of all federal law enforcement around him. Terrorist runs up to him, through a security perimeter armed to the teeth, and blasts him in the stomach. Then, as terrorist is fleeing, Authority agent nails him with a perfect shot in the back and kills him.

I'm not buying it. And I'm going over the line to find out exactly what the hell happened.

June 22, 2021

I've been hitting my gang contacts hard in last couple of weeks. "Open mouths get fed," I tell them. You see, all these kiddie gangs are connected up with the terrorists, and they don't even know it. I read my flow charts at the FBI presentations. The gangs are raising their money, washing it, carrying out contract killings without asking any questions.

They don't know much about the kid, even though they saw him get killed on TV and watched the video on YouTube. A couple of my sources saw him at a couple of meetings, but he was just a face. Tell me about some of the other faces, I ask them. I show them a couple of pictures. I get a match, and since I did my homework on my roster of terror suspects, that match hit about eight more matches for me. Now I'm in business.

July 7, 2021

Today the chief calls me into his office and tells me he heard about what I've been up to. "Lay off this one, Luca," he says. "It's nothing but trouble."

"Why?" I ask him. "I mean, this is serious stuff, we've got terrorists running in our backyard. I think the President may even be in danger."

"Then give it to the Authority," he says.

I can't tell him what I think the Authority is up to. If I do, I go from trusted detective to kook, and trust means everything to me.

I have two choices here. I can try and argue with him, or button up and keep investigating on the sneak. Giving up isn't on the list.

I decide to go the button-up route. "I'll lay off," I tell him. "Anything you say, chief."

And then the old chief smiled at me. "Look, Luca," he says. "We've been working together now what, twelve, thirteen years? You're a good cop. Let's be there to see our grandkids play together."

It was the way he said it. I can't explain it, I guess it just threw me a little. "You think I might not make it 'til then?" I said.

The smile went away. "Just think about it, Luca. These people don't mess around."

And that was it. I left and I went back to my desk. I kept trying to tell myself that when he said "these people," he meant Brigade 910, but I don't think so.

***

Johnny re-read the entry. The chief did mean Brigade 910, didn't he? Had to…

***

July 27, 2021

I think someone was tailing me today. Maybe it's just a paranoid feeling, because sneaking around with this investigation is really starting to stress me out, but I know how to tail another car, and I know what tailing feels like. I was on the job on the drug task force for a couple of years, I know this stuff.

Anyway, I had that feeling this morning on the way to work, so I decided not to go anywhere funny after-hours. Then I had that same feeling of being tailed on the way home from work.

It's hard to sleep at night when you think something like that might have happened. It's hard to live in two worlds when you can't tell anyone on the happy side about what life is like on the ugly side.

God, I wish I could.

***

You could've told me, Johnny thought. *I would've listened...*

Then he stopped himself: *Who am I telling? Who do I come home to and talk to about the ugly world?*

***

August 10, 2021

I haven't made much progress in the last month. I'm convinced I've been tailed every day since the last time I wrote. I'm really feeling the walls close in now. I'm afraid to make calls, afraid to go to websites, afraid to send the emails I want to send. If I'm really on their grid, they can see everything.

This is what they want. Even if I'm imagining all this and they've never heard of me before, this is the Anti-Subversion Authority's game. Don't go anywhere—don't say anything—don't read anything—don't think—don't breathe.

Freedom these days is just something you hear in speeches. It's not real; it's an illusion. The government can track my movements by my cell phone, they can read my emails and the websites I visit, they can throw total surveillance on me for months or even years without a warrant.

The Authority has two missions: 1) combat domestic terrorism, and 2) control 350 million people by keeping them afraid. Agenda number two is by far more important to them.

This is the group that I think has tailed me for the last month. This is also the group that I think is involved in a plot to assassinate the President. I think I am the only innocent person on earth who knows both of these things.

***

Johnny sighed. August 2021 was when Giovanni Sr. was on his way to committing suicide because of some sort of paranoid delusion.

Johnny picked the diary back up. This was his father in his last summer, his mind long gone.

***

August 25, 2021

Today I got my break. I don't care about being tailed anymore, even though they're still doing it. I got the piece of information I need, and it's time to make my move.

A couple of my sources came in, and my cross-checking matched up, and now I can say I know the real identity of the terrorist kid I interrogated at the beginning of all this. His name is Ryan Colgate, age 21 at the time of his death.

Why the mystery about the kid, even though he was shot in front of the national media? Because right away the media took the tack that "the terror suspect used various aliases, and not much is known about his background," all that. That came from the Authority. And the media never pursued it—that came from the Authority, too.

Funny what you can do when you make friends with independent journalists, like the ones who work for Gordon Bragg, and two-bit hustlers on the street. Ryan Colgate, I've got you.

But Colgate isn't the prize. What I wanted all this time was one little detail he mentioned to me at the end of the interrogation—a professor he'd told his story to. Now I've got him too.

I'm coming for you, Professor Anton Jacobs.

***

Professor... Anton... Jacobs.

That, of course, was impossible. It was the professor's murder, with Johnny listening on the headset in the armored SUV, that had midwifed Johnny into this world of clandestine operations.

First Sigma... now this. Except this wasn't a terrorist moniker, it was a *name*. A real name of a real person whom Johnny himself had surveilled before someone killed him in the middle of the night.

If his father had gotten this far in investigating Brigade 910... then he'd reached the edge of Johnny's work. Maybe even the edge... of Project Orion.

Dad, how can this be?

Johnny wanted to stop reading, he had to turn back now—but he knew he couldn't. He lowered his eyes to the page.

***

September 7, 2021

It took me awhile, but I paid Professor Jacobs a visit today at his college.

For the first time, I tried to slip the vehicles tailing me. A little weaving in and out of traffic, a little doubling back, stuff like that. I don't know if it worked, but I hope to God it did.

So I drove onto the campus, got directions, and walked right over to the English department. Right into the professor's office, in fact. I showed him my badge and asked if I could ask him a few questions.

He's kind of a prim and proper guy, blond hair, rectangular glasses, real nerdy like.

"What do you want to talk to me about, detective?" he asks me.

"Ryan Colgate."

The professor went pale. Now, I didn't come here to scare him. I don't think the guy's a criminal, it's just that a terrorist confided in him. I need to know what he knows.

"I guess you wouldn't believe it if I said I never heard of him," he says.

"Listen, professor." I looked the guy right in the eyes. "I'm off-duty here, off-the-record. My boss threatened me and told me not to bark up this tree, and I've been followed for the last two months. If you were in danger from me, you'd be dead by now, not talking to me face-to-face."

The professor cleared his throat. "He was a mixed-up kid, he had some prob—"

"He was a terrorist. And before they shot him, he came to you for help. That's why I'm here."

"He was a terrorist by association," the professor says.

"We arrested him with a stockpile of weapons. He was a member of Brigade 910."

"He was a mind control victim."

"What do you mean?"

"They lured him by posing as some political activist group, and then they indoctrinated him into terrorism by drugging him and threatening him."

"You believe that story?"

And then the professor looked <u>me</u> right in the eyes. "I swear by that story," he says.

"Tell me more."

And he did. He told me about how, according to Colgate, Brigade 910 taught him that the government murdered his brother by sending him off to die in an illegal war, that the government had carried out the Iowa attack and was preparing to take down our democracy and replace it with a totalitarian state. They drugged him, they told him they'd kill him and his family if he betrayed them, they made him kill a cop they'd captured and then told him he was sealed in by blood. He was an enemy of the industrialist pigs, they told him, a blood member of the revolution. Only Brigade 910 can protect you now, they said. And they drugged him and drugged him to the point that he didn't even remember his name.

"The President," I said to the professor. "Did he ever mention the President?"

The professor nodded, and he looked nervous again. "He did. He said the group planned to assassinate him."

"Why?"

"He didn't know. You think they'd tell him something like that? They were using him."

And for the first time, I felt a limitation with this Colgate stuff. He was just a pawn, after all. So I decided to try a different tack:

"Professor, was Ryan... in fear of his life when he came to you?"

"He told me he was already dead. And that I was the only chance he had to make sure he didn't die in vain... that he didn't go to hell when he died."

"Who did he think was going to kill him?"

"Brigade 910."

And now for the toughest question. "Who killed him that day, professor?"

"Another terrorist. He was a threat to them. He could've talked."

"He already did," I said. "And even the dumbest terrorist knows we interrogated him when we held him overnight. So why kill him then?"

"I can't answer that."

"I can. Or at least I have a guess."

"And what would that be?"

"I don't know, professor. But between you and me, I have the strongest feeling that the Anti-Subversion Authority let his killer slip through security. And then the Authority killed the shooter. The perfect—"

"Black op," the professor said.

I nodded. He knew his stuff. "Right. The perfect black op."

Jacobs laughed. "Come on, detective. We sound like a couple of conspiracy theorists."

"Professor... do you feel... that your life is in danger?"

Just then, he looked right at me, and he wasn't scared anymore. I can't describe it. He was just... almost shell-shocked I guess. "I'm already dead," he said.

"Come on, you can't mean–"

"I've been followed every night since Ryan came to see me. Someone has been in this office a few times—I can <u>feel</u> it, but I can't prove anything. My phone makes a faint clicking noise, every now and then, maybe once a week. My home—I think someone's been in my home."

"I won't let them kill you," I say. "And I won't let them kill the President."

"Turn back now. Because they'll kill you, too."

I leaned in close to him. "This is all I've got now. If I'm right—if we're right—that Brigade 910 wants to kill President Wilkins, this is all we have. And if I'm right that the Authority is somehow in on it—"

"There's nothing we can do about it, detective. We're just two teacups, two teacups in the middle of the sea."

And that was that. The professor had nothing more to say, and he had to go teach a class.

But I'm not giving up so easily. I'm no "teacup in the middle of the sea," whatever the hell that means.

I'm taking this to the Secret Service.

***

If this is true, Johnny thought, *then Dad, you just cracked a live case.*

That's why they killed the professor. Because he knew too much... about a plot to assassinate the President. Johnny snapped his fingers. And if they shot him just a few months ago, then they're still plotting it.

***

September 8, 2021

Called a Secret Service agent with their Newark Field Office, Agent Ramirez. Told him I'm a cop, told him everything I know, told him why I'm keeping it all a secret. He said he'd open an investigation and get back to me.

September 10, 2021

Agent Ramirez asked to meet me under a highway overpass in Newark.

Ramirez tells me that based on what the Service has learned so far, Brigade 910 is actively planning to assassinate the President of the United States.

For seven months I've had nothing but this diary, no one to talk to, no one to work with. Not anymore.

"So what will you do now?" I ask him.

"We've alerted the President's Protective Detail in Washington," he says, "and we told Director Chan."

Now I have to cover my last base. "Are you going to tell the Authority?" I ask him.

And just then, he got a funny look on his face, and he says, "No, we don't think they'd be much help in this whole thing."

Ramirez didn't know it, but I knew what he meant.

And then we shake hands. I'll never forget this moment—it's late at night, kind of misty out, a cool late summer night under the moon in Newark. Right at this second, shaking hands with a Secret Service agent as we work together to save the President—this is all I've ever wanted out of life as an investigator. I wish I could live forever in this second.

September 19, 2021

I met Ramirez under the overpass again tonight. "We've identified a Brigade 910 mole in your precinct," he says. "The one who broke into your file cabinet. It's Buchanan."

Buchanan is this patrolman, he's just a kid. "How can that be?" I say. "He's a cop."

"He might be a cop, but we're positive that they paid him off to get that file."

Jesus Christ. "What now?" I ask him.

"We watch him the same way he's watching you," Ramirez says. "If we have to black-bag him, we will."

I'd do it myself, I'm thinking. "How's the investigation going?"

"Running into roadblocks. We're trying to figure out the Brigade 910 chain of command, but it's a real bitch. Still working on it. I've been running surveillance on this Sigma."

"You'll get them. I know you guys will."

Ramirez flicked away his cigarette and looked at me square in the eye. "Luca, listen to me," he says. "Brigade 910 is talking about putting a hit on you. We'd love to lock them up for conspiracy, just for that. But we've got to do the deal straight. We have to wait and see what they're up to with POTUS. Then we'll get them, and you won't have anything to worry about."

I shook his hand. "Good luck, Ramirez."

I did my part. If they really are thinking of killing me... well, I should give them as little incentive as possible to actually do it.

***

Could this get any more intense? Any crazier? Johnny had shot it out with Brigade 910 in a gunfight last month—and they'd considered killing his father. Just the thought of it made Johnny want to grab Sigma, whoever he was, and strangle him.

***

October 11, 2021

Brigade 910 has struck. And at this point, there's no more standing on the sidelines.

Got an email at work today, one of those office-wide things. Secret Service agent killed last night, the heading says.

I think I knew what it said before I read it.

"Secret Service agent Andres Ramirez lost his life late last night in a car accident in Bayonne. He is survived by his wife Miranda, his son Diego, and his infant daughter Analisa. Condolences may be sent to..."

That was no accident, goddamn it. And here's how I know for sure: Because Brigade 910 was in my house sometime today.

I got home tonight, and right away I went up to my office to think about everything. I walk to my desk, and the drawer on the bottom right is sticking out a couple of millimeters. I haven't opened that drawer in a couple of years, it's just full of old junk. It should be closed all the way, nice and smooth. It's closed now, all right, but as if someone slammed it shut in a hurry. It bounced back out just enough for me to know the truth.

Someone's been in my home, in my office—in my papers and effects—and Agent Ramirez died last night.

October 30, 2021

I went to lunch with Johnny today. It didn't go so well.

I took it in a direction I shouldn't have. I started in about him being in the Authority, and I was almost begging him to give it up. How do I tell him to give it up without telling him all the crazy things I think about them? So we went back and forth for awhile, and then I finally said, "Listen to me. Just forget this whole federal thing, you have what it takes to get into a good school. Please, even if you hate my guts now and don't wanna be bothered with me, turn your back on them and don't look back. Please."

Johnny got mad. He said, "You don't get to tell me what to do, Dad. Leave me alone." And then he just got up and left. Walked right out of lunch.

It's my fault, because I can't make him understand. But he broke my heart today.

***

Tears streamed down both sides of Johnny's face, slicing down his cheeks, dripping off his chin. It was the last time he saw his father alive.

***

November 1, 2021

A letter came in to work from the professor today. It didn't have a return address. All it said was, "Come to my office and I'll tell you everything. A.J."

I shouldn't. But after all this time, if he held out on me, shouldn't I know everything? Isn't that what I wanted from the first night?

November 2, 2021

Went to see Professor Jacobs today. And he told me everything he knows. Everything about Brigade 910, how they operate, what they're planning, what their goals are.

He also told me that they'll kill me before long. If they're killing my sources— which he heard about through his own contacts—my time is running out. The one who kills me will be a professional, and he will be sent by Octavian.

"Then we have to get Octavian," I said.

Then the professor started to get tears in his eyes. "That's impossible. No one knows who he is."

"Then what the hell am I supposed to do?"

He didn't have an answer.

I didn't want to believe him. I just didn't want to believe that the road I started on the night I interrogated Ryan Colgate would end here. I had set out to save the President, to serve my country.

"Well, now you know everything," the professor said, holding out his hand. "That's all I have to give."

What could I do? I shook his hand. There really wasn't anything I could say.

November 16, 2021

Everyone who assisted in my investigation last spring is now dead, as of last night. I believe I will be killed within days.

I sent a package in the mail today to Miranda and Analisa Ramirez. It was a white rose, just a white rose, no note, no return address. I hope Miranda tries to figure out what it means. The men who resisted the Nazi regime in Germany called themselves the White Rose. And I believe Ramirez did nothing less– that I've done nothing less.

I'm bringing this diary to Marissa tonight, and I'm telling her that this is the end. I'll ask her to show it to Johnny when the time is right. I don't want Paul to see it, at least not for a long time. He's too young.

But Johnny, you're a man now. And when your mother shows this to you, it will be for a reason. The world is full of good and evil, and evil is having its moment right now. It won't always be that way. But think about which side you're serving, where you stand in all this. Who's killing people in the shadows? Who's fighting for freedom?

Johnny, I love you, and I'm so much more proud of you than you'll ever know. You're so much more than I deserve, so much more than I could have asked for.

And Paul, if this ever ends up in your hands, I love you too, with all my heart. I wish I could have seen the great man you will be.

I guess that's all I have left to say. I'm not keeping this diary anymore. If I die— when I die—it won't be a car accident. It won't be drowning, it won't be a shooting by a criminal I'm arresting. It won't be suicide. It will be murder, made to look like suicide, or an accident, or drowning.

It will be murder. I will be murdered by Octavian.

I'm taking this diary to Marissa tonight, and I'm telling her I love her. That's all I really have left to do on earth.

***

Johnny dropped the diary. His father died two days later. Murder, not suicide. Murder.

Chapter 24

Johnny bit his lip as he stood outside his mother's building, trying to dam back tears as snow whistled about him. He'd rushed out of his apartment, not calling his mother, and jumped in his car. Now he was shaking, his knees knocking.

Marissa answered the door, blinking awake. What time was it, anyway? Close to midnight, maybe...

"Baby, what's wrong?" she said.

It was the sight of his mother, her hair bundled, standing in her pajamas in the moonlight, that finished Johnny off, and now he was weeping, heaving, the last year and a half's hurt pouring out all over his face...

Marissa took her son in her arms. "Baby, what is it?" she said.

Johnny pushed off and held up the notebook, and then dug his head in his mother's shoulders, pulling on her, holding on tight...

"Mom, I read it," he said, sobbing, "I read it all, I read everything... "

"I'm so sorry," she said.

Later—Johnny didn't even know how much later, or remember how– he was sitting next to his mother on her couch, a blanket around him, a mug of hot chocolate in his quaking hand. "Mom," he said. "Everything I read... it's all... true?"

"Every word, honey." Marissa bit her lip, and she herself almost started to cry. "I wish it weren't."

What am I supposed to do? Oh God, tell me, what am I supposed to do now? "You never told me."

Marissa paused, measuring her words. "There was no way to tell you. Not any way that would've made sense. I... I almost fell apart when your father died. I was so afraid, and I was so angry..." And now she started to cry, little streams sliding down her cheeks. "But I couldn't tell you. I had to—" She choked up for a second, then continued— "I had to pretend that your father really died like they said, I had to let you think that he could take a gun and shoot himself like that... to keep you and your brother safe. And…" Marissa wiped away a tear. "To stay alive myself."

All this time, I've tried to figure out how he could do that. I've hated him,

I've spit on him, I've blamed him for everything... and now... it was all a lie...

"Why did you give me the diary?" he said. "Why now?"

"Because..." Marissa said. She paused. "Because I see what you're doing. I see how you're getting more involved in your work... how you're getting in deeper with the Authority. And I want you to turn back now."

"Why?"

"Because look what it did to your father!" Marissa sobbed for a moment, then steadied herself. "Getting mixed up in all that killed him, Johnny. And I don't want to lose you. I would die."

Johnny put down the hot chocolate. "Look at me. You're not going to lose me. There's no way."

"Tell me you'll resign tomorrow. Please."

Johnny turned it over in his head. His mother deserved to know her son was safe. He owed it to her to get out now, to stay alive...

But he owed his father something more. He owed him... vengeance.

"I can't," he said.

Marissa grabbed him. "*Yes you can.* You have to. Are you crazy? You read what your father wrote. My God, you have to get out!"

And through the tears, Johnny began to harden. He wasn't getting out of anything. Octavian and his thugs had murdered his father. And now, when Johnny reached down, and he felt his own broken heart... and he started to think of how cold his father must have been, crying in his sleep at night, and then dying alone after a bullet blasted out his throat...

Johnny had to avenge his father. There was no other way.

He saw the faces. The way his father looked when he was proud, how his whole face would brighten to life, dimples framing his smile. How Paul laughed when he roughhoused with them. How his mother shook her head and yelled to be careful, and then joined in herself and started laughing...

They butchered his father, made his mother and brother cry, cracked his own heart...

Johnny looked down. "I'm going to kill them all," he said.

Marissa touched his elbow. "Honey, no," she said. "That's not why I told you. You can't do that. That's... that's not you."

"Tell me everything you know."

Marissa looked away for a moment, the tears still streaming. "I don't know anything else."

Johnny arched his eyebrows. "Was there anything else Dad left behind?"

"I gave you all I have."

Johnny set his jaw. "Listen to me, Mom. Forget everything I just said about revenge. What you read is part of an ongoing criminal investigation. And if there's anything else, I need it now."

"Ongoing? How can it be ongoing? It's been more than a year—"

"He wrote about things that *I'm* investigating. Stuff he wrote a year and a half ago is still true today. It might even be worse now. And I need to know what else he knew."

Marissa paused, then shook her head. "I don't have anything else, Johnny." She stroked Johnny's hair. "I didn't want you to avenge him, honey. I just couldn't stand to see... what you thought of him."

Johnny lowered his head, sighed, and then hugged his mother. "Just let me do it my way, Mom. I have to. I have to... get the people who did this."

Marissa embraced him, entreated him, cried, pleaded... and as the pleas melted into hours, Johnny took hold of his new true north:

Machine-gunning every single bastard who murdered his father.

Chapter 25

Lizbeth Heathrow glided along the sidewalk with her boyfriend Richard as snow twisted through the midnight air. "This is beautiful," she said, squeezing his hand and smiling at him.

He shook his head. "It's cold," he said.

It was an unseasonal April snow, winter's last stand. "This is the last snow of the year," Lizbeth said. "Maybe the last snow of our lives."

It was true; tonight Lizbeth and Richard had decided to move out to Arizona together in June. Arizona was home for him, and he had job with a big-time law firm lined up. His father had helped line up a job for Lizbeth too, covering sports for a local newspaper. *Everything's perfect*, she thought.

"I hope it's the last snow of *my* life," Richard said. "I've been in this garbage dump state for too long."

Lizbeth looked at Richard. He was about Johnny's height, built a little thicker around the shoulders. His skin was fair, his eyes blue, his hair neat and blond.

"Don't hate!" Lizbeth said. "If you never went to school out here, you never would've met your future wife."

He hadn't proposed yet; but for the first time, they looked at rings together today. Lizbeth hesitated at first, but then she relented. How could she fight it? She had a guy who loved her, and she loved him back.

Is this what it's really about? Lizbeth had thought as she admired the ring that day. *Is this it?* Then she'd looked up at Richard smiling, more at the pricey ring than at her. *This must be it.*

"You," Richard said as he walked along tonight, "are definitely the hottest little thing in New Jersey. Everything else here is terrible. I'll make you a westerner yet."

Lizbeth squeezed his hand again. *A westerner.*

Just then, the wind gusted, and she shivered. A life without snow... Warmth and comfort and everything she could ever have asked for, forever.

"So you really liked that ring today, huh?" Richard said. "That's just the beginning for us, babe. I'm going to take care of you for the rest of your life. I love you."

Lizbeth closed her eyes. The words fell around her and wrapped her up, not quite so much like a blanket, but more like a brand new overcoat. Crisp and strong and something that might fit just right in a few years.

"I love you too," she said, closing her eyes again for a moment.

Just then, they walked past a tree on the sidewalk. Windblown specks of snow sprayed Lizbeth's face. She'd felt that mist before, on a different night, back in a different life.

She looked back at the tree as they walked on, the way the snow misted off the branches in the wind...

Lizbeth stopped, tugging on Richard.

"What are you doing?" he asked.

Lizbeth smiled. "Follow me for a second," she said.

Richard groaned. "Baby, I'm freezing my ass off."

"Just for a second." Lizbeth smiled again. "Come on."

She led Richard back to the tree, under its branches, clasping both his hands. She stood in silence for a moment.

"So... what are we doing?" Richard said.

"Wait for it," Lizbeth said. "Wait for it..."

"What am I waiting—"

The wind gusted again, and snowflakes drizzled about them. Lizbeth looked into Richard's eyes and stroked his hair, tracing her fingers over his jawline, down to his chest. Then she grabbed him by the lapels of his coat and kissed him as the snow swirled around them.

She felt his lips devour hers, pressing into her, sealing her mouth. Richard grabbed her around the waist and yanked her closer. The snow blasted the back of Lizbeth's neck, a chill ringing down her spine. Richard leaned back and smiled, still clasping her around the waist. "We've gotta get you upstairs," he said.

A second later, he was leading her away, back towards her apartment building. Lizbeth looked behind her as they trudged the first few steps, out at the snow swirling through the empty space under the tree.

Hours later, she was sitting by the window in her apartment, in the dark. It was near daybreak now, and the snow had melted away to raindrops that punched through the glow of false dawn.

Lizbeth gazed at the rivulets on the window, the way one hooked into another before sliding down the glass and crashing at the bottom. One silver raindrop after another, hooking and sliding and dying. She wondered if she would ever see anything this beautiful in Arizona.

She glanced back at Richard's form in the bed, tossing and snoring in the darkness. He'd make a good husband; he'd take good care of her. *But that's funny. I never thought I'd need a guy to take care of me.*

Over time, she figured, Richard had convinced her of it. It wasn't such a bad thing, it was just a kind of love she was still trying to understand. Soon they'd be engaged, and maybe then she'd understand it a little better, be more able to take it in her hands and turn it over for all it was worth.

Lizbeth stifled a sigh. What was it worth?

Lizbeth rubbed her face, pressed on her cheekbones. Was she the same old girl she used to be? Or was she falling away from her more each day, slipping into a new skin that felt like someone else's?

Every time Richard told her he loved her, every time he took her somewhere fancy, every time he kissed her, she felt special, almost as special as she wanted to feel.

But there was something more, something she closed her eyes and wished for sometimes—a certain kind of sweetness that perfumed the air, whispered in her ear, told her she was a princess and made her happy to believe it.

Lizbeth looked down. Richard could never provide that. But someone else out there could.

I'm crazy, she thought, staring out the window and then smiling to herself. *Completely crazy.*

But she couldn't help wondering the same thing every night: Was Gio safe tonight? Was he happy?

Lizbeth shook her head. *Get a grip, Heathrow.*

Lizbeth knew what she wanted; she'd known since she was a little girl. She knew how she wanted to feel when she floated to sleep, whether it was wrapped in the blankets herself or tangled in a man's arms. And she'd only met one guy in her life who made her feel that way.

Where are you, Lizbeth wondered. She sighed and gazed out the window, the rain pounding the night. *Where are you?*

Chapter 26

Johnny knelt in the snow before his father's grave, freezing rain slapping down on him through the dawn. He laid his hand on the marble headstone, frosted over from the night's snow, and swept it over the top of the semicircle.

I haven't been back here, he thought, closing his eyes for a second. *Not since they buried you.*

Johnny studied the inscription on the marker:

GIOVANNI LUCA

1971-2021

Laurel leaves framed the inscription. Johnny remembered that while they were making the funeral arrangements, his mother had urged him to include laurels in the inscription. *You have to do it, Johnny*, she'd said. *Laurels, to show his courage.*

It didn't make sense then; it made sense now. Just like everything else.

Johnny exhaled smoke, icy globs of rain pounding him. *I'm so sorry, Dad*, he thought, bowing his head. *I haven't come to see you once.*

Even if you died... the way I thought... I should have come here. I shouldn't have hated you... cursed you... given up on you. I gave up on you, Dad. I believed the worst about you when I should have fought for the best. And now… I know everything.

Johnny looked back up, out at the gravestones in the distance impressed in the snow like pockmarks. He wiped raindrops from his eyes.

I need your help with something, Dad. Help me make it right. Help me catch the people who did this to us. I can get them... just whisper in my ear, and I'll listen.

Johnny clutched the headstone for a moment, his eyes drifting shut. Exhaustion throbbed in his muscles; he felt his bones sink. All he wanted was to drop into the snow, sleep it all away...

But then he stiffened. Johnny forced his eyes open and pulled himself up. His lip began to quiver; he bit it shut.

I promise you, Dad. I'll get him. I'll kill Octavian.

Chapter 27

Hunter Peterson's shoes clicked on the icy path winding through Arlington Cemetery, drawing nearer the phalanx of Secret Service agents in the distance with each step. Yellow vapors illumined the bodyguards huddled around their President.

Peterson nodded to the detail as he approached, and then the President nodded himself. The phalanx broke formation, fanning out in a distant perimeter, leaving only Peterson, Wilkins, and Chan before the eternal flame.

"I think this might be the last time we meet like this," Wilkins said. "Every time I slip out of the White House like this, it feels harder and harder, like more eyes are looking for me out in the night." He shook his head and looked down, sighing out smoke. "Or maybe this is all starting to break me down."

"We won't let it break you down, Mr. President," Chan said. "That's what we're here for."

Peterson thought back to the newly minted "working President" who had smiled and shaken his hand two years ago. *Look what they've done to him. Look how they've beaten down such a good man.*

"Total Information Awareness is coming up for a vote in a few weeks," Wilkins said. "I need to know where we're at."

Peterson and Chan looked at each other. Peterson wondered if they each had the same thing to say, and really hoped not. He had accomplished nothing with Project Orion since the last meeting.

"We'll go by chain of command," Wilkins said. "Director Chan, brief me first."

Chan frowned. "It's gone cold, sir. We've only been able to crack the plot open to a point. Elements inside the government are moving against you, and they plan to do it with lethal force if you defy them. You know who they are. But we haven't figured out how they plan to do it."

The President nodded, then sighed again. He turned to Peterson. "And you? What have we learned about Project Orion?"

Peterson looked down. This wasn't how he wanted to brief the President, with failure. He bit his lip and looked back up. "We're getting nowhere, Mr. President," he said. "Like Chan said, we know what they plan to do, we just can't determine how they plan to deliver it."

Peterson saw a little more life fall out of Wilkins. *He's aging. Before our eyes, he's shriveling.*

"We've got two plots we're up against," Wilkins said, almost to himself, walking off a couple of steps. "Two plots coming from completely opposite sources, two sides that despise each other. A plot to kill me, and a plot to kill thousands of civilians in several different cities. Put them together... and there might not be a United States of America left." He dipped his head in his hands. "Jesus Christ." Wilkins rubbed his eyes, then turned back to Chan and Peterson. "I know I gave you an impossible mission. But we're running out of time." He looked skyward a moment, agony slashing across his face. "It's so much worse than we thought. So much worse."

Chan approached the President. "What do you mean?" he said.

Wilkins looked at Peterson. "What is the Anti-Subversion Authority?" he said.

"What... is... the Anti-Subversion Authority," Peterson repeated. "I don't understand the question."

Wilkins turned to Chan. "Then you tell me. What is the Anti-Subversion Authority?"

Puzzlement swept over Chan's face. "It's the agency Congress created after the Iowa attack to combat domestic terrorism," he said.

"Right. That's the best way to put it, I guess." Wilkins turned back to Peterson. "And *who* is the Anti-Subversion Authority?"

What are you talking about? "I'm not sure what you mean, sir."

"How many agents do we have in the Authority now?"

Where's he going with this? Peterson thought. "About two thousand," he said.

"Well, about that many *agents*," Wilkins said. "But now, let's talk about the uniformed officers we've deployed in the cities. I can't get a straight answer from anyone, but right now, my best estimate is that there are *fifteen thousand* on the streets. Ever wonder where they came from?"

Chan narrowed his eyes. "Recruitment, sir. Young guys who are looking for police work but want to serve their country."

"That's definitely what the Authority says, publicly. But think about it, Chan. We're talking about officers who tase children, pepper-spray civilians, crack people's skulls with batons for holding up the wrong sign at a rally. Like storm troopers, really. Who would do that to their fellow Americans? Or better yet, how did we find fifteen thousand of them?"

"It's just the times," Peterson said. "More people willing to get violent with subversives."

"I don't doubt that. Again, that's how the Authority would explain it. But leave the indoctrination behind for a second, Peterson. Unlearn what Bryson's been telling you in his memos. Can't you see that something's not right?"

All the time. "I've seen that for some time now, sir. But I don't know what."

"Well, I do." Wilkins paused. "The Authority uniformed officers you see patrolling the streets are part of a pilot program. A program that's going to triple after they pass Total Information Awareness."

"What kind of pilot program?" Chan asked.

"A recruitment program," Wilkins said. "But not the kind of recruitment you'd imagine. A kind of reverse recruitment, actually. Recruitment of thugs, miscreants, criminals, mentally ill, people who are easy to bend and won't hesitate to beat people up to make a few bucks. Real brown-shirt types. And then throw in recruitment of soldiers who fell on hard times, disillusioned federal agents, disillusioned police—people with top-flight training who are easy to bend."

"Easy to bend to the point that they use Gestapo tactics?" Peterson asked.

Wilkins set his jaw. "That's where the pilot program comes in. The training these officers receive… It's not standard training. It's mind-control—like those LSD experiments the CIA conducted on soldiers in the fifties. They use hallucinogenic drugs, water-boarding, sleep-deprivation—and they get their anti-subversion supermen. You see, it works like this." Wilkins sighed, almost in disbelief. "They find a good candidate, or maybe a candidate comes to them, says he wants to make a difference, serve his country. Authority brass screens him to see if he's the kind they're looking for. If he is, they lure him in. And then they break his mind into a million pieces and rebuild it into the machine they're looking for. There's your pilot program, gentlemen—fifteen-thousand-strong at last count, and jumping up to fifty thousand once they pass that goddamn law."

"Jesus Christ," Peterson said. "We're talking about a paramilitary unit, patrolling our streets."

Chan bit his lip and shook his head. "But who would do this? Why?"

Wilkins threw his shoulders back and cast out his arms. "Organized criminals," he said. "Organized criminals who sit on top of trillions of dollars of blood money extracted from the enslavement of billions of people."

He threw that one at us like a brick. "Enslavement, sir?" he asked.

"That's right, enslavement. I'm talking about narcotics... arms dealing... human trafficking... massive criminal empires... turning over more money than our GDP. Not like that mafia stuff you see on television. I'm talking about a criminal element that rules most of the countries of the world behind the scenes, and now it has its eyes on us."

"Why?" Chan asked.

"Power. Killing me and passing Total Information Awareness is supposed to be some kind of acceleration of a plan—a plan to whip this country into the most powerful dictatorship in the history of the world. Not for the sake of ruling America. It's more than that. It's about concentrating all of this country's power in a few hands, and then unleashing it to the ends of the earth."

"And Bryson is one of these people?" Peterson asked.

Wilkins shook his head again. "He's the part of them we can see. They're using him, Peterson. They have been, from the beginning."

"Sir," Chan said. "How do you know all this?"

"There's so much I have to tell you both," Wilkins said. "But as I'm telling you, keep one thing in mind. I have a plan. When I veto that bill, I'm going to make some moves, and I need you to go with them. I'll be making those moves because of everything I'm about to tell you. Do you understand?"

Peterson and Chan nodded.

Wilkins sighed. "All right, then. Now I'll tell you everything."

Peterson froze in the instant before the President started to speak.

He stared up at the Virginia sky, dots of constellations twinkling in the still. *No turning back now*, he thought as Wilkins' lips started to move. *No turning back, forever…*

Chapter 28

Johnny paced across the roof of an apartment building, his shoes grinding into the pitch. His quarry drifted into view below; he crouched at a parapet and spied Buchanan.

A year and a half later, he was Sergeant Buchanan, strutting out of the municipal building to his parking space. Johnny peered down at the man who had spied on his father for Brigade 910.

He'd tracked him every day and night for the last week, on breaks and after work, with both his own eyes and a long-range parabolic microphone that he'd smuggled out of the office. As he looked down on the traitor tonight, he knew he had him—who he was, his schedule, everything. Johnny had Buchanan the same way Brigade 910 had his father before they shot him.

Johnny stood up tall and drew the hood of his sweatshirt over his head. He gritted his teeth and glowered at the form below, who was easing into his new luxury SUV, about to drive home to wife Madeline and little Suzie.

Johnny stalked across the rooftop again, his eyes burning under the hood. Soon he'd make Madeline a widow and little Suzie fatherless. He'd shot someone before, hadn't he? Maybe. From behind a door.

He might have to abduct Buchanan for awhile, interrogate him, see what he knew. But ultimately Johnny would deliver justice to him. In the end, Sergeant Buchanan would have to answer for Giovanni Luca.

Two hours later, Johnny was sitting across from Justine at a cozy Italian restaurant. The flare of the candle at the table swirled through her wine glass and danced in her eyes. "Happy birthday," she said, smiling.

It was only a few days after Johnny's birthday, a few days after… everything. "Thank you," he said, smiling back. "You really didn't have to do this."

"Of course I do. You take me to so many nice places. I have to take care of my boyfriend on his birthday."

I'm her boyfriend, Johnny thought as he looked down at the candle for a moment, the flame gyrating behind glass. *And she's my girlfriend.*

He looked up, and Justine was holding out her wine glass. "To..." She paused. "I'm no good at these things!"

"Sure you are," Johnny said. "You're going to be a prosecutor, start practicing!"

"Okay, okay." Justine paused again, then smiled. "To us."

Johnny clutched the glass. They'd been together three months now, and things were good. What else could he ask for? He raised the glass and tapped it against hers. "To us."

They went on eating, laughing, celebrating his birthday. Justine looked so beautiful tonight, like she did every night.

Here and there he stole glances back at the candle, to avoid her eyes. *Everything about me is a lie to her.*

Could Johnny ever tell her the truth about how he'd been murdered? Would he ever *want* to tell her? He looked into her eyes again; he couldn't help it. They were smiling, loving.

But Johnny couldn't confide in her about what he was up against, what he'd done, what he planned to do...

After dinner, they drove back to his place. Justine stroked the nape of Johnny's neck. "You're so good to me," she said, a little drunk.

But he was starting to understand what he had to do. It had slipped into his mind earlier tonight, just a whisper, a little nudge telling him that he had to do the right thing.

Later that night, after more wine, they lay down in his bed, a single candle flickering on the dresser as a bulwark against the night. "You can hold your liquor a lot better than me," Justine said. "You don't say... the silly things I do..." She kissed his neck.

Johnny closed his eyes, her breath lulling him closer into her. "Silly things... like what?" he said.

"Like... that I'm falling for you, Johnny. I think you're sweeping me off my feet."

Johnny didn't answer, wrapping his arms around her instead. He wanted to say the same back, but he couldn't.

He held her as the minutes gave way to hours, the last night he'd spend in bed with Justine. The candle on his dresser bounced light off a picture frame.

Inside was a photograph of him and Lizbeth, Halloween night, sophomore year. She was hugging him, the robber to his cop.

Johnny gazed at the picture. If his father's death had broken something inside of him, learning the truth had mended it and made it even stronger than before. He had a duty to be upright and honest in everything he did.

We could've been almost good enough, he thought as he floated to sleep, *almost good enough—*

The next morning, Johnny told her that he couldn't see her anymore. She cried a little, first out of surprise and heartbreak, then out of frustration and indignance.

She shook her head, gathered her things, and crossed to the door. "I really wanted to know you, Johnny. And I think..." Justine bit her lip and paused. "I think I'm going to miss you more than any guy I ever met, and I hate it." She opened the door, walked out, and slammed it behind her.

Johnny lowered his head as her heard her heels click across the hallway outside, then die away. Tired, a little heartbroken, and almost in love with her, he let her go.

Chapter 29

A few nights later, Johnny fixed his eyes on Lizbeth, sitting next to him at Coogan's, her emerald eyes dancing behind rectangular glasses.

Lizbeth smiled. "I'm glad you met me tonight, Gio."

Johnny smiled back. "I'm glad you asked me to come, dork."

Lizbeth gazed at him a moment, smiling into his eyes. "I'm surprised I even recognized you when you came in." She shook her head. "You're a busy man these days, way too busy for your best friend."

"Come on, I always have time for Billy!"

Lizbeth slapped Johnny's arm. "F you, Luca. I'd totally punch you if I got to see you more than four times a year."

"You know I wish it were more than that," he said. *Shit, I said that out loud.* Johnny covered his mouth with his hand.

Lizbeth brushed her hand over his. "You don't mean that. But it's sweet." She gulped her beer. "So how's the girlfriend?"

"We broke up a couple of nights ago."

Lizbeth arched her eyebrows. "What happened?"

Where do I begin? "It's a long story. But nothing I want to talk about right now."

"I'm sorry, sweetheart. You know I'm here, always." Lizbeth rubbed Johnny's arm. "But... you're doing okay otherwise? Everything all right?"

I'm hanging on. "I'm okay, darlin'. Can't complain."

"Good. I worry about you, that's all. Can't help it, I guess." Lizbeth looked into Johnny's eyes. "Sometimes you're the last thing I think about before I fall asleep, you know? If you're doing okay, if you're happy."

Johnny returned the look. "And sometimes I think the same about you."

Lizbeth looked away for a moment, scanning the bar, and then she returned to him with a little blush on her face. "And do you think I'm doing okay?"

"I usually end up there."

"And sometimes you don't?"

Johnny poured beer down his throat. "Even *I* worry sometimes," he said. "I'm human, too."

"I know you are. Even if you make everyone think you're Superman... I know who you are. You're the same guy who held me when I broke up with my boyfriend freshman year."

That feels like six hundred years ago. "You think so?"

"Are you kidding? I swear, dude, whenever you stop running all over the place, and actually settle down..." Lizbeth paused, then smiled. "You're going to drive some chick up a wall."

Johnny again looked into Lizbeth's eyes. "So you don't think... I've turned into someone else?"

Lizbeth smiled. "Maybe you've tried to. But you're still my Gio. And you always will be."

Johnny closed his eyes, basking in the unconditionality of those words. *Would she still say that if she knew everything?*

Lizbeth clapped her hands. "So are we gonna blow some alien scum away?"

Their favorite arcade game was waiting for them in the corner of the bar, an alien shoot-em-up outfitted with two swiveling blasters. The two raced to their positions.

Johnny and Lizbeth made a spectacle of themselves for the next chunk of the night, elbowing each other for position, trading exclamations as they gunned down various alien life forms with big teeth and a taste for human flesh. "Get him, get him!" Lizbeth yelled. "Use the flame thrower! The flame thrower, damn it! Hurry!"

At one point, between stages, she turned to Johnny and narrowed her eyes. "You're shooting like a real pro tonight," she said. "They letting you carry a gun at the FBI lately?"

He winked. "Not yet," he said.

So they kept playing. As Johnny blasted away, he thought of a short story he'd read when he was a kid, after his mother had driven him to the library and forced him to take out a book. It was about a guy who made a deal with the devil: the devil gave him a stopwatch that could stop time and let him live forever inside his favorite moment; if the guy went his whole life without using the stopwatch, the devil got his soul.

If Johnny had that stopwatch tonight, he'd have clicked it while he and Lizbeth were playing. Outside was Project Orion and avenging his father's death. Inside was heaven: beer, a good video game, and most importantly, Lizbeth Heathrow.

Later, the two were back at the bar, spent from saving the world together. Lizbeth ordered up another round. "I brought you a birthday present, you know," she said.

Johnny feigned looking around. "That's funny, 'cause you look empty-handed to me, Heathrow."

Lizbeth slapped the inside of his shoulder, hard, her palm slamming against his leather jacket. "That's because it's in my bag, ass."

"Well give it up, man!"

Lizbeth rolled her eyes and dug into her purse. She pulled out a blue envelope and a small rectangle of tin foil. She handed both to Johnny.

Johnny slipped a finger into the foil. "No you don't," Lizbeth said. "Open the card first, like a good boy."

He did as asked. On the front of the card were a little boy and a little girl, their little hands cupped one on top of the other around the handle of an upside-down baseball bat, their little caps flipped backwards.

Johnny opened the card. "*To the friend who's always been the most fun to play with,*" it read. "*Happy birthday.*"

But Lizbeth had written her own missive in the space between: "*Dear Gio, Thank you for being the favorite part of my day, even when you don't know you are. Love, Lizbeth.*"

Johnny arched his eyebrows. "The favorite part?" he asked.

"That's what I said. Don't wear it out."

The favorite part of her day. Johnny felt like a twelve-year-old getting his first real Valentine's card. *I'm the favorite part of Lizbeth's day*, he thought, trying it on for size.

He tore open the foil, and there it was, an autographed rookie card of his favorite Yankee ever, Derek Jeter. *Good old Number Two*, Johnny thought, smiling.

"I'm still on a journalist's budget," Lizbeth said. "I'd give you the whole world, wrapped up, if I could. But I thought you might like this."

"I love it," Johnny said. He looked up and smiled. "He was the best of all time. My dad's favorite player, too." He pulled Lizbeth into an embrace. "It's perfect."

Lizbeth squeezed Johnny back, and then she pecked his neck. "I'm glad you like it," she said.

Johnny's neck caught fire; it spread to his face, his ears. He looked down into her eyes and edged her face up with his finger. For a moment—maybe just a split-second, maybe more—they drew closer together. She was breathing into him, her breath slipping through his lips, and he was breathing into her. Johnny's heart vibrated in his chest, shock waves rolling through him from his stomach to his forehead, as their lips neared each other.

Lizbeth pulled away. "I have to tell you something," she said.

Johnny stepped back. "What?"

Lizbeth measured her words. "I'm... Richard and I... we're moving."

Oh no. "Moving? Where?"

"Well..." Lizbeth looked down for a moment, then back up. "Richard has a chance to get an awesome job back home, and they're laying people off at my job, and... we're moving to Phoenix."

Johnny sank. "Phoenix." He paused. *Phoenix.* "When?"

"The first week of June."

Two more months… and then two thousand miles away.

"So he's finally going to pop the question," Johnny said. He forced a smile, even though he felt like he had to grab the wall or something. "Look at you, all grown up."

"You have to promise me something, Gio. You have to promise me I'll see you again before I leave."

"Lizbeth—"

"Because if tonight is the last night, I'm going to be totally heartbroken, and you haven't broken my heart yet, not once, not one time in all the years I've known you. You're the only person in the world who's never broken my heart. And I don't think you want to start now."

Johnny paused, and then he forced another smile. "You know I'll see you again before you leave."

Lizbeth hugged him. "In case you don't," she said. "Take this."

She handed him a sealed envelope. "Promise me you won't open it right away. You can't open it until you know just what you want out of life. Not until then."

Johnny narrowed his eyes as he took the envelope. "How do you know I don't?"

Lizbeth sighed. "Because I know everything about you, dork. Because if you *did* know—things might be different, that's all."

Johnny paused, then smiled and held up the baseball card. "Thanks for the card, beautiful."

Lizbeth hovered for a moment somewhere between crying and smiling, and then smiled. "You shouldn't call me that," she said. "Sometimes I melt a little… when you call me that." She rubbed Johnny's arm. "Goodnight, Gio. Happy birthday."

"Goodnight, Lizbeth."

Lizbeth stood there a moment, regarding her best friend. Then she smiled one last time and left.

Johnny sank into a stool. It was a terrible thing, he discovered—the second-most heartbreaking thing in his life, in fact—to wonder if he had just seen Lizbeth Heathrow walk out of a room for the last time.

"That's the last of it," Billy Hawkins said a few days later, pulling down the trailer door, slamming it, and flipping the latch. He stroked his red beard, his blond hair flapping in the wind. "Next stop, Miami."

Johnny shook his head. "I can't believe this is it, man. You made it."

"Not yet. I've still gotta survive I-95 for a thousand miles. It really blows that you can't road-trip, man." Billy slapped Johnny on the shoulder. "Too bad things didn't work out with you and Justine. Better luck next time, I guess... even if you do love dizzle."

Johnny laughed. "One of these days, something's going to work out. You'll see."

"And now Lizbeth is moving to Phoenix with that bone smuggler. Crazy, dude. Crazy." Billy shook his head and walked around to the cab of the moving truck. He popped open the door. "I'll tell you what I think."

"What's that?"

Billy yanked himself up into the cab. "You've got to tell her how you feel before she goes."

"Oh yeah? And how do I feel?"

"Listen to me, man. At some point you *have* to stop being so fucking indecisive, you know what I mean? You're going to lose her, *forever.* She's going be *gone*, dude, and by the time you de-bunch your panties she's going be saying 'I kinda do' on the altar with that lightswitch-for-genitals she calls a quasi-fiancé. If you love her like I know you do, *don't wait.* I can't help you with this one. Only you can. Make your move."

Of course, Johnny had thought of all of this already. He wasn't being indecisive, he was just doing the right thing, for him and for Lizbeth. "I'm trying to be noble here, asshole," he said.

Billy bellowed a laugh, then shook his head. "You've managed to turn the word 'noble' into a synonym for 'homosexual'!" He fired up the truck, jerked the door closed, then powered down the window.

Johnny looked at him. "You're the luckiest guy I know, Billy."

Billy grinned. "And why's that?"

"Because you wanted all your life to move to Miami, and now you're doing it, your way."

Billy shook his head. "It ain't luck, Luca. You figure out what you want to do... and you do it."

Johnny nodded. *Point A to point B.*

"Anyway, I've got to get out of this armpit state," Billy continued. "Happy birthday. Give that case of Guinness a good home." He pulled on the air horn, and its deep scream exploded into the afternoon. "I always wanted to do that," he said, smiling. "I asked them special for one of these."

Johnny smiled back. "See you on the flip side, brother."

Billy nodded, gripped the steering wheel as if grabbing reins on a chariot, and blasted out into the street. "Wooooo!" he yelped. "Wooooo!"

Johnny watched Billy Hawkins speed out of New Jersey, on his way to his life's dream, until the truck slipped out of view. Then he leaned back against his own truck. Billy was gone, leaving Johnny and the April air and all the things he was blood-sworn to do.

The next day, Johnny toiled at his desk, staring at the computer screen in his cubicle. He was poring over a blog titled "Clocks Striking 13," a subversive hotspot. Lately an anonymous contributor to the site had started posting names and photographs of Authority agents, including Peterson and Moloch.

Johnny clicked on Moloch's name. His picture popped up, revealing jet-black hair, bad-ass brown eyes, and middle-aged crags dug into his face. "Shepherd Moloch," read the caption. "Anti-Subversion Authority, Special Agent in Charge, New York Field Office." Then below the caption:

"Shepherd Moloch is the criminal in charge of the New York Field Office of the Anti-Democracy Authority. He is notorious for his brutal tactics in his post as head of the most active law enforcement office in the United States. Particularly renowned for his torture techniques and his sexual battery of women, he has also been known to experiment with ritual abuse methods in dealing with subjects. Moloch should be considered the second most wanted criminal in the illegitimate American regime, behind Authority Director Bryson, and should be captured or killed wherever encountered."

Johnny rolled his eyes. *Whatever, jackass.* He stared in at Moloch. He did not look like someone to be fucked with.

Johnny clicked on Peterson's name. And there was a picture of him, with his silver-brown hair and blue eyes, along with his title.

"Hunter Peterson is a patriot gone astray," the description read. "A former Secret Service agent who served with valor, he's prostituted his investigative talents to the Anti-Democracy Authority. He is a man of scruples who struggles to uphold the Constitution, but as long as he targets the innocent men and women his paymasters brand 'subversives,' he must be considered an enemy of the revolution. Given his position as an organ of the cabal of usurpers, Hunter Peterson must be targeted for capture or assassination wherever he is found."

Johnny closed out the page. *Fun stuff.*

He narrowed his eyes for a moment, then wheeled his chair to the edge of the cubicle and looked up and down the hallway. *Let's see if this total information stuff is any good.*

He googled "Sarah Chambers Andes", not for the first time. The first two words were the name of the daughter of the couple who'd been murdered up on that farm. The third word was the name of the upstate New York hamlet where they lived.

And like all the other times Johnny had done so, Sarah's social networking page came up, complete with a headshot, her blue eyes smiling, her blonde hair falling around her shoulders. He needed to know the girl behind the smiling eyes, the girl in the ballerina costume in that picture in the bedroom.

Sarah's page was password-protected, which ended Johnny's inquiry on his home computer. But not today, not here in the office. Johnny ran a program, copied and pasted the URL of Sarah's page into a field, and at the beaming of a progress bar, her page unlocked.

There it all was. Her favorite team was the Buffalo Bills, her favorite movie was *Pan's Labyrinth*, her favorite book was *To Kill a Mockingbird.* Her birthday was October 9, 2002—she was only twenty, a couple of years older than Paul.

Johnny shook his head. *Twenty years old. And her parents are gone.*

He clicked on one of her photo albums. He felt like a voyeur, but he couldn't turn back now. He needed to know her, he'd never meet her and tell her how sorry he was, but he needed to know life was going on, that she was okay.

There was a picture of Sarah out with her friends. She was short and slim, her blonde hair falling in wisps about her shoulders, an eyebrow ring fitted above one of her blue eyes. She was smiling and laughing in all of the pictures in the album, and Johnny saw a bit of Lizbeth in her, the serenity of her smile, the brightness of her eyes. He knew a good person when he saw one.

Johnny checked the date of the album. It was from Sarah's birthday party last October, before… everything. In fact, none of the albums were dated after December.

There was a blog. All of the entries were posted before December—except the last, which was posted two weeks ago.

"I believe that unarmed truth and unconditional love will have the final word," began one entry. *–Martin Luther King*

I used to think so.

Anyone close enough to me to be reading this blog knows that that used to be my favorite quote of all time. And you also know what I've been through the last few months. I'm sorry I haven't been more fun, that I just can't get back to being me. I think that person is gone.

The truth is, for everything I used to think I knew about the world, I never believed it was cruel. I always thought it was more kind than it was hateful, more just than unjust, more worthy of hope than despair. And it kills me to lay down my arms and admit I was wrong, but that's what I'm doing here.

This isn't just what happened to me and my family; it's the whole world. It's locked water taps in Africa, corporate militias in South America, tear gas in Tehran, the strong brutalizing the weak. It's the criminal-in-chief Wilkins sending his thugs to beat college kids for opposing his tyranny.

Everyone suffers, and all we are is hushed fear. Unarmed truth and unconditional love will never carry the day.

I guess what I'm saying is, to everyone who's been there for me these last few months, I love you very much, but you can stop asking me how I'm doing, telling me how sorry you are for what happened. It happened; asi es la vida. I'm starting to accept that I'm just never going to climb out of this hole I fell into. It's okay.

Johnny lowered his head. *I guess that answers my questions.*

He clenched his fist. *I could've stopped them. Or at least caught them before they left. Instead, I did nothing. Goddamn it, I did nothing.*

Johnny closed out of the blog and clicked on the picture of the smiling girl again. *Somehow, I'm going to pull you out of that hole.*

Chapter 30

The same day, in the Newark field office, Hunter Peterson had noticed an odd look on his secretary's face as he brushed past her on the way to his office. He had worked with Cynthia for eight or nine years now, and he could at least tell when she wanted to say something.

He ducked his head back out. "What is it?" he said.

Cynthia turned back to look at him, her blue eyes pouting. She was in her early forties, petite with short blonde hair.

"I can't believe you're not going," Cynthia said.

"Going to what?"

"Come on, Hunter. I've been reading the official messages. The dinner tonight."

"You know that's not my kind of thing."

"It's because you hate Moloch, and you hate Number One."

By "Number One," Cynthia meant Director Bryson, slated to give the keynote address at a commemorative dinner for federal law enforcement at the Waldorf-Astoria tonight. Instinctively Peterson bent a little lower towards her, but then he stiffened—they wouldn't have miked up the outside of his office, would they?

"I don't hate them," he said. "That's ridiculous."

Cynthia burst out laughing, and Peterson had to admit, she had a simply gorgeous smile, bright and perfect. "Stop talking to me like I'm a reporter or something. We both know they're awful." Her eyes danced up to his. "But I don't think you should let that keep you from going tonight."

"Come on. It's just a bunch of nonsense."

"Maybe... but you deserve to shine, Hunter. As hard as you work, no one recognizes you. Not since the old days."

Cynthia had been with Peterson back in the Secret Service, and she'd followed him to the Authority. "I don't need recognition," Peterson said. "I know what I'm doing back in that office there. That's enough."

"Well, I've decided that you deserve a special night in the city tonight, with a cocktail hour and fancy food and expensive wine. So you're going."

Peterson laughed. "Am I?"

"Actually, *we're* going."

Peterson arched his eyebrows. "We are?"

"Look, we've been working together nine years now. I haven't been out for a nice night on the town for a long time. And right now, you're the only guy I'd think to ask." Cynthia giggled. "Which may sound pathetic to you. But in any case, I'm dressing up tonight in a cute dress, and you're putting on a suit, and we're going to this event. And I don't care what anyone in this office says, because you're the boss, and I'm the head admin. So there."

Well, this was unexpected. His wife Patricia had passed away five years ago from cancer. And he'd gone out on a few dates in the last couple of years, but no second dates. "I don't know what to say," he said.

Cynthia stood up, and now her look was sad—not a coworker's look, but a friend's. She deepened her gaze into his eyes and put her hand to his elbow. "Say yes," she said. "Get out of the four walls of that office. Live a little with me." She paused. "You can't let them push you around forever, Hunter. Show them tonight that they can't."

And just then, Peterson realized that Cynthia knew more than he thought. Not the classified mission, not the secret visits—just that he was up against Moloch and Bryson, and it was grinding him down, trapping him in the office for late nights and then back at home for later nights. She knew, and she wanted to stand there with him. A knockout blonde who actually wanted to be at his side for a night. Not a bad deal, not bad at all.

"I guess it's a date," Peterson said.

Cynthia brightened. "Good, because I already put you down for the chicken," she said. She paused, then beamed again. "We'll show them," she said. "Tonight, Hunter. We'll show them."

Chapter 31

That night, there was a knock on Johnny's door. He opened it to find Marissa standing outside.

"So there *is* another diary," Johnny said.

Marissa stepped inside. "How did you—how did you know that's why I came?" she asked.

"Come on, Mom. You're not popping up to clean up the apartment."

Marissa looked around, grimacing at the mess. "Wouldn't hurt, though."

"Well, where is it?"

Marissa sighed. "Here." She reached into her bag and pulled out a notebook. "It's very short."

"Why didn't you tell me about it when I asked?"

Marissa frowned, and then she began to tear up. "Because the things he wrote, they're... they're..." She lowered her head in her hands.

Johnny leaned closer and stroked her hair. "Come on, don't cry. They're what?"

Marissa looked back up, waving him off. "They're dangerous."

"Dangerous how?"

"You'll see."

Johnny nodded. "This is the only other one? You promise?"

Marissa closed her eyes. "I promise." She handed him the notebook.

"You're doing the right thing, Mom." Johnny smiled. "I was getting worried I was gonna have to execute a search warrant at your place."

Marissa didn't smile back. "I'm gonna go. Be careful, Johnny. Please, be careful." She kissed him, then turned and left.

Johnny thought of walking after her, but he knew there was nothing reassuring he could say. He'd flown past careful already.

As the sound of his mother's footsteps died away outside, Johnny settled on his couch with the finale of his father's two-volume work.

Brigade 910 terrorists had murdered his father. He was still trying to wrap his head around it, still trying to think about it without his face flushing red and his heart zig-zagging in his chest, but he *knew* it. And if the old man had anything else left to say, Johnny was ready.

He opened the notebook.

***

November 2, 2021

Today I met with Professor Anton Jacobs, and he told me everything he knows about Brigade 910 and what they call Project Orion. I believe he's telling the truth. I also believe that I have to write all of this down tonight, because I may not be alive tomorrow at this time.

If you're reading this, then you've decided to stand up. Somehow my ex-wife has found you, and she's chosen you as our only hope. You are very brave, and you are very crazy—and that is the only combination that can save us now. Project Orion has claimed many lives to this point, and it will soon claim mine. But we are fighting—and dying—because eventually it will claim thousands of lives, and will shake this country to the point that there will be no republic left.

Chapter 32

At that moment, in the Waldorf-Astoria in Manhattan, Peterson fixed his eyes on Shepherd Moloch as he raised a glass to his lips. Scotch on the rocks—a Hunter Peterson standard from the old days—and hating Moloch from across the room, another old standard.

The partygoers, clad in suits and pretty dresses, were buzzing through cocktail hour in the Silver Corridor. Chandeliers dazzled from the arched ceiling above, flashes of light and gold tapering through three concentric tiers. The checkered black-and-white floor ran through the hall, red silk velvet sofas sitting sentry around each bay window. A pianist tapped notes into a baby grand at the mouth of the corridor.

Peterson glanced at Cynthia, stunning in a little black dress, and smiled; she knew how he felt about Moloch, but she didn't know why. Then Peterson stared again at Moloch, who this time stared back. He held up his wine glass and nodded at Peterson. Peterson grabbed his scotch and did the same.

Moloch looked good tonight, his shoulders filling out a charcoal pinstripe suit, a blue silk tie linking with an ice-blue pocket square. He clutched a blonde, who was about twenty-five years younger than him, round the wrist. Not the hand, Peterson noticed—she wasn't holding his hand back. It was around her wrist.

Peterson emptied some scotch into his throat. Standing across the room with that girl by the wrist was a monster, not a man.

Peterson had suspected as such early on in the academy, when he and Moloch were in the same class training for the Secret Service. The way he spotted you one second too late during weightlifting, the way he took sparring sessions one move too far, the way he didn't try just to outclass you, but to hurt you. *This is a guy*, young Peterson had thought back then, *who will terrorize people once he has power.*

Peterson turned out to be right, very early on. During their first run together, out of the New York field office, he had watched Moloch engage some drunken hick in a bar fight one night while they were out on a protection rotation in some lonely outpost in Oklahoma. Moloch had groped a woman, and her husband was out to avenge her honor. Before Moloch even threw a punch, Peterson realized that he didn't believe in a woman's honor—that he didn't believe in honor. Peterson and some of the other young agents tried to stop him, but he was no longer human at this point, no longer containable by anything other than a tranquilizer dart and a cage. He spun loose and roundhouse-kicked the hick in the face, then broke a beer stein over his head and sliced the back of his neck with a shard of glass. Moloch then grabbed the man by the arm; with one hand he clutched him by the wrist and twisted it back, and then he dug the elbow of his other arm into the man's tricep and muscled him over a stool.

Peterson stepped forward from the line of Secret Service agents. *Let him go, Moloch*, he said.

Moloch stared back, an animal instinct gleaming in his eyes. *I gotta learn him, first,* he said. He seethed into the hick's ear. *Ain't that right, boy? I gotta learn you good, or whup you!*

The wife scurried up. *Please*, she said. *Don't hurt him.*

Peterson stared back at Moloch. *You've got three seconds*, he said.

Moloch raised his elbow to break the husband's arm, and Peterson charged at him, tackling him. But Moloch kicked him off with one leg, and Peterson couldn't believe the strength. They stared at each other from different points on the dusty floor, and then several agents converged on Moloch as a few others tended to the injured husband.

All of the agents had been told a long time before that even *touching* a local could be enough for termination. It was at least enough for suspension.

Moloch suffered neither. The higher-ups instead transferred him to another field office—the first inexplicable step of an inexplicable rise to power. He never stopped hurting people, and rumors abounded that he'd added rape to his resume over the years. Just as the Secret Service hierarchy caught on to the fact that they had a maniac on their hands, Iowa happened and the Authority came along. Moloch beat out Peterson for the New York top spot, and now he was in line to become Director of the Anti-Subversion Authority once the Total Information Awareness Act became law.

A host began to ring a bell. Peterson smiled at Cynthia again, offered her his arm, and then headed towards the ballroom with her.

He crossed Moloch on the way. "Table four, Hunter," he said, a grin cutting across his face. "The Director promised me we could sit together."

Chapter 33

Brigade 910 is planning a terror attack on a scale we've never seen. They call it "Project Orion." The inner circle of the group likes to say it will be "9-11 squared." That gives you an idea of what we're up against.

But the trick is in the name. "Project Orion" is itself a code for the real terror plot, known only to the planners.

Orion is the Greek hunter. That's easy enough. That's what the foot soldiers of Brigade 910 think this attack means: hunting the corrupt U.S. government and making it pay for its crimes.

But the real meaning is in the first two letters of 'Orion': O and R. They stand for "Operation Reichstag." That's the name the leaders of Brigade 910 have given to their plan, and that is what they call it among themselves.

But it isn't clear why. The Nazis took over Germany in 1933 by what is known as the Reichstag fire. The Reichstag, the German parliament building, was set on fire the night of February 27, 1933. Inside the building the authorities found a single shirtless man, still alive, who claimed to have set the fire. He was a communist.

It turns out that undercover Nazis, posing as communist activists, had put the man up to setting the fire, and then double-crossed him. Nazi brownshirts set several other fires in the building, to make sure it was completely destroyed, and then left their patsy behind to be the only culprit discovered. Within a month Adolf Hitler was in complete control of Germany. Sixty million people died because of the Nazis in the twelve years following the Reichstag fire.

Brigade 910 is planning a massive attack, but why name it "Operation Reichstag"? The Reichstag fire was set by one group and blamed on another. Who would America blame for this horrific attack, here in 2021, besides Brigade 910? What can they gain from this? Cui bono?

The professor has a partial answer to this, and I think I'm coming around to it. As you go up the ranks in the terrorist hierarchy, the motives change, and things make less and less sense to an outsider, until they spiral off into total craziness. The Brigade 910 foot soldier today—or the al Qaeda bomber twenty years ago, for that matter—kills people because he thinks he has a cause so important that it's worth killing and dying for, whether it's Allah or overthrowing the American government. But higher up the ladder it may be about foreign relations, or money, or power. Maybe a terror deputy is ordering his subordinates to blow up targets in Iraq because he's an agent of the Iranian government whose job it is to destabilize Iraq. Maybe another commander is broke, or has a drug habit, or just wants to be rich, and he's managed to turn himself into a contract killer of civilians—someone who makes hundreds of thousands, or millions, devising terror attacks.

But we have no way of knowing what motivates the terrorists at the top. What could Osama bin Laden possibly have gained from spending millions of dollars of his own money to set up camps to train people to attack the greatest power on earth? What amount of money, what amount of power, was worth sparking the instant hate of three hundred million people and the blasting of a trillion dollars' worth of war to try and kill you?

Who is the head of Brigade 910, and what is he after? How can it possibly be worth it to him?

Well, I have an idea, and whoever you are, you're not going to like it.

Think about the names of the Brigade 910 commanders. Each commander, all the way up the ladder, is known to his subordinates as Octavian. That means that somewhere on this earth, there is a single leader of Brigade 910 trying to kill thousands of people and terrify hundreds of millions more—a single Octavian.

Octavian came to power after the murder of Julius Caesar. He fought vicious wars and emerged from the chaos as the absolute ruler of the Roman empire. He consolidated his rule, ended the republic for good, and crowned himself Rome's first emperor.

Think about it. Is Octavian a terrorist? Or is he inside the United States government?

Think about Colgate's murder. Shot in the stomach by a perfectly placed terrorist, who was shot in the back by a perfectly placed Authority agent.

Think about Ramirez's murder. A Secret Service agent who never did anything to get on Brigade 910's radar.

And think about what's happened to me. The guy in my department who's spied on me, Buchanan—a cop. Do you think a terrorist paid him off? Or maybe an Authority agent told him to keep tabs on me?

Octavian, whoever he is, is engineering a false-flag terror attack to consolidate the rule of himself and the Authority. Does any other explanation make sense?

Look at Operation Reichstag. Operation Reichstag will be a wide-scale attack aimed at mostly civilian targets. We don't have the specifics, but we know it will take place in several cities, on a preordained day, around lunchtime in New York, rush hour on the West Coast. They'll bomb buildings and soft targets like trains and buses. Brigade 910 will empty the arsenal that day. We think that could include chemical and biological weapons, and maybe even a dirty-bomb-type weapon.

Is that something a bunch of college kids and crackpots could pull off on their own?

Now you see why I can't go to the FBI, or the Secret Service, or any other agency. There's no one to trust. There's no way of knowing who's loyal and who's spying.

And the media? They're lackeys doing the bidding of their masters, lapping up whatever stories the government feeds them. Why do you think no one in the media reported on the connection between Colgate and a plot to assassinate the President? Why no one will report on the very obvious links between Brigade 910 and the Authority? The professor reached out to a reporter once, and that reporter was fired after bringing the story to his editor. A month later, the man moved out west after finding his dog poisoned to death.

This Operation Reichstag attack is not a new idea. Look at the Reichstag fire itself. Read up about something called Operation Gladio, when right-wing elements in the Italian government had a major train station bombed, and then blamed it on left-wing terrorists. They called it a "strategy of tension", a way to keep the people divided, keep them afraid, keep them running to the government for protection.

I don't know when Operation Reichstag will deploy, but you have to stop it. The cells will be waiting for a signal that day. When they get the signal, they will attack.

That's why we found Ryan Colgate sitting on a stash of weapons, with no idea when he'd use them. He was waiting, just like they're all waiting now, hiding behind their regular jobs, or sitting in a classroom somewhere, waiting for the signal that will detonate the worst terror attack in American history.

Except we know the signal, and now I'm giving it to you. It's up to you to stop it.

The assassination of President Wilkins will launch Operation Reichstag.

So there it is. Brigade 910 plans to launch numerous attacks around the country that will kill thousands of people. But they will not act—they are fixated on this—until they've killed the President. Then the terror begins.

***

Johnny dropped the notebook. A chill electrified his spine. *He can't be right. The Authority… and Brigade 910… can't be on the same side. They can't. God, they can't.*

A second chill bolted through Johnny. *The signal. Goddamn it, I know the signal.*

Chapter 34

Peterson glared across the table at Moloch, leaning back in his chair and snapping orders into the ears of his personal bodyguards, his top New York agents. Moloch was the only SAIC in federal law enforcement who was flanked by a gaggle of agents everywhere he went, in violation of federal law, actually. And the thugs he kept around him had a reputation as being the worst.

Cynthia tugged on Peterson's arm. "Having a good time?" she whispered in his ear.

He turned to her, and she smiled. "I'm trying," he whispered back.

The dinner was in the Grand Ballroom of the Waldorf, maybe the priciest venue on the East Coast, but then again, Director Bryson was now the most powerful man in the federal government. A red Persian rug inlaid with gold embroidering stretched in an enormous square in the center of the ballroom. Gold trim traced around the frames of the silk-upholstered chairs, threading to the legs, the chairs circling tables draped in white tablecloths that skirted to the floor. Balconies ringed the ballroom high up on the walls, navy blue curtains swaddled at the back of each, electric lanterns burning above. Bryson and his wife were the only ones sitting in a balcony.

Moloch smiled at Peterson and then rose in his seat. "I think we owe a toast here tonight," he said, raising his glass of red wine. "To Hunter Peterson, one of the President's best men, coming back to the scene to hang out with the boys after all these years."

"Here here!" cheered some of the men at the table, and there was a chorus of clanging glasses.

And then, when the attention was off of Moloch, he glared at Peterson.

This time it was Peterson who smiled back. *We'll play your game*, he thought, raising his glass and pouring back some Pinot Grigio. Across the table Moloch drank his red wine, and behind the vapor of good cheer he looked like a wolf drinking blood.

"You stay strong," Cynthia whispered in Peterson's ear as they all sat back down. "Tonight is your night."

Later, over dinner, Moloch kept his eyes trained on Peterson. He smiled as he cut into his steak, so rare that blood ran off the edge of his knife. "Cynthia," he called across the table. "I haven't seen you in years. I think you're the second-most gorgeous thing I've ever seen." He grinned out of the corner of his mouth and eyes back at his waifish date for the night, then turned back with a leer. "I had no idea you and Hunter were the government's newest power-couple. I guess I'm not as up on all the gossip as I should be." Moloch ran his knife over his fork, the teeth of the blade catching and bouncing, catching and bouncing. "But mostly, I hear everything." His eyes burned into Peterson's, laughing. "Everything."

Cynthia grinned. "Turning up the creep factor tonight, are we, Shep?" she said, rolling her eyes. "But Hunter and I aren't a power couple. He's not that lucky." She turned to Peterson and batted her eyelashes.

Peterson grinned. *I need to spend more nights out with this woman.*

The table fell silent for a few moments, the guests sinking into dinner. Peterson glanced up at Director and Mrs. Bryson dining in their balcony. *There he is, the king of kings, sitting in judgment on high.* Peterson shuddered.

"I expect him to deliver a brilliant speech," Moloch said, following Peterson's eyes. "Don't you think?"

Well, of course you do. You've got residue from his ass all over your hands. "What can we expect the director to discuss this evening?" he asked, still glancing up at Bryson in a tuxedo leaning close to his wife and nodding.

"I wouldn't want to give it away. But I'm sure he'll inspire you to round up the last of the subversives and end this war."

"Just me, Moloch?"

Moloch smiled. "All of us, Peterson."

Cynthia tapped Peterson's arm and stood up. "Please excuse me," she said. "I'll be back in a moment." She leaned into her date's ear. "Don't punch him out while I'm gone," she whispered. "The cheesecake here is to *die* for." With a smile and a nod, she was gone.

Moloch smiled after her, but Peterson deciphered a leer. "Hunter, let's get a drink at the bar," he said.

Peterson paused, then relented. "Love to," he said. *What's he up to?*

They strolled to the bar together through a sea of young agents elbowing to shake Moloch's hand. "Mr. Moloch, it's an honor," one said. "Sir, I've heard so much about you," another said.

Moloch and Peterson settled at the bar. "Two Grand Marniers, please," Moloch called to the bartender. He turned to his companion. "You still enjoy your after-dinner drinks, don't you?"

Peterson nodded.

"What a place," Moloch said, sweeping his arm wide. "New York City, Hunter." He sighed. "It's too bad we couldn't both rule here, you know. Maybe you should go back to the Service. You could be New York SAIC in a heartbeat." Moloch scooped the drinks from the bartender.

Peterson smiled at the bartender and then took his drink from Moloch. "And miss out on all the fun of being in the Authority?" He laughed. "Come on, I wouldn't give that up for anything."

Moloch held his drink up to the light for a moment, studying it. Then he took a sip and bored his eyes into Peterson's. "Well, maybe you should. I mean, a funny thing happens when you start opening doors. If there were three doors in a room, and you knew a lion was crouched behind one of them, would you take a shot on opening those doors?"

The fear started in Peterson's throat, sealing it shut; then it dropped through his esophagus and plunked into his stomach. "I'm not sure what you mean."

Moloch shook his head. "Peterson, we've been at this twenty years now. You know what I mean."

Peterson straightened up. "And you want me to stop opening doors? We're in the business of opening doors. We're fighting a war against a subversive element."

"One of us is. The other one is going his own way."

"Is that right?"

Moloch sipped more of his Grand Marnier and grinned as it burned through him. He leaned closer to Peterson. "That *is* right. We know you've been trying to reach out to the President. And we're telling you now to stop."

How could they know, Peterson thought, clutching his drink. *What do they know...*

"That's funny, I thought the director himself might want to come down from his throne to tell me that," he said. "I didn't think he'd need to send his jester to tell me."

Moloch drank again, a chuckle rolling through him. "You know, it's exactly that attitude that's put you where you are today. A second-rate has-been, eating my dust, showing up to an event where no one knows your name with some spinster from your office."

Peterson slammed the glass, his muscles tensing under his shirt, the blood shooting to his face.

"That's right, overreact," Moloch said. "And throw away what's left of your career. You could still be something, Peterson. The director has told me plenty of times, more than you would ever think—'Peterson could be an asset.' Why fight us?"

Peterson stole a breath. *I'm not twenty-eight, I'm forty-eight. I have to play him.* "Maybe if you told me where I went wrong, I could..." He looked away. "I could avoid that lion behind the door."

"You've been trying to brief the President, without going through the official channels. You've been reaching out to Director Chan. If you ever fed the President raw intelligence about Brigade 910, he might misconstrue things. Act rashly. The director's very concerned about upsetting President Wilkins without giving him the whole picture. We're working on very sensitive operations right now, with this Project Orion attack we're up against. We have to stick to our code."

Peterson looked at Moloch. *What the hell would you know about honoring a code?* But Peterson's eyes waved the white flag. "You know my heart was in the right place," he said. "But I won't reach out to Chan any more."

Moloch surveyed him a moment, then seemed to satisfy himself and smiled. "We need to know if you're going to come along with us in these things we have to do," he said. "With the move we're planning against Brigade 910, things could get rough."

"I'm on America's side. You know that. Not my own."

Moloch clinked his glass against Peterson's. "Good," he said. "I'm sure the director will be very happy to hear it."

They walked back to the table. *We're running out of time*, Peterson thought as more agents pressed Moloch for attention. *The window is closing on Chan... because the man next to me is at the right hand of the man who's going to kill the President of the United States. And he's on to us.*

Peterson left him behind and headed for the table. *Moloch knows, but not everything. Not that I've seen the President, that I've spoken to him—I don't think. I must've slipped them somehow. And however I did it... I have to figure out how to do it again.*

Peterson sat back down. "Where did you two go?" Cynthia asked. "I almost missed you while you were gone, you know. I think you're letting me have too many cocktails tonight."

"I think we're going to need more," Peterson said.

"Oh yeah? Did Moloch say anything that's going to force me to hit him with my famous right jab? Or maybe a swift kick to the groin?"

Peterson threw back some Grand Marnier. "No, he didn't say anything." He paused, and then sighed. Moloch was strolling back to the table. "Not anything worth listening to, anyway."

A few minutes later, they were feasting on dessert. Peterson mashed his cheesecake on his plate. His appetite was gone. *If Moloch knows everything*, he thought as he studied him charming the couples around him, *we might already be too late. I may already have failed.*

But I don't think he knows. He might suspect, but he doesn't know, not yet... There's still hope...

Just then, a thick-shouldered agent marched up behind Moloch and uttered something. Moloch leaned back, his ear meeting the young man's mouth as he bent forward to his boss. Moloch listened for a moment, then nodded. He turned to say something, then turned back to receive an answer in his ear, nodded again, and then waved the agent away.

Moloch addressed the table. "Everyone, please excuse me," he said, rising. "I'm afraid some business has come up tonight." He raised his date's hand to his lips and kissed it. "I'm sorry, sweetheart."

A chorus of the guests at the table entreated him to stay, asked him if everything was all right, if it couldn't wait. It couldn't, Moloch said. If only it could, he could hear the director's speech.

Moloch slapped Peterson on the shoulder. "It was good seeing you tonight, soldier," he said. "So good to see you come back to us."

He bowed to Cynthia, kissed her on the cheek, and after a final nod to the table, strode away. A second agent rushed up to Moloch and draped his coat around him while a third surged to his side.

Peterson glanced up at the balcony again. Just then, the first agent—the one who had caused Moloch to stir from the table—approached Director Bryson from behind, bent towards his shoulder, and said something into his ear. Bryson nodded.

Chapter 35

Alexander Bryson raised his hands to smooth down the applause as he stood at a podium before the Grand Ballroom in the Waldorf-Astoria. "Thank you," he said, the sheen of his black and white tuxedo gleaming in the spotlight. "Thank you so very much."

No, thank you, Peterson thought, his confrontation with Moloch still swirling in his stomach. Cynthia took his hand in both of hers.

"We have gathered in this room tonight some of the bravest men and women our fine country has called on in her time of need," Bryson said, triggering more applause. He tamped it down and continued. "And it is with the greatest honor that I stand before you as the Director of the United States Anti-Subversion Authority. You know, when I joined the Army about forty years ago, no one could have imagined there would be an agency with that name. 'Anti-Subversion Authority.' Back then, it would've sounded like something out of our worst nightmares. Some kind of Orwellian or Stalinist institution censoring everything and holding people in secret prisons."

But it's not? Peterson thought.

"But then again, in those days the worst thing we had to worry about was the Soviet Union, which was already falling apart. Terrorism was just getting started then. And it was something that happened *over there*—you know, the Israelis and the Palestinians, killing each other halfway around the world. September Eleventh hadn't happened yet. And most of the members of Brigade 910 weren't even born yet.

"But the attacks on the World Trade Center and the Pentagon changed our priorities. We woke up and realized that subversive elements, learning their trade in a cave in Afghanistan, were willing to inflict murder and destruction because they resented our role as the bearer of light and liberty to the globe. If someone were to suggest on September twelfth that we form an agency known as the Anti-Subversion Authority, I think we could've done it right then and there.

"But we didn't do it. Oh sure, we passed the Patriot Act, and we created the Department of Homeland Security, and we launched the

War on Terror. But let's be honest with ourselves. We lost our resolve. We wimped out. We got sick of watching our boys and girls come home dead or crippled from Iraq and Afghanistan, and we became guilty at the thought of keeping terrorists—*terrorists*!—in Guantanimo Bay and trying them before military commissions. All of a sudden terrorists had constitutional rights. Nine-Eleven was the past, we kept hearing. Let's get back to normal, the pundits said. I think that if someone had proposed forming the Anti-Subversion Authority back in 2008, he would've heard all of the old criticisms: 'That's insane. That's dictatorship. People have a right to say whatever they want, read whatever they want, gather wherever they want with whomever they want.'

"Well, in 2018 we learned our lesson. That do-whatever-you-want attitude bought us a generation of soulless brats who not only hated their own country, but were willing to resort to mass murder. Five years ago, these murderers put ricin in the water of a small town in Iowa, killing men, women, and children—babies and grandparents—and announced themselves as a group named Brigade 910. We were an evil empire, they said. We were oppressing innocent people around the world with our wars and our capitalism. And at home, Brigade 910 said, we had locked our own people in a nationwide prison, tracking their every move by GPS, collecting their phone records, all without warrants.

"Now we're all in this room tonight decent Americans, law-abiding, even before we got our badges. The attack on the innocents of Iowa was all of our worst nightmares, come to life: A homegrown terrorist group made up of our own young people, educated at our colleges, collaborating with each other in the shadows of the internet, smarter and more sophisticated than any of us ever imagined. We realized too late that they had fallen through every crack in our system, all of the holes left open by our liberal application of the Fourth Amendment, by our refusal to regulate the internet, by our lack of resolve to simply *monitor* people at the first sign of trouble. Almost overnight, this Brigade 910 group had fallen deep into our national arteries and hardened them.

"Brigade 910 began a campaign of murder and propaganda after Iowa. They bombed buses, they bombed trains. But then something incredible happened, something they thought was impossible: The men and women in this room fought back. *We answered the call.*"

The room exploded in applause, and Bryson swept his arm out, first to one wing of the ballroom, then another, hoisting the ovation to an orgiastic ecstasy. Cynthia squeezed Peterson's hand, and then she loosened and began to clap herself. She nodded at him as she applauded. Her eyes said everything, as they had all night. *Blend in, Hunter*, she was saying. *Show them you're with them—for now.*

Peterson applauded, watching the man who planned to kill President Wilkins address a room full of his best thugs on the subject of catching murderers.

"We know now that it's not a dirty thought to hate subversion," Bryson continued. "We know now that disagreement is one thing—look at those fat cats I left behind in Congress—but subversion is another. Subversion is unacceptable. It's like dirty water eating away at a foundation. It threatens all of us.

"Everyone in this room tonight is on the front lines of the most important war in our history. Are we going to be a superpower anymore? Or will we decline? Will we let the terrorists destroy our way of life? Will we surrender to fear?

"We on the front lines know what has to be done, and America is waking up to it now, too. We know that we have to confront subversion wherever we find it, and destroy it. But to do that we need the tools, and at this moment our government still hasn't given them to us. We've got the greatest technology in history waiting at our fingertips, enough to win this war tomorrow, but subversives and sympathizers are scaring citizens from doing what needs to be done, all in the name of so-called 'civil liberties.'

"Well, I've got my own idea about civil liberties, and I share it with all of you and millions of other people. I believe that I have a right to liberty from subversion and terrorism. I have a right to the liberty of knowing that the Anti-Subversion authority has the full power to monitor the population so that they can pull out dangerous criminals, investigate them, and apprehend them. I have a right to the liberty of having faith that my President will sign the law that can make this happen!"

Again the room thundered. Authority agents left their seats and applauded their overlord, and a table of Congressmen and another of Senators followed them. The guests in the room rose to their feet, whooping and cheering, in the name of the Total Information Awareness Act.

"You all know my position on President Wilkins's opposition to the proposed anti-terror law. I've gotten a reputation as being the only high-ranking member of the Executive Branch to criticize the President in public, over and over. And I say to that—I welcome that reputation! In the name of my civil liberties and everyone else's, I welcome the reputation as a troublemaker!

"The Total Information Awareness Act will give us the greatest power to break the back of subversives that the world has ever known. It offers the perfect marriage of technology and security. We can start to pull this Brigade 910 group, and any other terrorist swine we find, out of the population—out of our schools, our office buildings, our airports, wherever we find them—and break their backs.

"The days of sympathizer judges tying our hands in the name of the Constitution are coming to an end. We're writing a new Constitution, here in 2023, one that says that above and beyond everything else, we have a right to be *safe*.

"The days of ivory tower intellectuals telling us we're going too far are coming to an end. It's time to confront these people and call them out as what they really are—wannabe subversives who have been so spineless and weak all their lives that they've come to romanticize terrorists as the resistance against an evil empire. The Total Information Awareness Act will give us the power to identify these enemies of America, who are corrupting youth and molding recruits for Brigade 910 even as speak, and to eradicate their influence.

"The future we are preparing is one of unlimited victory over subversion. We'll end the bombings, the trafficking of chemical weapons and nuclear materials, the financing. But we won't stop there. We'll rip out this terrorist blight by the roots. We'll destroy the subversive element in our society so thoroughly that no one will ever even think of threatening our safety again. If someone hates America, if he sits in his home and collaborates with others who hate America, if he even *thinks* of doing anything to hurt this country—we'll find him!

"The future we are preparing is one of victory, security, and freedom. And when Congress passes the Act, as I predict it will, and President Wilkins drops his opposition to the Act, as I predict he will, we won't have to dream about the future anymore. It will be the glorious present, alive at our fingertips, and all of you in this room will finally have the chance to stand up and do your part to end this conflict!"

Waves of Authority agents jumped to their feet and cheered. The tables of Congressmen and Senators joined the ovation. Photographers crowded the stage and flashed away.

Peterson glanced back. Network and cable news crews were getting their share, cameramen swiveling and zooming in on cue from their producers.

Peterson was no political pundit, but it all seemed obvious now. Bryson had planted the press lapdogs, the Congressmen, everything. This was the latest and grandest stage from which to further embarrass and isolate the President.

Peterson shared a knowing look with Cynthia, then smiled at his tablemates and raised his glass in salute. Of all the things the director said tonight, he had to agree with one:

It was time to end this conflict, all right—before the usurper on that stage succeeded in overthrowing the republic.

Chapter 36

Johnny reached into a cabinet under his kitchen counter and pulled out a bottle of whiskey. This was what his father did when the going got rough sometimes, right? A little whiskey and a lot to think about.

He poured himself a shot. The liquid fell into the glass, bright and brown, a clean shot lapping against the edges of the glass and then settling in.

Johnny held it up. *I know everything now.*

He threw back the shot, swallowed hard, and then groaned as it burned in his chest. *I've got to do something,* he thought, his mind finally throwing down a bridge across the chasm. *I've got to tell the boss, tell him that I know everything now and we can stop them...*

His apartment buzzer screamed.

Johnny perked up, then put the glass down. He was a happening guy, but he'd had exactly one surprise visitor in the last six months—what's-her-name, the girl moving to Phoenix with a douchebag the first week of June.

The buzzer cut through the air again. Johnny crossed the room to the door and laid his finger on the intercom button. It couldn't be her, could it?

He pushed the button. "Who is it?" he asked.

"I got a delivery for you," a voice crackled back. "From Justine Newell."

Two thoughts jostled to slip through one shaft in Johnny's mind, and the first was, *She's so sweet.* But then came the second: *Damn it, I might have ex-girlfriend drama now.*

Johnny pushed the button. "Come up," he said.

He glanced down at the notebook on the couch. Justine sending him something tonight was perfect. Why? Because here she was reaching out to him again, and here he was walking with ghosts, tangled in revenge quests and terror plots. *Oh Justine,* Johnny thought, shaking his head. *Do you really want to know me? You really think you'd want to, if you saw this side of me?*

A moment later, the deliveryman knocked twice. *Maybe it's a bottle of wine. Or a teddy bear. Or a bill for our last date.*

He almost laughed out loud as he grabbed the doorknob, turned it, and began to pull. *Maybe it's a—*

The door blasted open, throwing Johnny back, and the deliveryman rushed in, followed by two others. Then the door slammed. But this wasn't a deliveryman, this wasn't—

Johnny cut off all thought. He slammed a foot into the first man's ankle and kicked out the back of his knee, dropping him.

Johnny clawed halfway back to his feet, all he saw were bodies, he couldn't even make out features—

Something smashed the back of his head, and he collapsed to his knees and hit the floor. He scratched back up and turned just as a club was swooshing down to meet his skull. He deflected it and grabbed the end, struggling for the weapon, then gaining the advantage—

Electric shocks ripped through the back of his shoulder and shot down his body. *Stun gun*, his failing mind mumbled...

"Get him!" a voice yelled. "Come on, put him to sleep!"

Another shock ripped through Johnny, and this time he convulsed. *This is them*, his brain blinked, *this is them—*

A pair of hands laced a rag around his mouth in a vise-grip. Vapors spat into Johnny's throat, first choking him, then clouding him. *This is them, this is them, this is—*

His eyes closed as his brain tried to warn him that he was now deep in the heart of Operation Reichstag.

Chapter 37

Paul's hair flapped in the wind as lightning flashed down from the sky above Yankee Stadium. *Why couldn't it be like this before*, he said. *Why couldn't we spend time like this before?*

There's so much to tell you, Johnny said. *So many reasons I've been away all this time.*

Thunder rumbled through the stadium, and there was another rip of lightning. The players on the field kept playing.

That's not good enough, Paul said. *You always say that.*

Johnny looked around. Black clouds strangled the sky above, and the stadium was empty except for him, his brother, and the players. *They killed Dad*, he said. *They shot him like an animal and made it look like suicide. I wasn't supposed to ever tell you that, but you're old enough now.*

Paul dug into his bag of Cracker Jacks and pulled out a revolver. *Then avenge him, he said.*

They're going to kill me, Paul, Johnny said. *They're going to kill me, and I won't be here to protect you and Mom. Don't go for revenge, you'll get yourself killed, please, please be care—*

Johnny woke up from his dream coughing. But he wasn't waking up from *real* sleep; it was like when he passed out from drinking. He'd just had his eyes closed for—how long was it?

"Give him more," a voice said. "We don't have all night."

A hand held a bottle under Johnny's nose. *Don't do it*, his brain told him. *Don't breathe, don't do anything for them—*

Johnny inhaled, and something noxious shot up his nose. He coughed again.

A man with a .357 in his waistband stood before him and folded his arms.

Johnny thrashed to jump to his feet—nothing. His wrists were bound behind him; just now he could feel the tightness of the manacles, slicing into his skin. His ankles were cuffed to the thick legs of a steel chair.

"The chair's bolted down, Luca," the man said. "A little better than the one you used on our operative in Irvington, no?"

He was in his mid to late thirties, about six feet tall with sandy blond hair and hazel eyes. He wore a white button-down shirt, the sleeves rolled halfway up his forearms, the tails tucked into khaki pants. But his voice—Johnny had heard it before, he knew it. Somewhere...

The man pulled out a cell phone. "I could leave you in here and bring the whole house down on you," he said. "I'd just have to hit a few buttons on this phone, right?"

And then Johnny remembered—the cadence of the voice, how each word had a biting edge of hate, how it had frozen him with fear once before. This was bad, so much worse than the worst he could've thought—

"Sigma," Johnny said.

The man smiled. "You're smart. That's why we've kept an eye on you for a long time."

Johnny scanned the surroundings. He was in a basement; he could tell by the pair of small windows cut into the top of the cinder-block walls on the far side of the room. A layer of dust wafted from the concrete floor throughout, giving the basement a chalky smell. Four men armed with machine guns stood guard at different points around the wide room, hoods swaddling their heads and faces except for their eyes. And in the distance was the only way the fuck out of here—a flight of stairs leading up.

"And we've kept an eye on *you* for a long time," Johnny said.

Sigma chuckled. "That's right. That's right." He plucked the gun from his waistband, and with his other hand he undid his belt and pulled it off. He pressed the gun against Johnny's forehead. "You've probably never felt a gun against you," he said.

Johnny felt his insides collapse. *Hold together*, he thought, but it almost sounded like a voice from somewhere else, whispering in his mind's ear. *Don't fall apart now...*

Sigma dug the barrel deeper into his forehead. "It would be over in three seconds, if I pulled the trigger. You'd feel a ripping through your whole body as everything shut down at once, and then you'd go to hell." He cocked the gun. "Maybe. Or maybe you'd sit here with half your skull blown off, and you'd bleed to death, nice and slow. I've seen both."

In one smooth motion, Sigma lowered the gun, took a step back, and whipped the length of the belt, the buckle smashing Johnny below the right eye. "But I'm leaving you a chance to live tonight," he said. He wound up backhand and smashed Johnny again, this time cracking the other side of his face.

Johnny thrashed, but he couldn't defend himself. Instead the four cuffs broke his skin in four different places. Something felt broken on the right side of his face, and he was already swelling up.

"So tonight we're going to find out if you can play the game, you federal pig," Sigma said, slipping behind Johnny and choking him with the belt. "We'll see how much your life means to you."

He let go, and Johnny gasped. *They killed Dad, I have to remember that, these fuckers killed Dad—*

"Fuck you, asshole," Johnny said.

Sigma pivoted back in front of him, folded his arms, and studied him for a moment. Then he laughed. "I guess we wouldn't be in this room together if you didn't have brass balls. But they won't be brass for long. In fact, they won't be balls for long, either, unless you work with me."

"And how would I do that?"

"That's easy. I've got some questions for you. And if you answer them to my satisfaction, you might live."

Fuck that. "I've got nothing to say to you."

"Oh, but you already have. I've already read over the notebook we found on your couch. And we found another one in your apartment just like it that we'll read over soon. So you're familiar with Operation Reichstag, is that correct?"

Johnny closed his eyes. "That's right."

"I want to know who wrote that."

"Well, I don't really give a shit what you want."

Sigma turned back to one of the hooded underlings and nodded. The henchman, still brandishing a machine gun, walked over behind Johnny. Then he plunged something into his shoulder.

Electric shocks lashed through him again. The man pushed the object harder, deeper into his shoulder, and the agony rolled through him, breaking his nerves apart, shearing his muscles into limp threads...

Sigma held up a hand, and the shocks stopped. Johnny convulsed against the cuffs. He thought he felt vomit barreling up his throat, but it settled back down. He felt his organs smoldering and smoking. "G-g-go to h-hell," he said. He couldn't stop shaking.

"I could have him keep hitting you until you're impotent for the rest of your life," Sigma said. "Or I could go past that. I know how to paralyze you. Or leave you brain damaged. Or in a vegetative state."

"They t-teach you th-that in the CIA?"

"More. And I think you'll experience most of it tonight." Sigma shook his head. "You're a hard man to leverage, you know. I mean, you broke up with that nice Justine girl. You must be a good little worker bee for the Authority, because it seems like you don't have any relationships at all."

Justine. They said they were bringing me something from Justine... they know Justine...

"I don't think we saw you spend time with a friend once, in all the time we watched you," Sigma continued. "But then again, we could go visit your mother in that little garden apartment of hers, or your brother at college. We could even do it right now."

I'll kill you, Johnny thought, the words rising up in his throat, vibrating on his tongue. *I'll fucking kill—*

But I'd just be giving him an empty threat, that second voice inside him said. And *he knows it. Come on, Sigma left the window of opportunity cracked open. Let's see if we can't crawl through it.*

Johnny bit his lip. "What do you want?" he said.

Sigma grinned. "Well, the first thing I wanted was to hear you say that. So we're off to a good start, aren't we?"

Johnny didn't answer. He glared into Sigma's eyes. *If I could just get loose, I'd kill you slow.*

Sigma snapped his fingers, and the guard behind Johnny buzzed his taser to life and shaved the air an inch above his shoulder. Johnny could feel the charge. "Aren't we?" Sigma said again.

He'll feel like he's already broken me if I go along here. Like I'm afraid of that taser. "We are," he said.

Was Johnny afraid of the taser? He thought he could take a few more bolts, if he had to. But he had to control the tempo of this interrogation, at least a little. Or he'd die a fuck of a lot more certainly—and quickly.

"Let's get to know you, Johnny Luca," Sigma said. "What position do you hold with the Authority?"

He knows that already. This is a test, like when they ask you something easy on the poly to see if it goes out of whack. Except if I answer this question wrong, they're gonna shock the shit out of me. "I'm a surveillance technician," he said.

"That's right. You sure are. And have you received any training as an agent?" Sigma's eyes looked past Johnny's shoulder in anticipation.

"I have."

Sigma's eyes fell back to Johnny's, surprised. "Weapons? Fighting techniques?"

"Both."

"How old are you, Luca?"

"I just turned twenty-five."

"A boy." Sigma shook his head. "How could a boy give me so much trouble?" He seemed to enrage himself at the thought, clenching his jaw and shaking his head again. "Do you know where I've been around the world? Do you know what I've done? You've let your boss send you into the lions' den, boy. He's gotten you into real trouble tonight."

I've got to keep playing with this dude. There's got to be some way to pull this off... He glanced over at the stairs.

"That's right, those stairs lead out of here," Sigma said. He grabbed Johnny around the chin, then reared back and slapped him across the face. "But I wouldn't even think about that until you tell me what I want to know."

The slap took root in Johnny's jaw and then exploded across the left side of his face. *God, help me kill this man...*

"Then what do you want to know?"

"How many times did you eavesdrop on my meetings?"

"Just once."

"Wrong answer."

Sigma nodded, and the taser plunged into Johnny's shoulder, blasting the meat on the back of his neck, shooting through his whole body again.

"Give him more!" Sigma yelled. "Teach him to lie to me!"

The guard pushed harder, and Johnny blacked out. *I believe in brain damage*, he thought, awash in a sea of mental gibberish. *I believe you can damage... my... brain...*

Sigma raised his hand, and the wrenching stopped. He shook Johnny. "How many times?"

"One," Johnny said. "I only d-did it one t-time, I f-fucking swear."

Johnny felt himself passed out on a raft, floating in the ocean amidst the wreckage of his mind. Just bobbing along, drifting under the sun with no way of ever getting home…

Sigma smiled, and then the look mutated into loathing. "It's too bad you had to listen in on me. You might not be here now." He gestured to the windows across the room. "You might be out there, sleeping in your little twin bed, thinking about how much you miss Justine." Sigma unsheathed the .357 from his waistband. "Now I want to know who wrote in that notebook about Operation Reichstag."

No fucking way. Shock me, kill me now, but I won't let you kill Dad twice. "Your mother," Johnny said.

Sigma shook his head at the guard, who must have automatically gone in for the kill. "Is this really how you want it to be? Can you be this stupid?"

"My bad. It was your sister, motherfucker."

Sigma bit his lip, and just then, Johnny could tell that he hadn't been defied like this for a really, really long time. *Time for what they call a "limited hang-out."*

"It was Ryan Colgate," Johnny said.

Sigma's eyes widened. "He's been dead for two years," he said. "Just how much do you know—"

"And Andres Ramirez."

The eyes widened further.

"And Anton Jacobs, too."

Sigma got a hold of himself. He took a step back, studied Johnny for a moment, then nodded. "One time, when I was in the Company, someone pushed me too far," he said. "It was over in Pakistan. You know those tribal areas, out in no-man's land? Well, someone pushed me too far once. His tribesmen found him with his back cut open and his legs cut off. And his head was at the entrance to their camp, on a pike."

"Well, guess what, douchebag. We're not in Pakistan."

"No... No, we're not. I can't exactly send your head to Hunter Peterson's office. I could just send you back in a body bag and then decapitate your brother for the hell of it."

This time Johnny lashed out, battling his bindings, but all he did was draw more of his own blood. "Motherfucker!" he yelled. "I swear, I'll fucking kill you, you piece of shit coward!" *Calm down,* that second voice said. *Don't lose control, or he'll beat you, and you'll die...*

"Hit him again!" Sigma yelled. "Don't stop until he's unconscious! We can wake him up and try again!"

The taser tore into Johnny again. He twisted in agony, the handcuffs slicing his extremities. His heart lurched in his chest, falling out of rhythm, out of time. His mind blinked in and out, began to power down...

He saw a flash of one of the guards walking up to Sigma, and Sigma raised his hand. The shocking stopped.

"Sir," the guard said. "Octavian is here. He's coming down to look at the prisoner now."

Johnny's muscles unspooled, and he twisted against the cuffs, unable to control his movements. He felt the hairs on his arms and legs shoot up; his eyes fluttered. *Octavian, I think he just said Octavian...*

If I can just... stop... shaking... He said Octavian... he killed Dad...

Footsteps creaked down the stairs, then crunched on the concrete floor behind Johnny. Johnny was still convulsing.

A figure in a long wool overcoat walked past him, then stood beside Sigma in front of him. Octavian was about six feet tall, just as tall as Sigma, and slim. His jet black hair was tinged with specks of silver, his dark brown eyes fixed in a glare on Johnny.

"So this is the famous Johnny Luca," Octavian said, still glaring.

"Yes, sir," Sigma said.

Octavian turned to his subordinate. "He's shaking. It looks like you've roughed him up pretty good."

"He's been recalcitrant, sir."

Johnny fixed his eyes on Octavian, and he shivered– and this shiver wasn't from the torture. *Holy shit, I've seen him before.*

"Of course he's recalcitrant," Octavian said. "He's one of Peterson's boys."

It was the face. That sallow face, the slight wrinkles, the jet black hair with the silver. A few strands dangled in front of the forehead like a soap opera star. But where, goddamn it, where?

"You've caused the Brigade a lot of trouble," Octavian said. "And tonight you'll have to answer for it."

Johnny tried not to say it, it was suicide, but he might not ever have the chance again—

"You killed my father, you son of a bitch," he said.

Octavian narrowed his eyes and tilted his head for a moment, studying Johnny. Their eyes met, and in that second they understood each other. Octavian seemed to figure out who Johnny's father was, and Johnny figured out who Octavian was.

I know you, I know where I've seen you, but I can't fucking believe it—

Octavian laughed, took a step back, and then threw a roundhouse kick. His shoe bashed into the side of Johnny's face, jolting his body back against his bindings. Johnny's face exploded in pain, and he could already feel blood pouring past his chin.

"That's for thinking your father was someone worth my time," Octavian said.

Purple spots vapored in front of Johnny's eyes. For a moment everything went black. Then he opened his eyes, and his gaze snapped on Octavian again.

Of course he'd seen him before. On the Clocks Striking Thirteen website. One of the Authority agents marked for death... the New York SAIC... Shepherd Moloch.

Shepherd Moloch was Octavian.

"I can see Sigma's been a little rough with you," Moloch said. "Because you've interfered with the revolution."

He opened his coat. For some reason he was wearing a charcoal suit with a blue silk tie. But it was him, goddamn it, Johnny knew the face. The agent in charge of the New York field office was the terrorists' leader... What the fuck?

"Sir, he knows about Colgate," Sigma said. "And Ramirez. And Jacobs."

"Is that so." Moloch nodded. "This kid's the best they've got, you know. He's Peterson's top asset—Peterson just doesn't know it yet." He snapped his fingers at one of the guards. "Bring me a baton."

One of the hooded men walked up to him and handed him a nightstick. Moloch took it in his hands, caressed it, and smiled.

"Luca, would you make me a bet that I could hit you with this all over your body and not make you lose your breath once?"

Johnny's lip quivered. This man killed his father... had him shot in the throat, ripped him away from his two sons... And now he was taunting him. Johnny felt something break inside him.

"I'll fucking kill you!" he screamed. "I'm gonna get out of this and *kill you*, motherfucker! I'll rip your fucking lungs out!"

And then there was that soothing, other voice again: *Calm down, don't waste your breath, be easy, think...*

Moloch laughed. "Let me show you something," he said to Sigma.

He walked up to Johnny. He traced the black baton over his ribcage, his arm, both his legs. "You feel it?" Moloch said. Johnny didn't answer. "You do," he continued. "It's strong. It can really hit." He ran the baton over Johnny's ribcage again. "You're strong, too. I can feel it. You could be trouble if we let you out of this chair. But don't you worry, you won't be getting out."

Moloch swung behind Johnny and drew the baton across his throat. "If I pull just right, I'll crush your voice box. Do you feel it?" He pulled the baton back a bit, and Johnny could feel it resting on his Adam's apple.

"I'll tell you what I can feel," Moloch went on. "I can feel your fear. It's pouring off of you... like pheromones." He inhaled. "I can smell it." He bent close to Johnny's ear and inhaled again. "It gives me one hell of a hard-on," he whispered.

Moloch crossed back in front of Johnny, turned and nodded at Sigma, and then stared back in at Johnny, his brown eyes bleeding hate. He drew back the baton and then whipped it into Johnny's ribcage. He exploded into a frenzy, bashing Johnny's chest, his shoulders, his ribs, the back of his neck. Each blow twisted into Johnny, bursting his skin under his clothes.

"You see?" Moloch said. "I didn't knock the wind out of you

once." Then he smashed Johnny's shin, and as a shock wave pulsed through him, he cracked the baton over his skull.

Johnny saw black again, and then Moloch and Sigma emerged behind another haze of purple. He was a mass of pain and bruises now. He could feel blood pouring off his scalp, from his face, under his shirt.

"Come over here for a second," Moloch said, gesturing to Sigma. "I need to tell you something."

They walked away for a moment. *This is really it. There's no way out. I can't get out of this chair, can't get to those stairs and escape... Can't do anything more than look at the fucker who killed my father...*

Please God, don't let me die being the only one who knows about this... about how the man we're all looking for is *inside* the government...

Moloch and Sigma returned, and now Sigma wore a grave look. Moloch handed him some kind of weapon. "Use this," he said. "He won't be so recalcitrant after you do."

Sigma bowed his head. "I won't let you down, Octavian."

Moloch nodded. "I trust you won't." He turned to Johnny. "I enjoyed our time, Luca. It's just too bad you didn't have more to say."

"I'll have something to say... when I kill you," Johnny said. "When I kill you."

Moloch grinned. "I'll be waiting."

He marched past Johnny, and then again there was crunching of concrete and creaking of wooden steps behind him.

Sigma waited for the steps to fade away. "You've crossed Octavian," he said to Johnny. "You've crossed me. And now you're going to tell me who's been tipping you off about Operation Reichstag."

And just then, Johnny knew. Sigma would never let him out of here; he intended to kill him tonight. It might have even been something Moloch told him in their conference in the corner. But this was it.

"I'm not telling you a goddamn thing," Johnny said.

Sigma nodded. "Well, no one's ever gotten through one of my interrogations without giving me what I wanted. Just you remember that." He paused. "Now I want you to tell me something very important. Were you listening in the night that Anton Jacobs died?"

That's a new one, Johnny thought through his agony. *His master Octavian must've wanted him to ask me that. They may actually need to know this.*

"Loosen up these cuffs, scumbag," he said. "Maybe I'll answer you."

"You're bargaining with something you don't have, Luca. Answer me." He clutched the handgun-looking weapon Moloch had handed him.

"Go fuck yourself." *He won't kill me yet, this can't be it...*

Sigma sighed, then drew Moloch's weapon. Except it wasn't a gun. It was *shaped* like a gun, and it had a trigger, but the barrel tapered off to a kind of satellite-antenna point. It looked like some kind of transmitter.

"Just remember, Luca," Sigma said. "You can stop all this whenever you want." He pointed the weapon and squeezed the trigger.

There was no projectile; no noise. Johnny narrowed his eyes. And then the wave blasted him.

His whole body was on fire. It felt like someone was pouring boiling water on his head and down his face, pressing his hands on gas burners, grinding a block of hot coals into his torso.

Sigma squeezed harder and stepped closer, bursting into laughter.

Johnny was burning, but there were no flames anywhere, no fire, just burning and agony and torture...

Sigma lowered the weapon. "It emits microwaves," he said. "In case you didn't notice, it makes you feel like you're on fire. But here's the beauty—it doesn't kill you. It doesn't even really injure you. The next time I could do it for a full minute. Or five. Or an hour."

"Goddamn you," Johnny cried. He felt consciousness slipping away. "Goddamn you to hell..."

Just then, there was rumbling upstairs, and a series of pops. Sigma raised his eyes, waited a moment, then looked back at Johnny.

He raised the weapon again. "Let's see if we can't get you to stop cursing like that."

An object clanged across the floor, and Sigma lowered his eyes towards it. It exploded in a flash of light and smoke.

Two more objects clanged into the basement and exploded into light that filled the room. Flares and smoke were everywhere.

A figure darted down the steps and popped off a shot; one of the hooded men looked like he went down. The figure then popped off two more shots, and two more guards went down.

"It's a smoker!" Sigma yelled. "Get him, goddamn it! Get him!"

A burst of machine gun fire peeled off. The figure in the haze tumbled to a different point on the floor, then popped off another shot—another guard slumped down. He raced across the floor and fired again, this time at Sigma.

The shot missed. Sigma fumbled for the gun in his waistband as the haze dissipated. The figure raced towards the windows, dodging another machine-gun burst, then drew his weapon and shot the last guard dead.

The last of the smoke thinned away to reveal Julius Fullerton, glock in hand, stalking Sigma.

Right on time, Johnny thought, adrenaline pumping through him now. *Get him, Fullerton, fucking get him...*

Sigma fired; Fullerton rolled out of the way and fired back. The shot tore across Sigma's sleeve, drawing blood, just a graze.

Fullerton raised the gun again, but Sigma raised the microwave device quicker.

He squeezed the trigger, and Fullerton dropped to his knees. "What the fuck!" he screamed, writhing. He dropped the gun.

No, goddamn it, no...

"Agent Viceroy," Sigma said with a sneer. "You survived."

"Fuck... you... Sigma," Fullerton said, forcing himself back to his knees.

"This all ends now. For both of you."

Sigma never saw what Johnny had seen the whole time Fullerton was down. As Sigma clutched at his handgun with his free hand, Fullerton reached into a holster on his hip, his arms trembling. Sigma aimed.

And then Fullerton reared back and hurled a knife through his chest.

Sigma looked down at the blade sticking in him, then fell over.

Fullerton fell back himself.

He pawed his way to his feet and raced over to Sigma, now thrashing on his back, trying to pull out the knife, a long blade at the center of a circle of red on his white shirt. "I owe you this one," Fullerton said.

He shot Sigma in the head, and Sigma stopped thrashing.

Fullerton turned to Johnny. "Yo, we gotta get out of here, straight *quick*."

"Fullerton, how did you—"

"Luca man, I got three dead bodies in my truck right now. That's how."

So that was it, Johnny thought, as his brain started to short-circuit. *They tried to kill us both...*

He was barely conscious when Fullerton blasted apart the handcuff chains. "Come on," he said, helping Johnny up. Johnny slumped in his arms. The muscles in his legs were shredded.

"Can't you walk?" Fullerton said. "Jesus Christ, what the fuck did they do to you—"

"The notebooks..." Johnny said. "Two blue notebooks in here somewhere... they were my father's, please..."

"Luca, we need to get–"

"I saw Octavian... he was here... Moloch was here..."

Johnny passed out.

Chapter 38

This time Johnny awoke of his own volition, in a bed. He couldn't make out the room, couldn't make out shapes; he could only make out the pain.

One body part after another fired off their missives, and the news wasn't good. Johnny felt a lump on the top of his head. His sides and his one shin throbbed. Bruises cracked into both sides of his face and geysered out pain. And he felt the rawness of wrists and ankles shredded by handcuffs.

Johnny couldn't move, couldn't speak, couldn't see—and then he could see, like that figure emerging from the haze in Sigma's basement. Who was that? Where was that?

Fullerton, he remembered. Appearing from the smoke of those flash grenades.

And Fullerton appeared now, this time from behind tides of purple swaying before Johnny's eyes. He was standing at the foot of the bed, a gaze burned into Johnny, his eyebrows twisted tight on his forehead. And standing beside him... Peterson. His gaze matched Fullerton's.

A hand massaged a compress onto Johnny's head. First the bag shocked his scalp with cold, then it started to ease him somehow.

"Dad," Johnny said, blinking away more purple. "Dad..."

"Not Dad," a voice said above him, the owner of the hand on Johnny's head. "Doctor."

"Doctor... Where am I?"

"You're safe," Peterson said, approaching him. "Just lay back. You're safe now."

"But... but... What the hell happened to me?"

Johnny started to remember. The handcuffs lashing his extremities to the bolted-down chair. The belt buckle... the taser... the nightstick on his skull. Wait—the nightstick—who did that?

Sigma was there, Johnny thought, still blinking as he tried to look up at Peterson. *And that other guy.. that other guy... Moloch.*

"Octavian," Johnny said, trying to sit up. Pain ripped through him and yanked him back down. "Octav–"

"Lay down," the doctor said with a nudge. Johnny still couldn't see his face.

"Where are we?"

Johnny could now make out white cinder-block walls and a wooden desk in the corner of the room. Otherwise the room was stripped.

"We're at an army base in Dover," Peterson said. "We're safe."

Not another fucking dream, Johnny thought, grinding his teeth. *In a second Peterson is going to turn into my mom or Dick or something.* "Come on, tell me the truth."

"He is," Fullerton said. "I brought us here. And you've been out for about four hours."

"Everything... tonight..."

"Everything you remember really happened," Peterson said. "Fullerton brought you here on my orders."

"An *army* base?"

"The President gave the commanding officers here orders... to give us a sanctuary."

"The *President*? Sanctuary for what?"

Peterson and Fullerton looked at each other. "There's a lot to tell you."

Then another recollection hit Johnny like a static spark. "The notebooks," he said. "Fullerton, did you bring back those notebooks?"

"I got 'em both, man," Fullerton said. He held them up.

Thank God. Johnny sighed.

Peterson turned to the doctor, still unseen to Johnny. "How is he?"

"They cracked three of his ribs," the doctor said. "But he's a tough kid. It could've been a lot worse."

"Give us a few minutes, please. And thank you, sir."

Peterson and the doctor saluted each other, and the doctor, wearing an officer's uniform, walked out.

Peterson waited for the door to close. "Are you all right?" he asked.

"They got me pretty good," Johnny said.

"What did they do to you?"

"They beat on me with a belt, kicked me in the face, hit me all over with a nightstick... used a taser on me."

"Goddamn it, Luca. Goddamn it."

"And Sigma did something else... He did it to Fullerton, too."

Peterson held up the microwave weapon. "This? I knew this was in development, but I didn't think it was finished yet. God, they're closer than I thought."

"To what?"

Peterson paused. He turned to Fullerton, nodded, then turned back. "How did they get you tonight?"

"One of them posed as a deliveryman," Johnny said. "He said he had a package from my ex-girlfriend."

"He knew her name?"

"He did." Johnny remembered. His last thoughts before the madness started were about Justine.

"You should've known right there," Fullerton said. "You just accept shit from your ex, man? It could've been a bomb!"

Johnny smiled. *Thank God this motherfucker saved my life.* "It was a good breakup, asshole."

"They chloroformed you?" Peterson said.

"They did. They used a rag or something. Next thing I knew, I was handcuffed to a chair, with Sigma in front of me."

"You're positive it was Sigma?"

"I capped him, boss," Fullerton said. "I told you, it was him. I could paint his face in my sleep."

"Sir," Johnny said. "I need to tell you what I saw–"

Peterson put a hand up. "Let's go in ord–"

"No, I need to tell you *now*, in case I drop dead in the next five seconds, *you need to know.*" Johnny's entire body was throbbing as much as ever; dying in the next five seconds wasn't too far-fetched.

"What is it?"

"I know who Octavian is. I met him tonight."

"He was there? *Octavian*? What does he look like?"

"I *know* him, boss. So do you."

"He was mumbling about that before, when I picked him up," Fullerton said. "I told you that."

Peterson narrowed his eyebrows. "Not what he was saying about—"

"It's Moloch," Johnny said. "The New York SAIC. Moloch is Octavian."

"That's impossible."

"It's damn possible. I met him face-to-face. One of the guards told Sigma that Octavian was coming, and the next thing I know, that Moloch dude walks in, and Sigma starts calling him sir. He roundhouse kicked me in the face and beat the shit out of me with the nightstick."

Peterson turned away and ran his hand through his hair. He shook his head. "How... how do you know it was him?"

"I've seen his face on that crazy website before, the Clocks Striking Thirteen, or whatever it is. He's got like black hair, a little gray, brown eyes, a little skinny—"

"What was he wearing?" Peterson advanced on Johnny, almost frenzied. "Do you remember what he was wearing?"

Johnny paused. Did he? He did, but just because it was so weird. "He had a fancy overcoat on. And a gray suit. A blue tie, I think."

"Jesus Christ." Peterson sank into a chair and dropped his head in his hands. "Jesus Christ, he left in the middle of dinner tonight, he didn't give us a reason..."

"Dinner? You were out to dinner with him?"

"It was a special dinner, over in the city, a big Authority event. He was there, and then he left..."

"That must be when he came to see me. He called me 'the famous Johnny Luca.' He's Octavian, sir."

"Luca, if this is true..." Peterson stood up and ran his hands through his hair again. "If this is true..." He heaved a breath. "This changes everything." He gestured palms-down, as if to settle himself. "Johnny, there was an attempt on Fullerton's life tonight."

"What happened to Fullerton?"

"They ran up on me, like they did to you," Fullerton said. "They tried ambushing me as I was driving up to my pad. I shot all three of them and threw them in my truck."

"Did they interrogate you, Luca?" Peterson said.

"They did," Johnny answered. "They wanted to know what I know about Project Orion. Except it's not called Project Orion."

"What do you mean?"

Johnny sighed. *How do I tell them about this one?* "They call it Operation Reichstag."

"That's impossible!" Peterson yelled. He punched his open hand. "That can't be true!"

"What? What do you mean?" *Old man's freaking out*, Johnny thought. "That's what they call it. I'm positive."

"Listen to me. What I'm about to tell you is *top secret*. Is that clear? If you even accidentally repeat it, I will kill you."

If there was a time for jokes, it was over now. Johnny nodded.

Peterson nodded himself. "I've been investigating a plot by rogue elements of the Authority to assassinate the President—named Operation Reichstag."

"That's funny," Johnny said. "I've been investigating a plot by Brigade 910 to assassinate the President—named Operation Reichstag."

"*Investigating*? What do you mean?"

Johnny tried to sit up; pain exploded from all points of his body. He forced himself up enough to sit back against his pillow.

"What I'm about to tell *you* is top-secret," he said. "And if you even accidentally repeat it, I'll kill you."

Peterson arched his eyebrows, then nodded. Fullerton nodded too.

"My father was a detective who investigated Brigade 910 before he died. Those notebooks over there that Fullerton saved for me were his diaries. They murdered him, but they made it look like suicide. Do you understand?"

Peterson and Fullerton nodded again.

"For the last year and half, I thought he shot himself. Then my mother made me read those diaries. Brigade 910 killed him... because somehow he got too close to Project Orion. Except he found out that's not what they call it. They call it Operation Reichstag. He died for that intel."

Peterson and Fullerton nodded yet again, this time with respect for a fallen comrade.

"The funny part is, I didn't read that last part about Operation Reichstag until tonight. But Sigma must've read it while I was knocked out, because when I woke up he started asking me what I know about Operation Reichstag, not Project Orion. He wanted to know who wrote the notebook."

"Did you tell him?" Fullerton asked.

"I didn't tell him anything." Johnny paused. "There's something else I found out tonight. And it's just as important."

"What's that?" Peterson asked.

"The signal. I know the signal."

Peterson's eyes shot up. "What is it?"

"They're going to kill Wilkins," Johnny said. "That's what my dad wrote. That's the signal to start the attack."

Peterson stepped back, shaking his head again.

"If he's right about all this, boss," Fullerton said, "we've got our signal, and we've got Octavian. It's Moloch. I believe it. It makes sense now."

"But how does it make sense?" Johnny said. "He's the Special Agent in Charge in New York, for Christ's sake, he—"

"It makes perfect sense," Peterson said. He punched his open hand. "It makes perfect goddamn sense. He's one of the ones we've been looking at in the plot against the President. It's him."

"But you're talking about an *Authority* plot against the President? A *government* plot against our own President?" Johnny thought back to his father's diary entry. How could it be?

"That's right, a government plot," Peterson said. "Not the government you know, though. A plot by evil bastards in high places who want to kill President Wilkins because he's standing in the way of the Total Information Awareness Act." Peterson laughed to himself, a bitter, broken laugh. "That's why it makes perfect sense that Moloch is Octavian."

What the hell is he talking about, Johnny thought. "What do you mean?'

"*Because*, Luca. Because..." Peterson braced himself for what he was about to say. "Because the Anti-Subversion Authority and Brigade 910 are the same entity. They're on the same side. The terrorists at the bottom and the agents at the bottom think differently, but at the top it's the same goddamn cancer."

"How can that be?" asked Fullerton.

"What I tell the two of you now, comes from the President

himself. Understand?"

Johnny and Fullerton nodded.

"The Authority is designed to be an agency that locks everyone in, not one that sets us free from terrorism," Peterson said. "The terror threat isn't meant to ever go away—it's supposed to be a permanent blank check for the Authority to grow stronger and stronger. The Authority is here to keep all of us in line, forever. And they've been planning it for a long time."

"Who?" Johnny said.

"We call them the 'invisible government.' Bryson's a part of it—the most powerful part we know. And they've been laying the groundwork for years, in ways we never even imagined, for this moment when they take complete control. This is the moment, boys. Operation Reichstag. The Nazis took over Germany with the Reichstag fire. That's where they get the name."

Johnny thought back to his father's diary. He wrote the same exact thing.

"And now you've shown me it's a two-sided coin," Peterson continued. "Brigade 910 is the second side. Come on, Moloch isn't some closet revolutionary moonlighting with a terror group. He's been installed there to coordinate their attacks in a way that maximizes the national panic. Bryson put him there." Peterson snapped his fingers. "Bryson's the real Octavian, boys. He's got to be. He's been running the assassination plot, why wouldn't he be running this, too? You put it all together, Luca. And I have to say—" Peterson picked up a night-table and hurled it across the room—"I feel like a fool for ever believing Brigade 910 was a real terrorist group. Goddamn those sons of bitches. God*damn* them, all the innocent people they've murdered all these years..."

"But why?" Fullerton said, arching his eyebrows at Peterson's rage. "Why would they do this? *Why*?"

"Because they're fascists, Fullerton."

Johnny thought of the girl who'd called him a "proto-fascist sympathizer" on the streets of Manhattan, an hour before she was blown away by a car bomb. "Fascists?" he asked.

Peterson paused. "I don't know how to tell you two this. I don't know how to rip down everything you believe about this country. But

I guess Moloch and Bryson have done that already." He sighed. "Your government isn't a democracy anymore, boys. It hasn't been since the Iowa attack. A secret group of ultra-nationalists—this invisible government, with Bryson as their mouthpiece—has hijacked the country. Why? Because they've decided for three hundred fifty million people that America works better as a fascist state, that if they beat us all down and whip us into shape they can turn us into the mightiest, most glorious, most feared empire in the history of the world. And wielding all their power at every level—in the government, in the media, at the top of corporations—and using Bryson as their frontman, they've almost done it." Peterson ran his hands through his hair, shaking his head. "You ever read the Gettysburg Address, boys? Well, if Bryson and the others pull this off, then Lincoln's worst fear will come true—government of the people, by the people, and for the people will perish. The three of us will be dead or in jail, along with thousands of other Americans, and most of the country will be too terrified by terrorism to question anything that the Authority does."

The world can't work this way. It just can't. "But how much can it be worth to them?" he said. "Aren't they already powerful enough?"

Peterson shook his head. "No. Not to them. You have to understand, there's one central pillar of everything they stand for—*The people must never control their own destiny.* According to fascism, we're too stupid, too weak. The state must be supreme over the individual, must crush the individual. These people believe America is the most powerful empire in the history of the world, and it's their job to keep it strong. They can't let us blow it for them, even if they have to throw the Constitution and democracy into the fire to keep it going." Peterson paused. "You see, it isn't about money for them—it's power. Power is their money. They worship it, like other people worship God."

Johnny slumped down against the pillow; he still ached all over. This was almost too much. If his father had gotten him into some heavy stuff, this was almost so heavy it broke him in half. And yet... Moloch was Octavian. Didn't that say it all? It was like a math equation. Moloch = Octavian. Wasn't that the answer to everything now?

"What's worst of all," Peterson continued, "is that they've discovered terrorism. It was like cavemen discovering fire. The Nazis practiced a little bit of it when they staged the Reichstag fire, but that's nothing compared to the impact that random bombings and hijackings could have on people's psyches. Terrorism shapes minds; that's what terrorists want. And when it falls into the hands of the powerful, it's like comparing a home movie to a Hollywood blockbuster. In the hands of Bryson and these bastards, terrorism is the ultimate symbolism, the ultimate way to get *everyone* to do *everything* they say." Peterson bit his lip. "If Luca here really did see Moloch tonight, they're planning Project Orion. The ultimate terror attack. The American Reichstag fire."

"Nine-Eleven squared," Johnny said.

The three fell silent for a moment, and then Fullerton's eyes widened. "They did Iowa," he said.

The words fell in the room like a grenade with the pin pulled. No one wanted to touch it, but it was there.

Peterson ran his hand through his head again. "They did," he said. "Goddamn them, they did."

"They formed the Authority right after that," Johnny said. "And all of a sudden Brigade 910 was the number one threat."

Peterson nodded. "The Authority is the most important part of all of this," he said. "Because they will be a police force like no one has ever seen in America. They'll be the ones storming houses in the middle of the night, stopping people for their national ID cards, abducting people off the street, beating protesters, listening in on our phone calls, reading our emails. They'll be the ones torturing people—" Peterson nodded at Johnny— "and liquidating them, killing them, by suiciding them, calling in drone strikes, whatever it takes. But the people we know now as cops and federal agents aren't willing to do that kind of stuff. It's unconstitutional, and it's cruel."

"But Authority agents do it now," Fullerton said.

"Because we're starting to see the shadows of what they've been planning. According to the President, the Authority uses a kind of reverse-recruiting. People we'd call miscreants—guys discharged from the military for being crazy, people rejected by police forces for being too violent, even convicted felons—are finding a home in the

Authority. The Nazis did the same exact thing in creating the brownshirts."

Brownshirts. Another word from Johnny's father's diary. "We're the brownshirts," Johnny said. "Us. The Authority."

Peterson nodded. "That's been the plan all along. Except Iowa expanded the labor pool. After most of an entire town was wiped out by a ricin attack, a lot more people were willing to crack subversive skulls. And Operation Reichstag will expand the labor pool exponentially."

"But we all know the Nazis were sick fucks," Fullerton said. "How can there be so many people willing to join up?"

"You did, didn't you?"

Fullerton didn't answer. He just nodded in understanding.

"When they get recruits for the uniformed officers on the streets, they brainwash them," Peterson explained. "They use mind-control drugs on them, they torture them to the point they can't even remember their names—and then they pump a new person into the one they just sucked out. And when this attack happens, and when that goddamn Act passes, that's what we'll have on all our streets. And then it'll be too late."

"But the President," Johnny said. "He's against them? How did someone against them ever become President?"

"Because President Wilkins played them. He kept his true colors close to the vest when he ran in the election. Now they know what he really is. Not only is he against the Act, but he knows that Bryson and the rest of them are the real enemy. That's why they have to kill him before they do anything else. And if we're right in what we've figured out tonight—" Peterson first looked up at Fullerton, then down at Johnny— "then they have to kill him before the Operation Reichstag attack, because he's the only one powerful enough to say they were responsible for it. That's why killing him is the signal."

But they tried to kill us tonight. If they're so powerful, they'll try again. "But how are we going to stop them? How *can* we stop them?"

Peterson smiled, and it was a smile of pride. "There are still patriots loyal to their President who are ready to fight," he said. "The Secret Service is completely loyal. They're on our side."

"Then let's arrest Bryson and Moloch now!" Fullerton said. "We can go get them tonight!"

Peterson touched his shoulder. "I said the same thing. But we can't. Bryson's been manipulating the people, and he's been manipulating the press. If we made a move, *we'd* end up in jail—or dead. We've got to beat him at his own game. That's what the President wants us to do. Beat him at his own game—catch him in the act."

If that's the plan, we're all dead. "How the hell are we going to do *that*?" Johnny said.

"We don't have a choice. We've cracked the signal. If we go after them before they make their move, they'll pull back and come up with a new plan—and a new signal, one we'll never figure out in time. Thousands of people will die, us and the President included. And the United States government will be a dictatorship."

Johnny saw the dread on Fullerton's face, and he felt it fall across his own.

"After Operation Reichstag and the Total Information Awareness Act, Bryson will be unstoppable," Peterson said. "The President, the Secret Service, us—we're the last hope. And we might die for it."

Johnny struggled to sit up. "They killed my father," he said. "And I want revenge."

"Then this is your stage." Peterson paused. "We killed one of their top guys tonight."

Sigma. Rest in peace, asshole.

"About damn time," Fullerton said.

And then Johnny remembered something about their confrontation. "You knew him," he said to Fullerton. "And he knew you. He called you 'Agent Viceroy.'"

Fullerton and Peterson shared a look. "'Viceroy' was my code name when I went undercover in the Brigade 910 cell," he said. "And when I flipped on them, the revolutionary-types named me 'Agent Viceroy,' kind of like the way you'd call a cop a 'pig.'" He shook his head. "That's all I can tell you about that, man. Maybe another time I can tell you more."

"This is the only protection I can offer you," Peterson said. "Here on this army base. They can't get you here. And if they can't find you—they can't use the ones you love to get to you. Remember that."

"Then what's our move?" Johnny said.

"Dig in here and figure out when they plan to launch the attack. That's our move. We've got Octavian, and we've got the signal—now we just need the date. We don't have a lot of time—now that Moloch knows that we know about him. It becomes a game of chicken now—we can't move too soon, or we'll blow the whole investigation, and Moloch knows that as long as we don't know the date, he's still in control. So we have to figure out the date and catch them in the act."

"Well, it'll be sometime between tomorrow and infinity," Fullerton said. "You put Luca and me on it, and we'll crack that shit, even with *those* odds."

Johnny smiled. "Goddamn right we can."

Peterson nodded. "We've got one hint. It won't be until after the President vetoes the Act, which is coming up soon. Once that happens, all hell is going to break loose." He paused, studying his young charges, almost, Johnny thought, like a father. "Listen to me," Peterson said. "All along, I've been playing with your lives. Our office—" He lowered his head— "is full of spies, full of those kinds of agents I described before. All along, you've both been the only hope I've had. And I couldn't even tell you until tonight. It took you both almost getting killed for me to tell you the whole truth. Your blood would've been on my hands. I know I haven't left you with much choice—but you can still turn back now. I can make arrangements—the President would understand. I could move you and your families out west—"

"Boss, I never knew you as one to trifle with damn nonsense," Fullerton said. "So don't start now. This isn't just us. It's our families. It's our country."

"He's right," Johnny said. "My father gave his life. And I'm ready to do the same." *Funny how those words weren't really true until I said them out loud.*

"I have to say," Peterson said, "after tonight, you two really might be unbreakable." He paused. "We're going to need you to be."

We'd better be, Johnny thought.

Then Fullerton gave the thought life: "We'd damn well better be," he said.

Chapter 39

Alexander Bryson approached the sea of votive candles. The candles ascended in staggered shelves, burning as points of light in the dark National Cathedral.

It's almost come to pass, Bryson thought, bowing his head. *The day I've been moving towards for the last twenty years.*

Bryson was the one they called "Octavian," the leader of both Brigade 910 and the Anti-Subversion Authority, the architect of Operation Reichstag. The entire nation rested on his shoulders, and in this most trying hour, he turned to God.

It had been Bryson, since the beginning. He had planned the Iowa attack—of course he had. It was a necessary step to pave the way for the Authority, for law and order, for preservation of the American empire. Every Brigade 910 attack since then, every Authority counter-measure, every pulling of political strings, had been his doing.

Except for Peterson's actions. When Bryson ascended to the position of Authority Director in 2019, he'd had his chief of staff prepare a list of agency figures who wouldn't fall in line going forward. It turned out to be a very short list, and it turned out that most of the troublemakers were easy to contain—a denial of a promotion here, a discovery of an indiscretion there, and there was no more trouble.

But this Peterson was different. He was spotless, he was powerful. His supporters in the government, especially in the Secret Service, were legion, and even worse, he was friends with the President. Bryson suspected early on that Wilkins had planted him in the Authority to foil his plans, but it turned out to be something so much more bare, more dangerous: Peterson fashioned himself a patriot, like Bryson himself did. And he had the one flaw Bryson had hoped to filter out, the flaw that metastasized as Peterson figured out little by little that something in the Authority wasn't quite right—he could think for himself.

In the future Bryson was preparing, *no one* would think for himself. Subversives had threatened the country for far too long, and they had to be crushed for once and for all. But this Peterson, who had slipped so high into the Authority ranks and who had taken direction from Wilkins, was like a dagger pointed straight at the heart of Operation Reichstag.

For the first time, Bryson's men had failed him last night. Peterson's two young agents—even now it made Bryson want to pound the railing and shake the candles from their shelves—had somehow *each* survived liquidation. Now they were nowhere to be found, and Peterson would doubtless be hemming even closer to the protection of Wilkins and Chan than before.

No one understood what was at stake. Not even Moloch understood, past his own lust for blood and power.

Bryson reached into his pocket and pulled out his wallet. He flipped it open and fished out a creased photograph.

He caressed it for a moment, tracing his finger over the image of a pretty brunette woman in her late thirties, smiling alongside a twelve-year-old brown-haired girl. The bespectacled girl smiled back, braces edging out from under her lips.

Twenty-two years ago, Bryson's wife and daughter vaporized into a fireball at the World Trade Center. Lindsey and young Emily were passengers on Flight 11, which exploded into the North Tower at 8:46 a.m.

The Brysons were living in Boston at the time. Lindsey's mother was dying, and she wanted to go to California to be with her at her deathbed. Emily begged her parents to let her go too, so she could see her grandmother for the last time, and eventually they relented. *She should go*, Bryson had told his wife. *She'll always be glad she did.*

Bryson himself booked the flight, to fly out of Logan Airport the morning of September 11, 2001.

He caressed the picture for another moment. *I can't imagine what it must have been like on that plane,* he thought.

Alexander Bryson was thirty-eight when terrorists murdered his wife, his daughter, and a piece of himself. As he looked down at his wife's empty casket at the wake that September, he almost cried. But when he looked down at Emily's, he steeled himself.

I can make it right, he thought that night. *I'm in a position to make it right.*

Bryson was, after all, a special forces officer—"Nightfox," they called him. He'd been tracking al Qaeda for years. And he'd failed his country and his family.

There'd be no more failure, forever. The morning after the funeral, he marched into his superior's office. "I want them all," Bryson told him. "I don't care where you send me, how long you send me there, I want them all."

Bryson got his chance. And over time, the Alexander Bryson of September 10 died, and only hate remained.

Eventually, fed up with the bureaucracy—with the hand-wringing over the treatment of detainees—with the legalese—with all of the goddamn rules—he began to go rogue. Bryson became a man apart, a vigilante, an assassin off the grid.

One day, when he was alone in a secure holding room with a handcuffed, hooded man, Bryson raised his handgun. And without a thought—of his family, or his hate, or anything at all—he shot him in the head. *He lunged at me*, he explained later.

From there, the killing became easier, the excuses smoother. The bodies piled up—dozens that Bryson killed around the world on top-secret "anti-terror" raids.

And when he came home years later, someone reached out to him from the shadows. *I've been following you*, he told Bryson. *I know what happened to your family. And I'm going to give you the chance to make things right, to make things right in this country.*

The man molded Bryson into a leader—the standard-bearer of anti-subversion testifying before congressional committees, arguing on cable news shows. Bryson's star rose. Before long, he was elected to the Senate. And the hate continued to ferment.

When the man asked Bryson to carry into effect his plan to transform America into the security state that it needed to be, Bryson responded by designing Brigade 910 and orchestrating the Iowa attack. He drafted the Anti-Subversion Act, organized the Authority, recruited Moloch to his cause, drew up every attack that Brigade 910 had launched—and wrote the Total Information Awareness Act.

And when Wilkins rose to stand in the way of the Act, Bryson sketched Operation Reichstag to life.

Thousands would die next month. It was of some concern, but, Bryson realized as he looked up at the candles, not much. *Let them all feel what I feel*, he thought. Operation Reichstag would end, for once and for all, the dissent and subversion that had allowed the 9/11 attacks, that had killed his family, that was destroying the fabric of the country, making it soft, making it *weak*. It made no difference if the people wouldn't consent to the surveillance state that Bryson had planned for the country. It wasn't up to them; it was up to *him*.

Next month Operation Reichstag would snap loose the guillotine towards the neck of subversion, and no one—not Wilkins, not Chan, not Peterson—would stop it.

Bryson looked at the photograph of Lindsey and Emily again, and he softened for a moment. If Wilkins would only change his mind…

Then he shook his head and shoved the picture back into his wallet. Bryson lit a candle, then turned and walked away.

Chapter 40

Johnny and Fullerton stood at attention and saluted as a man in an officer's uniform walked into the room.

"I told you, you don't have to do that," the man said.

"And I told you, sir, we'll be happy to salute you as long as you let us stay here," Fullerton said.

"I'm just following orders." The officer, an olive-skinned man in his late thirties with smooth light-brown hair and blue eyes, inclined his head and wiped sweat from his brow. "From the President."

They'd been here for a few days now, and would have to stay, Peterson had explained, until Operation Reichstag either was stopped or came to pass. Johnny was still on the mend. He had three cracked ribs and a deep laceration on his scalp. The medic had feared worse; he'd examined him for nerve damage and a broken jaw.

The first day, Peterson had entrusted him and Fullerton to the care of the man in the room, Colonel Shay Rutherford, the base commander. He'd furnished them with these quarters in a distant corner of the base. They hadn't seen or heard from Peterson since.

"In all my years in the service, I've never seen anything quite like this," Rutherford said. "But you all will be safe here, you can count on that much."

He spoke with a southern drawl, easy and smooth, that made Johnny believe it. Johnny fiddled with his shirt, the starch rustling at his touch.

That first day, Rutherford had brought them perfectly pressed officer's uniforms. *With more to follow,* he'd explained. *It's the only way to blend in here, as long as you all don't mind getting saluted from time to time.*

Johnny and Fullerton had tried to object, but Rutherford wouldn't hear it. *It's the only way,* he said. *You just mind the uniform, that's all. Men give their lives for that right there, the honor of wearing that.* Then he'd paused, screwed up his face, and added: *But you almost already gave your lives.*

"That computer is about to be up and running," Rutherford said, gesturing to a corner of the room. "Agent Peterson is fixing to send you intelligence reports, and he expects you to be reading them and working your damndest on them while you're here. He also expects you both to be working on your weapons training."

"Weapons training?" Fullerton said.

"For the day we deploy." Rutherford paused. "I just can't believe what's happening in this country," he said, shaking his head. "Alexander Bryson is a patriot, not a terrorist."

Peterson had briefed Rutherford on everything, explaining to Johnny and Fullerton that the President had assured him that he was loyal.

"You know Bryson?" Fullerton said.

"Only stories about him. He was a hell of a special ops officer, in his day. They called him 'Nightfox.'" Rutherford wiped more sweat from his brow. "But if he's a traitor, then we'll deal with his treason, I can tell you that."

"We're working on it, sir. Even though we're stuck with an Italian cripple over here."

"I won't be a cripple for long," Johnny said, but then his side singed him. He wondered.

"Well, you'll be safe here," Rutherford said again. "The men and women on this base aren't much into politics. They're loyal."

"Do they... Will they know?" Fullerton said.

"They won't know a thing." Rutherford paused. "Keep an eye out for those reports," he continued. "You've got encrypted email in here. And we can rig up that monitor over there—" he gestured to a flat-screen in the corner of the room—"for video conferencing, once Peterson figures out a secure way to get it done."

"So I guess we just wait," Fullerton said.

"That's right. And I'm sorry if you all get stir-crazy being stuck here, but that's the hand you've been dealt at this point. I can't let you off the base. But if your boss is right about all this, the end is coming soon. The hour is just about upon us."

Johnny and Fullerton looked at each other, that last sentence jarring them both, and then turned back to the colonel and nodded. The end was coming soon, all right, and it would be sudden and violent. People would die. Whether it would be innocent people, or the bastards who had murdered Johnny's father and plotted to kill thousands more, hung in the balance. *We can do this*, Johnny thought. *We have to. We have to.*

Chapter 41

That night, as Fullerton slept, Johnny pored over the desk in the corner of the room, cradling Lizbeth's envelope. *This can't be the last I hear from you*, he thought. He sighed. *But if it is…*

Johnny slipped a finger under the lip of the envelope and sliced it open.

***

December 10, 2019

Dear Gio,

I'm sitting here writing in my room on a Sunday night, watching the snow fall outside. The reason why I'm writing, instead of knocking on your door right now, is because I don't know how to tell you what I have to say.

Last night we were together at the Winter Ball. You were my date, as usual. We pregamed together, as usual. We acted silly together, we danced together. And then you took me out to that tree, with the snow falling around us.

It wasn't until that moment that I understood how it felt to have everything I ever wanted out of life, all at once. It wasn't being dressed up, or being with my friends, or having an amazing time at the ball. It was you, Gio. I looked into your eyes, smiling at me as the snow fell on us, and I realized that I'm in love with you.

You see, most of the time, I'm just plain old boring me, playing video games, watching old movies, and writing for the stupid newspaper. But when I'm with you, I can just feel the change in the room. I'm not plain and boring. I'm special.

So here's my little letter. I don't know if I'll ever give it to you. I don't know if I'll ever almost-kiss you again. But here, on this paper, in my head, in my heart, until I get the guts to tell you to your face, is the truth:

I love you, Gio, all the way down to my soul.

If you ever do read this letter, and we're not together yet, then (a) you've been a real ass all these years for not realizing how I feel about you, and (b) come sweep me off my feet, sweetheart. I'm pretty sure you're my soulmate, and I'm pretty sure I'm yours. It's a forever kind of thing.

Until then, I promise you, darling—wherever you go—wherever you rise—wherever you fall—I'll be there. You could fall through a bottomless pit, and I'd be there waiting for you. I promise.

Love always,

Lizbeth

***

I don't know if I'll live to see you again, sweetheart, Johnny thought, head lowered. *But if I do… I'll sweep you off your feet. I promise.*

Chapter 42

President Reed Wilkins sat at the desk in the Oval Office, thumbing through some papers. *Presidential papers*, he thought absently. He wondered if other Presidents, so far along into their terms, still stopped themselves from time to time to take in that they were sitting in the *Oval Office. This is where I work.*

Behind the President were three tall windows—the windows that Kennedy had stood before, head lowered, agonizing over the Cuban missile crisis as dusk rolled in. Straight ahead, at the north end of the room, was the fireplace, with two high-backed chairs upholstered in gold posted before it—the chairs where Americans saw him pose with foreign heads of state. To the right was the east door, which led out to the Rose Garden, and to the left was the west door, which led to the study. A twist of the oval, past the west door but before the fireplace, was the northwest door, which led to the West Wing. And a twist of the oval the other way, past the east door, was the northeast door, which opened to the secretary's office.

It's been like this for a long time, Wilkins thought. Long, but not too long, just since 1909—and since then, evolving and adapting. One thing he'd learned as President was that there was nothing so old in the Oval Office that it would be offended by change, yet there were some old things so worthy of veneration that no President would ever change them. That was the beauty of serving as Chief Executive of a young, strong republic—the benefit of knowing what worked, and the freedom to discard what didn't.

That was the story of this Oval Office: built in 1909, burned by fire in 1929, redesigned once more and tinkered with ever since. Some things in the room were strong and immutable, like the doors topped with substantial pediment hoods, the bookcases set into niches, the deep bracketed crown molding, the ceiling medallion of the presidential seal, the portrait of Washington above the fireplace. Others were left to each President's discretion, like the gold oval carpet Wilkins had picked out, with the seal threaded into the middle, gold drapery at the windows behind him to match. Simple and elegant, oval and baroque, regal—not for himself, but for the ones who had come before him, and for the country that had raised him up.

Wilkins surveyed his office, the people's office. *I want to stay here*, he thought. *I want to stay here until I'm asked to leave, or I serve out my time. Just like how I want to die peacefully in bed—not at the point of a gun.*

It wasn't much to ask for. There was still the people's work to be done, and there was still living to be done. He had two beautiful, gifted children—Garrett, who'd be starting at Yale Law in the fall, and Gabrielle, pursuing a master's in international relations at Princeton. And his wife—God, Delilah.

So it wasn't too craven a thought, he supposed, to want to leave the White House in peace and to die in peace. But he knew it wasn't his choice. Soon he'd have to make his stand in history—and it could mean death. And if it had to be death... He'd die for this. Maybe his enemies hadn't yet understood him—he'd die for this, if he had to.

Wilkins lowered his head. Sometimes his hands shook; but they were still today. That's what passed for a good day in the presidency of Reed Wilkins, lately.

"Mr. President," a woman's voice called from his right. "Mr. President..."

Wilkins looked up. It was Ms. Timmins, his secretary, a white woman just as old as he. "Yes, Sally?"

"It's Director Bryson. He's arrived without an appointment, and he's waiting in the West Wing. He says he's here to see you."

Wilkins set his jaw. *So the hyena comes to meet the lion in his pride.* "Send him in."

Ms. Timmons frowned. "I'm sorry. I don't know what's gotten into him, disturbing you like this. I'll tell his staff that this is completely unacceptable."

Wilkins smiled. It was nice, in this small way, to see someone so fiercely loyal. "That's quite all right, Sally," he said. "Let's see what Mr. Bryson's business is."

The President sat back, and a pit opened in his stomach. He'd been nervous when he asked out Delilah for the first time; when he entered his first combat zone, in Kuwait; when he took the bar exam; when he'd spoken at the national convention; and he was nervous now.

He could hear pleasantries outside the northwest door, to his left.

Authority agents stood post there, now—not Secret Service. "Good afternoon, sir," Wilkins heard one heard one of them say.

The door creaked open, and there he was, the Director of the United States Anti-Subversion Authority, his gray eyes fixed on Wilkins.

The President rose. "Mr. Director," he said. He gestured to a chair in front of the desk. "Please, sit down."

Bryson nodded. "Thank you, Mr. President."

The two sat, Wilkins behind the desk, Bryson in front. "So what brings you here today?" the President said.

Bryson stared at him. "The business of the Total Information Awareness Act."

But of course. "What about it?"

"Well, the vote is only a few days away. And I expect it to pass."

"So do I."

Bryson sharpened his glare. "I also expect you to sign it."

Wilkins arched his eyebrows. "Is that right?"

"That's right, Mr. President. Because a lot of important people are counting on that bill becoming law, people who feel you owe them something."

"That's funny, because I was under the impression I don't owe anyone a goddamn thing."

Surprise and anger cut across Bryson's face. "A mistaken impression," he said. "And now is the wrong time for mistakes."

"Then drop your support for the bill. Because that's the real mistake here."

"The *real* mistake, actually, is a sitting President who would condemn his own people to death by refusing to provide them the safety they deserve."

"Oh, take off the mask," Wilkins said. "We're face-to-face now, so why don't you take off the mask?"

Bryson stiffened up, and there was that look again—surprise and anger, salted with hate. "And what would I say if I were to take off the mask?"

"You'd say that the Total Information Awareness Act is your tool to swindle everyone into a permanent prison of technology and surveillance. It's your way to destroy dissent and take control of everyone's lives, forever—to teach everyone to live under the boot of a master with a gun. It's a writ for the government to make war on its own people."

Bryson studied Wilkins for a moment, almost as if looking at a zoo exhibit. *No one has said anything like that to him in a long, long time*, Wilkins thought.

"Mr. President," Bryson said, "even you would admit that this country is in crisis right now."

"The crisis is of your own making, Bryson. You've created the panic."

Easy there. He doesn't know that I know about him and Brigade 910. He doesn't know about the coded message I received by courier a few days before. ATTEMPT ON MY AGENTS' LIVES, it read when decoded. TALK TO C. –H.P.

And Chan had told the President the rest, about the attempted murder of Peterson's young agents, how Moloch was Octavian and Bryson was a higher Octavian, how Operation Reichstag wasn't just a plot to kill Wilkins, it was a plot by Bryson to rend the curtain of democracy in two through calculated mass murder.

Things were so very much worse than Wilkins ever thought, and the tragedy was at hand. And here sat the devil himself, across from him in the Oval Office, demanding one last time that the President capitulate.

"The crisis is real," Bryson said. "And you'd be a fool to ignore it."

Wilkins burned a gaze into Bryson's eyes, delivering two laser-guided brown missiles into twin lakes of ice gray. "Believe me, I haven't."

"Then you have to understand that you court danger every day you oppose this law."

"Danger to whom?"

"Danger to the American people, Mr. President. In ways you don't even understand."

Oh, but now I do. "How's that?"

"Because you're making some kind of stand for freedom, when the only freedom that matters is freedom from attack by your enemies. That's what we want to provide. And you're standing in our way."

"It's what the Constitution tells me to do."

"You don't get it, do you?" Bryson shook his head, and for a moment his look of anger and hatred gave way to something unexpected—empathy, actual empathy. "The world is full of dangers you don't comprehend. All you ever did for the Army was lob shells at defenseless Iraqis in that toy-soldier war in ninety-one. I was in special ops. Have you ever interviewed an al Qaeda terrorist who swore to Allah he'd incinerate New York City with a suitcase nuclear weapon, if he had the chance? Well, I have. How about someone planning to hijack a plane and crash it into a building? Or buying packs full of powder he thought was weapons-grade anthrax? Who's going to stop people like this, you?"

I am. By stopping you. "We're bound to stay within the law. You swore the same oath as me. As soon as we cross the boundaries, we become something we're not. Something like the terrorists. *Principles of law, once bent, do not snap back easily.* Justice Oliver Wendell Holmes."

"We don't plan for them to ever snap back. Surely you must know that by now. The War on Terror will never end, no matter what we tell the people. You may call that dishonesty, but I call that saving people's lives. The firefighters and policemen buried under the rubble at the World Trade Center would have appreciated it. What we need is a paradigm shift, and you're going to deliver it for us. A permanent shift away from this wishy-washy liberty you think you're fighting for, towards a future of never-ending security."

"The security won't be never-ending," Wilkins said. "But what we stand to lose—*that* will be permanent. The things you want us to throw away are going to be gone forever, just to buy us a few more degrees of security. What happens when the next terrorist finds a way through what you're planning? Tanks rolling through the streets?"

"Whatever it takes," Bryson said.

"*No. Not* whatever it takes. Some things are sacred. Maybe not to you or whoever you're mouth-piecing for, but they are to me and millions of people living here. You're trying to get me to whiteout the Bill of Rights from the Constitution, which is like ripping out someone's brain and expecting him to live. It's a lobotomy—and it won't work. Even if you do pass this law, you won't be able to stop people from rising up to take their freedom back."

"There'll be no uprising. Look what we've gotten them to accept already! We both know two shooters killed Kennedy, don't we? There were never any protests in the streets for him. We gave al Qaeda billions of dollars so they could fight the Soviets, and later so they could fight the Serbs. The Supreme Court has held the police can search your bags with a drug-sniffing dog, track your location by cell phone GPS, and even *fly a helicopter over your home,* all without invading your privacy. When did the people find out the NSA was storing all of their phone records, seventeen, eighteen years ago? No protests then. You, the President, have the power to detain people as terror suspects, hold them without charge, send them to a gulag, and have them executed by a military tribunal—or if you don't feel like detaining them, you can blow them away in a drone strike. You could have protested all of this. But you went to work in a big law firm after you graduated law school, and lived in a big, comfortable house, didn't you? Did you protest? Did anyone else?"

He's pulling back the mask now, Wilkins thought. *Finally, who he is, what he stands for, what he wants to do—*

"I think the American people will take our little law just fine," Bryson said. He sneered at Wilkins. "There's nothing left. Everything has been stripped away, little by little. What you see as some sort of sudden coup is really just the final little step in a slow little progression."

Wilkins felt Bryson battering him, wearing him down, winning. "Then why is half the country against you?" he asked.

Bryson smiled. "Shouldn't you be asking yourself why it's only half?"

Wilkins felt the strength shoot back in. "Because you've manipulated everyone. Because you've terrified them all into thinking you're the only one who can save them from Brigade 910, that your tactics are the only way to save their lives. That they *need* this bill, even if they don't want it."

"If anyone doesn't want this bill, it's because *you've* manipulated them. Because *you've* filled their heads with ideas about freedom that haven't existed since a time when people picked up their muskets and peeled off shots at the Redcoats. But you won't stop me. You're too late. More congressmen believe the Authority is their friend than those who don't. That's enough."

"Not without my signature, it's not."

"But I'll have your signature, Wilkins."

"You'll address me as *Mr. President*, you treasonous son of a bitch," Wilkins said, blood rushing to his face. "Because *I am* your President, until I'm not. Now get the hell out of this office, or I'll have you removed."

Bryson grinned. "By whom? The Authority agents outside that door, who answer to me? The ones around the perimeter of the White House, who call me sir? Or the ones who set up sniper positions around your motorcades?"

I'll kill you. I'll see you tried for treason and I'll execute you myself.

Bryson took hold of a picture frame at the corner of the President's desk and turned it towards himself. "The First Family," he said. He stroked the glass for a moment. "This is the height of American beauty, Mr. President. Truly the best stock our nation has to offer."

Bryson jabbed the picture frame into the corner of the desk, cracking the glass, and ground it into the wood. Then he flung it to the floor.

"Wait for tonight, *Mr. President*," Bryson said. "Wait for a special report on the news. You'll know my power then."

The Director of the Anti-Subversion Authority rose, nodded with a smile, and marched out the northwest door.

Later that evening, the news broke. A car bomb had exploded in Chicago, ripping through a downtown street. Brigade 910 claimed responsibility: "Tonight, we struck at one of the many black hearts of the criminal regime in Washington. We will not stop until the victory of truth and liberty is complete."

The news commentators pounced. "In case anyone was stupid enough to forget, we're in a war here," one said. "If the President vetoes that law, Congress should impeach him and a grand jury should indict him as an accessory to murder," another said.

And in the West Wing, as advisors flocked to the President to receive his orders, Wilkins thought back to Bryson smashing the picture frame. *He's pulled off the mask all the way. There can be no mistake between us now.*

He looked at his best friend, Attorney General Sharpe. "Maybe it's time to sign the law," Sharpe said, when the others had left. "I think it's the only choice we have."

I can't tell him, how could I ever begin to make him understand...

It's up to me to kill the monster behind that mask.

Chapter 43

On Wednesday, April 28, 2023, the Total Information Awareness Act came up for a vote in the United States House of Representatives. It had already passed in the Senate.

There were histrionics and perorations on both sides, exhortations to defend the Constitution to the death, clarion calls to destroy the forces of terror for once and for all. Capital police and Authority officers ejected protesters from the gallery several times during the floor debate. Hundreds of others crowded in front of the Capitol outside, dammed back by concrete barricades and Authority officers brandishing machine guns.

Thousands more flooded the National Mall, a human sea ebbing around both sides of the Reflecting Pool, swinging placards and chanting on the same ground on which crowds had huddled to hear Martin Luther King, Jr. tell the nation he had a dream. People clashed, with screams, with fists, with feet. Authority officers sliced through the throngs with bomb-sniffing dogs, tasers, and batons, beating subversives and arresting them, firing paintballs at troublemakers to track those who slipped the perimeter. Helicopters buzzed the sky above.

Set up at select points around the Mall was a battery of elite Authority counter-assault agents, ready to level the protesters to their knees with tear gas and clubs if the crowd got too out of hand.

"Nothing less than our national fiber is at stake," Representative Rivera said on the floor of the House that day. "We can sign away our money, but we can't sign away our freedom. We can't sign away our honor. We can't sign away that which is inalienable."

"If we don't halt Brigade 910 here, while we have the capability, we will continue to bury our dead," Representative Davis said. "If we allow the terrorists to inflict so much fear on our people that we become paralyzed, they will succeed in destroying America's greatness and in making us a nation of dependents, weak in the eyes of the world and vulnerable to outside attack."

"We are the freest nation in history," Representative D'Onofrio said. "Even if we've done things in the past to make other nations question our commitment to that ideal, I'd like to think that victims of oppressive regimes still look to us as the light of the world. Let's not extinguish that light. Let's not lose their faith. Let's continue to show the world that we can live free and still prosper."

"The enemy is no longer at the door, he's in the living room," Representative Chalmers said. "He's in the college classroom, he's in the church pew, he's on the internet, reaching out to our children. We've wrung our hands at this problem and gone through this charade for long enough. We're past the point of trying to extend our constitutional freedoms to terrorists and murderers. I defy anyone in this chamber to tell one of the loved ones of a victim of the Chicago attack—of the New York attack—of the Iowa attack, and all the other attacks—that he or she supports freedom for terrorists. We all love freedom, and we all hate war. But there's no other way. We have to take the fight to Brigade 910 and root out every subversive element in our society. Only the terrorists themselves have something to fear from this act. Our innocent constituents can go on with their lives as if no law had been passed at all."

"The right of the people to be secure in their persons, houses, papers, and effects," Representative McDonnell said, "against unreasonable searches and seizures, shall not be violated, and no warrants shall issue, but upon probable cause, supported by oath or affirmation, and particularly describing the place to be searched, and the persons or things to be seized. James Madison and the American people, 1789."

Eventually, the Speaker of the House closed the debate and called for order. The Representatives dug in to vote, and the spectators and crush of media fell to a hush to watch.

That afternoon, congressmen voted for freedom; they voted for security; they voted because they were from districts that resented federal authority; districts that cried out for national security; districts that demanded civil rights; districts that had been victimized by terror attacks; districts that were liberal, conservative, libertarian, blue collar, professional, poor, wealthy, middle class.

On April 28, 2023, the roll was called, and the United States House of Representatives voted on the Total Information Awareness Act. And by a vote of 219-216, it passed.

The official, enrolled bill reached the President's desk shortly thereafter, the same day. He stared down at the bill.

He'd gotten word that protests had erupted on the National Mall, but he was sure Bryson had already taken care of that, as well as any protests that had broken out anywhere else. *I can't help the ones getting beaten and arrested right now*, Wilkins thought. *I can't help them all, I can't save everyone...*

But he could, for the future. He could give the people their republic back, if they could keep it.

Wilkins sighed in agony, still staring at the parchment. *If I do what I'm about to do, I could be signing my own death warrant, and the death warrant for thousands of people.*

He trembled. *Lord, help me...*

The President's veto that day was quick, and his veto message curt: "As President, I have sworn an oath never to sign unconstitutional legislation. I find the bill which the Congress has passed to be offensive under the First, Second, Fourth, Fifth, Sixth, and Eighth Amendments to the United States Constitution."

And there was a second message which the President sent out to the press that day:

"I have signed an Executive Order relieving Mr. Alexander Bryson of his duties as Director of the United States Anti-Subversion Authority. In the same Order, I have appointed Mr. Hunter Peterson as the new Acting Director."

Chapter 44

Hunter Peterson led a troop of U.S. Marshals down H Street to Authority Headquarters so that he could assume office as director, the international media in tow. "Mr. Peterson!" correspondents shouted, jostling against the marshals to get close to him. "Mr. Peterson! What are your comments on this development? How do you respond to the perception that you are forcing out the best man for the job in a time of national crisis? Can you comment on charges you are completely unqualified to hold this position? Mr. Peter—"

Wilkins hadn't even alerted him. Peterson had huddled in his office, waiting for word that the President had vetoed the Act. And then there it was—a red bar shot across the top of the TV screen, screaming "Breaking News: Wilkins Vetoes Total Information Awareness Act, Ousts Bryson as Authority Director." That alone had been enough to trigger goosebumps. A moment later, Cynthia ran in: "Hunter, my God, why didn't you tell me?"

A crush of media had swarmed around him as he left the federal building that first night. Before Peterson could utter a "no comment," a motorcade had pulled up and whisked him away.

Late that night, he was with Wilkins in the Oval Office. *Just do everything I say,* the President told him. *Everything that happens from this point on, I can see it coming a mile away. Bryson can't surprise me.*

So here Peterson was, leading practically an entire field office of U.S. Marshals dispatched to enforce the President's order, international media demanding attention. And when Peterson and his entourage reached headquarters, they were confronted by a ring of Authority agents brandishing machine guns.

Peterson stepped ahead of his pack. "Stand down," he said to the agents blocking the door.

An agent clad in body armor and a riot helmet stepped forward. "Agent Peterson," he said, glowering behind his visor. "We have a federal court order barring you from the premises." He handed Peterson a piece of paper.

"Temporary Restraining Order," it read. Peterson scanned the rest—the agent was right. The order prohibited him from entering the premises and from assuming office as director in any way. The caption of the suit? *Bryson v. Wilkins*, naming Peterson, Attorney General Sharpe, and other officials as additional defendants.

So Peterson stood there, before the eyes of the world, a detachment of federal agents behind him standing opposed to another detachment of federal agents. And then he remembered the President's words: *Everything that happens from this point on, I can see it coming a mile away.* Bryson can't surprise me.

Peterson nodded and turned around. The media erupted into more questions, and then something flattened them into silence.

"Agent Peterson," a familiar voice called behind him.

Peterson turned around to face Bryson. "That's *Director* Peterson," he said.

Bryson smiled at the reporters, then at Peterson. "I'm afraid you're mistaken, Agent Peterson."

Peterson felt the moment mounting, carrying him up, and he realized why the President had sent him here. The words flowed through him: "You're disobeying a direct order of the President, Mr. Bryson."

"The President is disobeying the Anti-Subversion Act, which says that the President can only remove me for cause." Bryson rolled his eyes, and the reporters laughed. "I'm sorry, all you marshals, that the President put you in this position."

Peterson paused, and again he felt instinct taking over. *Don't let it go any farther.* He turned around to the marshals and nodded. "Let's go," he said.

The reporters split into two camps, one besieging Peterson, the other staying behind with Bryson. Peterson walked in silence towards the White House.

Chapter 45

Later that afternoon, Peterson was sitting across from Wilkins in the Oval Office. "So was that part of your plan?" he said, grinning.

"All of it," Wilkins said. "He's right about the Act. I can't terminate him, unless I can show legal cause, which I can't, even though he's trying to kill me. And you'll never get in that office—he'll get a preliminary injunction in the next few days."

"So what are you going to do?"

"Argue that the Act is unconstitutional because it limits my powers as the President. The Supreme Court'll take the case plenty quick. And I'll lose."

Please tell me this isn't the plan. "Then what can we accomplish with all this?"

"Well, your argument with Bryson on live television just saved you from any unfortunate accidents which might have befallen you otherwise. And I think I can say the same for Chan and your two young agents."

Genius.

"But that's not the only thing," Wilkins said. "There's something else. Something even bigger than that."

"What?"

Wilkins leaned closer. "I found a way to beat Bryson at his own game."

"How?"

"By bugging *him*. Chan's IT experts found a way to backdoor into the Authority headquarters computer system." Wilkins smiled. "When I dismissed Bryson, I shook up their operations. Let's see what they do now."

"You think we can recover any intelligence?"

"I'm sure of it. Bryson can't be running Operation Reichstag out of his basement. He needs ultra security, which he can only get in that fortress on H Street, using what he thinks is a secure computer system. He needs building blueprints, flight plans, reconnaissance reports—and details about every move I'll be making in the next few weeks."

"Weeks?"

"It's down to weeks, Hunter. The Supreme Court's going to get that case soon. And Congress is about to set a date to vote to override my veto. They don't have enough votes to override—not even close. So sometime between the Supreme Court decision and the override vote, I'll be assassinated." Wilkins set his jaw. "It's the only way. The Court will give Bryson his power back, and then the Operation Reichstag attack will happen. Thousands of people will die, including me. And then with the entire nation completely terrified, Congress will vote to override the veto."

They've scared him so much, they've made him fearless. He's running on animal instinct now—and he's winning. "You've turned the tide, sir," Peterson said.

"We can't afford to lose," Wilkins said. "Saving my life is one thing. Saving the lives of all those people—that's another. *We can't afford to lose,* Hunter."

"I understand, Mr. President."

"Good. You should go back to New Jersey—I'm going to take a ton of heat from the pundits for looking weak by trying to appoint you, but I'll worry about that. Reestablish contact with your young agents and get them ready. In the coming weeks, you and Colonel Rutherford will be responsible for briefing and training the Operation Reichstag counter-assault force. We'll be concentrating our men and women on that base you've got your agents on."

"When can I expect this force?"

"Very soon. Bryson's very strong, Hunter. We're still trying to figure out who's loyal, who's disloyal, who's been lied to, who's been blackmailed into spying for him. But there are still heroes in this country, patriots who are ready to lay their lives on the line for this thing. We're assembling them now, and soon they'll be under your command." Wilkins ran his hand through his hair. "But for now, go back home and wait for my orders—we've set up a secure video-conferencing line in your home and rigged the place with such strong anti-bugging technology that you can expect to get cancer next week."

"My *home*?"

Wilkins laughed—the first time Peterson had seen that in years. "We're quick. When you're racing the devil—you've got to be quick. Get on the first train back home. You'll have round-the-clock Secret

Service protection, with your detail posing as Authority agents. And you'll have something even better than that at keeping you safe—I've made you a celebrity. Go on like you did today whenever the reporters come up to you. Maybe when all this is over, Delilah'll see you on the cover of *Us Weekly*."

Wilkins laughed again, and Peterson joined him. They were both terrified, Peterson was sure. But maybe now they were so afraid and so desperate, Bryson had knocked a screw loose. It was making them stronger, giving them a second sight, helping them lock in on their target...

Chapter 46

Things went just as Wilkins had prophesied.

Byte by byte, Chan and his team harvested the Operation Reichstag plan from the Authority computer system. There were target cities in every region: New York, Boston, Philadelphia, Washington, Atlanta, Miami, Chicago, Detroit, Houston, Denver, Las Vegas, Los Angeles, and San Francisco.

From the files and documents, Wilkins, Chan, and Peterson were able to draw up a skeleton of the false-flag attack—but just a skeleton. For one thing, they didn't know who the President's assassin was. They could only hypothesize that it would be a drugged-out lone-gunman type who fired the shot, with support from an Authority agent—maybe logistical, maybe a second shot.

And second, the files often alluded to "other theaters" and "other flashpoints" in the Operation Reichstag attack. So even though Wilkins had issued the order to hit all the suspects the morning of the attack, there were potentially dozens of other attacks which the good guys wouldn't discover in time.

As Detective Giovanni Luca, Sr. observed in his diary—and as Peterson had observed in examining the diary after Johnny had handed it over—the assassination meant everything to the attack. Bryson was serious about holding off until a bullet ripped through the President's skull. Then the mass murder would begin.

So, the President and his men concluded, their only chance was to prevent the assassination. That would drive the unknown attackers underground to await further orders—orders which would never come. The counter-assault force would round up all of the *known* attackers and interrogate the hell of them, while Wilkins, alive and kicking and suddenly the brave survivor of an assassination attempt, would expose Bryson before three hundred fifty million people and destroy the surveillance state superstructure.

There was some hope. Deep in Bryson's files, they found a weakness, a bottleneck in the plans. It seemed that Bryson had drawn things up so that Moloch would be the one who delivered the signal that day. The assassin or assassins would kill Wilkins, and then an Authority meta-agent on scene would relay the news to Moloch.

Moloch, posing as Octavian, would then transmit the signal to Brigade 910 and other Authority meta-agents embedded in their terror network.

So stopping Moloch that day would have to be part of the plan. Because if Moloch succeeded in transmitting the signal, there would be no United States of America left.

The first attack planned after the assassination of the President was the detonation of a dirty bomb on 34th Street in New York. In another attack, a terrorist was to shoot down a passenger jet over the city with a shoulder-fired missile, and in another, a backpack bomb would destroy a subway line.

Down the Atlantic coast, car bombs would explode at the National Mall, the State Department, and IMF world headquarters, and another two bombs would explode in the DC Metro. A Brigade 910 terrorist—particularly identified in the files as a complete triumph of mind control experiments—would open fire with a machine gun on Pennsylvania Avenue until he was shot dead.

Simultaneously, across the Mississippi, two truck bombs would level the Sears Tower. Shooters would open fire at the airports in San Francisco, Atlanta, Houston, and Denver. The terrorists would then unleash biological attacks in Miami, Philadelphia, and Los Angeles, and a sarin gas attack on the Las Vegas strip.

And there were other attacks planned, unknown to Wilkins and his men, but alluded to in the files. Attacks on soft targets, more planes shot down, perhaps other biological and chemical attacks. In some cases the terrorists would use hired couriers who wouldn't even know what they were carrying and dropping off, in other cases they'd use ultra-nationalist Authority agents who'd cut their teeth fomenting civil wars in third-world countries, in others they'd simply use zealous terrorist maniacs or more of their army of mind-control victims.

Bryson's casualty estimate for the day: ten thousand killed.

The President also proved prophetic on the case of *Bryson v. Wilkins*. The district court ordered a preliminary injunction against Wilkins's order dismissing Bryson, then reached the merits of the matter on an expedited schedule and permanently enjoined the President from dismissing Bryson. The Court of Appeals for the D.C. Circuit took the case and quickly decided that the President lacked authority under the Anti-Subversion Act to dismiss Bryson without good cause.

The Supreme Court promptly issued a writ of certiorari to review the matter, and ordered the case argued and briefed on an expedited schedule. Most Court observers expected a decision by the third week of May.

Meanwhile, the Senate had set aside the last week of May to debate overriding the President's veto of the Total Information Awareness Act, and had set June 2 as the day it would vote.

So that was the assassination window—between the third week of May, which began May 17, and June 2.

Wilkins had planned to split most of that time between the White House and Camp David. He, Chan, and Peterson deduced—in a huge gamble, but a smart gamble— that they wouldn't dare kill him at one of those impregnable sites, because it would destroy the imagery of the lone gunman-wacko taking a potshot at the President. It would have to be at one of the three speaking engagements the President had planned outside of Washington for that seventeen-day span.

The engagements were planned for Dallas, St. Louis, and New York. Bryson had the respective motorcade route maps, blueprints of the respective visit sites, and even the names of the Secret Service agents who were to support the Authority detail on each visit.

And late one May night at Camp David, President Wilkins, Director Chan, and SAIC Peterson decided that Wilkins would cancel the Dallas and St. Louis visits. That left New York, into which Peterson could easily move the counter-assault force stationed in New Jersey. Chan would stay behind to defend Washington, and other counter-assault units, consisting of FBI, Secret Service, ATF, and Marshals, would defend the other sites.

On May 18, the Supreme Court decided for Director Bryson in *Wilkins v. Bryson*, by a 5-4 vote, just as Wilkins had predicted. The court held that the Anti-Subversion Act plainly provided that the President could not terminate the director of the Authority without good cause, and that the statute did not unconstitutionally limit the President's powers.

Bryson's official statement was brief: "Today the Supreme Court has resolved a constitutional crisis which the President had unfortunately precipitated himself. With this dispute behind us, I can get back to my work of defending the nation from terror, free from the influence of Washington politics."

It was small comfort, but cold comfort, that everything had gone as Wilkins had foreseen it. It was he who had proposed breaking into the Authority computer system, he who had thought to fire Bryson in order to prick him into making a mistake, he who had predicted the outcome of the legal and congressional wrangling, he who had figured out that they'd only kill him between the Supreme Court decision and the override vote, and in public.

Bryson's fatal mistake—if Wilkins got out of this alive, and if they stopped Operation Reichstag, and if Wilkins would indeed eventually see him executed for treason—would be that he took the President to be a grunt who had served in a "toy-soldier war." Wilkins had served as an officer in the United States Army during the Gulf War under President Bush I, and just now, when he needed it most, he discovered he was so much more brilliant a tactician than he ever thought he was. His commanding officers had given him the carriage of a soldier, the fiber of a President, and the tactical mind of a five-star. This hour—if Wilkins' counter-assault force prevailed in crippling Bryson's forces—would be as much theirs as it would his.

Lying next to Delilah the night of the Supreme Court decision, Wilkins trembled. He wanted to believe Heaven was real, and that maybe God would be merciful enough to admit him there—but how could there be a Heaven, he wondered, if he couldn't lie next to Delilah and watch her sleep there?

That morning, when he arose, he steeled his resolve. In the heart of his terror, there was clarity. Operation Reichstag would begin in New York City on May 27, 2023.

Chapter 47

On May 22, Johnny and Fullerton were out on the shooting range at the base. They had adjusted to the seclusion, and used their time analyzing Bryson's intercepted documents, sharpening their firearms and combat skills, and working out. Johnny was now fully recovered from Sigma's torture.

"You ain't gonna top *that* performance," Fullerton said, gesturing to a target fifty yards away which he'd riddled with bullet holes throughout the legs and mid-section.

Johnny cocked his MP-5 and dug its buttstock into his shoulder. Knees bent a bit, leaning forward, he clutched the underside of the barrel with his left hand and wrapped his right finger around the frame of the trigger. He then tilted his right cheek down towards the rear sight and lasered a look through the front sight. The target swam, then locked into view. Johnny squeezed the trigger and pumped a round through the target's leg.

"Hit the stomach," Fullerton said.

Johnny edged up the weapon and laced a round through the stomach.

"Hit him in the head," Fullerton called. "Shoot to kill."

Johnny edged up again, and in a nanosecond the head locked into view in the back sight. He blasted a hole through the middle of the forehead.

"Burst," Fullerton said.

Johnny turned a switch near the trigger clockwise, picked up the target, and sprayed the target with three rounds, a recoil forcing the weapon up a bit.

This submachine gun was a part of his body now, an extension of his arms. It felt so light and slender when he cradled it, and so true when he fired it. He was a marksman like his father before him, and in five days he knew he'd be drawing on that skill to save the world.

Peterson had told them everything by video conference. Operation Reichstag, he'd explained, was to deploy on May 27. The President would be giving an award to some crime victims' advocate at a luncheon in New York, and that was where an assassin would attempt to kill him. Johnny and Fullerton would be part of the counter-assault force dispatched to thwart Bryson.

It was only six months ago that Johnny had chased that Authority vehicle into the night, he remembered as he popped off more rounds at Fullerton's direction. Six months ago that he was a surveillance technician... washing cars for the bosses... a boy who didn't know anything about his father, his agency, or his country.

Johnny emptied the magazine. He looked off to his left and noticed another pair of shooters on the range. Like he and Fullerton, they didn't quite fit in here; he'd noticed more and more of these types on the base lately. Peterson told him to expect it in the run-up to Operation Reichstag.

"Tell me about your father," Fullerton said.

Johnny turned around. "What?"

"Your father, man. What was he like?"

I don't think anyone's asked me that since he died. "He was a cop... a detective. Real patriotic type."

"You were close?"

Johnny looked downrange. "Closer than you can imagine."

Fullerton patted him on the shoulder. "I'm sorry about what they did to him, man. I know you've got to be tired of hearing that. But I'm sorry."

"It's all right." Johnny turned back to him. "Or maybe it isn't all right yet. But it will be. In five days."

Fullerton nodded, then he looked away himself. "I can't believe this shit, man. I can't believe how far we allowed this to get." He shook his head. "This motherfucker Bryson is going to kill ten thousand people. Holy *shit*."

"We never knew. It's all been lies. Since Iowa. All lies, from the beginning."

"You're slacking with that firearms training," a familiar voice called.

They turned around to face Peterson.

"Boss," Fullerton said.

"How are we looking out here?" Peterson said.

"How did you get here?" Johnny said. "Last I saw, the media was following you around everywhere."

"I left the federal building in a Secret Service motorcade. The drivers split up and diverted the press." Peterson surveyed Johnny, weapon in hand. He turned to Fullerton. "Can the kid shoot?"

Fullerton smiled. "Luca, show the boss your move."

Johnny didn't have to think. He turned around, locked onto the target fifty yards downrange, and blasted rounds right through the heart.

"Good shot," Peterson said. "Good shot, Agent Luca." He paused, studying his two young proteges with a grave look. "Listen to me, both of you. I've decided to make you part of the team I'm sending in to save the President's life." He paused again. "You've both got the training," he continued. "And hell, you've seen more action than most agents. You're both almost perfect shots. And you've been with this since the beginning, so maybe you've got a sixth sense for it now. I'll get you blueprints and layouts of the place, and I'll have you training on this base with more of our guys for this op." Peterson's face hardened. "I need you to pick out the assassin in this big room and take him down. I need you to spot him before he shoots. I can get you the Authority creds to get in, and I can get you suits to look like protective detail guys—but only you can spot the shooter. Whoever he is, the Authority is going to let hide his weapon somewhere in the place, and seat him somewhere where he can get off the shot. Free your minds when you're in there. That's all I can say. You'll have other guys with you, looking for the killer along with you. But my money's on you two, because you're young, because your minds can expand when something new is thrown at you. *Free your minds in there*, and you can do this."

"Where will you be?" Johnny asked.

Peterson smiled. "Arresting Shepherd Moloch in his office in the World Trade Center."

Johnny and Fullerton looked at each other, and Johnny knew they were thinking the same thing. *Let's get them, let's do this now, we can beat these motherfuckers*—but then it was Fullerton who filled the silence, just as he had all along:

"We're gonna get you that brass ring, boss. Ain't that right, Agent Luca?"

Johnny nodded. "You can count on us, sir."

Chapter 48

The day of May 25, Johnny sat in a briefing room full of Secret Service, FBI, ATF, and Marshals. Over the last several days, they'd all gotten acquainted with each other, this New York counter-assault force which Peterson and Rutherford had cobbled together. All of the men and women in the room were there on the recommendation of Chan and the President.

They were all older than Johnny and Fullerton, and had all launched counter-terrorism and contraband raids. They were here first because they were damn good, and second because Peterson, Chan, or Wilkins could vouch for their loyalty.

As Peterson and Rutherford explained in their briefing, the force would be divided into six units. First, agents of the Secret Service Counter-Assault Team would waylay the New York Authority agents assigned to work the presidential visit site that morning and incapacitate them, clearing the way for other Secret Service agents to arrive at the site and pose as Authority protective agents. Peterson and Chan had devised the strategy after poring over Authority internal memoranda and divining a weakness in the plans—Authority agents were still very green at organizing protective assignments for presidential visits, and most of Wilkins's DC-based Authority detail didn't know the New York agents who'd be hosting them. Once in place, the Secret Service team on site would facilitate the entry of the good guys.

The second unit consisted of ATF, who would sweep Thirty-Fourth Street in Manhattan, apprehend the dirty bomber and his accomplices, secure the bomb, and defuse it. The third unit, comprised of ATF and FBI, would thwart the subway attack. ATF and FBI also made up the fourth unit, which would halt the terrorist who was to shoot down a plane from an obscure point along the Hudson River. The fifth unit, made up of Marshals, would support Peterson as he effected a full custodial arrest of Shepherd Moloch at the New York field office.

And the sixth, comprised of Secret Service and two young Authority agents, would save the President of the United States.

Johnny could feel older eyes assessing him and Fullerton with incredulity when Peterson explained they'd be part of the presidential team. It was Rutherford who read their looks and called them on it: "I just want you all to know these boys are two of the best we've got going on this operation. I've seen 'em train myself. They belong."

And that was all that needed to be said. The incredulity hardened into nods.

"I wish we had more intel for the sixth unit than the goddamn layout of the room," Peterson said as the plasma monitor beamed a picture of the ballroom where the President would be presenting the award. "But we don't. It's a clean slate. The second shooter could be Authority or he could be civilian. But you can be sure that somewhere in that room will be the patsy, the one they'll want everyone to believe was the only assassin. *Key in on the patsy.* Without him, the assassination is impossible." Peterson pressed his remote, and the perspective of the picture twisted and zoomed in on a balcony. "We believe this balcony," he said, "will be sealed off by the President's Authority detail for the event, and if we try to unseal it, we'll create massive suspicion. This is the most likely point of origin for any second shot, and maybe even the first, if we stop the patsy shooter. It will be impregnable as long as it's controlled by Wilkins's detail, even with the Authority credentials we've given you. The next best thing is to man a post under the balcony. Agent Troy, that's where I want you to be. You get your pick of three more to stand post at different points along the floor in front of the balcony. If any of you see the sniper, shoot him, and shoot to kill." Peterson tapped the remote again, and stretched the picture into a long view from the back of the room, with a graphic representing the President's podium in the background. "Everyone else will be split into two squads. Agent Garcia, choose up a squad that will be combing the room for other possible Authority snipers. And again, I want you to shoot to kill, because they will be. Agent Wolfe, round up a squad that will be looking for the civilian shooter. And I want Fullerton and Luca on that team."

"Yes, sir," said Wolfe, a thick-shouldered, middle-aged black man.

Johnny set his jaw. *This really is it. The final hour.*

"Members of this squad, expect to take a bullet. Expect to dive on the President, knock him over, do whatever it takes. It may mean your life, because you have the most important job of all. And again, I wish I could provide you with intel, but I can't. I've got nothing. It could be anyone. And that's no help." Peterson pointed to his head.

Free your minds.

"Free your minds," Peterson said. "You'll be tense, you'll barely be able to breathe, but free your minds. Let your eyes be the transmitters, and your brain the receiver. Point A to Point B. If someone doesn't look right to you—if he's one degree unhinged, if his eye is one percent shifty, if he swallows a little too hard or fiddles a little too much—he's probably the one we're looking for. Don't be afraid to look at him. If he's got the mental profile we think he has, he could break and get rash. Force him into a mistake. And then, be quick. He might be quick himself; but *you can be quicker.* You're elite. If you find this bastard, and you're quicker than him, and Troy and Garcia's squads contain the professionals, we've got them. And we'll all be back here smoking stogies Thursday night and making plans to visit Moloch and Bryson in the can. And we can all kiss our spouses and hug our kids again."

Peterson powered down the hologram, and the lights came up. "We'll stop Operation Reichstag in its tracks," he said. "I spoke to the President earlier, and he has every confidence in you all. He wants you to realize that this is our moment. This is Lexington and Concord, Saratoga, Midway. This is it. We know now that elements of our own government have been plotting to inflict terror on our own people. We were fooled by their lies, we all were. But we're not too late. In forty hours we'll show them we're not too late. We'll show them that freedom still rings."

Chapter 49

Steven Cadbury stared at the message on the computer screen:

"Tomorrow is zero hour."

It was 7:00 PM, May 26. The thirty-eight-year-old Anti-Subversion Authority agent was working late tonight in the Chicago field office, though poring over intercepted electronic communications between terrorists wasn't exactly a nine-to-five job. He ran a hand through his thinning brown hair, pushed up his glasses on his nose, picked at the Authority emblem on his navy blue polo shirt.

"Tomorrow is zero hour."

This was really it, wasn't it? Brigade 910 hadn't said anything like that before, in all this time.

Cadbury knew exactly what it meant. Here, at the end, he knew it all too well.

Over the last year and a half, he'd tracked the development of something the terrorists called "Project Orion." In the intelligence reports he prepared for his superiors, the plot went from terrorist pipe dream to credible blueprint to active planning. Somewhere along the way it kicked into operational stage.

But, Cadbury's superiors told him, it couldn't be real. It was too ambitious, too much of an overreach for the relatively nascent terror group. It was so ambitious, in fact, that it would require abetment by a well-placed government insider. And Brigade 910 had no presence in the government.

But that wasn't good enough for Cadbury. Because the intelligence told him otherwise, time and again. Brigade 910 was cultivating new cells, training operatives, and procuring all kinds of weapons. And the plot continued to radiate out to new cities, in every region.

Cadbury wouldn't let the matter lie, and he urged it upon his superiors again. In time, they went from dismissing his reports to warning him. "Just lay off it," his boss told him. "That comes from the top."

"The top," of course, was the Washington chieftains. Someone had handed down the edict from on high, and such edicts were unwritten law in the offices and cubicles of the Authority.

Steven Cadbury was a good man. He was a faithful husband and a good father. He went to church, paid all his taxes, and gave to charities. And when his supervisor gave an order, he followed it.

So even as he watched Project Orion mushroom into the most devastating terror plot in American history, he held his tongue. The higher-ups were taking care of it, after all. That's why it had been squashed from the top. Some high-ranking official wanted to parade Brigade 910 suspects in front of the cameras at a press conference after their arrest, to make some political hay. Typical government turf war.

Except the squashing never came. Project Orion thrived, took deeper root, snaked out in more directions. There were specific cities and specific modes of attack outlined. And finally, there was chatter that the attack would happen in the spring, probably sometime in May.

For Cadbury, the U.S. map was a mass of throbbing red lights dotting several cities throughout the country, with each light promising hundreds or thousands of casualties. Someone had to stop this thing.

But it couldn't be him. What could he do? Who was Steven Cadbury, but a teacup in the middle of the sea? There was no one he could tell, no one he could rally to his side.

Tonight, the night of May 26, as Cadbury stared in at the monitor, he realized it was all over. That mental map full of throbbing red lights was about to explode in a hail of dirty bombs, shoulder-fired missiles, and chemical attacks. The cavalry wasn't coming.

He thought back to his supervisor's first impression of Project Orion: It was impossible to pull off without the assistance of a well-placed government insider. Hmm.

Thousands and thousands and thousands of people... in one day... horrible, painful, violent deaths... what have I done, what have I done...

Tomorrow was zero hour. And now nothing could stop it.

Shepherd Moloch arched back in his leather chair, massaged his temple for a moment, then checked his watch. Seven-thirty P.M.,

May 26. He laughed.

The field office was empty now, and all the lights were out. Here in Moloch's office on the ninetieth floor of One World Trade Center, sunlight tumbled through two windows, one near where he sat, the other at the far end of the room. The shades were drawn on all the others, cloaking most of the room in darkness.

Moloch held up a two-way phone and studied it for a moment. Shortly before noon tomorrow, word would crackle through that the President had been fatally shot. Then he would click the phone and send the word:

"Brigadier One, commence Operation Reichstag."

Those five words would cascade from sea to shining sea, leveling America in between. It would be a bloodletting. Thousands would die in order to cleanse the nation of subversion forever. What did the masses know, what did they know, of government's lonely and austere offices?

Moloch knew. He would never forget how Bryson had explained it all to him, slowly at first, then in a final, orgasmic burst. *We've chosen you for an important mission*, he'd said. *A long time ago, we chose you. And now this is the hour.*

As Bryson had explained the reality about Brigade 910 and what he had planned, Moloch didn't feel outrage. Instead he felt privilege. Privilege that he had reached the inner circle of the highest council of government, that the power brokers considered him a good enough soldier that they had fingered him for their plans.

Tonight, as Moloch lounged back in the chair, all the work was done. In sixteen hours they'd stage the greatest act of this long play. His heart pounded, not at the mass death that act would occasion, but at the thought that their grand op was so near deployment.

And behind that, a more naked craving powered his heartbeat–the nearness of so much power, *unlimited power.*

Moloch laughed again, then held up the phone to his lips without clicking it.

"Brigadier One," he said to the empty room. "Commence Operation Reichstag."

Miranda Ramirez cradled a white rose as she sat at her kitchen table.

"Mama, what is it?" Diego, her oldest, asked.

"It's nothing, baby. Go watch some TV. Bedtime is in fifteen minutes, and I *mean* it."

The eight-year-old skulked off at the mention of bedtime. Anna looked up at the wall. It was 8:45 now.

She looked down at the white rose again, and panic rolled through her. Who was doing this? Why? She'd gotten one of these two-and-a-half years ago, right after... Andres died. Just like tonight, there had been no name on the delivery.

It had scared her so much then, so soon after her husband's accident. But concluding the sender really intended the flower as a token of his mourning and had just neglected to include his name, she forgot about it.

In the time since, a suspicion sometimes gnawed at her by night. Andres didn't die in an accident, she'd think to herself as she lay awake in bed. They killed him, someone killed him, I can *feel* it. I love him so much... Then she'd cry herself to sleep. Come morning, she was back to working two jobs and taking care of the children, until the next time the suspicion gnawed at her.

Tonight a second white rose had come. But this time she wasn't afraid, she realized as she caressed it.

It was something in the way it looked, in the way its cool petals rested on her skin. It wasn't meant to scare her, it was meant to soothe her. It was good and pure and safe. The man at the other end of this flower—it just *felt* like a man—was watching over her. And he wanted justice as she did.

But why today, she wondered. Why send it today?

Then Miranda chased the thought away. This was all craziness. Maybe she should go to the police and file a stalking complaint.

Instead she resolved to hustle Diego to bed, check on Analisa, her three-year-old, one more time, and try and sleep herself. *Someone knows. That's what this white rose means, that's the only thing it could mean—*

Tonight, when the terror came, she'd feel safe.

President Wilkins held his wife's hand up to his lips and kissed it.

"What was that for?" Delilah asked.

"Do I need a reason?" Wilkins said. "I love you, baby. That's all. You've got to let me run my game on you *sometimes*."

Delilah laughed. "I didn't know you *had* game."

They were in the White House residence, sitting on a couch together, a dormant fireplace on the far side of the room. Two Authority agents were posted outside the room, as usual. *She loves to sit by the fire during Christmastime. Please Lord, let me see another Christmas with her—*

But the worst thing to do now was to love his life on earth more than the life the Lord had breathed into him. Bryson couldn't take that life from him.

Wilkins looked at the First Lady. But I need you to spare me, Lord. *So I can love this woman and our children, protect them…*

And strike down Alexander Bryson.

Here, at the end, he could almost let go of his life. His mother had raised him up well enough to have faith that he'd be saved if he believed. But he *had* to survive tomorrow, because his country needed him.

Wilkins gazed at his wife. Her skin was a dark cream, her cheekbones as fine and delicate as an angel's sculpture, her brown eyes softened with a gaze of pure love.

Got to be strong, can't let her see that I'm so afraid.

"Tell me about our B & B again," he said, taking her hand.

The night he proposed, they'd mapped out the their life together and dreamed that it would end with them running a bed and breakfast in the country, anywhere from Florida to Alaska, as long as they were together. Since then, it had become code between them, a way of saying, *I'm stressed, baby, please help me forget my troubles...*

Delilah smiled, her eyes a little worried now. "I think I see us in Montana, boo," she said.

"Montana!" Wilkins laughed. "The only black folks in Montana!"

"We're the only ones in this White House, aren't we?" Delilah smiled again. "All the people are going to come from far and wide to see us, the only President and First Lady to ever open a bed and breakfast and receive all the citizens of the country, whenever they want to see us. We'll fix them flapjacks and grits... and I'll tell our guests the story about the time I had to holler at you for leaving the toilet seat up in the White House."

Wilkins laughed again. "I told you about repeating that story!"

Delilah laughed along, but then she stopped and looked into his eyes. "Everything going okay, baby?" She rubbed his arm.

"Just a little stress with that bill, that's all. Nothing we can't handle, right?"

Delilah rubbed his arm again. "Every President has his troubles, you know that. And in my opinion, you've handled them with grace. Strong and steady."

Wilkins smiled, and tried not to let a tear slip loose. *If she only knew what that meant to me.*

All he wanted was to tell her everything. But he couldn't, not her, or Sharpe, or the kids. Tomorrow he would, if there was a tomorrow.

"Strong and steady, eh?" he said. "Big words from such a pretty girl. I have to say, I'm flattered."

Delilah smiled again. "You should be. I had a couple of other suitors, you know. My mother always told me, 'Lay off that Reed, he ain't going nowheres.'"

"You should've listened. You might've been living in a nicer place."

Delilah laughed. "We're going to get through everything just fine, you'll see. Our son is going to be the best lawyer in the country, and our daughter is going to be Secretary of State someday, and you and I—"

"We'll be in Montana. Fixing those flapjacks."

"That's right. You just remember that."

I will. Tomorrow... I'll think of nothing else.

The hour approached. In his pocket was a pill that would lull him to eight hours of peaceful sleep. And then he'd wake up early tomorrow morning, dress, kiss Delilah goodbye, and wake the kids like he used to when they were little, just to tell them he was going. After that he'd stroll out to his motorcade, leave for New York, and meet his destiny.

Wilkins thought of the militiamen on the Lexington green that April afternoon in 1775, staring down seven hundred of the finest imperial troops on earth. *Disperse, you rebels!* redcoat Major John Pitcairn yelled at them. *Damn you, throw down your arms and disperse!*

And still they stared, clutching their muskets, in that moment resolving that they'd rather die than live under an empire.

Stand your ground, Captain John Parker told them that day. *Don't fire unless fired upon, but if they mean to have a war, let it begin here.*

They mean to have a war, Wilkins thought. *And I'm going to give it to them.*

He thought of George Washington's reflections when he heard about Lexington and Concord, the words of the first President beaming out to the sitting President across the centuries:

The once-happy and peaceful plains of America are either to be drenched in blood or inhabited by slaves. Sad alternative! But can a virtuous man hesitate in his choice?

No, Wilkins thought. *And I don't hesitate in mine. Tomorrow, we'll stand our ground before an empire one more time.*

May the right prevail.

Hunter Peterson sat up in bed, awash in a sea of black. It was 10:00 PM on the eve of Operation Reichstag, and he was thinking of his father.

Hank Peterson was on President Kennedy's detail as his motorcade wound through Dealey Plaza in Dallas on November 22, 1963. He left the Secret Service soon after, and never spoke of his time on the inside. Young Hunter could approach Hank about anything—football, girls, school—but not that. Until the end.

"That was the most false-flag bullshit that ever was," his father told him, when he was dying of pancreatic cancer. "The whole thing was a goddamn frame-up, ordered by all those bastards on the inside."

Hank didn't have much else to say. Nothing about who would run such a black op, and why– because he really didn't know. But he knew enough to figure out that the Warren Commission flat-out lied when it declared there had only been one shooter, and that if there was one crack in the foundation, the whole building had to come down.

Peterson stared up at the ceiling. *Tricia, can you see me now? Please, honey, stand by my side tomorrow, I need you...*

The pill he had ingested began to cradle him to sleep. His muscles eased loose, his bones sank into the cool sheet.

Hunter Peterson wasn't huddled in the basement poring over a flow chart in the dark anymore. He was the leader of the main counter-assault force deployed to defend his country from its worst attack ever. Tomorrow he'd thwart Bryson and deliver justice to Moloch... or die trying.

Here, at the end, he accepted that. He would die trying, if he had to.

We'll get them, Dad, he thought, as the blackness cascaded through his eyes and brushed them shut.

Brittany Owen blinked away a tear as she gazed at her computer screen at 10:45 p.m, the night of May 26. The monitor flashed a slideshow of images of her and her best friend, Suzie, in various locales—drinking in Suzie's dorm room; splashing on the beach; holding up lighters at a concert.

Suzie had been killed in a terrorist attack five months ago. One minute she was volunteering at a "Freedom Now!" stand in Manhattan, urging passersby to protest the Total Information Awareness Act, and the next a car bomb blew her up beyond recognition.

Brittany wiped another tear from her cheek. *It's so hard down here, Susu,* she thought as a picture of the two at Yankee Stadium shimmered onscreen. *So hard here on earth without you.*

Brittany was nineteen years old. Red streaked through her blonde hair, in honor of Suzie. Three piercings poked through each ear, and another twinkled on her eyebrow. She still couldn't understand it, how her best friend could have been murdered like that. Suzie had stood out on the freezing street that night, just trying to help people. And then… gone.

All because of those terrorist assholes. She caught herself; she and Suzie both knew that the real world wasn't an action movie, divided into terrorists and heroes. *But goddamn it. They killed her, they never even gave her a chance…*

Brittany was a typical college student. She drank a lot; smoked pot sometimes; resented authority; and was passionate about politics. She'd been to other countries—not just rich European countries, but places like Eritrea and Vietnam. She'd stared into the wrinkled face of suffering, marveled at the clenched fists of hunger.

And thus it only made sense that Brittany loathed the Anti-Subversion Authority. The world *wasn't* terrorists vs. heroes; it was the oppressed vs. tyranny, a knock-down, drag-out fight to the finish between the downtrodden and men with guns. The Authority was the enemy, an agent of the power-elites, designed especially to beat and arrest people Brittany's age to keep them in line.

But since Suzie's killing, she'd begun to rethink that. She had to admit, sometimes a warm feeling kindled in her chest when she saw the Authority hauling in another terror suspect. Take *that*, she'd think.

A growing part of Brittany liked the idea of a government boot stomping across a subversive's face. It was time to leave behind the stupid idealism of protesting the Total Information Awareness Act. After all, her best friend was *killed.*

What had Suzie protested the Act for? To be killed by a terrorist? And Brittany had protested along with her—for what? For this agony she felt now, this emptiness, this hate?

Brittany sighed and clicked off the pictures. The world just felt so miserable sometimes, so hopeless.

She chided herself for the times she'd admired the Authority agents on television. *I don't want to take the Authority's side. I don't want to sell out. I don't want to turn into a cookie-cutter security mom who worships every poser tough guy who comes along and pretends he can keep us safe if we just give him more power.*

Brittany sighed again. But where were the real heroes anymore? Was there anyone left who could make a stand?

She turned off the lights and turned over the same thought in bed. *I don't know anymore,* Brittany thought as she wrapped herself in her blanket. *I just don't know.*

Johnny sat on his bed, his head in his hands.

"You take the pill yet?" Fullerton said, strolling in from his bathroom wearing white longjohns.

"No, man," Johnny said, laughing at the longjohns.

"Oh, you think this is funny? You probably got Spiderman drawers on now or some shit."

"Spiderman drawers would be manlier that what you got on,

sucka!"

"There's nothing manly about you, Luca. I've come to that conclusion. But I'm cool with that. I always wanted a partner with an alternate lifestyle. I'm all about diversity, man."

At least one of us is loose tonight. "Then I feel sorry for you. Because tomorrow night, I'm putting in a request to break us up. I've been through enough shit with you."

Fullerton looked into his eyes. "Almost."

You had to bring that up, Johnny thought. He nodded. "Almost."

"How are you feeling, man?"

"Fan-fucking-tastic."

And by "fan-fucking-tastic," Johnny meant completely terrified. So terrified he couldn't breathe. *I keep thinking this is going to go away tomorrow, just evaporate at the last minute. What if it doesn't?*

Fullerton sighed. "Yeah, man." He kicked at the air. "I know."

Johnny shook his head. "I didn't even vote in the last election, you know that?" he said. He shook his head again. "All of this happened right under my nose. And I never paid attention."

"It happened under all our noses. For a long time. Under our parents' noses, our grandparents'. Lying is a straight powerful thing, Luca. It's the most powerful thing in the world. Once you find a way to scare people so much that you can make them believe anything you say, you got 'em. That's what happened. But we're gonna bust that shit up tomorrow. We *caught* 'em, man. Think about that. For once, we *caught* 'em. Just think of what we can do if we can pull this thing off."

Johnny looked at Fullerton, his arms folded, dressed down, as ready for bed as he was to save the world. "Can we pull it off, Fullerton?"

Fullerton paused, and the moment's delay gave him away to Johnny.

"You don't think we can," Johnny said.

Fullerton looked at him a moment, a parent about to tell his son that Santa Claus didn't exist. "Would it stop you if I said it was a longshot?"

Johnny's stomach wrenched into a knot. "We're going to die," he said, looking down.

Fullerton crossed the room and laid a hand on his shoulder. "Look. Bad shit could happen. You've known that for a long time. This ain't a drill, like when I was throwing you around in that gym. This ain't even like up on that farm, or that night in Irvington, or the night I capped Sigma. This is more than us. And this is more than just a few people. This is the *country*, man, and it's thousands of lives on the line, and three hundred fifty million people who could be sleeping under a dictatorship tomorrow night. And I've got to be straight with you, 'cause you deserve it—chances are, something in our op's gonna get fucked up tomorrow. Look at everything we need to go our way. We could all die." Fullerton shook Johnny. "But look at the way we've been *living*! We can't stay on the run forever. If they don't kill us, they're going to arrest us, us and the boss. They're going to get our families. So even if we only got a small shot—it's the only shot. Would you take that shot for your mom? For your brother? Would you die for this?"

I would, Johnny thought.

For family. For love. For freedom—he would die.

"I would," he said.

Fullerton studied Johnny a moment, then he smiled. "Must be an Italian thing," he said. "That macho shit's in your blood, just like body hair."

Johnny laughed. "Now you've got to come back with the diss. This is what I get for saving your fucking life. Racial hatred."

Fullerton smiled. "You got a girl, man?"

Can't say that I do. "No."

"Now don't bullshit me, Luca. I know you like to use your pimp hand mostly on yourself, but you sure you don't got something going on? What happened to that chick you were digging a few months back?"

He means Justine. "Didn't work out."

Fullerton grinned. "You really are a man of few words. Why didn't it work out? Performance issues?"

Why didn't it work out? "I don't know. I didn't love her, I guess."

Fullerton nodded. "Fair enough, man. Fair enough. Then who do you love?"

"What do you mean?"

"Come *on*, kid. Everybody loves somebody."

Can't argue there, Johnny thought. "I might be sweet on this one girl. But I'm not going to claim *love* or anything like that."

"That's because you're a commitment-phobic bitch. But that's all right, man, that's cool too." Fullerton grinned. "So why aren't you with her?"

"Because she's with someone else."

"And does she love the dude?"

Maybe not. "Enough to move out west with him."

Fullerton shook his head. "You're just full of half-ass, jive answers. You know what I think? I think all this time, all these months we've been together, you've been in love with one chick. And you've been fighting for her. Every move you've made, every risk you took—it's been for her, even if you never even thought about it. That's the kinda dude you are. And I don't hold it against you. It's admirable."

"And what makes you so sure about this?"

"Don't ever play me in poker, 'cause I got the sickest read ever on you. I told the boss my little theory about you. You see, you just *act* like you don't give a fuck, like you're all tough and shit. But the truth is that you feel everything right down to your soul. And I don't know who this chick is, but I know you got it bad for her. A dude like you can't live any other way." Fullerton took a step back. "And if I had to guess your scenario a little more, I'd say this chick doesn't love her man, and she really loves you. Just like in all those white-bread romantic comedies. And you haven't made your move." Fullerton paused. "But if this is the last night of your life, you can at least go to bed admitting to yourself that you're in love with this chick."

Johnny nodded. *I can do that. I can at least do that much.* "What about you? Do *you* have a girl?"

"Of *course*, man. Don't ask stupid questions." Fullerton reached into a drawer and pulled out a little black box, velvet and square.

"What's that?"

Fullerton rolled his eyes. "Get the rigatoni bolognese out of your eyes, dog. What does it look like?" He opened the case, and a diamond burst out in sparkles. "If I get out of this tomorrow, I'm going to pop the question."

So maybe you do plan on surviving. "What's her name?"

"Alicia."

"Alicia and Julius... I like it." Johnny paused, then looked up at Fullerton. "Are you scared, Fullerton?"

Probably not. Dudes like him, they just jump into the fire.

"Fucking terrified, man," Fullerton said. "But the only thing I can do is control the fear. I can't make it go away."

"How do you control it?"

"That's easy. Just think on your girl tomorrow. Fix your mind on her, and she'll show you the way."

Johnny nodded again. *I can do that.*

"It's time for lights out," Fullerton said. "I'm going to say some prayers, but I like to do my praying in the dark. So let's swallow those pills down."

On the count of three, they gulped down the angels that would sing them to their rest—pills that would give them eight hours' sleep. Fullerton clicked off the light.

Lying in the dark, Johnny thought of the white rose he'd sent to Mrs. Ramirez. If that was his last bit of business on earth, it was good enough.

"Tomorrow night," Fullerton called out from bed in the dark, already yawning. "No more... slavery... tomorrow night. We'll live free... live free or die... finally..."

Johnny stared up into tender black as he melted to sleep. *We'll live free*, he thought. *Or die…*

Bryson sat on a pew in the back of the National Cathedral. It was 11:30 PM, the night of May 26.

I can still stop it. All I have to do is give the order. It's not too late.

He steeled himself. Now wasn't the time to lose resolve, or faith. He didn't make the world; this was how it was handed to him, all those years ago. *This is how things are, Nightfox*, he was told. *There are no Republicans, no Democrats, no Constitution, no United Stated States of America, not in the way you think of it—there's only power. And I'm inviting you to share in that power, to make the world how you want it to be. You can help people. But tough decisions have to be made, and I'm going to teach you how to make them.*

I'll do anything you say, Bryson had said, all those years ago. And now, tonight, as he sat in the Cathedral, he pondered how he was about to become bound in blood.

Sometimes he felt like a toy soldier, fighting someone else's war. But he wasn't. Because in a year and a half, he'd be President of the United States—and then, finally, he could make things the way he wanted them to be.

Bryson was sixty years old. He'd started at twenty-two, helping run weapons for the Contras, and now tomorrow he'd clinch the crowning achievement of his career—a perfectly drawn and executed false-flag terror attack, just as he'd been tasked to do. *My greatest achievement is bloodshed. He looked down. Mass killing.*

When Bryson was President, things would be different. The subversive element would be gone, and the conflict would be over. He could preside over the safekeeping, at long last, of the American empire.

No, there'd be no calling off Operation Reichstag. And there really was no way to stop it now. Bryson knew that Peterson was going to move against him—he was ready. He didn't know where Peterson was, but it didn't matter. Tomorrow he'd crush Peterson's insignificant little rebellion, and either kill him or jail him.

Because Bryson had preemptive strikes planned, and Peterson didn't know it. But tomorrow Peterson would learn that Bryson was three steps ahead of a fool like him. Peterson's plans would be eviscerated like a woodchip slamming into a buzzsaw.

And tomorrow night, when smoke was rising over the nation, Bryson would reconcile what he'd done. Many thousands would be dead, yes. But the job begun on September 11, 2001 would finally be done—the job Americans didn't have the spine to finish themselves—the job Lindsey's and Emily's murders cried out for.

The sun would rise on America's destiny the morning of May 28, 2023. Day one of the age of American Empire.

Steven Cadbury stood up.

It was after midnight now, and he was still at the office. Operation Reichstag was so close he could feel it breathing on his neck, hot and corrosive. It infested his skin, flushed his face, blotted his eyes.

Nothing can stop it. And I let it happen... I stood by, and I let it happen...

His desk chair sank a little under his weight. The rope rested on his neck, bristling his skin, tied to a pipe above the drop ceiling.

The red lights still throbbed all over map burned into his brain. A dirty bomb in New York... Chicago… San Francisco… so many cities…

Cadbury looked at his cubicle, then scanned from the calendar on the wall to the picture of his wife and kids on his desk. *I can still undo this*, he thought. *All I have to do is slip off this rope, put the chair back, and stick my head in the sand tomorrow.*

Then his eyes fell back on the calendar. "Remember OPSEC!" it read.

OPSEC. Operational Security.

Cadbury swung the wheeled chair out from under him, and the noose crushed his neck.

At 12:23 AM, Steven Cadbury became the first casualty of Operation Reichstag.

Chapter 50

Johnny Luca stood in the puddle of sunlight that pooled below the window in the room. The early morning of May 27, 2023 was bright, streaks of tangerine stretching across the azure canopy above. Just then, he thought of a poem he read once in high school, about a boy who climbed through a hole in the vault of the sky, wriggled through the three wires of the world, and then glanced down once last time before hoisting himself out. *I wish I were that guy.* He had been awake for three minutes, and the centrifuge was cycling in his stomach already. *God, I wish I were that guy.*

"Luca," Fullerton said from across the room, rubbing his eyes. "Wash and suit up. Let's go."

Johnny glanced at the tactical gear in the middle of the room, and thought again of the boy climbing through the sky.

Chapter 51

Brigadier One sat by the window of his Brooklyn apartment, running his fingers over the peeling white paint of the windowsill. Sitting on a chair across the room was a package that the media would call a "dirty bomb." In a few hours, he'd hop on the subway, get off at Herald Square, and drop the package in a trash can. He'd then stroll for several blocks and man his post inside a coffee shop, a wireless headset in his ear. When Octavian issued the order, he would punch a few buttons on his phone, and a corner of Thirty-Fourth Street would explode in a hail of radiation. All too easy.

Brigadier One gazed out the window. The city was just waking up, the rumbling of trucks and the tapping of car horns puncturing the chirping of birds. And he wanted nothing more than to rupture that morning song into a dissonance of emergency sirens and panic.

Inside the apartment it was still. In a moment he'd get up to fix a little breakfast, brew a cup of coffee. But for now he just wanted to meditate on the death blow he would strike to the criminal American regime, on how historians would etch his name into the annals of revolutionaries, on how—

The front door blasted open and an object clanged on the floor, exploding in light.

"Move in!" a voice yelled as smoke and light choked Brigadier One's eyes. "Take him down! *Take him down*!"

A hand pinioned his arms behind his back while another dug into neck, driving him to the floor. The intruder snapped zip ties around his wrists and ground a boot into his back. "Don't move!" he yelled. "*Don't move*!"

Through the haze, Brigadier One could make out shapes clad in black, brandishing shotguns and taking up positions around the apartment, one guarding the door. "You're under arrest, fucker," a voice said above him.

It's over, Brigadier One thought, *someone's betrayed us, they've destroyed Project Orion—*

And then he saw the figure at the door reach into his waistband and pull out two handguns fitted with silencers.

Clack! The man who had arrested Brigadier One stumbled

backwards, then dropped to the floor next to Brigadier One.

"What the—" another man said, before a bullet pierced a hole in his forehead.

Clack! *Clack*! The man at the door shot with one handgun, then pivoted and fired with the other, and two more black-clad comrades hit the floor.

The last member of the team cocked his shotgun and aimed– his last two movements before the traitor peeled off a shot that ripped through his forehead.

Gun smoke burned through the room, mingling with the fading haze of the flash grenade. *What the hell is going on*, Brigadier One thought, scurrying to his feet, wrenching against the zip ties.

The black-clad man met his eyes for a moment and nodded. Then he circled the room, stopping at each fallen comrade and popping a fresh bullet into his head.

He approached Brigadier One.

"Who are you?" Brigadier One asked.

The man stuck one of the guns back in his waistband and drew a knife. "Turn around," he said.

Brigadier One edged away. "Tell me who you are."

The man closed his eyes in agony, then opened them. "Octavian sent me to stop this raid."

"But you were with them."

"Octavian…" The man closed his eyes again. "Octavian embedded me with them." He cut off the zip ties. "Now call him and tell him you're all right. Tell him we've repelled the attack."

Project Orion's saved. Brigadier One picked up his two-way. "Octavian," he said. "Brigadier One in place. We've repelled the government attack and we're awaiting your orders."

Chapter 52

Johnny stretched his starched white shirt across his chest and buttoned up, sealing it over a layer of Kevlar. He reached for a blue tie.

"When was the last time you put on a suit, man, your frat formal?" Fullerton said, already clad in a black suit.

"Fuck off, Fullerton," Johnny said. "It's been awhile."

Fullerton adjusted his earpiece. "The CAT team better take those dudes down, man. Otherwise we'll be walking into a trap."

By "CAT team," Fullerton meant the Secret Service Counter-Assault Team, an elite group assigned to disable the Authority lead site agents that morning as they left their homes. Johnny popped his collar and wrapped the tie around. "And you're telling me that if the CAT guys take them down and set up Secret Service agents working the perimeter, the Authority agents onsite aren't going to be suspicious?" he asked.

"It's a critical flaw in their setup, brother. Those Authority dudes don't know how to do protective assignments for the President. They're thugs, man, legbreakers— they ain't Secret Service agents. They just got that job 'cause Bryson fixed it that way. If you ask me, there's only gonna be three bad guys in that room, and everyone else is gonna be straight oblivious."

"And who are those three?"

"The patsy, the second shooter, and the one who relays the signal to Moloch. And I don't reckon any of those three are gonna be in any position to make a lot of noise if they see us in there."

Johnny cinched the knot on his tie and yanked it into form, then lowered the collar.

"Don't you look nice!" Fullerton said, pinching his cheek. "Your mama would be so proud!"

I don't know how he stays so loose.

A serious look fell across Fullerton's face. "Here, man," he said, handing Johnny his MP-5. "Get a good feel for it. We're going to roll out soon."

Johnny clutched the weapon. It was no longer the extension of himself that it was when he peppered the bull's-eye at will on the range. Now it was an alien appendage jutting out of his chest.

When is this going to feel right? Johnny thought.

Chapter 53

CAT agents Proctor and Stiles sat in a vehicle parked on a sunny street in the North Jersey suburbs. "You ready?" Proctor said.

"Let's go," Stiles said.

They debarked from the truck and crept up the black driveway lined with stone blocks. They closed in on the front door, just a few steps away now...

Just then, a dog barked behind them.

It was an old man walking his beagle; the block was just waking up now. He fixed his eyes on them from behind his square-rim glasses, his gray mustache screwed in suspicion. "Morning!" he called.

The two agents turned to face him, handguns weighing down their waistbands under the tails of their polo shirts. One put his hand on his hips, fingering the handle through the shirt, and waved. His partner did the same.

The old man held the look for another moment, then smiled and strolled away with his dog.

The two waited for him to disappear around the corner, throwing glances over their shoulders at the front door. If the door opened, they were caught, they'd have to draw their weapons…

Just another morning in the life of two CAT agents on a black-bag assignment. They turned back to the subject home and prepared to neutralize the Authority agent within.

The two crept to the front door, one behind the other. They exchanged nods, and then Proctor rang the bell.

There was a commotion within, a shuffling of feet, and then a woman answered. "Hel—"

Proctor surged through the door, knocking her over, and Stiles rushed in, handgun drawn. The woman screamed—Proctor jerked her up by her collar, then slammed the door, sealed her mouth with his hand, and pressed the barrel of the gun against her temple.

The subject, dressed in an undershirt and suit pants, darted across the hall above and reached for his hip. "Don't move!" Stiles screamed. "Move and you fucking *die*!"

The Authority agent, fair-haired, blue-eyed, in his early thirties, reached again for his hip, and a bullet ripped through his right shoulder. He dropped.

The wife thrashed against Proctor, stomping her feet; he wrestled her to the ground. Stiles bounded up the stairs, swept his hand around the subject's hip and tossed away a handgun, and then plunged a syringe into his arm. He then nodded at Proctor.

Proctor pulled out a syringe and dug it into the wife's arm. She struggled, then slumped down.

Then a little boy, no older than five, emerged at the far end of the top floor hallway, his hair a blond mop, his little feet padding on the green carpet. "Daddy?" he said. Instantly his face burst into red and exploded in tears. "*Daddy*!"

"Put him down," Proctor called from the floor below.

Stiles nodded, swallowed up the boy in his arms—as old as his own son—and plunged a syringe into him. A second later, all was quiet.

"That's the only kid," Proctor called from downstairs. "They'll all be up and about in about six hours." He gestured at the subject. "How is he?"

"He might go," Stiles said. "Try and get that bullet out of him. I've got to get out of here."

"You have the keys to his ride?"

"Check." Stiles held them up. He had to take the vehicle and drive it to the visit site, because Moloch likely was tracking it by GPS.

"Good. Let's cuff them."

The two cuffed husband, wife, and son to different fixtures in the house.

"I'll take care of them," Proctor said. He shook Stiles's hand, then pulled him into an embrace. "Try and live out there, brother," he said. "This is all our lives on the line today."

Stiles nodded. "See you when I see you, partner."

He headed for the door. Seven other CAT duos had to do what they just did, if this op was going to work...

Stiles stiffened for a moment. *I shot the guy in front of his wife. Goddamn him, he reached for his weapon—*

Then he clicked his two-way. "Logan," he said, addressing Peterson by his code name. "This is Freedom One. Subject neutralized, on my way to site in subject's g-ride."

Chapter 54

A gunshot blasted through the back of an ATF agent's head in an apartment in Chicago.

Before any of his partners could fire back, single bullets split their skulls one by one. The handcuffed Brigade 910 terrorist, who planned on truck-bombing the Sears Tower that morning, trembled in the corner. A moment later, he was free and radioing Octavian that the government attack had been repelled.

City-by-city, traitors decimated the counter-Operation Reichstag teams. In Boston, Philadelphia, Detroit, Los Angeles—everywhere—raid agents turned on their own comrades and gunned them down.

That morning, the last thoughts of many federal agents was *What's happening, how can this be*—and then they knew no more as lead seared through bone and into their brains.

And in New York, as the good news poured in over the radio that each operative was in place, Moloch leaned back in his chair and smiled. He and Bryson had cut Peterson's legs out from under him.

Chapter 55

Director Chan clenched his weapon as the SUV rumbled along a back road in Winchester, Virginia, an hour and a half west of Washington. It had been a long time since he'd ridden in the passenger seat on the way to an arrest.

A few days ago, he'd gotten intelligence that Director Bryson would be coordinating Operation Reichstag from a secure facility in the backwoods of Winchester, near the West Virginia border. From this location he'd rain down a symphony of murder and treachery on his country.

But he wouldn't. Because Chan and his ten-vehicle convoy of Secret Service, ATF, and FBI agents were on their way to storm the facility and finally arrest the Director of the Anti-Subversion Authority. *He'll pay for his crimes*, Chan thought as the truck bounced along dirt roads through the woods.

The woods were thick, choking out the morning sun. To the right they plunged to a death-drop into a rocky creek.

Devil's drop, Chan thought absently. *We had a drop like that in our town when we were kids... we called it Devil's Drop.*

He thought of Theresa, at home with Katie and Joanna. Last night they went to sleep by light of a tyrant's moon, and they didn't even know it. Tonight the moon would shine freedom, pure and bright, finally.

The truck came to a clearing. In the light that poured into the open woods, Chan could see a ranch house, with a little satellite dish poking off the side. A few government vehicles were parked in front, all in a row. And at the end of that row—Chan could see it now, he'd waited so long to finally see it—was Alexander Bryson's.

Chan knew exactly where Bryson was. In the backyard, there was an entrance to a bunker, a rusting trap door. Chan knew it; he *knew* it. He had Bryson, and finally, there was nowhere for him to run.

Chan's stomach knotted. He wasn't nervous; he couldn't be nervous. That was for rookies out on their first raid. This was different; this buzzed past the frontiers of anything he'd ever felt. It was like he'd been pounding on the door to heaven with a battering ram for twenty years, and the hinges had just busted, and the light of a sunrise sky was streaking through, spreading wider, shining brighter...

The car parked. "This is it," the driver said. "We've got him, sir. On your mark."

You swore the same oath as me, you bastard, Chan thought as he glared at the ranch. *I swear to defend the Constitution from all enemies, foreign and domestic...*

"Let's do it," Chan said.

"We're going in," the driver radioed to the rest of the convoy.

Chan popped open the door and stepped out to the melody of other truck doors popping open and slamming shut. Thirty agents armed with shotguns and machine guns awaited his orders.

The grass dripped with the misty smell of pure morning. Birds sang to each other. A passenger jet streaked overhead through the ripples of the cloudless sky.

And in the cacophony of the newborn day, Chan heard a whistling.

The whistling split the air as a rocket crashed into one of the convoy trucks and incinerated it into a fireball. The blast knocked Chan back twenty feet as it vaporized a handful of the agents.

Another rocket slammed into another truck and exploded into a conflagration. *Ambush,* Chan thought through a concussed fog. *Ambush...*

He felt for his weapon, grabbed it, and struggled to his feet. "Ambush!" he yelled. "Ambush!"

Chan felt as if an aluminum bat had smashed him in the face. He stumbled, then pumped his shotgun as secondary explosions burst in the distance. Through the smoke, he could see that several of his men and women were down.

He heard a shotgun blast to his right; one his agents had fired into the woods, the rockets must have come from the woods...

Then he heard another shotgun blast, and the shattering of glass. Another of his agents had shot an approaching SUV right through the windshield, and the truck had slowed to an ominous roll.

A shootout erupted on different points of the front lawn. Chan's agents traded rounds with shooters who had taken cover behind a wave of armored trucks which had rolled up after the initial explosions. He could hear the sounds of automatic fire coming from the other side and could see his agents dropping in sheets.

I've got to save them, Chan thought, aiming at one of the armored cars ahead, *I've got to save them—*

He picked up an enemy sniper in his sights and pulled the trigger, the shotgun slamming into his shoulder. The sniper geysered blood as he fell.

Another two SUVs raced up on Chan's left side. They were surrounded now: the fire behind them, the woods to the right, the shooters straight ahead, and the new arrivals to the left.

And then, as bullets exploded all over the lawn, Chan resolved his only choice: charging straight ahead, right at Bryson. He would have to shoot his way through, and he could only pray his agents covered him. Bryson wasn't getting out of this alive.

But a few paces ahead, one of his men was down, lying prone in the grass. Chan fired two blasts at the trucks to his left and then ran forward. He grabbed his agent as he ran, dragged him for a few steps, and then dove on top of him. He might've broken one of the young man's bones; it was better than a bullet.

Chan's left arm burned. He'd been shot; he'd just taken a bullet that would've hit the young man in the head.

The move had cost him a few steps—he still had to get to the bunker. "Play dead," he whispered to the fallen agent.

Chan pumped his shotgun and charged forward again. A shooter in full body armor, clad in all black up to a kerchief wrapped around his face, took aim at him. Chan blew him away and kept running, gunfire erupting behind him, the ranch growing nearer with each step...

Another shooter ran up to him. Chan raised his weapon; his finger curled around the trigger; his finger started to squeeze—

And then a swarm of bullets ripped through his chest.

Chan fell back in an explosion of agony. *Armor-piercing bullets*, he thought. *Only the government... only the government... uses them...*

He thrashed against his own body, squeezed the grass, grabbed his shotgun, started to push off the ground—

And in the throes of this surge to halt Operation Reichstag, Chan died.

Chapter 56

Bryson put down his radio. He had just received word that Chan was dead.

He was in his office in downtown Washington, of course. It was he who had leaked the false intelligence to Chan about the Winchester ranch through back-channels, he who had set up the ambush with a corps of fanatical Brigade 910 terrorists armed to the teeth and lusting to massacre as many federal agents as they could.

It was perfect. Chan had to die, and now he was dead. It was much better for Operation Reichstag that the Director of the Secret Service was killed in a firefight in the middle of the woods near West Virginia than in an ambush in the heart of Washington.

Everything was going as planned. Around the country, his saboteurs had destroyed all of the anti-Operation Reichstag teams, and all of his men were in place.

Bryson had planted the moles by having Brigade 910 terrorists abduct their families and threaten to kill them if they didn't do what they were told. And with perfect efficiency, they'd done it.

Of course, all of the hostages were already dead, down to the last child. And when the moles tried to get them back later in the day, they'd all be killed, too.

Chan was dead, and so was Peterson's counter-assault force. The only person on Earth who stood in Bryson's way now was President Wilkins.

In a couple of hours, he'd be dead too. It would only take one bullet to kill him, maybe two, maybe three. He was just one man; a single man was easy to kill. And Bryson didn't even have to lure him, like he did Chan. He'd have Wilkins boxed in a room, surrounded by a legion of his own agents.

It was America's destiny, and it was unstoppable now. It had been all along.

Chapter 57

One black SUV bounced out of the driveway and ripped up the tree-lined street, scattering a stream of cherry blossoms in its wake. A moment later, another black SUV peeled out in pursuit.

Freedom Seven had failed to apprehend its subject at his townhouse, and the subject Authority agent had shot one of the CAT agents in terror and bounded away. Now they were giving chase, the wounded agent bleeding from the arm in the passenger seat, the healthy driver sweeping around the first corner, the United States of America in the balance.

"Jam that fucking radio and his cell signal!" yelled Thorpe, the driver, a crew-cut former Army Ranger in his mid-thirties.

"I'm jamming it!" yelled Blake, the wounded one, a fair-haired agent in his late twenties. "Catch the fucker!"

The Authority agent in the truck ahead blazed through the development, sideswiping a silver convertible, popping over a sewer grate, rumbling towards the main drag ahead.

"Come on!" Thorpe yelled, flooring it and yanking the steering wheel with one hand. The engine's scream was like the squawk of an eagle banging against the Grand Canyon. "You've got to fire on him, Blake. Can you do it? Your arm all right?"

"I can do it," Blake said. "Keep up with him." *But I don't know if I can. I can barely move it.*

The two trucks tore onto the main drag, and now Thorpe cut on the siren to get everyone out of the way. This was one-on-one.

Blake grabbed his handgun, wrapped his finger around the trigger, and raised his arm. A nuclear blast of pain shot up the arm and clustered in his shoulder. "God-*damn* it!"

The truck ahead twisted left through a red light, cutting across an oncoming bus. Thorpe hardened his face and surged through the light himself, first swinging to the right to miss the bus, then lurching to the left to dodge traffic speeding from the other direction, triggering a symphony of honking horns.

The CAT truck fish-tailed, then righted itself. Ahead the Authority agent sideswiped another car, burst onto the sidewalk, brained a fire hydrant, then landed back in the street as the hydrant exploded into a cascade.

"He's headed for the Turnpike," Thorpe said, maneuvering to a rush of more horns. "If he makes it over the bridge..."

Blake grabbed his gun with his left hand. Thorpe meant the George Washington Bridge. If the subject made it over the bridge into the city, even if they could stay close enough to jam him, it was over. He'd find help. And then the bad guys would be waiting at the hotel, where they'd ambush the good guys and arrest or kill them. And then the President would be shot.

Blake stuck his head out the window and lined up a lefty sidearm shot. *I'm about to shoot at a federal agent.*

He closed his eyes. He'd never shot lefty before, he'd never rip off a good one... *Fuck it. I was a switch hitter in high school.*

Blake aimed at the driver's side rear tire and pulled the trigger. The recoil wrenched the gun out of his hand; it clanged into the street. The shot exploded at the base of the tire—about two inches wide right. The subject raced ahead, unimpaired, towards the Turnpike ramp.

"Fuck!" Blake yelled. "I lost the weapon, Thorpe. It's gone."

"I've got to keep him in range," Thorpe said. "We have to stay close enough to keep jamming his radio and his cell signal. If he gets a message out, this whole op is fucked." He looked at Blake, gritted his teeth at the sight of his bleeding partner who'd just gutted out the first lefty sidearm shot he'd ever seen, and then set his face on the road. *There's only one thing left to do*, he thought.

"Hold on," Thorpe said.

Ahead the subject vehicle whirled onto the Turnpike ramp, slowing down a touch to avoid spinning out, then straightening out at the base and speeding ahead.

Thorpe took the curve harder. The truck edged off the asphalt, started to spin, began to tip—

Then the first angel to which Jeff Thorpe had ever prayed nudged the truck back onto the road, and the vehicle raged ahead, truer and faster than before, headed straight out onto the New Jersey Turnpike.

Thorpe cut across two left lanes; the Authority agent bogged down a few mph's slower in the right lane. The CAT truck picked up a speck of distance; then a step; then a car length. The subject was still in the far right lane.

"Hold on, partner," Thorpe said. He swooped back across one right lane, and now they were just to the left of the subject, about halfway up the length of his truck.

And in that second, Blake realized what Thorpe was about to do.

Thorpe sped up some more, set his jaw one last time, then slashed to the right into the back half of the Authority vehicle, a textbook pit maneuver.

Their vehicle bounced off the subject's with a thud. Airbags exploded in front of Thorpe and Blake as their truck spun; in the distance the Authority truck spun out and crashed into the wall abutting the shoulder.

And after Thorpe and Blake's truck spun one complete revolution, a car smashed directly into the driver's side at a right angle and flipped them.

Blake opened his eyes. He was lying on his side, but not really. Instead of flipping all the way, the truck had tipped onto the passenger side. The snap was Blake's arm, already shot, bashing against his window as it pounded the pavement.

With his good left hand, he unsheathed his seatbelt. He'd never been at this angle in a car in his life; the sun rained through Thorpe's broken window, the only way out now.

"Thorpe?" Blake called. "Thorpe, we gotta get—"

Blood bubbled from Thorpe's mouth.

No, Blake thought. *Oh no...*

"My... weapon," Thorpe gasped. "Take it. Finish this."

"Thorpe, come on, I've got to get you out of here, just let me—"

"The... mission. The President. Finish the mission."

And with that, Thorpe gasped again, and his eyes rolled back in his head.

A wave of agony strangled Blake. Thorpe was dead. *This can't be, this can't be...*

But then the wave melted away. *If I don't get out of here, I'm dead too.*

Blake looked down at Thorpe's holstered weapon. He couldn't do this, could he?

Just then, he gagged, then blacked out for a second. When he opened his eyes again, his lap was covered in blood.

I think I'm dying.

He took hold of Thorpe's gun and unholstered it. Then he grabbed the frame of Thorpe's window—now the roof of the truck—and yanked himself up. He wriggled against his partner's corpse, up and over, out into the wreckage of Thorpe's last stand.

The car that had hit them was totaled; the driver was probably dead. *Forgive me*, Blake thought, looking up.

Then he skulked towards the Authority truck, crumpled at the wall several feet away. The Turnpike was now a mass of traffic which had bottled up behind the accidents; Blake could feel hundreds of eyes on him as he dragged himself towards the steaming heap on the shoulder.

He started to shake as he closed in on the subject. Maybe it was fear for what he was about to do. But, as another stream of blood poured out of Blake's mouth, it was more likely that his body was going into shock.

Blake thought of his fiancee as he ripped open the door with his one good arm. She was beautiful and sweet, a shy dimpled smile lighting her face, the woman he was to marry in two months.

He craned his head into the driver's side. The Authority agent, brown-haired, olive-skinned, and no older than he, was unconscious, but still breathing.

Blake shivered; he felt his lungs filling up. *I didn't ask for this, I don't know if this is wrong or right—*

He fired two shots at the console radio, destroying it. Then he pointed the barrel at the Authority agent's head.

I don't want to do it, oh God, I don't... But if he talks, so many people will die today—

He pulled the trigger, and turned away from the sight of the exploding skull.

Blake sank against the truck. He saw flashing lights ahead; first they looked red and blue, but then they looked silver and gold, orange and green, everything all at once, swimming together...

He pulled out his two-way, shivering. "Logan," he said. "Freedom Seven... mission accomplished."

Blake collapsed.

Chapter 58

Johnny clutched his weapon as he sat next to Fullerton in the back of the truck, the SUV motoring northbound up the far left lane of the West Side Highway, lights flashing. Peterson had advised the sixth unit that all seven CAT teams had succeeded in their mission and had given them the go-ahead to proceed to the presidential visit site and crush the terror plot.

Trees lined the median to the left, cast in the shadow of skyscrapers hulking above the city. *I haven't been out here since Brigade 910 set off that car bomb. The night I met Justine.*

"A lot of history out here," Fullerton said. "Part of the World Trade Center collapsed onto here. Right around here, actually. Look, man." He tapped Johnny and pointed out to the tallest skyscraper of them all, a cuboid bursting with swirls of prismatic light, a massive spire jutting up towards the azure vault above. "One World Trade Center. That's where the boss is going to bust Moloch."

Johnny looked up at the tower and held the gaze a moment, the truck slowing down a bit as traffic in front made way. *We're finally going to bust Moloch.*

Just then, a car honked its horn to the right. A sedan had stopped beside the truck, and the driver had rolled down his window and begun gesturing at them.

"I know him," said Wolfe, sitting in the passenger seat. "He's FBI." He powered down his window. "Harris," he called. "What's going—"

Agent Harris tossed a grenade into the truck and blazed away.

"It's live!" Wolfe yelled. "Everybody out! *Everybody out*!"

What the fuck, Johnny thought, popping open the door and dropping out.

"Back!" Wolfe screamed. "As far as you can!"

Johnny jumped onto the median and tore behind the others, weapon in hand.

Wolfe ran several paces out into the street, flashed his badge, and held up his gun. "Stay back!" he screamed, halting oncoming traffic. "*Back*!"

The truck exploded, a fireball ripping it apart and raining down debris on the West Side Highway.

The blast rattled Johnny's bones, all the way to the tips of his teeth, as it hurled him and the others to the grass of the median. It knocked Wolfe onto the hood of a car.

"What the hell was *that*?" said Austin, the driver, a balding man with a ruddy face.

"A sneak attack," said Kleibeck, a red-haired agent, getting to his feet.

Other trucks in the sixth unit convoy pulled over, and a chorus of popping doors filled the city air, which had fallen silent as traffic froze before a burning hunk of the boulevard.

"He was FBI," Wolfe said, a bead of sweat snaking across his black forehead. "I know him. But why? Why?"

"They fucking made us," Fullerton said. "And we gotta break up outta here, 'cause we can't stay all in one place like this. Who knows what the fuck else they got planned."

"You're right." Wolfe flagged down two of the approaching agents. "Dyer, Tompkins," he called. "You need to stay with the scene here and work it out with the NYPD. We've got to make it to the site. Time is running out." The two nodded at him. "Fullerton," Wolfe called. "Get Peterson on. Tell him what just happened."

Fullerton clicked the two-way. "Boss," he said. "Boss, we need you."

Johnny's hands strangled his weapon. He was a mass of hushed fear, sweating in a suit under the May sun a half a block away from near-death. *If they made us, we could be walking right into a trap.*

"What is it?" Peterson said.

"Take me off speaker," Fullerton said. "I need to talk to you one-on-one."

Police sirens tore through the silence. Two cruisers were already on the scene.

Johnny walked close to Fullerton. *What are we going to do?* he thought.

"Someone tried to stop us," Fullerton said. "Pulled up in a car beside us and threw a grenade through the window." He paused. "I'm serious, boss. He honked the horn and rolled down the window. Wolfe said he recognized him, he was FBI. Agent Harris I think. So

Wolfe rolls down the window to see what's up, and the dude tossed out the grenade and booked." Fullerton paused again. "Yeah, boss, he's gone. Everyone's all right. The truck's burning up on the West Side Highway." He wiped sweat from his brow, shook his head, then continued. "Boss, listen to me. If they made us... They made you too. You might have a mole with you right now. Check on that. You could be in danger." Fullerton paused again, a deeper pause, as if listening to directions. He nodded several times. "Copy," he finally said. "You be safe, sir. Remember, you and me are supposed to be popping some bub tonight for my engagement. Don't stand me up."

Fullerton put the phone in his pocket and looked at Johnny. "If you don't ask for a raise after today, you're even more sorry than I thought," he said. He whistled at the others. "Listen up," he called. "Boss says take NYPD transport to the site, 'cause they might be looking for us all over the roads. Except he wants one decoy driver for each vehicle we got." He paused. "Any volunteers?"

"This ain't no time for volunteers," Wolfe said. He picked out three drivers, then turned back to Fullerton. "How are we supposed to get this transportation?"

"Captain Monahan. He said mention Captain Monahan to the cops."

"You hear that?" Wolfe called out to Dyer and Tompkins, who were already explaining the situation to the police on the scene. "Tell them Hunter Peterson and Captain Monahan want us to get NYPD transport to the site. Throw in a full police escort, too."

Chapter 59

"Pull over," Peterson said, shoving his phone into his pocket.

"Here?" the driver said.

"That's what I said."

They were in downtown Brooklyn, on the way to arrest Moloch. They'd taken an alternate route so they wouldn't get caught up with the others.

Compromised, Peterson thought as the truck lurched to a stop. *The op's been compromised. All of the CAT teams reporting into me this morning, the team that took down the dirty bomber, the others—what if they were lying to me? And Chan... Where is he? Why isn't he answering me?*

"Everybody out," Peterson said.

There's a mole in this truck. And I think I know who it is.

Everyone stepped out of the car and stretched out on the bustling street. Glass office buildings stood as bulwarks against the sun for a row of courthouses as old as the republic itself.

"One of you is a traitor," Peterson said.

"Sir?" one of them said. "What do you—"

"*Shut up*!"

Peterson scrutinized his men for a moment, all dressed in tactical gear. He scanned across hardened eyes, squared jaws, heavy breathing. *Which one is it? Who could it be?*

"You the mole, Gittens?" he asked. He narrowed his eyes. "How about you, Lundquist? You sell us out?"

"Sir," Agent Lundquist said. "I don't know what you're—"

The words evaporated as time slowed to a crawl. Lundquist's lips undulated in slow motion. A breeze fluttered a strand of hair across another agent's forehead. And then another agent reached into his waistband—

Peterson unholstered and fired, hitting him in the shoulder.

"Take him down!" he yelled. "He's the traitor!"

The rest of the team grabbed the agent Peterson had shot.

"Pull him up," Peterson said.

As the others held the traitor, Lundquist cuffed him and pulled him up. *Agent Gacy. He just didn't look right to me all morning.*

He grabbed Gacy by the shirt, clenched his fist, then swallowed.

"Gacy, how could you? Why? *Why*?"

Gacy began to cry. "They got my family," he sobbed. "They're... they're holding them..."

"*Who*?"

"Brigade 910."

"Do you realize what you're doing? How many people you're going to kill?"

Gacy wept. "My wife, my kid—"

Peterson grabbed his collar again. "Shut up! I want to know if we're being followed. *Tell me*!"

Gacy closed his eyes. "GPS on the truck."

Oh no. They know where we are. They could be watching us now. They could be up in one of those buildings. Jesus Christ, we're in the middle of the street here—

Just then, a shot pierced the driver's side window.

"*Get down*!" Peterson yelled, diving for cover. "Behind the truck!"

Three more shots sliced the body of the truck as pedestrians began to scream and run.

"Sniper," Peterson called to the others. "They're watching us. Goddamn it, they're watching us."

Got to keep moving, come on, Hunter, think—

He bolted out into the street in front of an oncoming car and whipped out his gun. The car froze in front of him. He ran to the driver's side and flashed his badge; the driver didn't respond.

Peterson smashed the window with his forearm, raining glass on the driver, and pried open the door. "Official business," he said, yanking the driver out and throwing him to the ground. "Run to those men by the truck over there and *get down*." He turned to his agents. "Miller!" he called. "Toss me the red light."

Miller threw him the magnetic police light. Peterson slapped it on the roof of the car and dropped in.

"Where are you going?" Lundquist said.

"To the World Trade Center. I'll arrest Moloch myself. They can't track this car." Peterson gestured to the others. "Fan out and *find that sniper*. And take Gacy into custody and bring him to the field office."

Just then, another shot tore into back door of the car on the driver's side, and more people screamed. *Christ,* Peterson thought, ripping into drive and blazing up the street.

He blared his horn at cars in front of him, weaved around them, and shot through a red light. *I've got to get Moloch.*

Chapter 60

The sixth unit, with a full police escort, pulled up to the service entrance of the Prescott Hotel.

The agents, all clad in suits and armed with machine guns, stepped out of the paddy wagon. The policemen nodded at them, almost saluting.

"Thanks for the ride, boys," Fullerton said to the officers. "Just so y'all know, I'm gonna have the sickest bachelor party ever in a little while, and all ya'll are invited."

"Come on, Fullerton," Johnny said, walking up to him. "Let's get to work."

Fullerton smiled. "You ready to save the world?"

You fucking bet. "I'm ready."

Wolfe walked ahead of them to the service door, with Johnny, Fullerton, and the others in tow.

A young agent halted them at the door. "Let's see the creds," he said. He examined them with narrowed eyes.

They all pulled out their doctored Authority IDs and presented them to him. The agent perused the cards, then studied Wolfe and the others again. "I don't know you," he said, clutching his gun. He tugged the radio on his chest, pressing it against his cheek.

"With a firm reliance on the protection of Divine Providence," Wolfe said.

The agent paused. He then stared at the men of the sixth unit, still clutching his gun, the radio receiver still poised at his lips. He rested his thumb on the transmitter.

"We mutually pledge to each other our Lives, our Fortunes and our sacred Honor," the agent said, still holding his stare. Then he nodded.

Wolfe nodded back, then turned to the others. "Let's go," he said.

They all marched towards the door. Just as Johnny approached, the agent turned back inside to a counterpart manning a metal detector within, and nodded. "It's them," he said.

The agent turned back around. "We had a hell of a morning getting here," he said. "I shot a guy in front of his kid. And we might've lost two men... I'm not sure." He shook his head. "Make us proud, guys. Finish the job."

Wolfe led Johnny and the others through the bowels of the building, along dirty concrete floors, past loading docks forced empty to make way for the President's security apparatus.

"Remember," Wolfe said. "You're all agents out of the Authority Newark Field Office, if anyone asks you. The New York agents upstairs, they're probably already scratching their heads a little bit, because they're getting here and their lead site agents aren't here. We disabled them all. As we speak, Secret Service agents are explaining that they're sharing today's protection assignment. So the Authority's antennas are already up a little bit. We need full undercover skills, boys." Wolfe pointed at his earpiece. "We're off the Authority radio grid," he said. "We've got our own channel. Anything you say over the radio, the only person who can hear it is another guy in this unit. So don't hold back."

They came to a service elevator. "Troy, you take up a position with your guys near that balcony," Wolfe continued. "Garcia, you and your men start casing the room for any other Authority agents who could be a sniper. And my guys, we'll be searching the crowd for the civilian shooter. We believe the Authority planted a weapon here last night, and one of them will help the patsy retrieve it when he gets here. So he'll be armed. We have no profile whatsoever on who it might be. So use your instincts, and pray."

Wolfe paused, then nodded and punched the service elevator button.

Chapter 61

Peterson stole a glance at his phone as he raced towards the Brooklyn Bridge. He punched the last of the letters of his text message with one hand, steering with the other.

Approaching bklyn brdg, the message read. *Ambushed earlier. Alone now driving civilian car. Will ditch car in lwr manhattan and walk to WTC. Be ready.*

Peterson beamed the message out to his mole in the New York office, Officer Duffy, then sighed and dropped the phone back into his pocket. He swirled from lane to lane, the Brooklyn Bridge getting closer with each car he whipped past.

Chapter 62

The sixth unit marched towards the hotel ballroom in lockstep, Johnny Luca in tow.

He clutched his machine gun as they crossed an anteroom towards their journey's end. Wolfe then raised a fist to a swinging door, turned back and nodded at his comrades, then pounded open the door and marched on.

Johnny trailed the others across the threshold, and then the ballroom burst open in front of him. A mass of guests, fidgeting on folding chairs, filled the room from the back up to the three-quarter point. The crowd formed a wedge, wrapping around the room in triangular slices lined with red carpets, tapering to a small row in the front, several feet from where Johnny stood. Strung before the front row were black velvet ropes, Authority agents hulking behind them with assault weapons drawn.

Johnny looked to his left. There was the makeshift stage, black wood panels crafted into a platform onto which the President of the United States would soon walk. A banner stretched across and above the back of the stage, the phrase "Honoring Everyday Heroes" etched against a stars and stripes background. Closest to Johnny, to the far left of the stage for anyone facing front, was the President's podium, one mahogany rectangular block standing vertically, a square piece sloping down from the top for the President's papers, and another square piece jutting across the front– bearing the presidential seal.

Johnny glanced up at the balcony at the back of the room; as Peterson had predicted, it was roped off and deserted. Then he glanced back to the podium. From somewhere in this crowd—and maybe from somewhere up in that balcony—would blast the bullet that might snuff out the President's life.

"Needle, meet haystack," Fullerton said, elbowing Johnny and tilting his head towards the crowd.

"Tell me about it," Johnny said.

"Look, man. You and your pops got us this far. Just one last mile, kid. One last mile."

Johnny sighed as he looked at the stage. Some crime victim organization was sponsoring the event, and the President was to honor a little girl who had fought off an abductor.

"When's POTUS going to be here?" he asked Fullerton.

"Soon, man," Fullerton replied. "Should just be a few minutes out now."

"You ever stand this close to a President before?"

"Nah. But my mom met Clinton once. Book signing." Fullerton smiled. "You should buy that book. You might get some pointers on how to get laid for a change!"

Johnny grinned. "At least I'm not the one popping the question tonight."

Fullerton laughed, then grew stern. "So you think there's going to be a tonight?"

Johnny glanced up at the balcony again, empty but for the red curtains. "I don't know, man. But I'll die to get you there."

Fullerton looked into Johnny's eyes, and for the first time in all their months together, Johnny saw tears welling up. "Same here, man," he said. "Same here."

Chapter 63

Peterson craned his head up at One World Trade Center, swirling to the sky before him in majesty. *Ninetieth floor. Moloch's on the ninetieth floor.*

After Congress created the Authority, the government had seized the top inhabited floor of One World Trade Center for the New York field office, the most prime real estate in the city.

Peterson craned his head up one last time, sunbeams raking his eyes, then nodded to himself. *Time to bring you to justice.*

He pulled out his phone and texted Duffy: *Coming up now.* He then clenched his fist and strode through the revolving door.

Peterson crossed the lobby, flashing his badge at the security guards stationed at a desk in the middle. He continued to the elevator banks, punched the button at a deserted elevator, waited, waited. Forty-one... down to thirty... twenty... ten...

The doors opened, and Hunter Peterson walked through to meet his destiny.

The elevator climbed the Freedom Tower, ticking past each floor. Passengers embarked and debarked along the way, but they were only ghosts, specters of a world Peterson was no longer part of, and might never rejoin.

Ninety.

The doors slid open again, and the great seal of the United States Anti-Subversion Authority, cut in gold trim on the glass-paneled wall, greeted Peterson.

He stepped off, crossed to the solid wood lobby door, and pulled it open, the latch clicking, the door yielding. He didn't even throw a look at the receptionist, stationed behind a wall of bulletproof glass to the left, as he headed for the white ballistic door straight ahead. Duffy, please be here now...

One pace, two paces–

The door opened, and holding it for Peterson was middle-aged Duffy, the man who had, unbeknownst to Peterson, lent a hand to Johnny Luca the night he was beaten by Authority agents for trying to get to the scene of a car bombing, who had told the young surveillance technician that the agents in his field office were "animals."

Peterson and Duffy shared a nod as Peterson entered the field office. "I'll take you to him," Duffy said.

Peterson could feel strange eyes slicing into him as the two wound their way through. *I wish I didn't have to do this alone*, he thought as they walked, his face burning, his heart snapping in and out.

Duffy stopped at a closed door. "This is it," he said.

Peterson nodded. He reached into his pocket and held out a piece of paper. "This is the warrant," he said. "Hold the door, Duffy."

Duffy took the paper. "Yes, sir."

Both their eyes fell on a keypad of nine clear squares jutting out a bit from the wall. This was Duffy's moment. Peterson had tasked him with spying on Moloch and harvesting the door passcode.

Duffy gulped, then hit a button on the keypad. Red LED numbers swirled to life on the clear squares, from one to nine, but in jumbled order– a security measure. Duffy punched square after square, some combination of six. Nothing happened.

Oh no.

But then there was a snap in the door catch. Peterson breathed deeply.

He pushed open the door, and there was Moloch, sitting at his desk, staring right at him. "Peterson," he spat, his eyes sharpened into disbelief and hate.

Peterson stepped inside and held up the warrant. *Find the words, find the words—*

"Shepherd Moloch, you're under arrest for providing material support to a terrorist organization, conspiracy to commit murder, and conspiracy to assassinate the President of the United States."

Moloch clenched his teeth. "You're arresting me, Peterson?"

"You have the right to remain silent. Anything you say can be used against you. You have—"

Just then, the door snapped shut, pushing Peterson inside. Moloch stood up and smiled. "I control it from my desk," he said. "A little button that closes the door and scrambles the code. A nice intimate setting for the two of us."

Peterson drew his handgun. "It's over, Moloch. Everything. Get your hands up."

Moloch laughed. "Now why would you want me to do that? I'm not going to hurt you. We're on the same side!" He stepped out from behind his desk.

"We're not on the same side. I'm not on the same side as terrorists and killers. I'm not guilty of treason."

Moloch's eyes flashed with hate again. "And neither am I." His eyes bored into Peterson's. "Put down that gun like a good dog and bow down right in front of me. You might get it in the back of the head instead of the face. Not like it matters. No one's going to miss Hunter Peterson when he's gone, certainly not your dead wife, anyway."

Peterson cocked the gun. *Don't let him goad you*, he thought. "You're under arrest, Moloch. Put your hands up, or I'll kill you."

Moloch glared at him another moment, then dove behind his desk. Peterson scanned the room, but then something knocked him to the floor. He scrambled, but then a wave of pain blasted him back down. He dropped his gun.

Moloch was on his feet, clutching the same handheld microwave device Luca and Fullerton had taken off Sigma. He focused it on Peterson and strangled the trigger, a sneer curled around his lips.

Peterson felt his insides incinerate, his guts smoldering, his bones smoking under his skin. He writhed on the floor. *Fight him*, came the thought cutting through the pain, *fight him, you have to get up...*

Moloch pulled out a handgun. "I've waited a long time for this," he said. "You failed, Peterson. I want you to think about that as you die. You failed." He blasted Peterson with another charge out of the pain weapon, then aimed the firearm, narrowing his eyes.

Not here, not here, not like this, not here–

He fumbled at his waistband, slipped out the same microwave weapon, aimed it straight up at Moloch, and pulled the trigger.

Moloch's narrowed eyes held steady a moment, then widened open in agony. Peterson, now flat on his back, aimed higher, truer, still yanking on the trigger.

Moloch's body shook, and then he fell to the floor, dropping both weapons.

The gun, Peterson thought, still writhing. *The gun—*

He crawled, his body a mass of pain, then lunged at Moloch's handgun, only for his hand to curl around Moloch's wrist. Moloch, crawling himself, had grabbed the gun first.

Peterson drained his strength into keeping Moloch's hand down as Moloch thrashed against his grip. He raised his hand off the floor, overcoming Peterson as he shook, starting to pivot, to turn the gun towards him...

Peterson head-butted him, then slammed his hand into the floor until he dropped the weapon. Peterson swiped at it, knocking it across the room.

Moloch stumbled to his feet, and before Peterson could respond, he kicked him in the face. Peterson felt a crack spray across his cheek.

"You shouldn't have come," Moloch said, huffing. "You should've... stayed out of my way. Now you'll learn." He reared back for another kick, then laid it into Peterson.

Peterson caught the leg and dropped him in one motion. "You're under arrest," he said, punching him in the face. "You're under—"

Moloch caught the next punch, then flexed his quad muscles and flipped Peterson over him and onto his back.

Peterson slammed to the floor, first the trauma jarring him, then the adrenaline firing through him. He and Moloch snapped back to their feet.

"You're too late," Moloch said. "Can't you see you're too late? They're all dead, Peterson. Even Chan. All dea—"

"Son of a bitch!" Peterson rushed forward and caught hold of him, the momentum sending them bounding across the room. He grabbed Moloch by the shirt and slammed him against a cabinet door, shattering the glass.

Then Moloch swung loose. He punched Peterson in the face, then in the stomach, then kneed him in the jaw. He grabbed him and charged forward, sending Peterson back on his heels, Moloch still clutching him.

The two crashed through a glass-paneled door, spilling out onto the terrace outside Moloch's office.

Chapter 64

Johnny surveyed an old man's face a few seats away as he patrolled the carpeted aisle. He was about seventy-five, blue-eyed, wrinkles etched into his face, white hair flaring out from under an Army baseball cap, the grandfather he never met. As Johnny studied him, the old man turned to face him, and his eyes softened with admiration for the boy with the machine gun.

Johnny continued to scan the crowd in his aisle. There were old ladies in their Sunday best, old men in sweater vests, soccer moms huddled with little kids, professionals in their suits, school-aged boys who eyed Johnny's gun and earpiece with awe. But there was no one who looked anything like an assassin.

He started to sweat. *Free your mind, Luca. Look behind them, look through them...*

There's no way. He gazed out at the crowd stretching in every direction. *How the hell are we going to pick this maniac out of all these people?*

He turned to his right; there was a woman bouncing her little daughter on her lap, looking up at him and smiling. *Thank you for keeping me safe*, the look said.

Johnny wiped the sweat from his brow. *Free your mind.*

"How's it going over there, Luca?" Fullerton said, his voice crisp in the earpiece. He was patrolling a few aisles away.

"Nothing," Johnny said. "Nothing, man."

"Be patient. We're going to do this. Stay strong over there."

Johnny looked up at the balcony, empty as it was before.

At that instant, the house microphone rumbled, and then:

"Ladies and gentlemen, the President of the United States!"

The crowd jumped to its feet, hooting and hollering, as "Hail to the Chief" burst over the sound system.

Chapter 65

Peterson twisted loose of Moloch's grip, glass strewn along his forehead and scalp. He pivoted to his feet, and New York city rose behind him.

Moloch kipped up. "You won't stop me," he said. "Not when I'm this close!"

Peterson spit out a bit of glass. "Close to what? You're going to kill ten thousand people!"

"You could've shared in this, Peterson. You know what we're going to have after today? We're going to have it all. *Power.* All the power we ever dreamed of."

Peterson took a few steps back, the staggered towers of the World Financial Center shimmering across the street. "I never dreamed of power, you son of a bitch."

Moloch nodded, almost as if at a child's naiveté. "I know. I know." He brushed off glass and lowered into attack formation. "Which is too bad, you know. Because we would've given you so much of it. Instead I'm going to kill you."

Peterson lowered into formation. "Here I am, Moloch. Come kill me."

They shared one last glare, then surged together in the middle of the observation deck.

Moloch hit first, a roundhouse kick into Peterson's stomach. Peterson keeled over; Moloch went for another; Peterson caught his leg and punched his inner thigh, dropping him. Peterson staggered back, choking for air.

He thought back to the young agent who had almost broken that yokel's arm in that bar in Oklahoma. *I've got to stop this monster, I've got to stop him, I've got to stop him.*

He charged Moloch, who rolled him into a hip throw. Peterson slammed on his back again, hard, his head bouncing on the concrete. He could hear Moloch bounding towards him.

Come on, legs, if you've got anything left in you—

Hunter Peterson, forty-eight years old, swept out his legs as his adversary approached, sending him flying.

He stumbled back to his feet and stalked the fallen Moloch.

Chapter 66

"This is for the heroes," President Wilkins said at the podium. "This is for the ones who get up every morning, struggle in silence, and forge ahead, even though no one's watching. Even though no one knows how you're struggling, or how you're forging. This is for the ones who carry themselves through the day with courage and pride, even though you might be full of fear. You are the backbone of this nation, and the award I present today is for all of you."

The crowd roared its applause. Johnny was still patrolling, but he had to let some wonder spill in. He'd never been this close to a President before, and he was pretty sure he never would be again. Johnny looked around at the crowd. *They love their President. Low approval ratings, protests, riots... They still love their President.*

The balcony; that man in the suit at the end of the row with the short brown hair; that kid in the row behind him with spiked hair and earrings; that middle-aged dude who was clapping a little less than the others. It could be anyone, that shot could come from anywhere, and all Johnny could do was look, try and spot a false move...

Come on, pick someone, make a move...

"We've got him," said a voice in the earpiece. "Suspect observed. Get over here right away."

"Location?" said another voice.

"Center aisle. Come on, double-time."

"On my way," Fullerton said.

"On the way," said another.

Johnny took a deep breath. "On the way," he said.

Chapter 67

Moloch smiled, bleeding from the nose now, baring at last all of his mania. "I don't have to wait, Peterson," he said. He held up his two-way. "I won't wait!"

"*No*!" Peterson screamed, taking off.

Moloch clicked the two-way; it beeped; he leaned in—

And Hunter Peterson tackled him, knocking the phone loose.

Moloch's finger's curled around the phone. He clicked it again, and it beeped again. "Brig—" He struggled against Peterson, still clicking, still beeping. "Brigadier—" He thrashed against Peterson. "Brigadier One—"

Peterson punched him in the face; he felt Moloch's skin blanche. He hit him again, and again, and again, and the last blow plunged Moloch into unconsciousness. He let go of the phone.

Peterson rear-cuffed him, then stood up. *What next?*

Chapter 68

Johnny joined his comrades at the center aisle. "That's him," Wolfe said, looking out at a thirty-something male halfway into the row. "He keeps reaching into his jacket pocket and swallowing hard, looking up and down. He's sweating like crazy. Let's take this motherfucker down."

"Let's do it," Fullerton said.

"You and Luca, get him from behind. We'll get him from the front. Wrestle him down."

Johnny and Fullerton nodded.

"Before the presentation of the main award," the emcee said into the microphone, "we have a presentation that isn't on your program. This special young lady..."

The voice droned off as Johnny and Fullerton climbed over guests' feet, the words melting into the cacophony of the room. The subject reached into his jacket and clutched his hand inside, gritting his teeth. Johnny and Fullerton shuffled closer, seat by seat...

"Ladies and gentlemen, a young woman who has truly shown courage in the face of adversity, Sarah Chambers!"

Johnny slowed a step. *Sarah Chambers*, he thought as the crowd applauded.

He turned to the stage, and he saw a blonde girl, about Paul's age, striding towards the President. *Sarah Chambers*, he thought. The girl who'd walked in on that carnage at the farm that December morning, the girl Johnny had cyberstalked all these months. Here, in this room, about to receive an award from the President, standing right next to him on stage. As the crowd continued to clap, Johnny saw tears stream down her face. *I don't believe it.*

He took another step towards the suspect, then locked in place. *The criminal-in-chief Wilkins*, Sarah had posted on her page.

And now she was walking towards to the President, crying and shaking, and she was reaching into a pocket in her slacks.

It's her. "It's the girl," he said out loud, to himself. He grabbed Fullerton.

"Come on!" Fullerton whispered, tugging on him.

Just then, Wolfe and two others grappled with the subject in the jacket.

It's not him, it's the girl on the stage—

"It's the girl!" he yelled.

Fullerton turned around. "Luca—"

Johnny took off back towards the aisle. "It's the girl!" he yelled. He tore out to the aisle. "The girl, Fullerton, the girl, on the stage!"

The gun was concealed behind her right thigh—a revolver. Johnny saw her arm start to twitch, tears still streaming—

"The girl!" Johnny yelled again, running up the aisle. He didn't know if anyone was running with him; he didn't know anything. All he could see was Sarah's arm shaking, then rising, clutching the gun—

Johnny pounded up the aisle, tried aiming his weapon. He raced faster—

And as he raced, everything slowed down; he was running in a quicksand of time. Sarah raised the gun, her movements in waves, as if behind a wall of water; a look of horror dragged across the President's face, frame-by-frame; the crowd gasped, one person at a time.

She's going to kill him, she's really going to do it—

Johnny reached the steps, bounded up to the stage, just as Sarah was pointing—

He lunged at the President and his assassin, his hand seizing Sarah's wrist, his shoulder crashing against the shoulder pad of the President's suit. The three of them spilled to the ground.

In that second, he looked into Sarah's eyes, the girl in the bedroom picture now flesh. She scrambled to her feet and ripped away towards an outside terrace as the crowd screamed.

"Sarah!" Johnny yelled.

Just then, a shot rang out from the back of the room. Something hot and metal seared into his shoulder, burrowed and lodged. Johnny could feel it twisting in his muscles as he stumbled.

"Stay down!" Fullerton yelled. He'd been following Johnny the whole time, and now he was covering President Wilkins with his body.

"Was he hit?" Johnny said.

"I'm all right, I'm all right," Wilkins said, before Fullerton could answer.

Another shot rang out, splintering somewhere on stage. Then

there was an exchange of shots in the back of the room, near the balcony.

Sarah, Johnny thought, clutching his shoulder. He got up and took off for the terrace. *What did they do to her? I have to find her...*

"Luca, stay down!" Fullerton yelled behind him.

Johnny raced outside, pain slicing in sharp angles through his right arm and into his chest, his shirt moistening with blood.

Sarah held the gun to her head.

"No," Johnny called.

"Leave me alone," she said, crying. "Please let me die, *please*."

Johnny looked into her eyes. "I believe that unarmed truth and unconditional love will have the final word."

Sarah's eyes widened. "How did you… who are you?"

"I'm someone who cares about you. Truth and love can still have the final word, Sarah. The world… can still be more just than unjust. You have to believe me. Put the gun down."

Sarah shook her head. "He... he killed my parents. They told me... they told me I could make it right, I could make him pay for what he did."

"They lied to you. He didn't kill your parents. *They* did. Whoever made you do this. I was there... when they died. I know."

Sarah pressed the gun against her temple, fresh tears streaming down her cheeks. "You're lying."

"They killed my father, Sarah. They killed your parents. And they tricked you, they made you into something you're not. Put the gun down. I can save you. I can make it all right. You're safe now." Johnny's knees started to knock. *I think I'm losing a lot of blood*, he thought.

Sarah held the gaze another moment, still pressing the gun against her head, and then she relented. She lowered it to her side.

And then a bullet tore through her forehead, spraying blood behind her, cutting a circle in her flesh.

"No!" Johnny yelled. He turned back to the shooter.

It was a man he'd never seen before, not anyone from the sixth unit or the counter-assault force. He had to be an Authority assassin. He'd just killed Sarah, and now he was aiming his weapon at Johnny.

Johnny shrank away. *I hope it's quick. Please God, let it be quick—*

Then there was another shot, and the man collapsed.

Fullerton emerged onto the terrace, his gun smoking. He kicked the fallen shooter's gun away. "Seal this all off!" he yelled behind him. "We've got a man down here! Get help!"

He turned back to Johnny, wearing a grave look. "You're going to be okay, man," he said. But his eyes said something different.

Johnny tried to answer, but his thoughts started to mist over. He looked down at a pool of red in front of him as everything began to spin. *I think that's my blood.*

Fullerton and the terrace spun faster, danced into different colors, swirled into waves—and then everything faded to black.

Chapter 69

Johnny Luca plunged through the ocean, and it was black and enveloping and never-ending.

Where am I, he thought as he plunged deeper. He felt himself twisting through water like a corkscrew, headed straight down, but he couldn't see anything, it was all black, black everywhere.

The water rushed over him, swallowing him, forcing him down. He stopped twisting and plunging. Now he just sank, swaying towards black endless bottom like a feather drifting to an unmarked grave in a distant corner of the earth.

As Johnny sank, he saw flashes. The President of the United States standing at a podium with his seal—a crying blonde girl pulling out a gun. And then the President and the girl flashed bigger, closer, until Johnny met them, all three of them falling down on the stage.

Johnny felt the water filling him up, bubbling down his esophagus, pouring into his lungs like milk babbling out of a creamer. And now he *was* the water, black and endless.

He saw more flashes. The blonde girl holding a gun to her head, then lowering it to her side; a red circle opening up in her forehead, red spraying behind her. Then Johnny saw a man pointing a gun at him, then Fullerton dropping him, then Fullerton looking down at Johnny like he was about to weep.

Johnny merged into the ocean, dissipated beneath its waves, the pulse of his thought slowing, then falling silent. Johnny Luca, twenty-five years old, diffused through the end of time.

Through his nothingness, he felt a stroking, as if on his head, as if he had a head.

Darling, a voice called.

He was air, a rivulet already streaked down a window, scattered at the bottom. But he'd heard a voice.

Darling, the voice called again, and there was more stroking, smooth fingers melting into him, easing him. *You're with me. I'm here.*

I can't see you, he said.

But I can see you, the voice said. *I can hold you.*

It was a young woman's voice, a voice from the other end of time, a voice that used to make his knees knock—

It can't be you, he said. *I let you go. I let you walk away from me.*

And now I'm down here with you, she said.

Am I dead?

There was a pause, as heavy as infinity. *You might be.*

But I don't want to be.

Why not?

Now he was the one who paused. She was still stroking his hair; he could feel her fingers radiating warmth. Just then, he felt his heart beat. *Because I need to see you again*, he said.

He felt a rocking, as if he were swaying away from nothingness, drifting closer to substance.

Right answer, Gio, the girl said. *What took you so long?*

He laughed, a giggle resonating through a vacuum. *Don't tell me I'm stuck down here with you forever.*

Don't you want to be?

Not here, he said. *Not like this. I want to feel your breath on my neck again. I want to feel my fingers in your hair. I want to know what it's like to wake up next to you.*

And then he *did* feel breath on his neck, and then tugging—an embrace. The smell of her hair, dancing with notes of spring, filled his nostrils, which had just tingled to life. He felt fingers trace across his chest; he could feel his chest again.

Hold on, she said.

He felt more rocking, and then he gathered the force of a pendulum, cresting and falling and cresting, cresting and falling and cresting—

Hold on, she said again.

And then he exploded back through the end of time, and the black ocean was cascading over him again, twisting him, forcing him down—

But Johnny began to crack up through the black, slicing through it, then surging.

I'm here, Lizbeth said. *I'm here, I won't leave you, I never would*—

Johnny could see light ahead, first sparkling in points, then streaming in ribbons, swirling and sparkling.

Come find me, Lizbeth said as the light raced ahead, bursting throughout the black, gobbling Johnny up. *Find me on the other side…*

Johnny exploded through the surface.

Chapter 70

Johnny blinked his eyes open.

There was light, artificial and cold, first streaming before him in tiny bubbles, then expanding and filling the room as his pupils re-calibrated. Its source: a plate of florescent tubes overhead.

Johnny felt something in his right hand—a squeezing. He shifted his eyes, unable to move otherwise.

And broadcasting the squeezing was Julius Fullerton's hand.

"He's up!" Fullerton yelled.

There was a rush of figures to where Johnny lay.

"Fullerton," Johnny half-whispered.

"It's me, man." Fullerton squeezed again, wearing the same grave look he had before Johnny lost consciousness.

Johnny looked down at the hand again. *Holy shit, I think I'm alive.* "You can..." He gathered the strength in his windpipe. "You can let go of my hand now." He forced a smile, the muscles cracking in his face like grinding rocks.

Fullerton paused, then smiled and let go. He turned back to Peterson, who had led the gaggle of strangers to the foot of the bed.

"You're going to be all right," Peterson said, smiling. "An inch or two closer to your neck, and probably not."

Fullerton grinned. "We've got to stop meeting like this, Luca. You're turning out to be a little too brittle for this job."

Johnny tried to roll his eyes, but they were sunk in their sockets. "You ever get shot, asshole?"

Fullerton laughed. "He really *is* going to be all right, boss!"

Peterson smiled, but then seriousness cut across his face. "There's something you should know, Luca."

That's never a good thing. Johnny looked at Peterson. He had a black eye, along with lacerations on his face and split skin on all of his knuckles, and his shirt collar was stained with blood. "It must be about the op," Johnny said.

Peterson nodded. "That's right, it's about the op." He turned around to the others, then back to Johnny. He paused a moment, measuring the words. Then he looked into his eyes. "You saved the lives of ten thousand people today."

Johnny closed his eyes. *I need to hear that again. God, let me hear those words again.*

"The President is safe," Peterson went on. "Not a scratch. And it's because of you."

Johnny felt his eyes welling up. *That can't be. That can't—*

"We lost a lot of men on our side," Peterson said. He shook his head and swallowed hard. "One of my best friends, in fact. But we stopped everyone else. Even Moloch is in custody. We *stopped* them."

"You should've seen the way you ran," Fullerton said. "You were on point the whole way."

I can hardly remember it. I just remember... Sarah, on the stage, and the way she was shaking... reaching into her pocket...

Peterson narrowed his eyes. "You knew who she was. Whose daughter she was."

Johnny closed his eyes, then opened them. "So do you."

"Well, we had to ID her… when she died."

Johnny swallowed hard, thinking of the circle sliced into her forehead.

"But how did *you* know?" Peterson asked.

"Because I've been checking up on her." Johnny sighed. "I found her web page. I needed to know how she was doing… after what happened. I needed to know if she was all right."

Peterson turned back to the others again. "That's what saved the President's life," he told them. He turned back to Johnny. "That extra mile, Luca. Kind of reminds me of a Jersey cop who cracked the Project Orion case."

And at that, Johnny beamed—the final vindication of his father.

"Where are we, anyway?" he asked.

"We're in a bunker under the Empire State Building. We smuggled you here through a tunnel and got a surgeon on you. This is the only time in your life you'll ever be here, so soak it in."

There wasn't much to soak in. It was dim and white and full of people he'd never seen before, in pressed shirts and slacks and blazers.

Johnny sighed again. "And I'm... going to be all right?"

Peterson nodded. "You'll be in a sling for awhile. But we got the bullet out of you."

"Who shot her, sir?"

"It was one of the embedded Authority meta-agents. And he was going to kill you, too. But Fullerton took him down."

Johnny looked up at Fullerton, who was grinning. "It's all right," Fullerton said. "You can buy me a value meal some time. I won't even ask you to super-size it."

Johnny laughed. "Did you pop that question yet?"

The grave look fell across Fullerton's face again. "Nah, man. I've been by your side the whole time."

"How long has it been?"

"It's about seven-thirty at night. Sundown soon."

"There are some people I want you to meet," Peterson said. He turned back and nodded at a fifty-something woman in a pantsuit, who stepped forward.

"This is Congresswoman Rivera," Peterson said. "She led the fight in the House against the Total Information Awareness Act."

The congresswoman stroked Johnny's hand for a moment. "It's an honor," she said. "Thank you."

Johnny gulped. A congresswoman was thanking him?

"And this is Congressman Richards," Peterson said. "And Congressman O'Roarke."

Two middle-aged men stepped up to greet Johnny and thank him.

Johnny gulped again.

"And this is the mayor," Peterson said. "You stopped a dirty bomb from going off on Thirty-Fourth Street today."

A balding, Italian-looking man stepped towards Johnny and shook his hand. "Nice job, kid," he said.

Just then, Peterson's lip quivered. "I wanted you to meet the Secret Service Director tonight," he said. He sat his jaw. "But we lost him today. He would've been the first one here to thank you, Luca."

There were others, and they were practically lining up in the small bunker to meet him. They all looked important.

"You see, I guess you could call us the rebellion," Peterson said. "We've all been fighting this plot for months." He smiled. "And today we won the fight."

There wasn't any pain anymore; only light. It swirled through Johnny, like water over rock, and radiated out through his eyes. "It wasn't me," Johnny said. "It was everyone else. I just finished their work." *Like Dad.*

"That's just the kind of attitude that makes you the hero you are," Congresswoman Rivera said. "That sense of duty."

Hero? Sense of duty? Shouldn't I be home playing video games right now?

"Everyone in this room," Peterson said, "has promised to keep your identity a secret. After the attack, we locked down the hotel and confiscated every camera. We destroyed every picture of the incident, to protect you."

What a trip. Who the hell would want to know who I am?

"Just sit back for now," Peterson said. "We'll get you out of here tomorrow morning, and then you can go back home. You'll be safe." He smiled again, then turned and walked out through a door in the back of the room, the others following him. Only Fullerton remained.

Johnny grinned at him. "Is this the part where you put a pillow over my head and shoot me?" he asked. "Like in those movies where there's always those crazy twists and turns?"

Fullerton shook his head and laughed. "I should," he said. "For all the grief you gave me all this time. But you damn sure made up for it today, man. You came correct, Agent Luca."

Johnny's eyes fluttered, suddenly heavy. He'd be passing out again soon. Would he plunge beneath the waves again? Out of the blue, and into the black?

"What's it like outside, Fullerton?" He paused. "I mean... tonight. After everything."

"Quiet. Paralyzed, kind of. Everyone's waiting for what's going to happen next. And right now, we're the only ones who know that nothing bad's going to happen."

Johnny closed his eyes. "And I did that?"

"You did, man. You sure did."

Fullerton might have said something else then; Johnny wasn't sure. The words melted into a sweet breeze, here in the secret bunker beneath the Empire State Building, bearing him to his first peaceful sleep since his father died.

Chapter 71

That night, President Wilkins clicked off the light in the presidential bedroom, and in the same instant the fibers of the sheets tinged his arm hairs, Delilah grabbed him. "Promise me," she said in the dark. "Promise me, Reed. *Promise* me."

"Promise you what?"

"Promise me I can hold onto you like this every night for the rest of my life. Promise me nothing bad's going to happen to you." Delilah choked back sobs. "*Promise* me."

Wilkins pulled her close. "I promise."

"Nothing's worth losing you over. I want you to remember that. Just shut up and let me be selfish. You might have some higher notions about your oath and your duty, but you're my husband. You're the father of my children. And that's the man I want. In one piece, in bed with me every night."

"And that's where I'll be."

The two fell silent for a moment. And then Delilah spoke up again in the dark:

"Who was that boy who saved you today?"

Wilkins smiled in the black. "A hero, beautiful. A real-life hero. And I reckon he doesn't even realize how much of a hero he is."

And that was it. There would be no creeping into the closet tonight, no rendezvous in the tunnel beneath the capital. He'd signed an executive order restoring full presidential protective duties to the Secret Service, and there was nothing Bryson could say to squawk about it. For the first time in Wilkins's presidency, only Secret Service agents were guarding the White House.

There, in the dark, the President knew. It glowed in him, an ember in his brain. He knew exactly what was left to be done, and how to go about doing it.

Tomorrow Hunter Peterson would begin his second tenure as Director of the Anti-Subversion Authority, and he'd be tasked with the most important job of all: dismantling the Authority, piece-by-piece, until there was nothing left. And in case Bryson had any court maneuvers planned, Wilkins had signed an order authorizing the Army to force him from the Authority building and install Peterson as

Director.

Also tomorrow, Wilkins would hold a meeting in the Oval Office with Gordon Bragg, the billionaire media magnate. Bragg had made a name for himself over the last year as the only media figure with the guts to confront Bryson, haranguing him from his columns and ordering his publications to focus their fire on Bryson and expose the rotten core of the Authority. Bryson had thrived all these years with the aid of a servile media's propaganda, but now Wilkins, with Bragg by his side, would bring a gun to that gunfight.

And Bryson? Wilkins had a surprise headed his way, not the least of which was the fact that Wilkins had just provided Attorney General Sharpe with the massive Operation Reichstag investigative file.

It's not an iron cage locking us in, Wilkins thought as he faded to sleep. *It's a rotten old latticework… and we're all going to grab a slat and rip it down… this Octavian latticework…*

Chapter 72

At that moment, Bryson was sitting at his desk at Authority headquarters. He pushed a button on the desk, and steel shutters rang down every window in the room. Then he pushed another button, and there was a buzz, then a steady hum ringing the perimeter of the room—electromagnetic debugging and soundproofing.

He didn't know how many more times he'd be in the comfort of his office like this, how much more often he'd be able to isolate himself at a switch. But for now—at least for tonight—his office was impregnable.

Bryson pushed another button, and there was a rumbling of a motor within the desk. The surface of the back half of the desk parted, and a flat-screen monitor rose from the chasm. It stopped at just above his eye level.

The monitor flashed on, and there on the screen was the most important figure in Alexander Bryson's life.

"You should've established contact sooner," the man on the screen said.

"It couldn't be helped, sir," Bryson said.

"It seems that a lot can't be helped these days, doesn't it? Operation Reichstag was a complete failure."

Bryson lowered his head. "I know."

"You'd better have more for me than that. You'd better have our next moves mapped out."

"Our press sources are using the attack on Wilkins and Chan's killing as a pretext for pushing Total Information Awareness, even with Wilkins's approval ratings so high. And we've got a source monitoring Moloch at the prison, in case he decides to talk."

"I want him alive, Bryson. He won't talk. He knows we'll provide for him if he's loyal. How are our other operations coming?"

"We're making the right inroads with the right people. And Project Scorpion is proceeding on schedule."

"Good work, Nightfox."

Bryson closed his eyes for a moment; he hadn't been called that in years. It was a name from a different time, a different life, before all of this.

The man flashed a lecherous grin. "You just bear down for now," he told Bryson. "If they remove you from your office, I'll reach out to you another way. Count on it."

Bryson bowed his head. "Yes, Octavian."

The transmission cut off.

Chapter 73

The next day, his arm in a sling, Johnny strolled through the cemetery to his father's grave, then stopped short and gulped. Before the headstone was a white rose.

Johnny knelt down, the moist grass spreading out and gathering him up. *Who the hell left this here?* he thought as he brushed the petals. He shook his head. *There's so much I still don't know.*

He couldn't let anything surprise him now. Not this white rose, not the way his mother had insisted Johnny have laurel leaves inscribed on the headstone a year and half ago.

Johnny kissed the top of the headstone. "You did it," he whispered. *The President is safe, Dad. All because of you and Mom. You saved everyone's lives. You saved the country.*

Johnny stood up straight. *And I know what to do*, he thought, beaming. "I know what to do, Dad," he whispered.

He kissed the headstone again, stole one last glance at the white rose resting on the grass, and then turned and walked away.

That afternoon, federal agents massed outside of Alexander Bryson's home in McLean, Virginia. Earlier that morning, Bryson had gone quietly when Peterson again showed up to take his place as Director.

One of the agents raised a battering ram. "Breach the door," the leader said.

That night, President Wilkins sat at the Oval Office desk, a teleprompter standing sentry a few feet away, a gaggle of television cameras trained on him. The White House had announced a "major address to the nation on yesterday's attempt on the President's life and the thwarted terror attacks on several cities."

Wilkins closed his eyes and thought of John Adams's words after the Battles of Lexington and Concord: *The die is cast, the Rubicon crossed.*

"Five, four," the television crewman called. "Three, two…"

Wilkins looked into the camera. "My fellow Americans," he began.

Chapter 74

As the President was giving his speech that night, Johnny walked through his undergraduate campus, forging through a drizzle along paths lit by ankle-height lamps. He ambled past the theater, clad in red brick, Shakespeare quotes adorning the stone wall in front. He passed the library, three stories of red brick, a ramp angling down to a basement where he had an economics class once.

The campus was empty tonight; school had been out for a couple of weeks. Johnny walked on, further into the humid black.

The rain intensifying, Johnny approached the deep grassy bowl in the heart of campus. It was just him and the tall oaks and the night. He crossed the bowl, the blades of grass slick with raindrops, to one of the oaks, *the* oak.

Johnny laid a hand on its bark. If he stared long enough, like at one of those drawings where the patterns suddenly gave way to shapes, he could almost see the boy and the girl shivering in the snow. *I noticed this on the way over to your place tonight,* Johnny had told her that night. *Right where the tree hangs over us here.*

And a moment later, the snow had sprayed all around them, and they'd slow-danced together, and drawn closer.

"Gio," a voice called behind him.

Johnny closed his eyes, the rain picking up, and breathed slowly. He turned around.

"Lizbeth."

She smiled, but it was forced, plaintive. Then seriousness sliced through the smile, and she ran to him. "Your arm," she said, embracing him. "What happened?"

Johnny closed his eyes again as he held her. "I…" He leaned back and looked into Lizbeth's eyes, emeralds shimmering behind her wet glasses. "I crashed into the catcher in softball the other night. Dislocated my shoulder." He shook his head. "She held on to the ball, though. She squared right up, and I went right down."

"What the hell is wrong with you?"

Johnny arched his eyebrows. "What?"

Lizbeth stepped back. "Do you ever take care of yourself? I mean, look at you. Do you ever stop and think that there are people who worry about you?"

"Hey, it was a close game!"

Lizbeth's look softened, and then she laughed. "Did you say it was a girl who took you out?"

"That's right. She was a tank."

Lizbeth shook her head and laughed again. "I didn't even know the FBI had a team." She laid her hand on Johnny's shoulder. "I'm one of those people who worry, in case you didn't notice. Ever since you told me you were in the city the night of the bombing. You could've been killed. I think about it all the time—you were only three blocks away. God, I'm crazy." Lizbeth shook her head, and the seriousness returned. "I don't know what you do, or where you go, ever. Except I know that you're trying to become a federal agent who fights terrorists, and they tried to kill the President yesterday. And I'm moving two thousand miles away next week." Lizbeth looked down. "And there won't be anyone to take care of my Gio." She shook the rain from her hair, then laughed. "Did you bother to check the weather before asking me to meet you out here?"

Johnny poked her. "Did *you*, dork?"

Lizbeth slapped his finger away, then sighed. "Well, we're all packed up to go. Leaving in a few days."

"Ready to cover those Diamondbacks? They don't play in October, unless they're getting their asses kicked by the Yankees in the World Series, so you won't be able to lead in with Darnell Williams and the fixings."

Lizbeth laughed, her look again salted with plaintiveness. "Who else but you would remember that stupid article?" She turned away from Johnny and stroked the tree bark. "This old tree," she said. "We were some good-looking couple that night, let me tell ya." Lizbeth turned around to face Johnny, taking off her glasses and drying them on her shirt, then looking into his eyes.

"You spoke French to me…" Lizbeth laughed to herself. "The only French you knew, anyway. And then it snowed." Lizbeth looked up at the branches. "We're not going to get any snow tonight, unless you have one hell of a trick up your sleeve."

"I think I'm all out of fancy moves," Johnny said.

Lizbeth sighed. "And so am I." She paused, and then her lips trembled. "I should be going to Arizona next week with you, Gio," she said. "Or Italy. Or Africa. Or anywhere in the world. Or staying right here… with you." Lizbeth closed her eyes, and a tear mingled with the raindrops streaming down her cheeks. "Why did you ask me to come here tonight?" She began to sob. "Why here? When you know I could never live with myself if I said goodbye to you here?"

Johnny feathered Lizbeth's chin upwards with his finger, just as he had under the same tree those three and a half years ago, then reached into his pocket and pulled out her letter. "Because I'm here to tell you that I'm not an ass," he said.

"My letter! Gio, you weren't supposed to read it until—"

"Until I knew just what I wanted out of life. I heard you the first time, Heathrow."

Lizbeth stepped back. "And?"

Just then, everything slowed down, just like when Johnny sprinted towards that stage in that ballroom in New York. The raindrops, the tree's swaying leaves, the flutter in Lizbeth's hair, everything dragging frame-by-frame as every star in Johnny Luca's universe aligned:

"And I want you, Lizbeth. I've wanted you from the second I saw you."

More tears streamed down Lizbeth's face. "Then you should have told me the second you saw me," she said. "We'd be a lot dryer right now."

"We would be," Johnny said, approaching her. "And everything would be way less complicated. But I don't do simple, Lizbeth." He took her in his arms.

"Neither of us do," she said, gazing into his eyes.

"And *this* won't be simple, either." Johnny kissed her, their lips melting together, the rain drenching them as he pulled her closer to him.

This was the world, this was everything, this was every answer to every question Johnny had ever had. They each rocked back. Johnny couldn't speak; he couldn't breathe. He wasn't on earth.

Lizbeth smiled. "And you said you were out of fancy moves."

"Say you'll stay," Johnny said. "Or go with me to Italy. Or Africa."

"Gio—"

"Because I came a long way to see you tonight, Lizbeth." Johnny closed his eyes for a moment, then opened them. "And I'd like to tell you all about just how far I came."

That moment, Johnny supposed, was when it all slowed down for Lizbeth, the instant when she had to make her own decisions about what her own life was going to be. And he allowed himself to hold his breath.

"My God, I love you so much," Lizbeth said, throwing her arms around him. "And I want to hear everything about everything. You've got me, Gio. You've had me from the night we danced here."

Johnny kissed her again. "Then let me tell you about the time I fell into a bottomless pit," he said. "And I found you there waiting for me."

The End

www.ingramcontent.com/pod-product-compliance
Lightning Source LLC
Chambersburg PA
CBHW020302030826
48979CB00027B/1934/J

* 9 7 8 0 9 8 9 1 7 7 5 1 1 *